"I am a libertine, but I am neither *a criminal* nor *a murderer*"
—Marquis de Sade, 1781

Sade's most famous novel, *Justine, or Good Conduct Well Chastised*, was written while Sade was a prisoner in the Bastille and first published in 1791. That year, Sade told a friend that he wrote it for money, tailoring it to the wishes of the printer, who asked that it be "well-spiced." Ten years later, when he was arrested for writing *Justine*, he denied being its author. The book focuses on Justine and her sister, Juliette, young orphans who represent the two sides of human nature: virtue and vice. Justine the Virtuous suffers for her goodness; she is robbed, raped, and framed. Her tormentors are never punished; in fact, Justine brings only good fortune to her abusers—they become a minister, surgeon to the king, and a millionaire.

DONATIEN ALPHONSE FRANÇOIS DE SADE, known as the Marquis de Sade, was born in 1740 in France. He was educated by Jesuits, then entered the military, participating in the Seven Years' War. After his marriage in 1763, he became embroiled in several sexual scandals and feuds that landed him in prison. Among his crimes were spanking a prostitute, feeding aphrodisiac sweets to women, and seducing his sister-in-law. In 1801, he was again arrested, this time for writing obscene literature, and he spent the rest of his life behind bars. Most of his work was written while he was incarcerated, and many of his manuscripts were reportedly destroyed by the police and the courts. Sade, ever the logician, noted that, if the police were more astute, they would not have locked him up, allowing him time to create literature and thus corrupt others. Instead, Sade reasoned, the authorities should have set him free and surrounded him with a harem on which to feast.

Madame de Sade remained loyal to her husband for many years, visiting him often in prison. Finally, in 1790, she petitioned to separate from him, and he later blamed her for the destruction of numerous manuscripts—13 years worth of work—because it took her ten days to retrieve his belongings from the Bastille when he was transferred to Charenton asylum. (The Bastille was attacked, and Sade's belongings destroyed, on the tenth day.) Like Machiavelli, Sade was for many years considered to have a criminal mind, but he is now viewed as an original philosophical thinker and a precursor to Freud, Nietzsche, and existentialism. His other major works include *Eugénie de Franval* (1788), *Philosophy in the Bedroom* (1795), *Juliette* (1797), and *The 120 Days of Sodom* (1931-35). Sade died in 1814 in Charenton.

Justine

Justine

Marquis de Sade

BOOK-OF-THE-MONTH CLUB
NEW YORK

Justine

*T*he most famous of all Sade's works is the novel Justine. *It is also probably the one he cared most about—Sade dedicated it to the faithful companion of the last twenty-five years of his existence, Marie-Constance Quesnet. It was also the book which caused him the most difficulty with the authorities during his lifetime.*

Sade finished the first draft of this "philosophical novel" while he was a prisoner in the Bastille. Working uninterruptedly over the two-week period from June 23 to July 8, 1787, in his cell in the "Second Liberty," Sade completed the hundred-and-thirty-eight-page manuscript, which he entitled Les Infortunes de la Vertu. *Originally intended to become a part of the volume he was then preparing,* Contes et fabliaux du XVIIIe siècle, *this "first Justine" underwent considerable revision in the course of the following year, and Sade soon determined to strike it from his list of tales and make it a work unto itself.*

Writing to his lawyer-friend Reinaud on June 12, 1791, a little more than a year after the Revolutionary government had rendered him his liberty, Sade noted: "At the moment a novel of mine is being printed, but it is a work too immoral to be sent to so pious and so decent a man as yourself. I needed money, my publisher said that he wanted it well *spiced, and I gave it to him fit to plague the devil himself. It is called* Justine, or Good Conduct Well Chastised. *Burn it and do not read it, if perchance it falls into your hands. I am disclaiming the authorship. . . ."*

In fact, the original edition of Justine—*the author's first work published during his lifetime—did not bear his name. Printed in Paris, chez Girouard*[1] *on the rue du Bout-du-Monde,* Justine *first appeared in two octavo volumes, with a frontispiece depicting Virtue between Licentiousness and Irreligion, and at the place on the title page generally reserved for the publisher's imprint there appeared the vague description:* In Holland, At Associated Booksellers.

What of the admission by the author that he wrote the novel to order? This, as Lely points out, seems hardly likely. First, the general outline and somber pessimism of the 1791 Justine *were already evident in the 1787 version. Second, the novel does figure in the* Catalogue raisonné *which Sade himself drew up roughly three years before its publication. And finally—perhaps the most convincing argument of all—Sade dedicated the novel, as we have noted, to his dear friend Marie-Constance Quesnet, an indication that he himself valued the work highly, well understood its importance, and would never have dared compromise the merit of the work by spicing it to suit the publisher's taste.*

"Will it not be felt," writes Sade in his dedication, "that Virtue, however beautiful, becomes the worst of all possible attitudes when it is found too feeble to contend with Vice and that, in an entirely corrupted age, the safest course is to follow the others?" If this be the impression, says Sade, it is wrong: this work is intended to combat such "dangerous sophistries," such "false philosophy," and show how Virtue afflicted may turn a thoroughly depraved and corrupt spirit wherein there yet remain a few good principles, back toward the path of righteousness.

During the decade following its publication, Justine *went through six printings (one of which, actually done in Paris, bore as the unlikely place of publication: "Philadelphia"), eloquent testimony to its early popularity. Doubtless prompted by its success, an enterprising Paris publisher, Nicolas Massé, brought out, in 1797, the monumental ten-volume work entitled* La Nouvelle Justine . . . suivie de l'Histoire de Juliette, sa soeur, *which was freely offered, at*

---

[1] *Girouard was later to perish, under the Reign of Terror, on January 8, 1794.*

least for a year following its publication, in the leading Paris bookstores. Then, in the waning two years of the eighteenth century, searches and seizures began, ending with the arrest, on March 6, 1801, of the man who was purported to be, but adamantly denied he was, the author of both works. On that day, both Sade and Massé were arrested on the latter's premises. A search of Massé's offices revealed a number of manuscripts in Sade's handwriting, as well as printed volumes of Justine *and* Juliette *annotated in his hand. Massé, after being detained for twenty-four hours, was released upon condition that he reveal the whereabouts of his stock of* Juliette, *and there is evidence to indicate that the publisher, to save himself, had denounced Sade to the police. Be that as it may, Sade was once again incarcerated, first in Sainte-Pélagie and then, two years later, in the Charenton Asylum, where he was to remain a prisoner until the end of his life.*

O thou my friend! The prosperity of Crime is like unto the lightning, whose traitorous brilliancies embellish the atmosphere but for an instant, in order to hurl into death's very depths the luckless one they have dazzled.

Yes, Constance, it is to thee I address this work; at once the example and honor of thy sex, with a spirit of profoundest sensibility combining the most judicious and the most enlightened of minds, thou art she to whom I confide my book, which will acquaint thee with the sweetness of the tears Virtue sore beset doth shed and doth cause to flow. Detesting the sophistries of libertinage and of irreligion, in word and deed combatting them unwearingly, I fear not that those necessitated by the order of personages appearing in these Memoires will put thee in any peril; the cynicism remarkable in certain portraits (they were softened as much as ever they could be) is no more apt to frighten thee; for it is only Vice that trembles when Vice is found out, and cries scandal immediately it is attacked. To bigots Tartuffe was indebted for his ordeal; Justine's will be the achievement of libertines, and little do I dread them: they'll not betray my intentions, these thou shalt perceive; thy opinion is sufficient to make my whole glory and after having pleased thee I must either please universally or find consolation in a general censure.

The scheme of this novel (yet, 'tis less a novel than one might suppose) is doubtless new; the victory gained by Virtue over Vice, the rewarding of good, the punishment of evil, such is the usual scheme in every other work of this species: ah! the lesson cannot be too often dinned in our ears!

But throughout to present Vice triumphant and Virtue a victim of its sacrifices, to exhibit a wretched creature wandering from one misery to the next; the toy of villainy; the target of every debauch; exposed to the most barbarous, the most monstrous caprices; driven witless by the most brazen, the most specious sophistries; prey to the most cunning seductions, the most irresistible suborna-

7

tions; for defense against so many disappointments, so much bane and pestilence, to repulse such a quantity of corruption having nothing but a sensitive soul, a mind naturally formed, and considerable courage: briefly, to employ the boldest scenes, the most extraordinary situations, the most dreadful maxims, the most energetic brush strokes, with the sole object of obtaining from all this one of the sublimest parables ever penned for human edification; now, such were, 'twill be allowed, to seek to reach one's destination by a road not much traveled heretofore.

Have I succeeded, Constance? Will a tear in thy eye determine my triumph? After having read Justine, *wilt say: "Oh, how these renderings of crime make me proud of my love for* Virtue! *How sublime does it appear through tears! How 'tis embellished by misfortunes!"*

Oh, Constance! may these words but escape thy lips, and my labors shall be crowned.

$\mathcal{T}$he very masterpiece of philosophy would be to develop the means Providence employs to arrive at the ends she designs for man, and from this construction to deduce some rules of conduct acquainting this wretched two-footed individual with the manner wherein he must proceed along life's thorny way, forewarned of the strange caprices of that fatality they denominate by twenty different titles, and all unavailingly, for it has not yet been scanned nor defined.

If, though full of respect for social conventions and never overstepping the bounds they draw round us, if, nonetheless, it should come to pass that we meet with nothing but brambles and briars, while the wicked tread upon flowers, will it not be reckoned —save by those in whom a fund of incoercible virtues renders deaf to these remarks—, will it not be decided that it is preferable to abandon oneself to the tide rather than to resist it? Will it not be felt that Virtue, however beautiful, becomes the worst of all attitudes when it is found too feeble to contend with Vice, and that, in an entirely corrupted age, the safest course is to follow along after the others? Somewhat better informed, if one wishes, and abusing the knowledge they have acquired, will they not say, as did the angel Jesrad in *Zadig,* that there is no evil whereof some good is not born? and will they not declare, that this being the case, they can give themselves over to evil since, indeed, it is but one of the fashions of producing good? Will they not add, that it makes no difference to the general plan whether such-and-such a one is by preference good or bad, that if misery persecutes virtue and prosperity accompanies crime, those things being as one in Nature's view, far better to join company with the wicked who flourish, than to be counted amongst the virtuous who founder? Hence, it is im-

9

portant to anticipate those dangerous sophistries of a false philosophy; it is essential to show that through examples of afflicted
virtue presented to a depraved spirit in which, however, there remain
a few good principles, it is essential, I say, to show that spirit quite
as surely restored to righteousness by these means as by portraying
this virtuous career ornate with the most glittering honors and the
most flattering rewards. Doubtless it is cruel to have to describe, on
the one hand, a host of ills overwhelming a sweet-tempered and
sensitive woman who, as best she is able, respects virtue, and, on
the other, the affluence of prosperity of those who crush and
mortify this same woman. But were there nevertheless some good
engendered of the demonstration, would one have to repent of
making it? Ought one be sorry for having established a fact whence
there resulted, for the wise man who reads to some purpose, so useful a lesson of submission to providential decrees and the fateful
warning that it is often to recall us to our duties that Heaven
strikes down beside us the person who seems to us best to have fulfilled his own?

Such are the sentiments which are going to direct our labors,
and it is in consideration of these intentions that we ask the reader's
indulgence for the erroneous doctrines which are to be placed in the
mouths of our characters, and for the sometimes rather painful
situations which, out of love for truth, we have been obliged to
dress before his eyes.

Madame la Comtesse de Lorsange was one of those priestesses
of Venus whose fortune is the product of a pretty face and much
misconduct, and whose titles, pompous though they are, are not
to be found but in the archives of Cythera, forged by the imperti-
nence that seeks, and sustained by the fool's credulity that bestows,
them; brunette, a fine figure, eyes of a singular expression, that
modish unbelief which, contributing one further spice to the passions, causes those women in whom it is suspected to be sought
after that much more diligently; a trifle wicked, unfurnished with
any principle, allowing evil to exist in nothing, lacking however
that amount of depravation in the heart to have extinguished its
sensibility; haughty, libertine; such was Madame de Lorsange.

Nevertheless, this woman had received the best education;

daughter of a very rich Parisian banker, she had been brought up, together with a sister named Justine, by three years younger than she, in one of the capital's most celebrated abbeys where, until the ages of twelve and fifteen years, the one and the other of the two sisters had been denied no counsels, no masters, no books, and no polite talents.

At this period crucial to the virtue of the two maidens, they were in one day made bereft of everything: a frightful bankruptcy precipitated their father into circumstances so cruel that he perished of grief. One month later, his wife followed him into the grave. Two distant and heartless relatives deliberated what should be done with the young orphans; a hundred crowns apiece was their share of a legacy mostly swallowed up by creditors. No one caring to be burdened with them, the convent's door was opened, their dowry was put into their hands, and they were left at liberty to become what they wished.

Madame de Lorsange, at the time called Juliette, whose mind and character were to all intents and purposes as completely formed then as at thirty, the age she had attained at the opening of the tale we are about to relate, seemed nothing but overjoyed to be put at large; she gave not a moment's thought to the cruel events which had broken her chains. As for Justine, aged as we have remarked, twelve, hers was of a pensive and melancholy character, which made her far more keenly appreciate all the horrors of her situation. Full of tenderness, endowed with a surprising sensibility instead of with her sister's art and finesse, she was ruled by an ingenuousness, a candor that were to cause her to tumble into not a few pitfalls. To so many qualities this girl joined a sweet countenance, absolutely unlike that with which Nature had embellished Juliette; for all the artifice, wiles, coquetry one noticed in the features of the one, there were proportionate amounts of modesty, decency, and timidity to be admired in the other; a virginal air, large blue eyes very soulful and appealing, a dazzling fair skin, a supple and resilient body, a touching voice, teeth of ivory and the loveliest blond hair, there you have a sketch of this charming creature whose naive graces and delicate traits are beyond our power to describe.

They were given twenty-four hours to leave the convent; into their hands, together with their five score crowns, was thrown the responsibility to provide for themselves as they saw fit. Delighted to be her own mistress, Juliette spent a minute, perhaps two, wiping away Justine's tears, then, observing it was in vain, she fell to scolding instead of comforting her; she rebuked Justine for her sensitiveness; she told her, with a philosophic acuity far beyond her years, that in this world one must not be afflicted save by what affects one personally; that it was possible to find in oneself physical sensations of a sufficiently voluptuous piquancy to extinguish all the moral affections whose shock could be painful; that it was all the more essential so to proceed, since true wisdom consists infinitely more in doubling the sum of one's pleasures than in increasing the sum of one's pains; that, in a word, there was nothing one ought not do in order to deaden in oneself that perfidious sensibility from which none but others profit while to us it brings naught but troubles. But it is difficult to harden a gentle good heart, it resists the arguments of a toughened bad mind, and its solemn satisfactions console it for the loss of the *bel-esprit*'s false splendors.

Juliette, employing other resources, then said to her sister, that with the age and the figure they both of them had, they could not die of hunger—she cited the example of one of their neighbors' daughters who, having escaped from her father's house, was presently very royally maintained and far happier, doubtless, than if she had remained at home with her family; one must, said Juliette, take good care to avoid believing it is marriage that renders a girl happy; that, a captive under the hymeneal laws, she has, with much ill-humor to suffer, a very slight measure of joys to expect; instead of which, were she to surrender herself to libertinage, she might always be able to protect herself against her lovers' moods, or be comforted by their number.

These speeches horrified Justine; she declared she preferred death to ignominy; whatever were her sister's reiterated urgings, she adamantly refused to take up lodging with her immediately she saw Juliette bent upon conduct that caused her to shudder.

After each had announced her very different intentions, the two girls separated without exchanging any promises to see each another again. Would Juliette, who, so she affirmed, intended to become a lady of consequence, would Juliette consent to receive a little girl whose virtuous but base inclinations might be able to bring her into dishonor? and, on her side, would Justine wish to jeopardize her morals in the society of a perverse creature who was bound to become public debauchery's toy and the lewd mob's victim? And so each bid an eternal adieu to the other, and they left the convent on the morrow.

During early childhood caressed by her mother's dressmaker, Justine believes this woman will treat her kindly now in this hour of her distress; she goes in search of the woman, she tells the tale of her woes, she asks employment . . . she is scarcely recognized; and is harshly driven out the door.

"Oh Heaven!" cries the poor little creature, "must my initial steps in this world be so quickly stamped with ill-fortune? That woman once loved me; why does she cast me away today? Alas! 'tis because I am poor and an orphan, because I have no more means and people are not esteemed save in reason of the aid and benefits one imagines may be had of them." Wringing her hands, Justine goes to find her curé; she describes her circumstances with the vigorous candor proper to her years. . . . She was wearing a little white garment, her lovely hair was negligently tucked up under her bonnet, her breast, whose development had scarcely begun, was hidden beneath two or three folds of gauze, her pretty face had somewhat of pallor owing to the unhappiness consuming her, a few tears rolled from her eyes and lent to them an additional expressiveness. . . .

"You observe me, Monsieur," said she to the saintly ecclesiastic . . . "Yes, you observe me in what for a girl is a most dreadful position; I have lost my father and mother. . . . Heaven has taken them from me at an age when I stand in greatest need of their assistance. . . . They died ruined, Monsieur; we no longer have anything. There," she continued, "is all they left me," and she displayed her dozen *louis,* "and nowhere to rest my poor head. . . . You will have pity upon me, Monsieur, will you not? You are Religion's minister and Religion was always my heart's virtue; in the name of that God I adore and whose organ you are, tell me, as if you were a second father unto me, what must I do? . . . what must become of me?"

The charitable priest clapped an inquisitive eye upon Justine, and made her answer, saying that the parish was heavily loaded; that it could not easily take new charges unto its bosom, but that if Justine wished to serve him, if she were prepared for hard toil, there would always be a crust of bread in his kitchen for her. And as he uttered those words, the gods' interpreter chucked her under the chin; the kiss he gave her bespoke rather too much worldliness for a man of the church, and Justine, who had understood only too well, thrust him away. "Monsieur," said she, "I ask neither alms of you nor a position as your scullion; it was all too recently I took leave of an estate loftier than that which might make those two favors desirable; I am not yet reduced to imploring them; I am soliciting advice whereof my youth and my misfortunes put me in need, and you would have me purchase it at an excessively inflated price." Ashamed thus to have been unmasked, the pastor promptly drove the little creature away, and the unhappy Justine, twice rejected on the first day of her condemnation to isolation, now enters a house above whose door she spies a shingle; she rents a small chamber on the fourth floor, pays in advance for it, and, once established, gives herself over to lamentations all the more bitter because she is sensitive and because her little pride has just been compromised cruelly.

We will allow ourselves to leave her in this state for a short while in order to return to Juliette and to relate how, from the very ordinary condition in which she sets forth, no better furnished with resources than her sister, she nevertheless attains, over a period of fifteen years, the position of a titled woman, with an income of thirty thousand pounds, very handsome jewels, two or three houses in the city, as many in the country and, at the present moment, the heart, the fortune and the confidence of Monsieur de Corville, Councilor to the State, an important man much esteemed and about to have a minister's post. Her rise was not, there can be no question of it, unattended by difficulties: 'tis by way of the most shameful, most onerous apprenticeship that these ladies attain their objectives; and 'tis in all likelihood a veteran of unnumbered campaigns one may find today abed with a Prince: perhaps she yet carries the humiliating marks of the brutality of the libertines into whose hands her youth and inexperience flung her long ago.

Upon leaving the convent, Juliette went to find a woman whose name she had once heard mentioned by a youthful friend; perverted was what she desired to be and this woman was to pervert her; she arrived at her house with a small parcel under her arm, clad in a blue dressing gown nicely disarrayed, her hair straggling carelessly about, and showing the prettiest face in the world, if it is true that for certain eyes indecency may have its charms; she told her story to this woman and begged her to afford her the sanctuary she had provided her former friend.

"How old are you?" Madame Duvergier demanded.

"I will be fifteen in a few days, Madame," Juliette replied.

"And never hath mortal . . ." the matron continued.

"No, Madame, I swear it," answered Juliette.

"But, you know, in those convents," said the old dame, "sometimes a confessor, a nun, a companion . . . I must have conclusive evidence."

"You have but to look for it," Juliette replied with a blush.

And, having put on her spectacles, and having scrupulously examined things here and there, the duenna declared to the girl:

"Why, you've only to remain here, pay strict attention to what I say, give proof of unending complaisance and submissiveness to my practices, you need but be clean, economical, and frank with me, be prudent with your comrades and fraudulent when dealing with men, and before ten years' time I shall have you fit to occupy the best second-story apartment: you'll have a commode, pier-glass mirrors before you and a maid behind, and the art you will have acquired from me will give you what you need to procure yourself the rest."

These suggestions having left her lips, Duvergier lays hands on Juliette's little parcel; she asks her whether she does not have some money, and Juliette having too candidly admitted she had a hundred crowns, the dear mother confiscates them, giving her new boarding guest the assurance her little fortune will be chanced at the lottery for her, but that a girl must not have money. "It is," says she, "a means to doing evil, and in a period as corrupt as ours, a wise and well-born girl should carefully avoid all which might lure her into any snares. It is for your own good I speak, my little one," adds the duenna, "and you ought to be grateful for what I am doing."

The sermon delivered, the newcomer is introduced to her colleagues; she is assigned a room in the house, and on the next day her maidenhead is put on sale.

Within four months the merchandise is sold successively to about one hundred buyers; some are content with the rose, others more fastidious or more depraved (for the question has not yet been decided) wish to bring to full flower the bud that grows adjacently. After each bout, Duvergier makes a few tailor's readjustments and for four months it is always the pristine fruits the rascal puts on the block. Finally, at the end of this harassing novitiate, Juliette obtains a lay sister's patents; from this moment onward, she is a recognized girl of the house; thereafter she is to share in its profits and losses. Another apprenticeship; if in the first school, aside from a few extravagances, Juliette served Nature, she altogether ignores Nature's laws in the second, where a complete shambles is made of what she once had of moral behavior; the triumph she obtains in vice totally degrades her soul; she feels that, having been born for crime, she must at least commit it grandly and give over languishing in a subaltern's role, which, although entailing the same misconduct, although abasing her equally, brings her a slighter, a much slighter profit. She is found agreeable by an elderly gentleman, much debauched, who at first has her come merely to attend to the affairs of the moment; she has the skill to cause herself magnificently to be kept; it is not long before she is appearing at the theater, at promenades, amongst the elite, the very *cordon bleu* of the Cytherean order; she is beheld, mentioned, desired, and the clever creature knows so well how to manage her affairs that in less than four years she ruins six men, the poorest of whom had an annuity of one hundred thousand crowns. Nothing more is needed to make her reputation; the blindness of fashionable people is such that the more one of these creatures has demonstrated her dishonesty, the more eager they are to get upon her list; it seems that the degree of her degradation and her corruption becomes the measure of the sentiments they dare display for her.

Juliette had just attained her twentieth year when a certain Comte de Lorsange, a gentleman out of Anjou, about forty years of age, became so captivated by her he resolved to bestow his name upon her; he awarded her an income of twelve thousand pounds and assured her of the rest of his fortune were he to be the first to die; he gave her, as well, a house, servants, lackeys, and the sort of mundane consideration which, in the space of two or three years, succeeded in causing her beginnings to be forgot.

It was at this point the fell Juliette, oblivious of all the fine feelings that had been hers by birthright and good education, warped by bad counsel and dangerous books, spurred by the desire to enjoy herself, but alone, and to have a name but not a single chain, bent her attentions to the culpable idea of abridging her husband's days. The odious project once conceived, she consolidated her scheme during those dangerous moments when the physical aspect is fired by ethical error, instants when one refuses oneself much less, for then nothing is opposed to the irregularity of vows or to the impetuosity of desires, and the voluptuousness one experiences is sharp and lively only by reason of the number of the restraints whence one bursts free, or their sanctity. The dream dissipated, were one to recover one's common-sense mood the thing would be of but mediocre import, 'tis the story of mental wrongdoing; everyone knows very well it offends no one; but, alas! one sometimes carries the thing a little farther. What, one ventures to wonder, what would not be the idea's realization, if its mere abstract shape has just exalted, has just so profoundly moved one? The accursed reverie is vivified, and its existence is a crime.

Fortunately for herself, Madame de Lorsange executed it in such secrecy that she was sheltered from all pursuit and with her husband she buried all traces of the frightful deed which precipitated him into the tomb.

Once again become free, and a countess, Madame de Lorsange returned to her former habits; but, believing herself to have some figure in the world, she put somewhat less of the indecent in her deportment. 'Twas no longer a kept girl, 'twas a rich widow who gave pretty suppers at which the Court and the City were only too happy to be included; in a word, we have here a correct woman who, all the same, would to bed for two hundred *louis,* and who gave herself for five hundred a month.

Until she reached the age of twenty-six, Madame de Lorsange made further brilliant conquests: she wrought the financial downfall of three foreign ambassadors, four Farmers-general, two bishops, a cardinal, and three knights of the King's Order; but as it is rarely one stops after the first offense, especially when it has turned out very happily, the unhappy Juliette blackened herself with two additional crimes similar to the first: one in order to plunder a lover who had entrusted a considerable sum to her, of which the man's family had no intelligence; the other in order to capture a legacy of one hundred thousand crowns another one of her lovers granted her in the name of a third, who was charged to pay her that amount after his death. To these horrors Madame de Lorsange added three or four infanticides. The fear of spoiling her pretty figure, the desire to conceal a double intrigue, all combined to make her resolve to stifle the proof of her debauches in her womb; and these misdeeds, like the others, unknown, did not prevent our adroit and ambitious woman from finding new dupes every day.

It is hence true that prosperity may attend conduct of the very worst, and that in the very thick of disorder and corruption, all of what mankind calls happiness may shed itself bountifully upon life; but let this cruel and fatal truth cause no alarm; let honest folk be no more seriously tormented by the example we are going to present of disaster everywhere dogging the heels of Virtue; this criminal felicity is deceiving, it is seeming only; independently of the punishment most certainly reserved by Providence for those whom success in crime has seduced, do they not nourish in the depths of their soul a worm which unceasingly gnaws, prevents them from finding joy in these fictive gleams of meretricious well-being, and, instead of delights, leaves naught in their soul but the rending memory of the crimes which have led them to where they are? With what regards the luckless one fate persecutes, he has his heart for his comfort, and the interior ecstasies virtues procure bring him speedy restitution for the injustice of men.

Such was the state of affairs with Madame de Lorsange when Monsieur de Corville, fifty, a notable wielding the influence and possessing the privileges described further above, resolved entirely to sacrifice himself for this woman and to attach her to himself forever. Whether thanks to diligent attention, whether to maneuver, whether to policy on the part of Madame de Lorsange, he succeeded, and there had passed four years during which he dwelt with her, entirely as if with a legitimate wife, when the acquisition of a very handsome property not far from Montargis obliged both of them to go and spend some time in the Bourbonnais.

One evening, when the excellence of the weather had induced them to prolong their stroll beyond the bounds of their estate and toward Montargis, too fatigued, both, to attempt to return home as they had left, they halted at the inn where the coach from Lyon stops, with the intention of sending a man by horse to fetch them a carriage. In a cool, low-ceilinged room in this house, looking out upon a courtyard, they took their ease and were resting when the coach we just mentioned drew up at the hostelry.

It is a commonplace amusement to watch the arrival of a coach and the passengers' descent: one wagers on the sort of persons who are in it, and if one has gambled upon a whore, an officer, a few abbots and a monk, one is almost certain to win. Madame de Lorsange rises, Monsieur de Corville follows her; from the window they see the well-jolted company reel into the inn. There seemed to be no one left in the carriage when an officer of the mounted constabulary, stepping to the ground, received in his arms, from one of his comrades poised high on top of the coach, a girl of twenty-six or twenty-seven, dressed in a worn calico jacket and swathed to the eyes in a great black taffeta mantle. She was bound hand and foot like a criminal, and in such a weakened state, she would surely have fallen had her guards not given her support. A cry of surprise and horror escaped from Madame de Lorsange: the girl turned and revealed, together with the loveliest figure imaginable, the most noble, the most agreeable, the most interesting visage, in brief, there were there all the charms of a sort to please, and they were rendered yet a thousand times more piquant by that tender and touching air innocence contributes to the traits of beauty.

Monsieur de Corville and his mistress could not suppress their interest in the miserable girl. They approached, they demanded of one of the troopers what the unhappy creature had done.

"She is accused of three crimes," replied the constable, " 'tis a question of murder, theft and arson; but I wish to tell your lordship that my comrade and I have never been so reluctant to take a criminal into custody; she's the most gentle thing, d'ye know, and seems to be the most honest too."

"Oh, la," said Monsieur de Corville, "it might easily be one of those blunders so frequent in the lower courts . . . and where were these crimes committed?"

"At an inn several leagues from Lyon, it's at Lyon she was tried; in accordance with custom she's going to Paris for confirmation of the sentence and then will be returned to Lyon to be executed."

Madame de Lorsange, having heard these words, said in lowered voice to Monsieur de Corville, that she fain would have from the girl's own lips the story of her troubles, and Monsieur de Corville, who was possessed of the same desire, expressed it to the pair of guards and identified himself. The officers saw no reason not to oblige, everyone decided to stay the night at Montargis; comfortable accomodations were called for; Monsieur de Corville declared he would be responsible for the prisoner, she was unbound, and when she had been given something to eat, Madame de Lorsange, unable to control her very great curiosity, and doubtless saying to herself, "This creature, perhaps innocent, is, however, treated like a criminal, whilst about me all is prosperity. . . . I who am soiled with crimes and horrors"; Madame de Lorsange I say, as soon as she observed the poor girl to be somewhat restored, to some measure reassured by the caresses they hastened to bestow upon her, besought her to tell how it had fallen out that she, with so very sweet a face, found herself in such a dreadful plight.

"To recount you the story of my life, Madame," this lovely one in distress said to the Countess, "is to offer you the most striking example of innocence oppressed, is to accuse the hand of Heaven, is to bear complaint against the Supreme Being's will, is, in a sense, to rebel against His sacred designs. . . . I dare not. . . ." Tears gathered in this interesting girl's eyes and, after having given vent to them for a moment, she began her recitation in these terms.

Permit me to conceal my name and birth, Madame; without being illustrious, they are distinguished, and my origins did not destine me to the humiliation to which you see me reduced. When very young I lost my parents; provided with the slender inheritance they had left me, I thought I could expect a suitable position and, refusing to accept all those which were not, I gradually spent, at Paris where I was born, the little I possessed; the poorer I became, the more I was despised; the greater became my need of support, the less I was able to hope for it; but from amongst all the severities to which I was exposed at the beginning of my woeful career, from amongst all the terrible proposals that were made me, I will cite to you what befell me at the home of Monsieur Dubourg, one of the capital's richest tradesmen. The woman with whom I had lodgings had recommended him to me as someone whose influence and wealth might be able to meliorate the harshness of my situation; after having waited a very long time in this man's antechamber, I was admitted; Monsieur Dubourg, aged forty-eight, had just risen out of bed, and was wrapped in a dressing gown which barely hid his disorder; they were about to prepare his coiffure; he dismissed his servants and asked me what I wanted with him.

"Alas, Monsieur," I said, greatly confused, "I am a poor orphan not yet fourteen years old and I have already become familiar with every nuance of misfortune; I implore your commiseration, have pity upon me, I beseech you," and then I told in detail of all my ills, the difficulty I was having to find a place, perhaps I even mentioned how painful it was for me to have to take one, not having been born for a menial's condition. My suffering throughout it all, how I exhausted the little substance I had . . . failure to obtain work, my hope he would facilitate matters and help me find the wherewithal to live; in sum, I said everything that is dictated by the eloquence of wretchedness, always swift to rise in a sensitive soul. . . . After having listened to me with many distractions and much yawning, Monsieur Dubourg asked whether I had always been well-behaved. "I should be neither so poor nor so embarrassed, Monsieur," I answered him, "had I wished to cease to be."

"But," said Dubourg upon hearing that, "but what right have you to expect the wealthy to relieve you if you are in no way useful to them?"

"And of what service are you speaking, Monsieur? I asked nothing more than to render those decency and my years will permit me fulfill."

"The services of a child like yourself are of no great use in a household," Dubourg replied to me. "You have neither the age nor the appearance to find the place you are seeking. You would be better advised to occupy yourself with giving men pleasure and to labor to discover someone who will consent to take care of you; the virtue whereof you make such a conspicuous display is worthless in this world; in vain will you genuflect before its altars, its ridiculous incense will nourish you not at all. The thing which least flatters men, that which makes the least favorable impression upon them, for which they have the most supreme contempt, is good behavior in your sex; here on earth, my child, nothing but what brings in gain or insures power is accounted; and what does the virtue of women profit us! It is their wantonness which serves and amuses us; but their chastity could not interest us less. When, to be brief, persons of our sort give, it is never except to receive; well, how may a little girl like yourself show gratitude for what one does for her if it is not by the most complete surrender of all that is desired of her body!"

"Oh, Monsieur," I replied, grown heavy of heart and uttering a sigh, "then uprightness and benevolence are to be found in man no longer!"

"Precious little," Dubourg rejoined. "How can you expect them still to exist after all the wise things that have been said and written about them? We have rid ourselves of this mania of obliging others gratuitously; it was recognized that charity's pleasures are nothing but sops thrown to pride, and we turned our thoughts to stronger sensations; it has been noticed, for example, that with a child like you, it is infinitely preferable to extract, by way of dividends upon one's investment, all the pleasures lechery is able to offer—much better these delights than the very insipid and futile ones said to come of the disinterested giving of help; his reputation for being a liberal man, an alms-giving and generous man, is not, even at the instant when he most enjoys it, comparable to the slightest sensual pleasure."

"Oh, Monsieur, in the light of such principles the miserable must therefore perish!"

"Does it matter? We have more subjects in France than are needed; given the mechanism's elastic capacities for production, the State can easily afford to be burdened by fewer people."

"But do you suppose children respect their fathers when they are thus despised by them?"

"And what to a father is the love of the children who are a nuisance to him?"

"Would it then have been better had they been strangled in the cradle?"

"Certainly, such is the practice in numerous countries; it was the custom of the Greeks, it is the custom in China: there, the offspring of the poor are exposed, or are put to death. What is the good of letting those creatures live who, no longer able to count upon their parents' aid either because they are without parents or because they are not wanted or recognized by them, henceforth are useful for nothing and simply weigh upon the State: that much surplus commodity, you see, and the market is glutted already; bastards, orphans, malformed infants should be condemned to death immediately they are pupped: the first and the second because, no longer having anyone who wishes or who is able to take care of them, they are mere dregs which one day can have nothing but an undesirable effect upon the society they contaminate; the others because they cannot be of any usefulness to it; the one and the other of these categories are to society what are excrescences to the flesh, battening upon the healthy members' sap, degrading them, enfeebling them; or, if you prefer, they are like those vegetable parasites which, attaching themselves to sound plants, cause them to deteriorate by sucking up their nutritive juices. It's a shocking outrage, these alms destined to feed scum, these most luxuriously appointed houses they have the madness to construct quite as if the human species were so rare, so precious one had to preserve it down to its last vile portion! But enough of politics whereof, my child, you are not likely to understand anything; why lament your fate? for it is in your power, and yours only, to remedy it."

"Great Heavens! at the price of what!"

"At the price of an illusion, of something that has none but the value wherewith your pride invests it. Well," continued this barbarian, getting to his feet and opening the door, "that is all I can do for you; consent to it, or deliver me from your presence; I have no fondness for beggars. . . ."

My tears flowed fast, I was unable to check them; would you believe it, Madame? they irritated rather than melted this man. He shut the door and, seizing my dress at the shoulder, he said most brutally he was going to force from me what I would not accord him voluntarily. At this cruel moment my misery endowed me with courage; I freed myself from his grasp and rushed toward the door:

"Odious man," said I as I fled from him, "may the Heaven you have so grievously offended some day punish your execrable heartlessness as it merits to be. You are worthy neither of the riches you have put to such vile use, nor of the very air you breathe in a world you defile with your barbarities."

I lost no time telling my hostess of the reception given me by the person to whom she had sent me; but what was my astonishment to have this wretch belabor me with reproaches rather than share my sorrow.

"You idiotic chit!" said she in a great rage, "do you imagine men are such great dupes as to dole out alms to little girls such as you without requiring something for their money? Monsieur Dubourg's behavior was far too gentle; in his place I should not have allowed you to leave without having had satisfaction from you. But since you do not care to profit from the aid I offer you, make your own arrangements as you please; you owe me money: pay it tomorrow; otherwise, it's to jail."

"Madame, have pity—"

"Yes, yes, pity; one need only have pity and one starves to death."

"But what would you have me do?"

"You must go back to Dubourg; you must appease him; you must bring home money to me; I will visit him, I will give him notice; if I am able, I'll repair the damage your stupidity has caused; I will convey your apologies, but keep it in mind, you had better improve your conduct."

Ashamed, desperate, knowing not which way to turn, seeing myself savagely repulsed by everyone, I told Madame Desroches (that was my landlady's name) that I had decided to do whatever had to be done to satisfy her. She went to the financier's house and upon her return advised me that she had found him in a very irritable mood, that it had not been without an effort she had managed to incline him in my favor, that by dint of supplications she had at least persuaded him to see me again the following

morning, but that I would have to keep a strict watch over my behavior, because, were I to take it into my head to disobey him
again, he himself would see to it I was imprisoned forever.

All atremble, I arrived; Dubourg was alone and in a state yet
more indecent than on the previous day. Brutality, libertinage, all
the characteristics of the debauchee glittered in his cunning glances.

"Thank Desroches," he said harshly, "for it is as a favor to
her I intend to show you an instant's kindness; you must surely be
aware how little you deserve it after your performance yesterday.
Undress yourself and if you once again manifest the least resistance
to my desires, two men, waiting for you in the next room, will
conduct you to a place whence you will never emerge alive."

"Oh Monsieur," say I, weeping, clutching the wicked man's
knees, "unbend, I beseech you; be so generous as to relieve me
without requiring what would be so costly I should rather offer you
my life than submit to it. . . . Yes, I prefer to die a thousand times
over than violate the principles I received in my childhood. . . .
Monsieur, Monsieur, constrain me not, I entreat you; can you
conceive of gleaning happiness in the depths of tears and disgust?
Dare you suspect pleasure where you see naught but loathing? No
sooner shall you have consummated your crime than my despair will
overwhelm you with remorse. . . ."

But the infamies to which Dubourg abandoned himself prevented me from continuing; that I was able to have believed myself
capable of touching a man who was already finding, in the very
spectacle of my suffering, one further vehicle for his horrible passions! Would you believe it, Madame? becoming inflamed by the
shrill accents of my pleadings, savoring them inhumanly, the wretch
disposed himself for his criminal attempts! He gets up, and exhibiting himself to me in a state over which reason is seldom
triumphant, and wherein the opposition of the object which causes
reason's downfall is but an additional ailment to delirium, he seizes
me brutally, impetuously snatches away the veils which still conceal
what he burns to enjoy; he caresses me. . . . Oh! what a picture,
Great God! What unheard-of mingling of harshness . . . and
lewdness! It seemed that the Supreme Being wished, in that first
of my encounters, to imprint forever in me all the horror I was to
have for a kind of crime whence there was to be born the torrent

of evils that have beset me since. But must I complain of them? No, needless to say; to his excesses I owe my salvation; had there been less debauchery in him, I were a ruined girl; Dubourg's flames were extinguished in the fury of his enterprises, Heaven intervened in my behalf against the monster before he could commit the offenses he was readying for, and the loss of his powers, before the sacrifice could occur, preserved me from being its victim.

The consequence was Dubourg became nothing if not more insolent; he laid upon me the blame for his weakness' mistakes, wanted to repair them with new outrages and yet more mortifying invectives; there was nothing he did not say to me, nothing he did not attempt, nothing his perfidious imagination, his adamantine character and the depravation of his manners did not lead him to undertake. My clumsiness made him impatient: I was far from wishing to participate in the thing, to lend myself to it was as much as I could do, my remorse remained lively. However, it was all for naught, submitting to him, I ceased to inflame him; in vain he passed successively from tenderness to rigor . . . from groveling to tyranny . . . from an air of decency to the profligate's excesses, in vain, I say, there was nothing for it, we were both exhausted, and happily he was unable to recover what he needed to deliver more dangerous assaults. He gave it up, made me promise to come the next day, and to be sure of me he refused absolutely to give me anything above the sum I owed Desroches. Greatly humiliated by the adventure and firmly resolved, whatever might happen to me, not to expose myself a third time, I returned to where I was lodging. I announced my intentions to Desroches, paid her, and heaped maledictions upon the criminal capable of so cruelly exploiting my misery. But my imprecations, far from drawing the wrath of God down upon him, only added to his good fortune; and a week later I learned this signal libertine had just obtained a general trusteeship from the Government, which would augment his revenues by more than five hundred thousand pounds per annum. I was absorbed in the reflections such unexpected inconsistencies of fate inevitably give rise to, when a momentary ray of hope seemed to shine in my eyes.

Desroches came to tell me one day that she had finally located a house into which I could be received with pleasure provided my comportment remained of the best. "Great Heaven, Madame," I cried, transported, throwing myself into her arms, "that condition is the one I would stipulate myself—you may imagine how happy I am to accept it." The man I was to serve was a famous Parisian usurer who had become rich, not only by lending money upon collateral, but even by stealing from the public every time he thought he could do so in safety. He lived in the rue Quincampoix, had a third-story flat, and shared it with a creature of fifty years he called his wife and who was at least as wicked as he.

"Thérèse," this miser said to me (such was the name I had taken in order to hide my own), "Thérèse, the primary virtue in this house is probity; if ever you make off with the tenth part of a penny, I'll have you hanged, my child, d'ye see. The modest ease my wife and I enjoy is the fruit of our immense labors, and of our perfect sobriety. . . . Do you eat much, little one?"

"A few ounces of bread each day, Monsieur," I replied, "water, and a little soup when I am lucky enough to get it."

"Soup! Bleeding Christ! Soup! Behold, deary," said the usurer to his dame, "behold and tremble at the progress of luxury: it's looking for circumstances, it's been dying of hunger for a year, and now it wants to eat soup; we scarcely have it once a week, on Sunday, we who work like galley slaves: you'll have three ounces of bread a day, my daughter, plus half a bottle of river water, plus one of my wife's old dresses every eighteen months, plus three crowns' wages at the end of each year, if we are content with your services, if your economy responds to our own and if, finally, you make the house prosper through orderliness and arrangement. Your duties are mediocre, they're done in jig time; 'tis but a question of washing and cleaning this six-room apartment thrice a week, of making our beds, answering the door, powdering my wig, dressing my wife's hair, looking after the dog and the parakeet, lending a hand in the kitchen, washing the utensils, helping my wife whenever she prepares us a bite to eat, and daily devoting four or five hours to the washing, to mending stockings, hats, and other little household odds and ends; you observe, Thérèse, 'tis nothing at all, you will have ample free time to yourself, we will permit you to employ it to your own interest, provided, my child, you are good, discreet and, above all, thrifty, that's of the essence."

You may readily imagine, Madame, that one had to be in the

frightful state I indeed was in to accept such a position; not only was there infinitely more work to be done than my strength permitted me to undertake, but should I be able to live upon what was offered me? However, I was careful to raise no difficulties and was installed that same evening.

Were my cruel situation to permit me to amuse you for an instant, Madame, when I must think of nothing but gaining your compassion, I should dare describe some of the symptoms of avarice I witnessed while in that house; but a catastrophe so terrible for me was awaiting me during my second year there that it is by no means easy to linger over entertaining details before making you acquainted with my miseries.

Nevertheless, you will know, Madame, that, for light in Monsieur du Harpin's apartment, there was never any but what he got from the street lamp which, happily, was placed opposite his room; never did Monsieur or Madame use linen; what I washed was hoarded away, it was never touched; on the sleeves of Monsieur's coat, as well as upon Madame's dress, were old gauntlet cuffs sewn over the material, and these I removed and washed every Saturday evening; no sheets; no towels, and that to avoid laundry expenses. Never was wine drunk in her house, clear water being, declared Madame du Harpin, the natural drink of man, the healthiest and least dangerous. Every time bread was sliced, a basket was put beneath the knife so that whatever fell would not be lost; into this container went, also, and with exactitude all the scraps and leavings that might survive the meal, and this compound, fried up on Sunday together with a little butter, made a banquet for the day of rest; never was one to beat clothing or too energetically dust the furniture for fear of wearing it out, instead, very cautiously, one tickled about with a feather. Monsieur's shoes, and Madame's as well, were double-soled with iron, they were the same shoes that had served them on their wedding day; but a much more unusual custom was the one they had me practice once a week: there was in the apartment a rather large room whose walls were not papered; I was expected to take a knife and scrape and shave away a certain quantity of plaster, and this I next passed through a fine sieve; what resulted from this operation became the powder wherewith every morning I sprinkled Monsieur's peruke and

Madame's hair, done up in a bun. Ah! wouldst to God those had been the only turpitudes of which this evil pair had made habits! Nothing's more normal than the desire to conserve one's property; but what is not normal is the desire to augment it by the accession of the property of others. And it was not long before I perceived that it was only thus du Harpin acquired his wealth.

Above us there lodged a solitary individual of considerable means who was the owner of some handsome jewels, and whose belongings, whether because of their proximity or because they had passed through my master's hands, were very well known to him; I often heard him express regrets to his wife over the loss of a certain gold box worth fifty or sixty *louis,* which article would infallibly have remained his, said he, had he proceeded with greater cleverness. In order to console himself for the sale of the said box, the good Monsieur du Harpin projected its theft, and it was to me he entrusted the execution of his plan.

After having delivered a long speech upon the indifference of robbery, upon, indeed, its usefulness in the world, since it maintains a sort of equilibrium which totally confounds the inequality of property; upon the infrequence of punishment, since out of every twenty thieves it could be proven that not above two dies on the gallows; after having demonstrated to me, with an erudition of which I had not dreamt Monsieur du Harpin capable, that theft was honored throughout Greece, that several races yet acknowledge it, favor it, and reward it for a bold deed simultaneously giving proof of courage and skill (two virtues indispensable to a warlike nation), after having, in a word, exalted his personal influence which would extricate me from all embarrassments in the event I should be detected, Monsieur du Harpin tendered me two lock picks, one to open the neighbor's front door, the other his secretary within which lay the box in question; incessantly he enjoined me to get him this box and, in return for so important a service, I could expect, for two years, to receive an additional crown.

"Oh Monsieur!" I exclaimed, shuddering at his proposal, "is it possible a master dare thus corrupt his domestic! What prevents me from turning against you the weapons you put into my hands?

and what defense will you have if someday I make you the victim of your own principles?"

Du Harpin, much confused, fell back upon a lame subterfuge: what he was doing, said he, was being done with the simple intention of testing me; how fortunate that I had resisted this temptation, he added . . . how I should have been doomed had I succumbed, etc. I scoffed at this lie; but I was soon enough aware of what a mistake it had been to answer him with such asperity: malefactors do not like to find resistance in those they seek to seduce; unfortunately, there is no middle ground or median attitude when one is so unlucky as to have been approached by them: one must necessarily thereupon become either their accomplices, which is exceedingly dangerous, or their enemies, which is even more so. Had I been a little experienced, I would have quit the house forthwith, but it was already written in Heaven that every one of the honest gestures that was to emanate from me would be answered by misfortunes.

Monsieur du Harpin let more than a month drift by, that is to say, he waited until the end of my second year with him, and waited without showing the least hint of resentment at the refusal I had given him, when one evening, having just retired to my room to taste a few hours of repose, I suddenly heard my door burst open and there, not without terror, I saw Monsieur du Harpin and four soldiers of the watch standing by my bed.

"Perform your duty, Sirrah," said he to the men of the law, "this wretch has stolen from me a diamond worth a thousand crowns, you will find it in her chamber or upon her person, the fact is certain."

"I have robbed you, Monsieur!" said I, sore troubled and springing from my bed, "I! Great Heaven! Who knows better than you the contrary to be true! Who should be more deeply aware than you to what point I loathe robbery and to what degree it is unthinkable I could have committed it."

But du Harpin made a great uproar to drown out my words; he continued to order perquisitions, and the miserable ring was discovered in my mattress. To evidence of this strength there was nothing to reply; I was seized instantly, pinioned, and led to prison without being able to prevail upon the authorities to listen to one word in my favor.

The trial of an unfortunate creature who has neither influence nor protection is conducted with dispatch in a land where virtue is thought incompatible with misery, where poverty is enough to convict the accused; there, an unjust prepossession causes it to be supposed that he who ought to have committed a crime did indeed commit it; sentiments are proportioned according to the guilty one's estate; and when once gold or titles are wanting to establish his innocence, the impossibility that he be innocent then appears self-evident.[1]

I defended myself, it did no good, in vain I furnished the best material to the lawyer whom a protocol of form required be given me for an instant or two; my employer accused me, the diamond had been discovered in my room; it was plain I had stolen it. When I wished to describe Monsieur du Harpin's awful traffic and prove that the misfortune that had struck me was naught but the fruit of his vengeance and the consequence of his eagerness to be rid of a creature who, through possession of his secret, had become his master, these pleadings were interpreted as so many recriminations, and I was informed that for twenty years Monsieur du Harpin had been known as a man of integrity, incapable of such a horror. I was transferred to the Conciergerie, where I saw myself upon the brink of having to pay with my life for having refused to participate in a crime; I was shortly to perish; only a new misdeed could save me: Providence willed that Crime serve at least once as an aegis unto Virtue, that crime might preserve it from the abyss which is someday going to engulf judges together with their imbecility.

I had about me a woman, probably forty years old, as celebrated for her beauty as for the variety and number of her villainies; she was called Dubois and, like the unlucky Thérèse, was on the eve of paying the capital penalty, but as to the exact form of it the judges were yet mightily perplexed: having rendered herself guilty of every imaginable crime, they found themselves virtually obliged to invent a new torture for her, or to expose her to one whence we ordinarily exempt our sex. This woman had become

---

[1] O ages yet to come! You shall no longer be witness to these horrors and infamies abounding!

interested in me, criminally interested without doubt, since the basis of her feelings, as I learned afterward, was her extreme desire to make a proselyte of me.

Only two days from the time set for our execution, Dubois came to me; it was at night. She told me not to lie down to sleep, but to stay near her side. Without attracting attention, we moved as close as we could to the prison door. "Between seven and eight," she said, "the Conciergerie will catch fire, I have seen to it; no question about it, many people will be burned; it doesn't matter, Thérèse," the evil creature went on, "the fate of others must always be as nothing to us when our own lives are at stake; well, we are going to escape here, of that you can be sure; four men—my confederates—will join us and I guarantee you we will be free."

I have told you, Madame, that the hand of God which had just punished my innocence, employed crime to protect me; the fire began, it spread, the blaze was horrible, twenty-one persons were consumed, but we made a successful sally. The same day we reached the cottage of a poacher, an intimate friend of our band who dwelt in the forest of Bondy.

"There you are, Thérèse," Dubois says to me, "free. You may now choose the kind of life you wish, but were I to have any advice to give you, it would be to renounce the practice of virtue which, as you have noticed, is the courting of disaster; a misplaced delicacy led you to the foot of the scaffold, an appalling crime rescued you from it; have a look about and see how useful are good deeds in this world, and whether it is really worth the trouble immolating yourself for them. Thérèse, you are young and attractive, heed me, and in two years I'll have led you to a fortune; but don't suppose I am going to guide you there along the paths of virtue: when one wants to get on, my dear girl, one must stop at nothing; decide, then, we have no security in this cottage, we've got to leave in a few hours."

"Oh Madame," I said to my benefactress, "I am greatly indebted to you, and am far from wishing to disown my obligations; you saved my life; in my view, 'tis frightful the thing was achieved through a crime and, believe me, had I been the one charged to commit it, I should have preferred a thousand deaths to the anguish of participating in it; I am aware of all the dangers I risk in trusting myself to the honest sentiments which will always remain in my heart; but whatever be the thorns of virtue, Madame, I prefer them unhesitatingly and always to the perilous favors which are crime's accompaniment. There are religious principles within me which, may it please Heaven, will never desert me; if Providence renders difficult my career in life, 'tis in order to compensate me in a better world. That hope is my consolation, it sweetens my griefs, it soothes me in my sufferings, it fortifies me in distress, and causes me confidently to face all the ills it pleases God to visit upon me. That joy should straightway be extinguished in my soul were I perchance to besmirch it with crime, and together with the fear of chastisements in this world I should have the painful anticipation of torments in the next, which would not for one instant procure me the tranquillity I thirst after."

"Those are absurd doctrines which will have you on the dung heap in no time, my girl," said Dubois with a frown; "believe me: forget God's justice, His future punishments and rewards, the lot of those platitudes lead us nowhere but to death from starvation. O Thérèse, the callousness of the Rich legitimates the bad conduct of the Poor; let them open their purse to our needs, let humaneness reign in their hearts and virtues will take root in ours; but as long as our misfortune, our patient endurance of it, our good faith, our abjection only serves to double the weight of our chains, our crimes will be their doing, and we will be fools indeed to abstain from them when they can lessen the yoke wherewith their cruelty bears us down. Nature has caused us all to be equals born, Thérèse; if fate is pleased to upset the primary scheme of the general law, it is up to us to correct its caprices and through our skill to repair the usurpations of the strongest. I love to hear these rich ones, these titled ones, these magistrates and these priests, I love to see them preach virtue to us. It is not very difficult to forswear theft when one has three or four times what one needs to live; it is not very necessary to plot murder when one is surrounded by nothing but adulators and thralls unto whom one's will is law; nor is it very hard to be temperate and sober when one has the most succulent dainties constantly within one's reach; they can well contrive to be sincere when there is never any apparent advantage in falsehood. ... But we, Thérèse, we whom the barbaric Providence you are mad enough to idolize, has condemned to slink in the dust of humiliation as doth the serpent in grass, we who are beheld with disdain only because we are poor, who are tyrannized because we are weak; we, who must quench our thirst with gall and who, wherever we go, tread on the thistle always, you would have us shun crime when its hand alone opens up unto us the door to life, maintains us in it, and is our only protection when our life is threatened; you would have it that, degraded and in perpetual abjection, while this class dominating us has to itself all the blessings of fortune, we reserve for ourselves naught but pain, beatings, suffering, nothing but want and tears, brandings and the gibbet. No, no, Thérèse, no; either this Providence you reverence is made only for our scorn, or the world we see about us is not at all what Providence would have it. Become better acquainted with your Providence, my child, and be convinced that as soon as it places us in a situation where evil becomes necessary, and while at the same time it leaves us the possibility of doing it, this evil harmonizes quite as well with its decrees as does good, and Providence gains as much by the one as by the other; the state in which she has created us is equality: he who disturbs is no more guilty than he who seeks to re-establish the balance; both act in accordance with received impulses, both have to obey those impulses and enjoy them."

I must confess that if ever I was shaken it was by this clever woman's seductions; but a yet stronger voice, that of my heart to which I gave heed, combatted her sophistries; I declared to Dubois that I was determined never to allow myself to be corrupted. "Very well!" she replied, "become what you wish, I abandon you to your sorry fate; but if ever you get yourself hanged, which is an end you cannot avoid, thanks to the fatality which inevitably saves the criminal by sacrificing the virtuous, at least remember before dying never to mention us."

While we were arguing thus, Dubois' four companions were drinking with the poacher, and as wine disposes the malefactor's heart to new crimes and causes him to forget his old, our bandits no sooner learned of my resolution than, unable to make me their accomplice, they decided to make me their victim; their principles, their manners, the dark retreat we were in, the security they thought they enjoyed, their drunkenness, my age, my innocence— everything encouraged them. They get up from table, they confer in whispers, they consult Dubois, doings whose lugubrious mystery makes me shiver with horror, and at last there comes an order to me then and there to satisfy the desires of each of the four; if I go to it cheerfully, each will give me a crown to help me along my way; if they must employ violence, the thing will be done all the same; but the better to guard their secret, once finished with me they will stab me, and will bury me at the foot of yonder tree.

I need not paint the effect this cruel proposition had upon me, Madame, you will have no difficulty understanding that I sank to my knees before Dubois, I besought her a second time to be my protectress: the low creature did but laugh at my tears:

"Oh by God!" quoth she, "here's an unhappy little one. What! you shudder before the obligation to serve four fine big boys one after another? Listen to me," she added, after some reflection, "my sway over these dear lads is sufficiently great for me to obtain a reprieve for you upon condition you render yourself worthy of it."

"Alas! Madame, what must I do?" I cried through my tears; "command me; I am ready."

"Join us, throw in your lot with us, and commit the same deeds, without show of the least repugnance; either that, or I cannot save you from the rest." I did not think myself in a position to hesitate; by accepting this cruel condition I exposed myself to further dangers, to be sure, but they were the less immediate; perhaps I might be able to avoid them, whereas nothing could save me from those with which I was actually menaced.

"I will go everywhere with you, Madame," was my prompt answer to Dubois, "everywhere, I promise you; shield me from the fury of these men and I shall never leave your side while I live."

"Children," Dubois said to the four bandits, "this girl is one of the company, I am taking her into it; I ask you to do her no ill, don't put her stomach off the *métier* during her first days in it; you see how useful her age and face can be to us; let's employ them to our advantage rather than sacrifice them to our pleasures."

But such is the degree of energy in man's passions nothing can subdue them. The persons I was dealing with were in no state to heed reason: all four surrounded me, devoured me with their fiery glances, menaced me in a still more terrible manner; they were about to lay hands on me, I was about to become their victim.

"She has got to go through with it," one of them declared, "it's too late for discussion: was she not told she must give proof of virtues in order to be admitted into a band of thieves? and once a little used, won't she be quite as serviceable as she is while a virgin?"

I am softening their expressions, you understand, Madame, I am sweetening the scene itself; alas! their obscenities were such that your modesty might suffer at least as much from beholding them unadorned as did my shyness.

A defenseless and trembling victim, I shuddered; I had barely strength to breathe; kneeling before the quartet, I raised my feeble arms as much to supplicate the men as to melt Dubois' heart. . . .

"An instant," said one who went by the name of Coeur-de-fer and appeared to be the band's chief, a man of thirty-six years, of a bull's strength and bearing the face of a satyr; "one moment, friends: it may be possible to satisfy everyone concerned; since this little girl's virtue is so precious to her and since, as Dubois states it very well, this quality otherwise put into action could become worth something to us, let's leave it to her; but we have got to be appeased; our mood is warm, Dubois, and in the state we are in, d'ye know, we might perhaps cut your own throat if you were to stand between us and our pleasures; let's have Thérèse instantly strip as naked as the day she came into the world, and next let's have her adopt one after the other all the positions we are pleased to call for, and meanwhile Dubois will sate our hungers, we'll burn our incense upon the altars' entrance to which this creature refuses us."

"Strip naked!" I exclaimed, "Oh Heaven, what is it thou doth require of me? When I shall have delivered myself thus to your eyes, who will be able to answer for me? . . ."

But Coeur-de-fer, who seemed in no humor either to grant me more or to suspend his desires, burst out with an oath and struck me in a manner so brutal that I saw full well compliance was my last resort. He put himself in Dubois' hands, she having been put by his in a disorder more or less the equivalent of mine and, as soon as I was as he desired me to be, having made me crouch down upon all fours so that I resembled a beast, Dubois took in hand a very monstrous object and led it to the peristyles of first one and then the other of Nature's altars, and under her guidance the blows it delivered to me here and there were like those of a battering ram thundering at the gates of a besieged town in olden days. The shock of the initial assault drove me back; enraged, Coeur-de-fer threatened me with harsher treatments were I to retreat from these; Dubois is instructed to redouble her efforts, one of the libertines grasps my shoulders and prevents me from staggering before the concussions: they become so fierce I am in blood and am able to avoid not a one.

"Indeed," stammers Coeur-de-fer, "in her place I'd prefer to open the doors rather than see them ruined this way, but she won't have it, and we're not far from the capitulation. . . . Vigorously . . . vigorously, Dubois. . . ."

And the explosive eruption of this debauchee's flames, almost as violent as a stroke of lightning, flickers and dies upon ramparts ravaged without being breached.

The second had me kneel between his legs and while Dubois administered to him as she had to the other, two enterprises absorbed his entire attention: sometimes he slapped, powerfully but in a very nervous manner, either my cheeks or my breasts; sometimes his impure mouth fell to sucking mine. In an instant my face turned purple, my chest red. . . . I was in pain, I begged him to spare me, tears leapt from my eyes; they roused him, he accelerated his activities; he bit my tongue, and the two strawberries on my breasts were so bruised that I slipped backward, but was kept from falling. They thrust me toward him, I was everywhere more furiously harassed, and his ecstasy supervened. . . .

The third bade me mount upon and straddle two somewhat separated chairs and, seating himself betwixt them, excited by Dubois, lying in his arms, he had me bend until his mouth was directly below the temple of Nature; never will you imagine, Madame, what this obscene mortal took it into his head to do; willy-nilly, I was obliged to satisfy his every need. . . . Just Heaven! what man, no matter how depraved, can taste an instant of pleasure in such things. . . . I did what he wished, inundated him, and my complete submission procured this foul man an intoxication of which he was incapable without this infamy.

The fourth attached strings to all parts of me to which it was possible to tie them, he held the ends in his hand and sat down seven or eight feet from my body; Dubois' touches and kisses excited him prodigiously; I was standing erect: 'twas by sharp tugs now on this string, now on some other that the savage irritated his pleasures; I swayed, I lost balance again and again, he flew into an ecstasy each time I tottered; finally, he pulled all the cords at once, I fell to the floor in front of him: such was his design: and my forehead, my breast, my cheeks received the proofs of a delirium he owed to none but this mania.

That is what I suffered, Madame, but at least my honor was respected even though my modesty assuredly was not. Their calm restored, the bandits spoke of regaining the road, and that same night we reached Tremblai with the intention of approaching the woods of Chantilly, where it was thought a few good prizes might be awaiting us.

Nothing equaled my despair at being obliged to accompany such persons, and I was only determined to part with them as soon as I could do so without risk. The following day we lay hard by Louvres, sleeping under haystacks; I felt in need of Dubois' support and wanted to pass the night by her side; but it seemed she had planned to employ it otherwise than protecting my virtue from the attacks I dreaded; three of the thieves surrounded her and before my very eyes the abominable creature gave herself to all three simultaneously. The fourth approached me; it was the captain. "Lovely Thérèse," said he, "I hope you shall not refuse me at least the pleasure of spending the night with you?" and as he perceived my extreme unwillingness, "fear not," he went on; "we'll have a chat together, and I will attempt nothing without your consent.

"O Thérèse," cried he, folding me in his arms, " 'tis all foolishness, don't you know, to be so pretentious with us. Why are you concerned to guard your purity in our midst? Even were we to agree to respect it, could it be compatible with the interests of the band? No need to hide it from you, my dear; for when we settle down in cities, we count upon your charms to snare us some dupes."

"Why, Monsieur," I replied, "since it is certain I should prefer death to these horrors, of what use can I be to you, and why do you oppose my flight?"

"We certainly do oppose it, my girl," Coeur-de-fer rejoined, "you must serve either our pleasures or our interests; your poverty imposes the yoke upon you, and you have got to adapt to it. But, Thérèse, and well you know it, there is nothing in this world that cannot be somehow arranged: so listen to me, and accept the management of your own fate: agree to live with me, dear girl, consent to belong to me and be properly my own, and I will spare you the baneful role for which you are destined."

"I, Sir, I become the mistress of a—"

"Say the word, Thérèse, out with it: a scoundrel, eh? Oh, I admit it, but I have no other titles to offer you; that our sort does not marry you are doubtless well aware: marriage is one of the sacraments Thérèse, and full of an undiscriminating contempt for them all, with none do we ever bother. However, be a little reasonable; that sooner or later you lose what is so dear to you is an indispensable necessity, hence would it not be better to sacrifice it to a single man who thereupon will become your support and protector, is that not better, I say, than to be prostituted to everyone?"

"But why must it be," I replied, "that I have no other alternative?"

"Because, Thérèse, we have got you, and because the stronger is always the better reason; La Fontaine made the remark ages ago. Truthfully," he continued rapidly, "is it not a ridiculous extravagance to assign, as you do, such a great value to the most futile of all things? How can a girl be so dull-witted as to believe that virtue may depend upon the somewhat greater or lesser diameter of one of her physical parts? What difference does it make to God or man whether this part be intact or tampered with? I will go further: it being the intention of Nature that each individual fulfill on this earth all of the purposes for which he has been formed, and women existing only to provide pleasure for men, it is plainly to outrage her thus to resist the intention she has in your regard. It is to wish to be a creature useless in this world and consequently one contemptible. This chimerical propriety, which they have had the absurdity to present to you as a virtue and which, since infancy, far from being useful to Nature and society, is an obvious defiance of the one and the other, this propriety, I say, is no more than a reprehensible stubbornness of which a person as mettlesome and full of intelligence as you should not wish to be guilty. No matter; continue to hear me out, dear girl, I am going to prove my desire to please you and to respect your weakness. I will not by any means touch that phantom, Thérèse, whose possession causes all your delight; a girl has more than one favor to give, and one can offer to Venus in many a temple; I will be content with the most mediocre; you know, my dear, near the Cyprean altar, there is situate an obscure grot into whose solitude Love retires, the more energetically to seduce us: such will be the altar where I will burn my incense; no disadvantages there, Thérèse; if pregnancies affright you, 'tis not in this manner they can come about, never will your pretty figure be deformed this way; the maidenhead so cherished by you will be preserved unimpaired, and whatever be the use to which you decide to put it, you can propose it unattainted. Nothing can betray a girl from this quarter, however rude or multiple the attacks may be; as soon as the bee has left off sucking the pollen, the rose's calix closes shut again; one would never imagine it had been opened. There exist girls who have known ten years of pleasure this way, even with several men, women who were just as much married as anyone else after it all, and on their wedding nights they proved quite as virgin as could be wished. How many fathers, what a multitude of brothers have thuswise abused their daughters and sisters without the latter having become on that account any the less worthy of a later hymeneal sacrifice! How many confessors have not employed the same route to satisfaction, without parents experiencing the mildest disquiet; in one word, 'tis the mystery's asylum, 'tis there where it connects itself with love by ties of prudence. . . . Need I tell you further, Thérèse, that although this is the most secret temple it is howbeit the most voluptuous; what is necessary to happiness is found nowhere else, and that easy vastness native to the adjacent aperture falls far short of having the piquant charms of a locale into which one does not enter without effort, where one takes up one's abode only at the price of some trouble; women themselves reap an advantage from it, and those whom reason compels to know this variety of pleasure, never pine after the others. Try it, Thérèse, try, and we shall both be contented."

"Oh Monsieur," I replied, "I have no experience of the thing;

but I have heard it said that this perversion you recommend outrages women in a yet more sensitive manner. . . . It more grievously
offends Nature. The hand of Heaven takes its vengeance upon it
in this world, Sodom provides the example."

"What innocence, my dear, what childishness," the libertine
retorted; "who ever told you such a thing? Yet a little more attention, Thérèse, let me proceed to rectify your ideas.

"The wasting of the seed destined to perpetuate the human
species, dear girl, is the only crime which can exist—such is the
hypothesis; according to it, this seed is put in us for the sole
purpose of reproduction, and if that were true I would grant you
that diverting it is an offense. But once it is demonstrated that her
situating this semen in our loins is by no means enough to warrant
supposing that Nature's purpose is to have all of it employed for
reproduction, what then does it matter, Thérèse, whether it be
spilled in one place or in another? Does the man who diverts it
perform a greater evil than Nature who does not employ all of it?
Now, do not those natural losses, which we can imitate if we please,
occur in an abundance of instances? Our very ability to provoke
them, firstly, is an initial proof that they do not offend Nature in
the slightest. It would be contrary to all the equity and profound
wisdom we everywhere recognize in her laws for them to permit
what might affront her; secondly, those losses occur a hundred
hundred million times every day, and she instigates them herself;
nocturnal pollutions, the inutility of semen during the periods of
woman's pregnancy, are they not authorized by her laws, enjoined
by them, and do they not prove that, very little concerned for what
may result from this liquid to which we so foolishly attach a dis-
proportionate value, she permits us its waste with the same indifference she herself causes it every day to be wasted; she tolerates reproduction, yes, but much is wanting to prove reproduction is one
of her intentions; she lets us go ahead with our reproducing to be
sure, but it being no more to her advantage than our abstaining
therefrom, the choice we happen to make is as one to her. Is it not
clear that leaving us the power to create, not to create, or to
destroy, we will not delight her at all or disappoint her any more
by adopting toward the one or the other the attitude which suits
us best; and what could be more self-evident than that the course

we choose, being but the result of her power over us and the influence upon us of her actions, will far more surely please than it will risk offending her. Ah, Thérèse! believe me, Nature frets very little over those mysteries we are great enough fools to turn into worship of her. Whatever be the temple at which one sacrifices, immediately she allows incense to be burned there, one can be sure the homage offends her in no wise; refusals to produce, waste of the semen employed in production, the obliteration of that seed when it has germinated, the annihilation of that germ even long after its formation, all those, Thérèse, are imaginary crimes which are of no interest to Nature and at which she scoffs as she does at all the rest of our institutions which offend more often than they serve her."

Coeur-de-fer waxed warm while expounding his perfidious maxims, and I soon beheld him again in the state which had so terrified me the night before; in order to give his lesson additional impact, he wished instantly to join practice to precept; and, my resistances notwithstanding, his hands strayed toward the altar into which the traitor wanted to penetrate. . . . Must I declare, Madame, that, blinded by the wicked man's seductions; content, by yielding a little, to save what seemed the more essential; reflecting neither upon his casuistries' illogicalities nor upon what I was myself about to risk since the dishonest fellow, possessing gigantic proportions, had not even the possibility to see a woman in the most permissible place and since, urged on by his native perversity, he most assuredly had no object but to maim me; my eyes as I say, perfectly blind to all that, I was going to abandon myself and become criminal through virtue; my opposition was weakening; already master of the throne, the insolent conqueror concentrated all his energies in order to establish himself upon it; and then there was heard the sound of a carriage moving along the highway. Upon the instant, Coeur-de-fer forsakes his pleasures for his duties; he assembles his followers and flies to new crimes. Not long afterward, we hear cries, and those bandits, all bloodied over, return triumphant and laden with spoils.

"Let's decamp smartly," says Coeur-de-fer, "we've killed three men, the corpses are on the road, we're safe no longer." The booty is divided, Coeur-de-fer wants me to have my share; it comes to twenty *louis,* which I am compelled to accept. I tremble at the obligation to take such money; however, we are in a hurry, everyone snatches up his belongings and off we go.

The next day we find ourselves out of danger and in the forest of Chantilly; during supper, the men reckon what their latest operation has been worth to them, and evaluate the total capture at no more than two hundred *louis*.

"Indeed," says one of them, "it wasn't worth the trouble to commit three murders for such a little sum."

"Softly, my friends," Dubois answers, "it was not for the sake of their purses I exhorted you not to spare those travelers, it was solely in the interests of our security; the law's to be blamed for these crimes, the fault's not ours; so long as thieves are hanged like murderers, thefts shall never be committed without assassinations. The two misdeeds are punished equally; why then abstain from the second when it may cover up the first? What makes you suppose, furthermore," the horrid creature continued, "that two hundred *louis* are not worth three killings? One must never appraise values save in terms of our own interests. The cessation of the victims' existences is as nothing compared to the continuation of ours, not a mite does it matter to us whether any individual is alive or in the grave; consequently, if one of the two cases involves what in the smallest way affects our welfare, we must, with perfect unremorse, determine the thing in our own favor; for in a completely indifferent matter we should, if we have any wits and are master of the situation, undoubtedly act so as to turn it to the profitable side, entirely neglecting whatever may befall our adversary; for there is no rational commensuration between what affects us and what affects others; the first we sense physically, the other only touches us morally, and moral feelings are made to deceive; none but physical sensations are authentic; thus, not only do two hundred *louis* suffice for three murders, but even thirty *centimes* would have sufficed, for those thirty *centimes* would have procured a satisfaction which, although light, must necessarily affect us to a much more lively degree than would three men murdered, who are nothing to us, and by the wrongs done whom we are not in the least touched, no, not even scratched; our organic feebleness, careless thinking, the accursed prejudices in which we were brought up, the vain terrors of religion and law, those are what hamper idiots and confound their criminal careers, those are what prevent them from arriving at greatness; but every strong and healthy individual, endowed with an energetically organized mind, who preferring himself to others, as he must, will know how to weigh their interests in the balance against his own, will laugh God and mankind to the devil, will brave death and mock at the law, fully aware that it is to himself he must be faithful, that by himself all must be measured, will sense that the vastest multitude of wrongs inflicted upon others cannot offset the least enjoyment lost to himself or be as important as his slightest pleasure purchased by an unheard-of host of villainies. Joy pleases him, it is in him, it is his own, crime's effect touches him not, is exterior to him; well, I ask, what thinking man will not prefer what causes his delectation to what is alien to him? who will not consent to commit this deed whereof he experiences nothing unpleasant, in order to procure what moves him most agreeably?"

"Oh Madame," I said to Dubois, asking her leave to reply to her execrable sophistries, "do you not at all feel that your damnation is writ in what you have just uttered? At the very most, such principles could only befit the person powerful enough to have nothing to dread from others; but we, Madame, perpetually in fear and humiliated; we, proscribed by all honest folk, condemned by every law, should we be the exponents of doctrines which can only whet the sword blade suspended above our heads? Would we find ourselves in this unhappy position were we in the center of society; were we to be where, that is to say, we ought to be, without our misconduct and delivered from our miseries, do you fancy such maxims could be any more fitting to us? How would you have him not perish who through blind egoism wishes all alone to strive against the combined interests of others? Is not society right never to suffer in its midst the man who declares himself hostile to it? And can the isolated individual fight against everyone? Can he flatter himself he is happy and tranquil if, refusing to submit to the social contract, he does not consent to give up a little of his happiness to insure the rest? Society is maintained only by the ceaseless interexchange of considerations and good works, those are the bonds which cement the edifices; such a one who instead of positive acts offers naught but crimes, having therefore to be dreaded, will necessarily be attacked if he is the strongest, laid low by the first he offends if he is the weakest; but destroyed at any rate, for there is in man a powerful instinct which compels him to safeguard his peace and quiet and to strike whosoever seeks to trouble them; that is why the long endurance of criminal associations is virtually impossible: their well-being suddenly confronted by cold steel, all the others must promptly unite to blunt the threatening point. Even amongst ourselves, Madame, I dare add; how can you lull yourself into believing you can maintain concord amongst ourselves when you counsel each to heed nothing but his own self-interest? Would you have any just complaints to make against the one of us who wanted to cut the throats of the others, who did so in order to monopolize for himself what has been shared by his colleagues? Why, 'tis a splendid panegyric to Virtue, to prove its necessity in even a criminal society . . . to prove for a certainty that this society would disintegrate in a trice were it not sustained by Virtue!"

"Your objections, Thérèse," said Coeur-de-fer, "not the theses Dubois has been expounding, are sophistries; our criminal fraternities are not by any means sustained by Virtue; rather by self-interest, egoism, selfishness; this eulogy of Virtue, which you have fabricated out of a false hypothesis, miscarries; it is not at all owing to virtuousness that, believing myself, let us suppose, the strongest of the band, I do not use a dagger on my comrades in order to appropriate their shares, it is because, thereupon finding myself all alone, I would deprive myself of the means which assure me the fortune I expect to have with their help; similarly, this is the single motive which restrains them from lifting their arms against me. Now this motive, as you, Thérèse, perfectly well observe, is purely selfish, and has not even the least appearance of virtue; he who wishes to struggle alone against society's interests must, you say, expect to perish; will he not much more certainly perish if, to enable him to exist therein, he has nothing but his misery and is abandoned by others? What one terms the interest of society is simply the mass of individual interests unified, but it is never otherwise than by ceding that this private interest can accommodate and blend with the general interest; well, what would you have him cede who has nothing he can relinquish? And he who had much? Agree that he should see his error grow apace with the discovery that he was giving infinitely more than he was getting in return; and, such being the case, agree that the unfairness of the bargain should prevent him from concluding it. Trapped in this dilemma, the best thing remaining for this man, don't you agree, is to quit this unjust society, to go elsewhere, and to accord prerogatives to a different society of men who, placed in a situation comparable to his, have their interest in combating, through the coordination of their lesser powers, the broader authority that wished to extract from the poor man what little he possessed in exchange for nothing at all. But you will say, thence will be born a state of perpetual warfare. Excellent! is that not the perpetual state of Nature? Is it not the only state to which we are really adapted? All men are born isolated, envious, cruel and despotic; wishing to have everything and surrender nothing, incessantly struggling to maintain either their rights or achieve their ambition, the legislator comes up and says to them: Cease thus to fight; if each were to retreat a little, calm would be restored. I find no fault with the position implicit in the agreement, but I maintain that two species of individuals cannot and ought not submit to it, ever; those who feel they are the stronger have no need to give up anything in order to be happy, and those who find themselves the weaker also find themselves giving up infinitely more than what is assured them. However, society is only composed of weak persons and strong; well, if the pact must perforce displease both weak and strong, there is great cause to suppose it will fail to suit society, and the previously existing state of warfare must appear infinitely preferable, since it permitted everyone the free exercise of his strength and his industry, whereof he would discover himself deprived by a society's unjust pact which takes too much from the one and never accords enough to the other; hence, the truly intelligent person is he who, indifferent to the risk of renewing the state of war that reigned prior to the contract, lashes out in irrevocable violation of that contract, violates it as much and often as he is able, full certain that what he will gain from these ruptures will always be more important than what he will lose if he happens to be a member of the weaker class; for such he was when he respected the treaty; by breaking it he may become one of the stronger; and if the laws return him to the class whence he wished to emerge, the worst that can befall him is the loss of his life, which is a misfortune infinitely less great than that of existing in opprobrium and wretchedness. There are then two positions available to us: either crime, which renders us happy, or the noose, which prevents us from being unhappy. I ask whether there can be any hesitation, lovely Thérèse, and where will your little mind find an argument able to combat that one?"

"Oh Monsieur," I replied with the vehemence a good cause inspires, "there are a thousand; but must this life be man's unique concern? Is this existence other than a passage each of whose stages ought only, if he is reasonable, to conduct him to that eternal felicity, the prize vouchsafed by Virtue? I suppose together with you (but this, however, is rare, it conflicts with all reason's informations, but never mind), I will for an instant grant you that the villain who abandons himself to crime may be rendered happy by it in this world, but do you imagine God's justice does not await that dishonest man, that he will not have to pay in another world for what he does in this? Ah! think not the contrary, Monsieur, believe it not," I added, tears in my eyes, " 'tis the misfortunate one's sole consolation, take it not away from us; forsaken by mankind, who will avenge us if not God?"

"Who? No one, Thérèse, absolutely no one; it is in no wise necessary that the misfortunate be avenged; they flatter themselves with the notion because they would like to be, the idea comforts them, but it is not on that account the less false: better still, it is essential that the misfortunate suffer; their humiliation, their anguishes are included in what Nature decrees, and their miserable existence is useful to the general scheme, as is that of the prosperity which crushes them; such is the truth which should stifle remorse in the tyrant's soul or in the malefactor's; let him not constrain himself; let him blindly, unthinkingly deliver himself up to causing every hurt the idea for which may be born in him, it is only Nature's voice which suggests this idea; such is the only fashion in which she makes us her laws' executors. When her secret inspirations dispose us to evil, it is evil she wishes, it is evil she requires, for the sum of crimes not being complete, not sufficient to the laws of equilibrium, the only laws whereby she is governed, she demands that there be crimes to dress the scales; therefore let him not be afraid, let him not pause, whose brain is driven to concerting ill; let him unheeding commit wrong immediately he discerns the impulsion, it is only by lagging and snuffling he outrages Nature. But let us ignore ethics for a moment, since it's theology you want. Be advised then, young innocent, that the religion you fall back upon, being nothing but the relationship between man and God, nothing but the reverence the creature thinks himself obliged to show his creator, is annihilated instantly this creator's existence is itself proven illusory.

"Primitive man, terrified by the phenomena which harried him, had necessarily to believe that a sublime being unknown to him had the direction of their operation and influence; it is native to weakness to suppose strength and to fear it; the human mind, then too much in its infancy to explore, to discover in Nature's depths the laws of motion, the unique springs of the entire mechanism that struck him with awe, found it simpler to fancy a motor in this Nature than to view Nature as her own mover, and without considering that he would have to go to much more trouble to edify, to define this gigantic master, than through the study of Nature to find the cause of what amazed him, he acknowledged this sovereign being, he elaborated rituals to worship it: from this moment each nation composed itself an overlord in conformance with its peculiar characteristics, its knowledge, and its climate; soon there were as many religions on earth as races and peoples and not long after, as many Gods as families; nevertheless, behind all these idols it was easy to recognize the same absurd illusion, first fruit of human blindness. They appareled it differently, but it was always the same thing. Well, tell me, Thérèse, merely because these idiots talk drivel about the erection of a wretched chimera and about the mode of serving him, must it follow that an intelligent man has got to renounce the certain and present happiness of life; like Aesop's dog, must he abandon the bone for the shadow and renounce his real joys for hallucinations? No, Thérèse, no, there is no God, Nature sufficeth unto herself; in no wise hath she need of an author; once supposed, that author is naught but a decayed version of herself, is merely what we describe in school by the phrase, a begging of the question. A God predicates a creation, that is to say, an instant when there was nothing, or an instant when all was in chaos. If one or the other of these states was evil, why did your God allow it to subsist? Was it good? Then why did he change it? But if all is now good at last, your God has nothing left to do; well, if he is useless, how can he be powerful? And if he is not powerful, how can he be God? If, in a word, Nature moves herself, what do we want with a motor? and if the motor acts upon matter by causing it to move, how is it not itself material? Can you conceive the effect of the mind upon matter and matter receiving motion from the mind which itself has no movement? Examine for one cold-blooded instant all the ridiculous and contradictory qualities wherewith the fabricators of this execrable chimera have been obliged to clothe him; verify for your own self how they contradict one another, annul one another, and you will recognize that this deific phantom, engendered by the fear of some and the ignorance of all, is nothing but a loathsome platitude which merits from us neither an instant of faith nor a minute's examination; a pitiable extravagance, disgusting to the mind, revolting to the heart, which ought never to have issued from the darkness save to plunge back into it, forever to be drowned.

"May the hope or fear of a world to come, bred of those primordial lies, trouble you not, Thérèse, and above all give over endeavoring to forge restraints for us out of this stuff. Feeble portions of a vile crude matter, upon our death, that is to say, upon the conjointure of the elements whereof we are composed with the elements composing the universal mass, annihilated forever, regardless of what our behavior has been, we will pass for an instant into Nature's crucible thence to spring up again under other shapes, and that without there being any more prerogatives for him who madly smoked up Virtue's effigy, than for the other who wallowed in the most disgraceful excesses, because there is nothing by which Nature is offended and because all men, equally her womb's issue, during their term having acted not at all save in accordance with her impulsions, will all of them meet with after their existence, both the same end and the same fate."

I was once again about to reply to these appalling blasphemies when we heard the clatter of a horseman not far away.

"To arms!" shouted Coeur-de-fer, more eager to put his systems into action than to consolidate their bases.

The men leapt into life . . . and an instant later a luckless traveler was led into the copse where we had our camp.

Questioned upon his motive for traveling alone and for being

so early abroad, upon his age, his profession, the rider answered
that his name was Saint-Florent, one of the most important mer-
chants of Lyon, that he was thirty-six years old, that he was on his
way back from Flanders where he had been concerned with affairs
relative to his business, that he had not much hard money upon his
person, but many securities. He added that his valet had left him
the preceding day and that, to avoid the heat, he was journeying
at night with the intention of reaching Paris the next day, where he
would secure a new domestic, and would conclude some of his
transactions; that, moreover, he was following an unfamiliar road,
and, apparently, he must have lost his way while dozing on his
horse. And having said that, he asked for his life, in return offering all he possessed. His purse was examined, his money was
counted, the prize could not have been better. Saint-Florent had
near unto a half a million, payable upon demand at the capital, had
also a few gems and about a hundred gold *louis*. . . .

"Friend," said Coeur-de-fer, clapping his pistol to Saint-Florent's nose, "you understand, don't you, that after having robbed
you, we cannot leave you alive."

"Oh Monsieur," I cried, casting myself at the villain's feet,
"I beseech you not to present me the horrible spectacle, upon my
reception into your band, of this poor man's death; allow him to
live, do not refuse me this first request I ask of you."

And quickly resorting to a most unusual ruse, in order to
justify the interest I appeared to take in the captive:

"The name Monsieur has just given himself," I added with
warmth, "causes me to believe we are nearly related. Be not astonished, Monsieur," I went on, now addressing the voyager, "be not
at all surprised to find a kinsman in these circumstances; I will explain it all to you. In the light of this," I continued, once again imploring our chief, "in the light of this, Monsieur, grant me the unlucky creature's life, I will show my gratitude for the favor by the
completest devotion to all that will be able to serve your interests."

"You know upon what conditions I can accord you what you
ask, Thérèse," Coeur-de-fer answered; "you know what I demand
from you . . ."

"Ah, very well, Monsieur, I will do everything," I cried,

throwing myself between Saint-Florent and our leader, who was still about to kill him. "Yes, I will do anything; spare him."

"Let him live," said Coeur-de-fer, "but he has got to join us, that last clause is crucial, I can do nothing if he refuses to comply with it, my comrades would be against me."

Surprised, the merchant, understanding nothing of this consanguinity I was establishing, but observing his life saved if he were to consent to the proposal, saw no cause for a moment's hesitation. He was provided with meat and drink, as the men did not wish to leave the place until daybreak.

"Thérèse," Coeur-de-fer said to me, "I remind you of your promise, but, since I am weary tonight, rest quietly beside Dubois, I will summon you toward dawn and if you are not prompt to come, taking this knave's life will be my revenge for your deceit."

"Sleep, Monsieur, sleep well," I replied, "and believe that she whom you have filled with gratitude has no desire but to repay it."

However, such was far from my design, for if ever I believed deception permitted, it was certainly upon this occasion. Our rascals, greatly overconfident, kept at their drinking and fell into slumber, leaving me entirely at liberty beside Dubois who, drunk like the others, soon closed her eyes too.

Then seizing my opportunity as soon as the bandits surrounding us were overcome with sleep:

"Monsieur," I said to the young Lyonnais, "the most atrocious catastrophe has thrown me against my will into the midst of these thieves, I detest both them and the fatal instant that brought me into their company. In truth, I have not the honor to be related to you; I employed the trick to save you and to escape, if you approve it, with you, from out of these scoundrels' clutches; the moment's propitious," I added, "let us be off; I notice your pocketbook, take it back, forget the money, it is in their pockets; we could not recover it without danger: come, Monsieur, let us quit this place. You see what I am doing for you, I put myself into your keeping; take pity on me; above all, be not more cruel than these men; deign to respect my honor, I entrust it to you, it is my unique treasure, they have not ravished it away from me."

It would be difficult to render the declarations of gratitude I had from Saint-Florent. He knew not in what terms to express his thanks; but we had no time to talk; it was a question of flight. With a dextrous movement, I retrieve the pocketbook, return it to him, and treading softly we walk through the copse, leaving the horse for fear the sound of his hoofs might rouse the men; with all possible dispatch we reach the path which is to lead us out of the forest. We had the good luck to be out of it by daybreak, without having been followed by anyone; before ten o'clock we were in Luzarches and there, free from all anxiety, we thought of nothing but resting ourselves.

There are moments in life when one finds that despite one's riches, which may be great, one nevertheless lacks what is needed to live; such was Saint-Florent's case: five hundred thousand francs might be awaiting him in Paris, but he now had not a coin on his person; mindful of this, he paused before entering the inn. . . .

"Be easy, Monsieur," I said upon perceiving his embarrassment, "the thieves have not left me without money, here are twenty *louis,* take them, please, use them, give what remains to the poor; nothing in the world could make me want to keep gold acquired by murder."

Saint-Florent, whose refinements of character I at the time did not exactly appreciate, was absolutely unwilling to accept what I tendered him; he asked me what my expectations were, said he would make himself bound to fulfill them, and that he desired nothing but the power to acquit himself of his indebtedness to me.

"It is to you I owe my life and fortune, Thérèse," he added, kissing my hands, "I can do no better than to lay them both at your feet; receive them, I beseech you, and permit the God of marriage to tighten the knots of friendship."

I know not whether it was from intuition or chilliness of temper, but I was so far from believing that what I had done for the young man could motivate such sentiments as these he expressed for me, that I allowed him to read in my countenance the refusal I dared not articulate; he understood, insisted no further, and limited himself to asking what he could do for me.

"Monsieur," said I, "if my behavior is really not without merit in your view, for my entire recompense I ask nothing more than to proceed to Lyon with you and to have you find me a place in some correct household, where my modesty will have no more to suffer."

"You could do nothing better," said Saint-Florent, "and no one is in a better position than I to render this service; I have twenty relatives in the city," and the young trader then besought me to divulge my reasons for having left Paris where I had mentioned to him I was born. I told my story with equal amounts of confidence and ingenuousness.

"Oh, if it is but that," said the young man, "I will be of use to you before we reach Lyon; fear not, Thérèse, your troubles are over; the affair will be hushed; you will not be sought after and, certainly, less in the asylum where I wish to leave you than in any other. A member of my family dwells near Bondy, a charming region not far from here; I am sure it will be a pleasure for her to have you with her; I will introduce you tomorrow."

In my turn filled with gratitude, I approve a project which seems so well suited to me; we repose at Luzarches for the rest of the day and on the morrow, it is our plan, we will gain Bondy, but six leagues distant.

"The weather is fine," Saint-Florent says to me, "trust me, Thérèse; it will be most enjoyable to go afoot; we will reach my relative's estate, will tell of our adventure, and this manner of arriving, I should think, will make you appear in a still more interesting light."

Having not the faintest suspicion of this monster's designs, and far from imagining that I was to be less safe with him than I had been when in the infamous company I had left, I agree to everything; we dine together; he not so much as murmurs when for the night I take a chamber separate from his, and after having waited until the warmest part of the day is past, certain of what he tells me, that four or five hours will suffice to bring us to his relative's, we leave Luzarches and strike out on foot for Bondy.

It was toward four o'clock in the afternoon when we entered the forest. Until then Saint-Florent had not once contradicted himself: always the same propriety, always the same eagerness to prove his sentiments for me; I should not have thought myself more secure had I been with my father. The shades of night began to descend upon the forest and to inspire that kind of religious horror which at once causes the birth of fear in timorous spirits and criminal projects in ferocious hearts. We followed mere paths; I was walking ahead, I turned to ask Saint-Florent whether these obscure trails were really the ones we ought to be following, whether perchance he had not lost his bearings, whether he thought we were going to arrive soon.

"We have arrived, whore," the villain replied, toppling me with a blow of his cane brought down upon my head; I fell unconscious. . . .

Oh, Madame, I have no idea what that man afterward said or did; but the state I was in when I returned to my senses advised me only too well to what point I had been his victim. It was darkest night when I awoke; I was at the foot of a tree, away from any road, injured, bleeding . . . dishonored, Madame; such had been the reward of all I had just done for the unlucky man; and carrying infamy to its ultimate degree, the wretch, after having done to me all he had wished, after having abused me in every manner, even in that which most outrages Nature, had taken my purse . . . containing the same money I had so generously offered him. He had torn my clothing, most of it lay in shreds and ribbons about me, I was virtually naked, and several parts of my body were lacerated, clawed; you may appreciate my situation: there in the depths of the night, without resources, without honor, without hope, exposed to every peril: I wished to put an end to my days: had a weapon been presented to me, I would have laid hands on it and abridged this unhappy life full only of plagues for me . . . the monster! What did I do to him, I asked myself, to have deserved such cruel treatment at his hands? I save his life, restore his fortune to him, he snatches away what is most dear to me! A savage beast would have been less cruel! O man, thus are you when you heed nothing but your passions! Tigers that dwell in the wildest jungles would quail before such ignominies . . . these first pangs of suffering were succeeded by some few minutes of exhaustion; my eyes, brimming over with tears, turned mechanically toward the sky; my heart did spring to the feet of the Master who dwelleth there . . . that pure glittering vault . . . that imposing stillness of the night . . . that terror which numbed my senses . . . that image of Nature in peace, nigh unto my whelmed, distraught soul . . . all distilled a somber horror into me, whence there was soon born the need to pray. I cast myself down, kneeling before that potent God denied by the impious, hope of the poor and the downtrodden.

"Holy Majesty, Saintly One," I cried out in tears, "Thou Who in this dreadful moment deign to flood my soul with a celestial joy, Who doubtless hath prevented me from attempting my life; O my Protector and my Guide, I aspire to Thy bounties, I implore Thy clemency, behold my miseries and my torments, my resignation, and hear Thou my entreaties: Powerful God! Thou knowst it, I am innocent and weak, I am betrayed and mistreated; I have wished to do well in imitation of Thee, and Thy will hath punished it in me: may Thy will be done, O my God! all its sacred effects are cherished by me, I respect them and cease to complain of them; but if however I am to find naught but stings and nettles terrestrially, is it to offend Thee, O my Sovereign Master, to supplicate Thy puissance to take me into Thy bosom, in order untroubled to adore Thee, to worship Thee far away from these perverse men who, alas! have made me meet with evils only, and whose bloodied and perfidious hands at their pleasure drown my sorrowful days in a torrent of tears and in an abyss of agonies."

Prayer is the misfortunate's sweetest comfort; strength reenters him once he has fulfilled this duty. My courage renewed, I raised myself up, I gathered together the rags the villain had left me, and I hid myself in a thicket so as to pass the night in less danger. The security I believed I enjoyed, the satisfaction I had just tasted by communing with my God, all combined to help me rest a few hours, and the sun was already risen high when I opened my eyes. For the wretched, the instant of awakening is hideous: the imagination, refreshed by sleep's sweet ministrations, very rapidly and lugubriously fills with the evils these moments of deceiving repose have smoothed into oblivion.

Very well, I said as I examined myself, it is then true that there are human creatures Nature reduces to the level of wild beasts! Lurking in this forest, like them flying the sight of man, what difference now exists between them and me? Is it worth being born for a fate so pitiable? . . . And my tears flowed abundantly as I meditated in sorrow; I had scarcely finished with my reflections when I heard sounds somewhere about; little by little, two men hove into view. I pricked up my ears:

"Come, dear friend," said one of them, "this place will suit us admirably; the cruel and fatal presence of an aunt I abhor will not prevent me from tasting a moment with you the pleasures I cherish."

They draw near, they station themselves squarely in front of me and so proximately that not one of their words, not one of their gestures is able to escape me, and I observe . . . Just Heaven, Madame, said Thérèse, interrupting herself, is it possible that destiny has placed me in none but situations so critical that it becomes quite as difficult for Virtue to hear them recited as for modesty to describe them? That horrible crime which equally outrages both Nature and social conventions, that heinous deed, in a word, which the hand of God has so often smitten, rationalized, legitimized by Coeur-de-fer, proposed by him to the unhappy Thérèse, despite her wishes consummated against her by the butcher who has just immolated her, in brief, I did see that revolting execration carried out before my own eyes, together with all the impure gropings and fumblings, all the frightful episodes the most meditated depravity can devise. One of the men, he who gave himself, was twenty-four years old, of such a bearing and presence one might suppose him of an elevated degree, the other, of about the same age, appeared to be one of his domestics. The act was scandalous and prolonged. Bending over, supported by his hands, leaning upon the crest of a little hillock facing the thicket where I lay, the young master exposed naked to his companion in debauch the impious sacrificial altar, and the latter, whom the spectacle filled with ardor, caressed the idol, ready to immolate it with a spear far more awful and far more colossal than the one wherewith the captain of the brigands of Bondy had menaced me; but, in no wise intimidated, the young master seemed prepared unhesitatingly to brave the shaft that was presented to him; he teased it, he excited it, covered it with kisses; seized it, plunged it into himself, was in an ecstasy as he swallowed it up; aroused by criminal caresses, the infamous creature writhed and struggled under the iron and seemed to regret it was not yet more terrible; he withstood its blows, he rose to anticipate them, he repelled them. . . . A tender couple lawfully

connected would not have caressed one another so passionately
. . . their mouths were pressed together, their sighs intermingled,
their tongues entwined, and I witnessed each of them, drunk with
lust, bring his perfidious horrors to completion in the very vortex
of delight. The homage is renewed, and in order to fire the incense
nothing is neglected by him who cries aloud his demand for it;
kisses, fingerings, pollutions, debauchery's most appalling refinements, everything is employed to revive sinking strength, and it all
succeeds in reanimating them five times in swift succession; but that
without either of them changing his role. The young lord was constantly the woman and although there was about him what suggested the possibility he could have acted the man in his turn, he had
not for one instant even the appearance of wishing to. If he visited
the altar corresponding to the one in him where sacrifices were
performed, it was in the other idol's behalf, and there was never
any indication the latter was threatened by assault.

Ah, how slowly the time seemed to pass! I dared not budge
for fear of detection; at last, the criminal actors in this indecent
drama, no doubt surfeited, got up and were prepared to start
along the road that was to take them home, when the master drew
near the bush which hid me; my bonnet betrayed me . . . he caught
sight of it. . . .

"Jasmin," said he to his valet, "we are discovered . . . a girl
has beheld our mysteries. . . . Come hither, flush the bitch into the
open, let's find out why she is here."

I did not put them to the trouble of dragging me from my
sanctuary; I stepped forward immediately and, falling at their
feet,

"Oh, Messieurs!" I cried, stretching my arms toward them,
"deign to have pity upon an unhappy creature whose fate more
deserves your compassion than you may think; there are very few
misfortunes which can equal mine; do not let the posture wherein
you discover me cause any suspicion to be born in you; it is rather
the consequence of my misery than of my faults; do not augment
the ills which overwhelm me, be so kind as to diminish them by
making available to me the means to escape the furies that hound
me."

The Comte de Bressac (that was the name of the young man

into whose hands I had fallen) possessed a mind containing a great fund of wickedness and libertinage; no very abundant amount of sympathy dwelled in his heart. Unfortunately, it is only too common to find men in whom pity has been obliterated by libertinage, whose ordinary effect is to harden: whether it be that the major part of his excesses necessitates apathy in the soul, or that the violent shock passion imparts to the nervous system decreases the vigor of its action, the fact always remains that a libertine is rarely a man of sensibility. But in addition to this harshness native to the species whose character I am sketching, there was also in Monsieur de Bressac a disgust for our sex so inveterate, a hatred so powerful for all that distinguishes it, that I encountered considerable difficulty introducing the affections into his soul wherewith I strove to move him.

"My little dove," said the Count, severity in his tone, "if you are looking for dupes, improve your style; neither my friend nor I ever sacrifice at your sex's impure temple; if it is money you are begging, look for people who are fond of good works, we never perform any of that description. . . . But, wretch, out with it: did you see what passed between Monsieur and me?"

"I saw you conversing together upon the sward," I replied, "nothing more, Monsieur, I assure you."

"I should like to believe it," said the Count, "for your own good; were I to imagine you had seen anything else, never would you emerge alive from where we are. . . . Jasmin, it is early, we have time to hear the girl's adventures, and afterward we will see what's to be done with her."

The young men sit down, they order me to sit near them, and thereupon very ingenuously I make them acquainted with all the woes that have afflicted me from the day of my birth.

"Well, Jasmin," said Monsieur de Bressac as soon as I had finished, "for once let us be just: the equitable Thémis has doomed this creature, let us not suffer the Goddess' designs to be thwarted so cruelly: let us expose the delinquent to the death penalty she has incurred: this little murder, far from being a crime, will merely take its place as a reparation in the moral scheme; since sometimes we have the misfortune to disturb that order, let us at least courageously make amends when the occasion arises. . . ."

And the cruel men, having laid hands upon me, dragged me toward the wood, laughing at my tears and screams.

"We'll tie each of her members to a tree—we need four trees placed in a rectangle," said Bressac, tearing off my clothes.

Then by means of their cravats, their handkerchiefs, their braces, they make cords wherewith I am tied instantly, in keeping with their plan, that is to say in the cruelest and most painful position imaginable. I cannot express to you what I suffered; it seemed they were rending me limb from limb and that my belly, facing downward and strained to the utmost, was about to split at any moment; sweat drenched my forehead, I no longer existed save through the violence of pain; had it ceased to compress my nerves, a mortal anguish would surely have seized me: the villains were amused by my posture, they considered me and applauded.

"Well, that's enough," Bressac said at last, "for the time being she may get off with a fright.

"Thérèse," he continued as he untied my hands and commanded me to dress myself, "show a little judgment and come along with us; if you attach yourself to me you shall never have reason to regret it. My aunt requires a second maid; I am going to present you to her and, upon the basis of your story, undertake to interest her in you; I shall make myself answerable for your conduct; but should you abuse my kindness, were you to betray my confidence, or were you not to submit yourself to my intentions, behold these four trees, Thérèse, behold the plot of earth they encompass: it might serve you for a sepulcher: bear it in mind that this dreadful place is no more than a league's distance from the château to which I am going to lead you and that, upon the least provocation, I will bring you back here at once."

I forgot my sufferings instantly, I embraced the Count's knees, tears streaming down my cheeks, I swore to behave myself well; but quite as insensible to my joy as to my pain,

"Let us be off," said Bressac, "your actions will speak for you, they alone will govern your fate."

We advance; Jasmin and his master exchange whispered remarks; I follow them humbly, without saying a word. In less than an hour we arrive at Madame la Marquise de Bressac's château, whose magnificence and the multitude of servants it contains make me see that whatever the post I must hold in the house, it will surely be more advantageous to me than that of drudge to Monsieur du Harpin. I am made to wait in an office where Jasmin most obligingly offers me everything conducive to my comfort. The young Count seeks out his aunt, acquaints her with what he has done, and a half-hour later himself comes to introduce me to the Marquise.

Madame de Bressac was a woman of forty-six years, still very beautiful, and who seemed highly respectable and sensible, although into her principles and remarks somewhat of austerity had entrance; for two years she had been the widow of the young Count's uncle, who had married her without any fortune beyond the fine name he brought with him. All the riches Monsieur de Bressac was able to hope for depended upon this aunt; what had come down to him from his father barely gave him the wherewithal to buy his pleasures: to which income Madame de Bressac joined a considerable allowance, but that scarcely sufficed; nothing is so expensive as the delights to which the Count was addicted; perhaps they are purchased at a cheaper rate than others, but they far more rapidly multiply. Fifty thousand crowns was the Marquise's revenue, and young Monsieur de Bressac was its sole heir. All efforts to induce him to find a profession or an occupation had failed; he could not adapt himself to whatever diverted his attentions from libertinage. The Marquise passed three months of the year's twelve in the country; the rest of the time she lived in Paris; and these three months which she required her nephew to spend with her, were a kind of torture for a man who hated his aunt and considered as wasted every moment he passed outside the city which was the home of his pleasures.

The young Count bade me relate to the Marquise the matter with which I had just made him acquainted, and as soon as I was done:

"Your candor and naïveté," Madame de Bressac said to me, "do not permit me to think you untruthful. I will inquire after no other information save what will authorize me to believe you are really the daughter of the man you indicate; if it is so, then I knew your father, and that will be one more reason to take an interest in you. As for the du Harpin affair, I will assume responsibility for settling it with two visits paid to the Chancellor; he has been my friend for ages. In all the world there is no man of greater integrity; we have but to prove your innocence to him: all the charges leveled against you will crumble and be withdrawn. But consider well, Thérèse: what I promise you now will not be yours save at the price of flawless conduct; thus, you see that the effects of the gratitude I require will always redound to your profit." I cast myself at the Marquise's feet, assured her she would be contented with me; with great kindness she raised me up and upon the spot gave me the post of second chambermaid in her service.

At the end of three days, the information Madame de Bressac had sought from Paris arrived; it corresponded with what I desired; the Marquise praised me for having in no wise imposed upon her, and every thought of unhappiness vanished from my mind, to be replaced by nothing but hope for the sweetest consolations it was permitted me to expect; but it did not consort with the designs of Heaven that the poor Thérèse should ever be happy, and if fortuitously there were born unto her some few moments of calm, it was only to render more bitter those of distress that were to succeed them.

We were no sooner arrived in Paris than Madame de Bressac hastened to work in my behalf: the first president judge wished to see me, he heard with interest the tale of my misfortunes; du Harpin's calumnies were recognized, but it was in vain they undertook to punish him; having made a great success of trafficking in counterfeit banknotes, whereby he ruined three or four families, and whence he amassed nearly two millions, he had just removed to England; as regarded the burning of the Palace prisons, they were convinced that although I had profited from the event, I was in no way to blame for causing it and the case against me was dropped, the officiating magistrates being agreed, so I was assured, that there was no need to employ further formalities; I asked no questions, I was content to learn what I was told, and you will see shortly whether I was mistaken.

You may readily imagine that as a consequence of what she did for me, I became very fond of Madame de Bressac; had she not shown me every kindness as well, had not such steps as those she had taken obligated me forever to this precious protectress? However, it was by no means the young Count's intention that I become so intimately attached to his aunt. . . . But this seems the moment for a portrait of the monster.

Monsieur de Bressac had the charms of youth and the most attractive countenance too; if there were some defects in his figure or his features, it was because they had a rather too pronounced tendency toward that nonchalance, that softness which properly belongs only to women; it seemed that, in lending him the attributes of the feminine sex, Nature had introduced its tastes into him as well. . . . Yet what a soul lurked behind those effeminate graces! All the vices which characterize the villain's genius were to be encountered in his: never had wickedness, vindictiveness, cruelty, atheism, debauchery, contempt for all duties and principally those out of which Nature is said to fashion our delights, never had all these qualities been carried to such an extreme. In the midst of all his faults predominated another: Monsieur de Bressac detested his aunt. The Marquise did everything conceivable to restore her nephew to the paths of virtue; perhaps she put too much rigorousness into her attempts; the result, however, was that the Count, further inflamed by that very rigor's effects, only the more impetuously gave himself up to his predilections and the poor Marquise gained nothing from her persecutions but his redoubled hate.

"Do not imagine," the Count would often tell me, "that it is of her own accord my aunt acts in all that concerns you, Thérèse; believe me, were it not for my constant badgering she would quickly forget what she has promised to do for you. She would have you feel indebted to her, but all she has done is owing exclusively to me; yes, Thérèse, exactly, it is to me alone you are beholden, and the thanks I expect from you should appear the more disinterested, for although you've a pretty face, it is not, and you know it very well, after your favors I aspire; no, Thérèse, the services I await from you are of a radically different sort, and when you are well convinced of what I have accomplished in behalf of your tranquillity, I hope I will find what I think I have the right to expect from your spirit."

So obscure were these speeches I knew not how to answer: however, reply to him I did, on a chance, as it were, and perhaps with too great a facility. Must I confess it? Alas! yes; to conceal my shortcomings would be to wrong your confidence and poorly to respond to the interest my misfortunes have quickened in you. Hear then, Madame, of the one deliberate fault with which I have to reproach myself. . . . What am I saying, a fault? It was a folly, an extravagance . . . there has never been one to equal it; but at least it is not a crime, it is merely a mistake, for which I alone have been punished, and of which it surely does not seem that the equitable hand of Heaven had to make use in order to plunge me into the abyss which yawned beneath me soon afterward. Whatever the foul treatment to which the Comte de Bressac had exposed me the first day I had met him, it had, all the same, been impossible to see him so frequently without feeling myself drawn toward him by an insuperable and instinctive tenderness. Despite all my recollections of his cruelty, all my thoughts upon his disinclinations toward women, upon the depravity of his tastes, upon the gulf which separated us morally, nothing in the world was able to extinguish this nascent passion, and had the Count called upon me to lay down my life, I would have sacrificed it for him a thousand times over. He was far from suspecting my sentiments . . . he was far, the ungrateful one, from divining the cause of the tears I shed every day; nevertheless, it was out of the question for him to be in doubt of my eagerness to fly to do his every bidding, to please him in every possible way, it could not have been he did not glimpse, did not have some inkling of my attentions; doubtless, because they were instinctive, they were also mindless, and went to the point of serving his errors, of serving them as far as decency permitted, and always of hiding them from his aunt. This behavior had in some sort won me his confidence, and all that came from him was so precious to me, I was so blinded by the little his heart offered me, that I sometimes had the weakness to believe he was not indifferent to me. But how promptly his excessive disorders disabused me: they were such that even his health was affected. I several times took the liberty to represent to him the dangers of his conduct, he would hear me out patiently, then end by telling me that one does not break oneself of the vice he cherished.

"Ah, Thérèse!" he exclaimed one day, full of enthusiasm, "if only you knew this fantasy's charms, if only you could understand what one experiences from the sweet illusion of being no more than a woman! incredible inconsistency! one abhors that sex, yet one wishes to imitate it! Ah! how sweet it is to succeed, Thérèse, how delicious it is to be a slut to everyone who would have to do with you and carrying delirium and prostitution to their ultimate period, successively, in the very same day, to be the mistress of a porter, a marquis, a valet, a friar, to be the beloved of each one after the other, caressed, envied, menaced, beaten, sometimes victorious in their arms, sometimes a victim and at their feet, melting them with caresses, reanimating them with excesses. . . . Oh no, Thérèse, you do not understand what is this pleasure for a mind constructed like mine. . . . But, morals aside, if you are able to imagine this divine whimsy's physical sensations, there is no withstanding it, it is a titillation so lively, it is of so piquant a voluptuousness . . . one becomes giddy, one ceases to reason, stammers; a thousand kisses one more tender than the next do not inflame us with an ardor in any way approaching the drunkenness into which the agent plunges us; enlaced in his arms, our mouth glued to his, we would that our entire being were incorporated into his; we would not make but a single being with him; if we dare complain, 'tis of being neglected; we would have him, more robust than Hercules, enlarge us, penetrate us; we would have that precious semen, shot blazing to the depths of our entrails, cause, by its heat and its strength, our own to leap forth into his hands. . . . Do not suppose, Thérèse, we are made like other men; 'tis an entirely different structure we have; and, in creating us, Heaven has ornamented the altars at which our Celadons sacrifice with that very same sensitive membrane which lines your temple of Venus; we are, in that sector, as certainly women as you are in your generative sanctuary; not one of your pleasures is unknown to us, there is not one we do not know how to enjoy, but we have in addition to them our own, and it is this delicious combination which makes us of all men on earth the most sensitive to pleasure, the best created to experience it; it is this enchanting combination which renders our tastes incorrigible, which would turn us into enthusiasts and frenetics were one to have the stupidity to punish us . . . which makes us worship, unto the grave itself, the charming God who enthralls us."

Thus the Count expressed himself, celebrating his eccentricities; when I strove to speak to him of the Being to whom he owed everything, and of the grief such disorders caused his respectable aunt, I perceived nothing in him but spleen and ill-humor and especially impatience at having to see, in such hands and for so long, riches which, he would say, already ought to belong to him; I saw nothing but the most inveterate hatred for that so gentle woman, nothing but the most determined revolt against every natural sentiment. It would then be true that when in one's tastes one has been able so formally to transgress that law's sacred instinct, the necessary consequence of this original crime is a frightful penchant to commit every other.

Sometimes I employed the means Religion provides; almost always comforted by it, I attempted to insinuate its sweetnesses into this perverse creature's soul, more or less certain he could be restrained by those bonds were I to succeed in having him strike at the lure; but the Count did not long tolerate my use of such weapons. A declared enemy of our most holy mysteries, a stubborn critic of the purity of our dogmas, an impassioned antagonist of the idea of a Supreme Being's existence, Monsieur de Bressac, instead of letting himself be converted by me, sought rather to work my corruption.

"All religions start from a false premise, Thérèse," he would say; "each supposes as necessary the worship of a Creator, but that creator never existed. In this connection, put yourself in mind of the sound precepts of that certain Coeur-de-fer who, you told me, used to labor over your mind as I do; nothing more just, nor more precise, than that man's principles, and the degradation in which we have the stupidity to keep him does not deprive him of the right to reason well.

"If all Nature's productions are the resultant effects of the laws whereof she is a captive; if her perpetual action and reaction suppose the motion necessary to her essence, what becomes of the sovereign master fools gratuitously give her? that is what your sagacious instructor said to you, dear girl. What, then, are religions if not the restraint wherewith the tyranny of the mightier sought to enslave the weaker? Motivated by that design, he dared say to him whom he claimed the right to dominate, that a God had forged the irons with which cruelty manacled him; and the latter, bestialized by his misery, indistinctly believed everything the former wished. Can religions, born of these rogueries, merit respect? Is there one of them, Thérèse, which does not bear the stamp of imposture and of stupidity? What do I descry in them all? Mysteries which cause reason to shudder, dogmas which outrage Nature, grotesque ceremonies which simply inspire derision and disgust. But if amongst them all there were one which most particularly deserves our scorn and hatred, O Thérèse, is it not that barbaric law of the Christianity into which both of us were born? Is there any more odious? one which so spurs both the heart and mind to revolt? How is it that rational men are still able to lend any credence to the obscure mutterings, to the alleged miracles of that appalling cult's vile originator? Has there ever existed a rowdy scoundrel more worthy of public indignation! What is he but a leprous Jew who, born of a slut and a soldier in the world's meanest stews, dared fob himself off for the spokesman of him who, they say, created the universe! With such lofty pretensions, you will have to admit, Thérèse, at least a few credentials are necessary. But what are those of this ridiculous Ambassador? What is he going to do to prove his mission? Is the earth's face going to be changed? are the plagues which beset it going to be annihilated? is the sun going to shine upon it by night as well as by day? vices will soil it no more? Are we going to see happiness reign at last?... Not at all; it is through hocus-pocus, antic capers, and puns[2] that God's envoy announces himself to the world; it is in the elegant society of manual laborers, artisans, and streetwalkers that Heaven's minister comes to manifest his grandeur; it is by drunken carousing with these, bedding with those, that God's friend, God himself, comes to bend the toughened sinner to his laws; it is by inventing nothing for his farces but what can satisfy either his lewdness or his gourmand's guts that the knavish fellow demonstrates his mission; however all that may be, he makes his fortune; a few beef-witted satellites gravitate toward the villain; a sect is formed; this crowd's dogmas manage to seduce some Jews; slaves of the Roman power, they joyfully embrace a religion which, ridding them of their shackles, makes them subject to none but a metaphysical tyranny. Their motives become evident, their indocility unveils itself, the seditious louts are ar-

---

[2] The Marquis de Bièvre never made one quite as clever as the Nazarene's to his disciple: "Thou art Peter and upon this Rock I will build my Church"; and they tell us that witty language is one of our century's innovations!

rested; their captain perishes, but of a death doubtless much too merciful for his species of crime, and through an unpardonable lapse of intelligence, this uncouth boor's disciples are allowed to disperse instead of being slaughtered cheek to jowl with their leader. Fanaticism gets minds in its grip, women shriek, fools scrape and scuffle, imbeciles believe, and lo! the most contemptible of beings, the most maladroit quacksalver, the clumsiest impostor ever to have made his entrance, there he is: behold! God, there's God's little boy, his papa's peer; and now all his dreams are consecrated! and now all his epigrams are become dogmas! and all his blunders mysteries! His fabulous father's breast opens to receive him and that Creator, once upon a time simple, of a sudden becomes compound, triple, to humor his son, this lad so worthy of his greatness; but does that sacred God stick at that? No, surely not, his celestial might is going to bestow many another and greater favor. At the beck and call of a priest, of, that is to say, an odd fellow foul with lies, the great God, creator of all we behold, is going to abase himself to the point of descending ten or twelve million times every morning in a morsel of wheat paste; this the faithful devour and assimilate, and God Almighty is lugged to the bottom of their intestines where he is speedily transmuted into the vilest excrements, and all that for the satisfaction of the tender son, odious inventor of this monstrous impiety which had its beginnings in a cabaret supper. He spake, and it was ordained. He said: this bread you see will be my flesh; you will digest it as such; now, I am God; hence, God will be digested by you; hence, the Creator of Heaven and Earth will be changed, because I have spoken, into the vilest stuff the body of man can exhale, and man will eat his God, because this God is good and because he is omnipotent. However, these blatherings increase; their growth is attributed to their authenticity, their greatness, their sublimity to the puissance of him who introduced them, while in truth the commonest causes double their existence, for the credit error acquires never proved anything but the presence of swindlers on the one side and of idiots on the other. This infamous religion finally arrives on the throne, and it is a weak, cruel, ignorant and fanatical emperor who, enveloping it in the royal mantle, soils the four corners of the earth with it. O Thérèse, what weight are these arguments to carry with an inquiring and philo-

sophic mind? Is the sage able to see anything in this appalling heap
of fables but the disgusting fruit of a few men's imposture and the
diddled credulity of a vast number? had God willed it that we have
some religion or other, and had he been truly powerful or, to frame
it more suitably, had there truly been a God, would it have been by
these absurd means he would have imparted his instructions to us?
Would it have been through the voice of a contemptible bandit he
would have shown how it were necessary to serve him? Were he
supreme, were he mighty, were he just, were he good, this God you
tell me about, would it be through enigmas and buffooneries he
would wish to teach me to serve and know him? Sovereign mover
of the stars and the heart of man, may he not instruct us by employing the one or convince us by graving himself in the other? Let him,
one of these days, upon the Sun indite the law, writ out in letters
of fire, the law as he wants us to understand it, in the version that
pleases him; then from one end of the universe to the other, all
mankind will read it, will behold it at once, and thereafter will be
guilty if they obey it not. But to indicate his desires nowhere but in
some unknown corner of Asia; to select for witnesses the craftiest
and most visionary of people, for alter ego the meanest artisan, the
most absurd, him of the greatest rascality; to frame his doctrine so
confusedly it is impossible to make it out; to limit knowledge of it
to a small group of individuals; to leave the others in error and to
punish them for remaining there. . . . Why, no, Thérèse, no, these
atrocities are not what we want for our guidance; I should prefer
to die a thousand deaths rather than believe them. When atheism
will wish for martyrs, let it designate them; my blood is ready to be
shed. Let us detest these horrors, Thérèse; let the most steadfast
outrages cement the scorn which is patently their due. . . . My eyes
were barely open when I began to loathe these coarse reveries; very
early I made it a law unto myself to trample them in the dust, I took
oath to return to them never more; if you would be happy, imitate
me; as do I, hate, abjure, profane the foul object of this dreadful
cult; and this cult too, created for illusion, made like him to be
reviled by everyone who pretends to wisdom."

"Oh! Monsieur," I responded, weeping, "you would deprive
an unfortunate of her fondest hope were you to wither in her heart
this religion which is her whole comfort. Firmly attached to its

teachings, absolutely convinced that all the blows leveled against it are nothing but libertinage's effects and the passions', am I to sacrifice, to blasphemies, to sophistries horrible to me, my heart's sweetest sustenance?"

I added a thousand other arguments to this one, they merely caused the Count to laugh, and his captious principles, nourished by a more male eloquence, supported by readings and studies I, happily, had never performed, daily attacked my own principles, without shaking them. Madame de Bressac, that woman filled with piety and virtue, was not unaware her nephew justified his wild behavior with every one of the day's paradoxes; she too often shuddered upon hearing them; and as she condescended to attribute somewhat more good sense to me than to her other women, she would sometimes take me aside and speak of her chagrin.

Meanwhile, her nephew, champing at the bit, had reached the point where he no longer bothered to hide his malign intentions; not only had he surrounded his aunt with all of that dangerous *canaille* which served his pleasures, but he had even carried boldness so far as to declare to her, in my presence, that were she to take it into her head to frustrate his appetite, he would convince her of their charm by practicing them before her very eyes.

I trembled; I beheld this conduct with horror. I strove to rationalize my reactions by attributing their origin to personal motives, for I wished to stifle the unhappy passion which burned in my soul; but is love an illness to be cured? All I endeavored to oppose to it merely fanned its flames, and the perfidious Count never appeared more lovable to me than when I had assembled before me everything which ought to have induced me to hate him.

I had remained four years in this household unrelentingly persecuted by the same sorrows, forever consoled by the same sweetnesses, when this abominable man, finally believing himself sure of me, dared disclose his infamous schemes. We were in the country at the time, I alone attended upon the Marquise, her first maid-in-waiting had obtained leave to remain in Paris through the summer to look after some of her husband's business. One evening shortly after I had retired, and as I was taking some air upon the balcony of my room, being unable to bring myself to go to bed because of the extreme heat, I suddenly heard the Count knock; he

wished to have a word or two with me. Alas! the moments that
cruel author of my ills accorded me of his presence were too precious for me to dare refuse him one; he enters, carefully closes the
door and flings himself into an armchair.

"Listen to me, Thérèse," and there is a note of embarrassment
in his voice, "I have things of the greatest importance to say to you;
swear to me you will never reveal any of them."

"Monsieur," I reply, "do you think me capable of abusing
your confidence?"

"You have no idea what you would be risking were you to
prove to me I had made a mistake in trusting you!"

"The most frightful of all my woes should be to lose your
trust, I have no need of greater menaces. . . ."

"Ah then, Thérèse, I have condemned my aunt to die . . . and
it is your hand I must employ."

"My hand!" I cried, recoiling in fright, "have you been able,
Monsieur, to conceive such projects? . . . no, dispose of my life
if you must, but imagine not you will ever obtain from me the horror you propose."

"Hear me, Thérèse," says the Count, reasoning with me
calmly, "I indeed foresaw your distaste for the idea but, as you have
wit and verve, I flattered myself with the belief I could vanquish
your feelings . . . could prove to you that this crime, which seems
to you of such enormity, is, at bottom, a very banal affair.

"Two misdeeds present themselves, Thérèse, to your not very
philosophic scrutiny: the destruction of a creature bearing a resem-
blance to us, and the evil with which this destruction is augmented
when the said creature is one of our near kinsmen. With regard to
the crime of destroying one's fellow, be persuaded, dear girl, it is
purely hallucinatory; man has not been accorded the power to
destroy; he has at best the capacity to alter forms, but lacks that
required to annihilate them: well, every form is of equal worth in
Nature's view; nothing is lost in the immense melting pot where
variations are wrought: all the material masses which fall into it
spring incessantly forth in other shapes, and whatsoever be our
interventions in this process, not one of them, needless to say, outrages her, not one is capable of offending her. Our depredations
revive her power; they stimulate her energy, but not one attenuates

her; she is neither impeded nor thwarted by any. . . . Why! what difference does it make to her creative hand if this mass of flesh today wearing the conformation of a bipedal individual is reproduced tomorrow in the guise of a handful of centipedes? Dare one say that the construction of this two-legged animal costs her any more than that of an earthworm, and that she should take a greater interest in the one than in the other? If then the degree of attachment, or rather of indifference, is the same, what can it be to her if, by one man's sword, another man is trans-speciated into a fly or a blade of grass? When they will have convinced me of the sublimity of our species, when they will have demonstrated to me that it is really so important to Nature, that her laws are necessarily violated by this transmutation, then I will be able to believe that murder is a crime; but when the most thoughtful and sober study has proven to me that everything that vegetates upon this globe is of equal value in her eyes, I shall never concede that the alteration of one of these creatures into a thousand others can in any sense upset her intentions or sort ill with her desires. I say to myself: all men, all animals, all plants growing, feeding, destroying and reproducing themselves by the same means, never undergoing a real death, but a simple variation in what modifies them; all, I say, appearing today in one form and several years or hours later in another, all may, at the will of the being who wishes to move them, change a thousand thousand times in a single day, without one of Nature's directives being affected for one instant—what do I say? without this transmuter having done anything but good, since, by dismantling the individuals whose basic components again become necessary to Nature, he does naught by this action, improperly qualified as criminal, but render her the creative energy of which she is necessarily deprived by him who, through brutish indifference, dares not undertake any shuffling, as it were, of the deck. . . . O Thérèse, it is man's pride alone erects murder as a crime. This vain creature, imagining himself the most sublime of the globe's inhabitants, its most essential, takes his departure from this false principle in order to affirm that the deed which results in his undoing can be nothing but an infamy; but his vanity, his lunacy alter the laws of Nature not one jot; no person exists who in the depths of his heart does not feel the most vehement desire to be rid of

those by whom he is hampered, troubled, or whose death may be
of some advantage to him; and do you suppose, Thérèse, that the
difference between this desire and its effect is very great? Now, if
these impressions come to us from Nature, can it be presumed they
irritate her? Would she inspire in us what would cause her downfall? Ah, be at ease, dear girl, we experience nothing that does not
serve her; all the impulses she puts in us are the agents of her
decrees; man's passions are but the means she employs to attain
her ends. If she stands in need of more individuals, she inspires lust
in us and behold! there are creations; when destructions become
necessary to her, she inserts vengeance, avarice, lechery, ambition
into our hearts and lo! you have murders; but she has not ceased
to labor in her own behalf, and whatever we do, there can be no
question of it, we are the unthinking instruments of her caprices.

"Ah, no, Thérèse, no! Nature does not leave in our hands the
possibility of committing crimes which would conflict with her
economy; has it ever been known to happen that the weakest were
able to offend the mightiest? What are we in comparison to her?
Can she, when she created us, have placed in us what would be
capable of hurting her? Can that idiotic supposition consort with
the sublime and sure manner in which we see her attain her ends?
Ah! were murder not one of the human actions which best fulfilled
her intentions, would she permit the doing of murder? May to
imitate then be to injure her? Can she be incensed to see man do to
his brethren what she herself does to him every day? Since it is
proven that she cannot reproduce without destructions, is it not to
act in harmony with her wishes to multiply them unceasingly? The
man who moves in this direction, who plunges ahead with all
possible zeal, will incontestably be the one who serves her best,
since it will be he who most co-operates with the schemes she manifests constantly. The primary and most beautiful of Nature's qualities is motion, which agitates her at all times, but this motion is
simply a perpetual consequence of crimes, she conserves it by means
of crimes only; the person who most nearly resembles her, and
therefore the most perfect being, necessarily will be the one whose
most active agitation will become the cause of many crimes; whereas, I repeat, the inactive or indolent person, that is to say, the
virtuous person, must be in her eyes—how may there be any doubt

of it?—the least perfect since he tends only to apathy, to lethargy, to that inactivity which would immediately plunge everything back into chaos were his star to be in the ascendant. Equilibrium must be preserved; it can only be preserved by crimes; therefore, crimes serve Nature; if they serve her, if she demands them, if she desires them, can they offend her? And who else can be offended if she is not?

"But my aunt is the creature I am going to destroy. . . . Oh, Thérèse, in a philosopher's view how frivolous are these consanguinary ties! Forgive me, but I do not even wish to discuss them, so futile are they. These contemptible chains, fruit of our laws and our political institutions—can they mean anything to Nature?

"Desert your prejudices, Thérèse, leave them behind, and serve me; your fortune is made."

"Oh Monsieur!" I replied, terrified by the Comte de Bressac, "your mind invents this theory of an impassive, indifferent Nature; deign rather to heed your heart, and you will hear it condemn all libertinage's false reasonings. Is not that heart, to whose tribunal I recommend you, the sanctuary where this Nature you outrage wishes to be heard and respected? If she engraves upon it the extreme horror of the crime you meditate, will you grant me it is a damnable one? Passions, I know, are blinding you at the present moment, but once they subside, how will you not be torn by remorse? The greater your sensitivity, the more cruelly shall it sting you. . . . Oh Monsieur! preserve, respect this tender, invaluable friend's life; sacrifice it not; you would perish of despair! Every day . . . at every instant you would be visited by the image of this cherished aunt, she whom your unthinking rage would have hurled into her tomb; you would hear her plaintive voice still pronouncing those sweet names that were your childhood's joy; she would be present during your waking hours and appear to torture you in your dreams; she would open with her bloodstained fingers the wounds wherewith you would have mutilated her; thereafter not one happy moment would shine for you while you dwelt upon this earth; you would become a stranger to pleasures; your every idea would be of trouble; a celestial arm, whose might you do not appreciate, would avenge the days you would have obliterated, by envenoming your own, and without having tasted happiness from your felonies, you would be slain by mortal sorrow for having dared accomplish them."

As I uttered these words tears returned to my eyes, I sank to my knees before the Count; by all that is most holy I did implore him to let fade into oblivion an infamous aberration I swore to him all my life I would conceal. . . . But I did not know the man with whom I was dealing; I knew not to what point passions had enthroned crime in that perverse soul. The Count rose and spoke in a voice of ice.

"I see very well I was mistaken, Thérèse," said he. "I regret it, perhaps as much on your account as on my own; no matter, I shall discover other means, and it will be much you shall have lost without your mistress gaining anything."

The threat changed all my ideas; by not accepting the criminal role proposed to me, I was exposing myself to great personal risk and my protectress was infallibly to perish; by consenting to be his accomplice, I would shield myself from the Count's wrath and would assuredly save his aunt; an instant's reflection convinced me I should agree to everything. But as so rapid a reversal would have appeared suspicious, I strove to delay my capitulation; I obliged the Count to repeat his sophistries often; little by little I took on an air of not knowing what to reply: Bressac believed me vanquished; I justified my weakness by the potency of his art and in the end I surrendered. The Count sprang into my arms. Ah, how I should have been overjoyed had his movement been inspired by another motive. . . . What is it I am saying? The time had passed: his horrible conduct, his barbarous designs had annihilated all the feelings my weakling heart had dared conceive, and I saw in him nothing but a monster. . . .

"You are the first woman I have ever held in my arms," said the Count, "and truly, it is with all my soul. . . . You are delicious, my child; a gleam of wisdom seems to have penetrated into your mind! That this charming mind has lain in darkness for so long! Incredible."

Next, we came to facts. In two or three days, as soon, that is, as an opportunity presented itself, I was to drop a dose of poison—Bressac gave me the package that contained it—into the cup of chocolate Madame customarily took in the morning. The

Count assured my immunity against all consequences and directly I consummated the deed, handed me a contract providing me with an annuity of two thousand crowns; he signed these promises without characterizing the state in which I was to enjoy their benefits; we separated.

In the midst of all this, something most singular occurred, something all too able to reveal the atrocious soul of the monster with whom I had to deal; I must not interrupt myself for a moment for, no doubt, you are awaiting the denouement of the adventure in which I had become involved.

Two days following the conclusion of our criminal pact, the Count learned that an uncle, upon whose succession he had not in the least counted, had just left him an income of eighty thousand pounds. . . . "O Heaven!" I said to myself upon hearing the news, "is it then in thuswise celestial justice punishes the basest conspiracy!" And straightway repenting this blasphemy spoken against Providence, I cast myself upon my knees and implored the Almighty's forgiveness, and happily supposed that this unexpected development should at least change the Count's plans. . . . What was my error!

"Ah, my dear Thérèse," he said that same evening, having run to my room, "how prosperity does rain down upon me! Often I have told you so: the idea of a crime or an execution is the surest means to attract good fortune; none exists save for villains."

"What!" I responded, "this unhoped for bounty does not persuade you, Monsieur, patiently to await the death you wished to hasten?"

"Wait?" the Count replied sharply, "I do not intend to wait two minutes, Thérèse; are you not aware I am twenty-eight? Well, it is hard to wait at my age. . . . No, let this affect our scheme not in the slightest, give me the comfort of seeing everything brought to an end before the time comes for us to return to Paris. . . . Tomorrow, at the very latest the day after tomorrow, I beseech you. There has been delay enough: the hour approaches for the payment of the first quarter of your annuity . . . for performing the act which guarantees you the money. . . ."

As best I could, I disguised the fright this desperate eagerness inspired in me, and I renewed my resolution of the day before, well persuaded that if I were not to execute the horrible crime I had engaged to commit, the Count would soon notice I was playing a trick upon him and that, if I were to warn Madame de Bressac, whatever would be her reaction to the project's disclosure, the young Count, observing himself deceived one way or another, would promptly resort to more certain methods which, causing his aunt equally to perish, would also expose me to all her nephew's vengeance. There remained the alternative of consulting the law, but nothing in the world could have induced me to adopt it; I decided to forewarn the Marquise; of all possible measures, that seemed the best, and I elected it.

"Madame," I said to her on the morrow of my last interview with the Count, "Madame, I have something of the highest importance to reveal, but however vital its interest to you, I shall not broach it unless, beforehand, you give me your word of honor to bear no resentment against your nephew for what Monsieur has had the audacity to concert. . . . You will act, Madame, you will take the steps prudence enjoins, but you will say not a word. Deign to give me your promise; else I am silent."

Madame de Bressac, who thought it was but a question of some of her nephew's everyday extravagances, bound herself by the oath I demanded, and I disclosed everything. The unhappy woman burst into tears upon learning of the infamy. . . . "The monster!" she cried, "have I ever done anything that was not for his good? Had I wished to thwart his vices, or correct them, what other motive than his own happiness could have constrained me to severity! And is it not thanks to me he inherits this legacy his uncle has just left him? Ah, Thérèse, Thérèse, prove to me that it is true, this project . . . put me in a way that will prevent me from doubting; I need all that may aid in extinguishing the sentiments my unthinking heart dares yet preserve for the monster. . . ." And then I brought the package of poison into view; it were difficult to furnish better proof; yet the Marquise wished to experiment with it; we made a dog swallow a light dose, shut up the animal, and at the end of two hours it was dead after being seized by frightful convulsions. Any lingering doubt by now dispelled, Madame de Bressac came to a decision; she bade me give her the rest of the poison and immediately sent a courier with a letter to the Duc de Sonzeval, related to her, asking him to go directly, but in secrecy, to the Secretary of State, and to expose the atrocity of a nephew whose victim she might at any moment become; to provide himself with a *lettre de cachet;* to make all possible haste to come and deliver her from the wretch who had so cruelly plotted to take her life.

But the abominable crime was to be consummated; some inconceivable permission must have been granted by Heaven that virtue might be made to yield to villainy's oppressions: the animal upon which we had experimented revealed everything to the Count: he heard it howling; knowing of his aunt's fondness for the beast, he asked what had been done to it; those to whom he spoke knew nothing of the matter and made him no clear answer; from this moment, his suspicions began to take shape; he uttered not a word, but I saw that he was disquieted; I mentioned his state to the Marquise, she became further upset, but could think of nothing to do save urge the courier to make yet greater haste, and, if possible, still more carefully to hide the purpose of his mission. She advised her nephew that she was writing to Paris to beg the Duc de Sonzeval to waste not a moment to take up the matter of the recently deceased uncle's inheritance for if no one were to appear to claim it, there was litigation to be feared; she added that she had requested the Duke to come and give her a complete account of the affair, in order that she might learn whether or not she and her nephew would be obliged to make a journey to Paris. Too skillful a physiognomist to fail to notice the embarrassment in his aunt's face, to fail to observe, as well, some confusion written upon mine, the Count smiled at everything and was no less on his guard. Under the pretext of taking a promenade, he leaves the château; he lies in wait for the courier at a place the man must inevitably pass. The messenger, far more a creature of the Count than his aunt's trustworthy minion, raises no objections when his master demands to see the dispatches he is carrying, and Bressac, once convinced of what no doubt he calls my treachery, gives the courier a hundred *louis,* together with instructions never to appear again at the Marquise's. He returns to the château, rage in his heart; however, he restrains himself; he encounters me, as usual he cajoles me, asks whether it shall not be tomorrow, points out it is essential the deed be performed before the Duke's arrival, then goes to bed with a tranquil air about which nothing is to be remarked. At the time I knew nothing, I was the dupe of everything. Were the appalling crime to be committed—as the Count's actions informed me later— he would of course have to commit it himself; but I did not know how; I conjectured much; what good would it do to tell you what I imagined? Rather, let us move ahead to the cruel manner in which I was punished for not having wished to undertake the thing. On the day after the messenger was intercepted, Madame drank her chocolate as she always did, dressed, seemed agitated, and sat down at table; scarcely was I out of the dining room when the Count accosted me.

"Thérèse," and nothing could have been more phlegmatic than his manner as he spoke, "I have found a more reliable method than the one I proposed to attain our objectives, but numerous details are involved, and I dare not come so often to your room; at precisely five o'clock be at the corner of the park, I'll join you, we will take a walk together in the woods; while on our promenade I'll explain it all."

I wish to affirm, Madame, that, whether because of the influence of Providence, whether owing to an excessive candor, whether to blindness, nothing gave me a hint of the terrible misery awaiting me; I believed myself so safe, thanks to the Marquise's secret arrangements, that I never for a moment imagined that the Count had been able to discover them; nevertheless I was not entirely at ease.

"Le parjure est vertu quand on promit le crime," one of our tragic poets has said; but perjury is always odious to a delicate and sensitive spirit which finds itself compelled to resort to it. My role embarrassed me.

However that may be, I came to the rendezvous; the Count was not late in getting there; he came up to me very gay and easy, and we set off into the forest; the while he but laughed banteringly and jested, as was his habit when we were together. When I sought to guide the conversation to the subject which he had desired to discuss, he told me to wait yet a little, he said he feared we might be observed, it did not seem to him we were in a safe enough place;

very gradually, without my perceiving it, we approached the four trees to which I had been so cruelly bound long ago. Upon seeing the place, a quiver ran through me: all the horror of my fate rose up before my eyes, and fancy whether my terror was not doubled when I caught sight of the preparations which had been made in that horrible place. Ropes hung from one of the trees; huge mastiffs were leashed to each of the other three and seemed to be waiting for nothing but me in order to fall to sating the hunger announced by their gaping foam-flecked jaws; one of the Count's favorites guarded them.

Whereupon the perfidious creature ceased to employ all but the very foulest epithets.

"Scum," quoth he, "do you recognize that bush whence I dragged you like a wild beast only to spare a life you deserved to lose? Do you recognize these trees unto which I threatened to lash you were you ever to give me cause to repent my kindness? Why did you agree to perform the task I demanded, if you intended to betray me to my aunt? and how could you imagine it was virtue you served by imperiling the freedom of him to whom you owe all your happiness? By necessity placed between two crimes, why have you chosen the more abominable?"

"Alas! I did not choose the less . . ."

"But you should have refused," the Count continued, in his rage seizing one of my arms and shaking me furiously, "yes, certainly, refused, and not consented to betray me."

Then Monsieur de Bressac told me how he had gone about the interception of Madame's messages, and how the suspicion had been born which had led him to decide to stop them.

"What has your duplicity done for you, unworthy creature? You have risked your life without having saved my aunt's: the die is cast, upon my return to the château I will find a fortune awaiting me, but you must perish; before you expire you must learn that the virtuous road is not always the safest, and that there are circumstances in this world when complicity in crime is preferable to informing." And without giving me time to reply, without giving evidence of the least pity for the frightful situation I was in, he dragged me toward the tree destined for me and by which his valet stood expectantly. "Here she is," he said, "the creature who wanted to poison my aunt and who may already have committed the terrible crime in spite of my efforts to prevent it; no doubt, it would have been better to have put her into the hands of justice, but the law would have taken away her life, and I prefer to leave it to her in order that she have longer to suffer."

The two villains then lay hands on me, in an instant they strip me naked. "Pretty buttocks," said the Count in a tone of cruelest irony, brutally handling those objects, "superb flesh . . . excellent lunch for the dogs." When no article of clothing is left upon me, I am secured to the tree by a rope attached around my waist; so that I may defend myself as best I can, my arms are left free, and enough slack is provided for me to advance or retreat about two yards. The arrangements completed, the Count, very much moved, steps up to have a look at my expression, he turns and passes around me; his savage way of handling me seems to say that his murderous fingers would like to dispute the rage of his mastiff's steel teeth. . . .

"Come," says he to his lieutenant, "free the animals, the time has arrived."

They are loosed, the Count excites them, all three fling themselves upon my poor body, one would think they were sharing it in such wise that not one of its parts would be exempt from assault; in vain I drive them back, they bite and tear me with renewed fury, and throughout this horrible scene, Bressac, the craven Bressac, as if my torments had ignited his perfidious lust . . . the beastly man gives himself up, while he regards me, to his companion's criminal caresses.

"Enough," said he after several minutes had gone by, "that will do. Tie up the dogs and let's abandon this creature to her sweet fate.

"Well indeed, Thérèse," says he as he severs my bonds, "virtue is not to be practiced at some expense; a pension of two thousand crowns, would that not have been worth more than the bites you are covered with?"

But in my state I can scarcely hear him; I slump to the foot of the tree and am about to lose consciousness.

"It is most generous of me to save your life," continues the traitor whom my sufferings inflame, "at least take good care how you make use of this favor. . . ."

Then he orders me to get up, dress, and quit the place at once. As my blood is flowing everywhere, in order that my few clothes, the only clothes I have, not be stained, I gather some grass to wipe myself; Bressac paces to and fro, much more preoccupied with his thoughts than concerned with me.

My swollen flesh, the blood that continues to stream from my multiple wounds, the atrocious pain I am enduring, everything makes the operation of dressing well nigh impossible; never once does the dishonest man who has just put me into this horrible state . . . him for whom I once would have sacrified my life, never once does he deign to show me the least hint of sympathy. When at length I am ready:

"Go wherever you wish," says he; "you must have some money left, I will not take it from you, but beware of reappearing at any one of my houses in the city or the country: there are two excellent reasons for not doing so: you may just as well know, first of all, that the affair you thought finished is not at all over. They informed you that the law was done with you; they told you what is not true; the warrant for your arrest still holds, the case is still warm: you were left in this situation so that your conduct might be observed. In the second place, you are going to pass, insofar as the public is concerned, for the Marquise's murderer; if she yet breathes, I am going to see to it she carries this notion into the grave, the entire household will share it; and there you have two trials still to face instead of one: instead of a vile usurer, you have for an adversary a rich and powerful man who is determined to hound you into Hell itself if you misuse the life his compassion leaves to you."

"Oh Monsieur!" was my response, "whatever have been your severities with me, fear not that I will retaliate; I thought myself obliged to take steps against you when it was a question of your aunt's life; but where only the unhappy Thérèse is involved, I shall never do anything. Adieu, Monsieur, may your crimes render you as happy as your cruelties have made me to suffer; and no matter what the fate reserved to me by Heaven, while it shall prolong my deplorable life, I shall only employ my days in uttering prayers for you."

The Count raised his head; he could not avoid glancing at me upon hearing these words, and, as he beheld me quavering and covered with tears and doubtless was afraid lest he be moved by what he saw, the cruel one went away, and I saw him nevermore.

Entirely delivered unto my agony, I fell back again and lay by the tree; there, giving free reign to my hurt, I made the forest resound with my groans; I pressed my stricken frame against the earth, and shed upon the sward all my tears.

"O my God," I cried out, "Thou hast so willed it; it was grained in Thy eternal decrees that the innocent were to fall unto the guilty and were to be their prey: dispose of me, O Lord, I am yet far away from what Thou didst suffer for us; may those I endure, as I adore Thee, render me worthy someday of what rewards Thou keepeth for the lowly, when he hath Thee before him in his tribulations, and let his anguishes be unto Thy greater glorification!"

Night was closing: it was almost beyond my power to move; I was scarcely able to stand erect; I cast my eyes upon the thicket where four years earlier I had slept a night when I had been in circumstances almost as unhappy! I dragged myself along as best I could, and having reached the very same spot, tormented by my still bleeding wounds, overwhelmed by my mind's anxieties and the sorrows of my heart, I passed the cruelest night imaginable.

By dawn, thanks to my youth and my vigorous temperament, some of my strength was restored; greatly terrified by the proximity of that baneful château, I started away from it without delay; I left the forest, and resolved at any price to gain the first habitation which might catch my eye, I entered the town of Saint-Marcel, about five leagues distant from Paris; I demanded the address of a surgeon, one was given me; I presented myself and besought him to dress my wounds; I told him that, in connection with some affair at whose source lay love, I had fled my mother's house, quit Paris, and during the night had been overtaken in the forest by bandits who in revenge for my resistance to their desires, had set their dogs upon me. Rodin, as this artist was called, examined me with the greatest attention, found nothing dangerous about my injuries; had I come to him directly, he said, he would have been able to guarantee that in the space of a fortnight he would have me as fresh and whole as I had been before my adventure; however, the night passed in the open and my worry had infected my wounds, and I could not expect to be well in less than a month. Rodin found space in his own house to lodge me, took all possible care of me, and on the thirtieth day there no longer existed upon my body a single vestige of Monsieur de Bressac's cruelties.

As soon as I was fit to take a little air, my first concern was to find in the town some girl sufficiently adroit and intelligent to go to the Marquise's château and find out what had taken place there since my departure. This apparently very dangerous inquisitiveness would without the slightest doubt have been exceedingly misplaced; but here it was not a question of mere curiosity. What I had earned while with the Marquise remained in my room; I had scarcely six *louis* about me, and I possessed above forty at the château. I did not suppose the Count would be unkind enough to refuse me what was so legitimately mine. Persuaded that, his first fury once passed, he would not wish to do me such an injustice, I wrote a letter calculated to touch him as deeply as possible. I was careful to conceal my address and I begged him to send back my old clothes together with the small sum that would be found in my chamber. A lively and spirited peasant girl of twenty-five undertook to deliver my letter and promised to do her best to bring me back all the information she could garner upon the various subjects about which I gave her to understand I needed to be enlightened. I insisted, that above all else, she hide the name of the place where I was, that she not breathe a word of me in whatever form or connection, and that she say she had taken the letter from a man who had brought it from somewhere fifteen leagues away. Jeannette left, and twenty-four hours later she came back with the reply; it still exists, I have it here, Madame, but before you read it, deign to learn what had transpired at the Count's château since I had been out of it.

Having fallen seriously ill the very day I left, the Marquise de Bressac had been seized by frightful pains and convulsions, and had died the next morning; the family had rushed to the château and the nephew, seemingly gripped in the greatest desolation, had declared that his aunt had been poisoned by a chambermaid who had taken flight the same day. Inquiries were made, and they had the intention to put the wretch to death were she to be found; as for the rest, the Count discovered that the inheritance had made him much wealthier than he had ever anticipated he would be; the Marquise's strongbox, pocketbook, and gems, all of them objects of which no one had known anything, put the nephew, apart from his revenues, in possession of more than six hundred thousand francs in chattels or cash. Behind his affected grief, the young man had, it was said, considerable trouble concealing his delight, and the relatives, convoked for the autopsy demanded by the Count, after having lamented the unhappy Marquise's fate and sworn to avenge her should the culprit fall into their hands, had left the young man in undisputed and peaceful possession of his villainy. Monsieur de Bressac himself had spoken to Jeannette, he had asked a number of questions to which the girl had replied with such frankness and decision that he had resolved to give her his response without pressing her further. There is the fatal letter, said Thérèse, handing it to Madame de Lorsange, yes, there it is, Madame, sometimes my heart has need of it and I will keep it until I die; read it, read it without shuddering, if you can.

Madame de Lorsange, having taken the note from our lovely adventuress' hands, read therein the following words:

> The criminal capable of having poisoned my aunt is brazen indeed to dare thus write to me after her execrable deed; better still is the care with which she conceals her retreat; for she may be sure she will be discomfited if she is discovered. But what is it she has the temerity to demand? What are these references to money? Does what she left behind equal the thefts she committed, either during her sojourn in the house or while consummating her final crime? Let her avoid sending a second request similar to this, for she is advised her ambassador will be arrested and held until the law acquaints itself with the place where the guilty party is taking cover.

Madame de Lorsange returned the note to Thérèse; "Continue, my dear child," said she, "the man's behavior is horrifying; to be swimming in gold and to deny her legitimate earnings to a poor creature who merely did not want to commit a crime, that is a gratuitous infamy entirely without example."

Alas! Madame, Thérèse continued, resuming her story, I was in tears for two days over that dreadful letter; I was far more afflicted by the thought of the horrible deed it attested than by the refusal it contained. Then, I groaned, then I am guilty, here am

I a second time denounced to justice for having been overly respect-ful of the law! So be it, I repent nothing, I shall never know the least remorse so long as my soul is pure, and may I never be responsible for any evil other than that of having too much heeded the equitable and virtuous sentiments which will never abandon me.

I was, however, simply unable to believe that the pursuits and inquiries the Count mentioned were really true, for they seemed highly implausible: it would be so dangerous for him to have me brought into court that I imagined there was far greater reason for him to be frightened at the prospect of having to confront me, than I had cause to tremble before his menaces. These reflections led me to decide to stay where I was and to remain, if possible, until the augmentation of my funds might allow me to move on; I communicated my plan to Rodin, who approved it, and even sug-gested I keep my chamber in his house; but first of all, before I speak of what I decided to do, it is necessary to give you an idea of this man and his entourage.

Rodin was forty years of age, dark-haired, with shaggy eye-brows, a sparkling bright eye; there was about him what bespoke strength and health but, at the same time, libertinage. In wealth he was risen far above his native station, possessing from ten to twelve thousand pounds a year; owing to which, if Rodin practiced his surgical art, it was not out of necessity, but out of taste; he had a very attractive house in Saint-Marcel which, since the death of his wife two years previously, he shared with two girls, who were his servants, and with another, who was his own daughter. This young person, Rosalie by name, had just reached her fourteenth year; in her were gathered all the charms most capable of exciting admira-tion: the figure of a nymph, an oval face, clear, lovely, extraor-dinarily animated, delicate pretty features, very piquant as well, the prettiest mouth possible, very large dark eyes, soulful and full of feeling, chestnut-brown hair falling to below her waist, skin of an incredible whiteness . . . aglow, smooth, already the most beautiful throat in all the world, and, furthermore, wit, vivacity, and one of the most beautiful souls Nature has yet created. With respect to the companions with whom I was to serve in this household, they were two peasant girls: one of them was a governess, the other the cook. She who held the first post could have been twenty-five, the other eighteen or twenty, and both were extremely attractive; their looks suggested a deliberate choice, and this in turn caused the birth of some suspicions as to why Rodin was pleased to accommodate me. What need has he of a third woman? I asked myself, and why does he wish them all to be pretty? Assuredly, I continued, there is something in all this that little conforms with the regular manners from which I wish never to stray; we'll see.

In consequence, I besought Monsieur Rodin to allow me to extend my convalescence at his home for yet another week, declaring that, at the end of this time, he would have my reply to what he had very kindly proposed.

I profited from this interval by attaching myself more closely to Rosalie, determined to establish myself in her father's house only if there should prove to be nothing about it whence I might be obliged to take umbrage. With these designs, I cast appraising glances in every direction, and, on the following day, I noticed that this man enjoyed an arrangement which straightway provoked in me furious doubts concerning his behavior.

Monsieur Rodin kept a school for children of both sexes; during his wife's lifetime he had obtained the required charter and they had not seen fit to deprive him of it after he had lost her. Monsieur Rodin's pupils were few but select: in all, there were but fourteen girls and fourteen boys: he never accepted them under twelve and they were always sent away upon reaching the age of sixteen; never had monarch prettier subjects than Rodin. If there were brought to him one who had some physical defect or a face that left something to be desired, he knew how to invent twenty excuses for rejecting him, all his arguments were very ingenious, they were always colored by sophistries to which no one seemed able to reply; thus, either his corps of little day students had incomplete ranks, or the children who filled them were always charming. These youngsters did not take their meals with him, but came twice a day, from seven to eleven in the morning, from four to eight in the afternoon. If until then I had not yet seen all of this little troupe it was because, having arrived at Rodin's during the holidays, his scholars were not attending classes; toward the end of my recovery they reappeared.

Rodin himself took charge of the boys' instruction, his governess looked after that of the girls, whom he would visit as soon as he had completed his own lessons; he taught his young pupils writing, arithmetic, a little history, drawing, music, and for all that no other master but himself was employed.

I early expressed to Rosalie my astonishment that her father, while performing his functions as a doctor, could at the same time act as a schoolmaster; it struck me as odd, said I, that being able to live comfortably without exercising either the one or the other of these professions, he devoted himself to both. Rosalie, who by now had become very fond of me, fell to laughing at my remark; the manner in which she reacted to what I said only made me the more curious, and I besought her to open herself entirely to me.

"Listen," said that charming girl, speaking with all the candor proper to her age, and all the naïveté of her amiable character; "listen to me, Thérèse, I am going to tell you everything, for I see you are a well brought up girl . . . incapable of betraying the secret I am going to confide to you.

"Certainly, dear friend, my father could make ends meet without pursuing either of these two occupations; and if he pursues both at once, it is because of the two motives I am going to reveal to you. He practices medicine because he has a liking for it; he takes keen pleasure in using his skill to make new discoveries, he has made so many of them, he has written so many authoritative texts based upon his investigations that he is generally acknowledged the most accomplished man in France at the present time; he worked for twenty years in Paris, and for the sake of his amusements he retired to the country. The real surgeon at Saint-Marcel is someone named Rombeau whom he has taken under his tutelage and with whom he collaborates upon experiments; and now, Thérèse, would you know why he runs a school? . . . libertinage, my child, libertinage alone, a passion he carries to its extremes. My father finds in his pupils of either sex objects whose dependence submits them to his inclinations, and he exploits them. . . . But wait a moment . . . come with me," said Rosalie, "today is Friday, one of the three days during the week when he corrects those who have misbehaved; it is in this kind of punishment my father takes his pleasure; follow me, I tell you, you shall see how he behaves. Everything is visible from a closet in my room which adjoins the one where he concludes his business; let's go there without making any noise, and above all be careful not to say a word both about what I am telling you and about what you are going to witness."

It was a matter of such great importance to familiarize myself with the customs of this person who had offered me asylum, that I felt I could neglect nothing which might discover them to me; I follow hard upon Rosalie's heels, she situates me near a partition, through cracks between its ill-joined boards one can view everything going on in the neighboring room.

Hardly have we taken up our post when Rodin enters, leading a fourteen-year-old girl, blond and as pretty as Love; the poor creature is sobbing away, all too unhappily aware of what awaits her; she comes in with moans and cries; she throws herself down before her implacable instructor, she entreats him to spare her, but his very inexorability fires the first sparks of the unbending Rodin's pleasure, his heart is already aglow, and his savage glances spring alive with an inner light. . . .

"Why, no, no," he cries, "not for one minute, this happens far too frequently, Julie, I repent my forbearance and leniency, their sole result has been repeated misconduct on your part, but could the gravity of this most recent example of it possibly allow me to show clemency, even supposing I wished to? A note passed to a boy upon entering the classroom!"

"Sir, I protest to you, I did not—"

"Ah! but I saw it, my dear, I saw it."

"Don't believe a word of it," Rosalie whispered to me, "these are trifles he invents by way of pretext; that little creature is an angel, it is because she resists him he treats her harshly."

Meanwhile, Rodin, greatly aroused, had seized the little girl's hands, tied them to a ring fitted high upon a pillar standing in the middle of the punishment room. Julie is without any defense . . . any save the lovely face languishingly turned toward her executioner, her superb hair in disarray, and the tears which inundate the most beautiful face in the world, the sweetest . . . the most interesting. Rodin dwells upon the picture, is fired by it, he covers those supplicating eyes with a blindfold, approaches his mouth and dares kiss them, Julie sees nothing more, now able to proceed as he wishes, Rodin removes the veils of modesty, her blouse is unbuttoned, her stays untied, she is naked to the waist and yet further below. . . . What whiteness! What beauty! These are roses strewn upon lilies by the Graces' very hands . . . what being is so heartless, so cruel as to condemn to torture charms so fresh . . . so poignant? What is the monster that can seek pleasure in the depths of tears and suffering and woe? Rodin contemplates . . . his inflamed eye roves, his hands dare profane the flowers his cruelties are about to wither; all takes place directly before us, not a detail can escape us: now the libertine opens and peers into, now he closes up again those dainty features which enchant him; he offers them to us under every form, but he confines himself to these only: although the true temple of Love is within his reach, Rodin, faithful to his creed, casts not so much as a glance in that direction, to judge by his behavior, he fears even the sight of it; if the child's posture exposes those charms, he covers them over again; the slightest disturbance might upset his homage, he would have nothing distract him . . . finally, his mounting wrath exceeds all limits, at first he gives vent to it through invectives, with menaces and evil language he affrights this poor little wretch trembling before the blows wherewith she realizes she is about to be torn; Rodin is beside himself, he snatches up a cat-o'-nine-tails that has been soaking in a vat of vinegar to give the thongs tartness and sting. "Well there," says he, approaching his victim, "prepare yourself, you have got to suffer"; he swings a vigorous arm, the lashes are brought whistling down upon every inch of the body exposed to them; twenty-five strokes are applied; the tender pink rosiness of this matchless skin is in a trice run into scarlet.

Julie emits cries . . . piercing screams which rend me to the soul; tears run down from beneath her blindfold and like pearls shine upon her beautiful cheeks; whereby Rodin is made all the more furious. . . . He puts his hands upon the molested parts, touches, squeezes, worries them, seems to be readying them for further assaults; they follow fast upon the first, Rodin begins again, not a cut he bestows is unaccompanied by a curse, a menace, a reproach . . . blood appears . . . Rodin is in an ecstasy; his delight is immense as he muses upon the eloquent proofs of his ferocity. He can contain himself no longer, the most indecent condition manifests his overwrought state; he fears not to bring everything out of hiding, Julie cannot see it . . . he moves to the breech and hovers there, he would greatly like to mount as a victor, he dares not, instead, he begins to tyrannize anew; Rodin whips with might and main and finally manages, thanks to the leathern stripes, to open this asylum of the Graces and of joy. . . . He no longer knows who he is or where; his delirium has attained to such a pitch the use of reason is no longer available to him; he swears, he blasphemes, he storms, nothing is exempt from his savage blows, all he can reach is treated with identical fury, but the villain pauses nevertheless, he senses the impossibility of going further without risking the loss of the powers which he must preserve for new operations.

"Dress yourself," he says to Julie, loosening her bonds and readjusting his own costume, "and if you are once again guilty of similar misconduct, bear it firmly in mind you will not get off quite so lightly."

Julie returns to her class, Rodin goes into the boys' and immediately brings back a young scholar of fifteen, lovely as the day; Rodin scolds him; doubtless more at his ease with the lad, he wheedles and kisses while lecturing him.

"You deserve to be punished," he observes, "and you are going to be."

Having uttered these words, he oversteps the last bounds of modesty with the child; for in this case, everything is of interest to him, nothing is excluded, the veils are drawn aside, everything is palpated indiscriminately; Rodin alternates threats, caresses, kisses, curses; his impious fingers attempt to generate voluptuous sentiments in the boy and, in his turn, Rodin demands identical ministrations.

"Very well," cries the satyr, spying his success, "there you are in the state I forbade. . . . I dare swear that with two more movements you'd have the impudence to spit at me. . . ."

But too sure of the titillations he has produced, the libertine advances to gather a homage, and his mouth is the temple offered to the sweet incense; his hands excite it to jet forth, he meets the spurts, devours them, and is himself ready to explode, but he wishes to persevere to the end.

"Ah, I am going to make you pay for this stupidity!" says he and gets to his feet.

He takes the youth's two hands, he clutches them tight, and offers himself entirely to the altar at which his fury would perform a sacrifice. He opens it, his kisses roam over it, his tongue drives deep into it, is lost in it. Drunk with love and ferocity, Rodin mingles the expressions and sentiments of each. . . .

"Ah, little weasel!" he cries, "I must avenge myself upon the illusion you create in me."

The whips are picked up, Rodin flogs; clearly more excited by the boy than he was by the vestal, his blows become both much more powerful and far more numerous: the child bursts into tears, Rodin is in seventh heaven, but new pleasures call, he releases the boy and flies to other sacrifices. A little girl of thirteen is the boy's successor, and she is followed by another youth who is in turn abandoned for a girl; Rodin whips nine: five boys, four girls; the last is a lad of fourteen, endowed with a delicious countenance: Rodin wishes to amuse himself, the pupil resists; out of his mind with lust, he beats him, and the villain, losing all control of himself, hurls his flame's scummy jets upon his young charge's injured parts, he wets him from waist to heels; enraged at not having had strength enough to hold himself in check until the end, our corrector releases the child very testily, and after warning him against such tricks in the future, he sends him back to the class: such are the words I heard, those the scenes which I witnessed.

"Dear Heaven!" I said to Rosalie when this appalling drama came to its end, "how is one able to surrender oneself to such excesses? How can one find pleasure in the torments one inflicts?"

"Ah," replied Rosalie, "you do not know everything. Listen," she said, leading me back into her room, "what you have seen has perhaps enabled you to understand that when my father discovers some aptitudes in his young pupils, he carries his horrors much further, he abuses the girls in the same manner he deals with the boys." Rosalie spoke of that criminal manner of conjugation whereof I myself had believed I might be the victim with the brigands' captain into whose hands I had fallen after my escape from the Conciergerie, and by which I had been soiled by the merchant from Lyon. "By this means," Rosalie continued, "the girls are not in the least dishonored, there are no pregnancies to fear, and nothing prevents them from finding a husband; not a year goes by without his corrupting nearly all the boys in this way, and at least half the other children. Of the fourteen girls you have seen, eight have already been spoiled by these methods, and he has taken his pleasure with nine of the boys; the two women who serve him are submitted to the same horrors. . . . O Thérèse!" Rosalie added, casting herself into my arms, "O dear girl, and I too, yes I, he seduced me in my earliest years; I was barely eleven when I became his victim . . . when, alas! I was unable to defend myself against him."

"But Mademoiselle," I interrupted, horrified, "at least Religion remained to you . . . were you unable to consult a confessor and avow everything?"

"Oh, you do not know that as he proceeds to pervert us he stifles in each of us the very seeds of belief, he forbids us all religious devotions, and, furthermore, could I have done so? he had instructed me scarcely at all. The little he had said pertaining to these matters had been motivated by the fear that my ignorance might betray his impiety. But I had never been to confession, I had not made my First Communion; so deftly did he cover all these things with ridicule and insinuate his poisonous self into even our smallest ideas, that he banished forever all their duties out of them whom he suborned; or if they are compelled by their families to fulfill their religious duties, they do so with such tepidness, with such complete indifference, that he has nothing to fear from their indiscretion; but convince yourself, Thérèse, let your own eyes persuade you," she continued, very quickly drawing me back into the closet whence we had emerged; "come hither: that room where he chastises his students is the same wherein he enjoys us; the lessons are over now, it is the hour when, warmed by the preliminaries, he is going to compensate himself for the restraint his prudence sometimes imposes upon him; go back to where you were, dear girl, and with your own eyes behold it all."

However slight my curiosity concerning these new abominations, it was by far the better course to leap back into the closet rather than have myself surprised with Rosalie during the classes; Rodin would without question have become suspicious. And so I took my place; scarcely was I at it when Rodin enters his daughter's room, he leads her into the other, the two women of the house arrive; and thereupon the impudicious Rodin, all restraints upon his behavior removed, free to indulge his fancies to the full, gives himself over in a leisurely fashion and undisguisedly to committing all the irregularities of debauchery. The two peasants, completely nude, are flogged with exceeding violence; while he plies his whip upon the one the other pays him back in kind, and during the intervals when he pauses for rest, he smothers with the most uninhibited, the most disgusting caresses, the same altar in Rosalie who, elevated upon an armchair, slightly bent over, presents it to him; at last, there comes this poor creature's turn: Rodin ties her to the stake as he tied his scholars, and while one after another and sometimes both at once his domestics flay him, he beats his daughter, lashes her from her ribs to her knees, utterly transported by pleasure. His agitation is extreme: he shouts, he blasphemes, he flagellates: his thongs bite deep everywhere, and wherever they fall, there immediately he presses his lips. Both the interior of the altar and his victim's mouth . . . everything, the before-end excepted, everything is devoured by his suckings; without changing the disposition of the others, contenting himself with rendering it more propitious, Rodin by and by penetrates into pleasure's narrow asylum; meanwhile, the same throne is offered by the governess to his kisses, the other girl beats him with all her remaining strength, Rodin is in seventh heaven, he thrusts, he splits, he tears, a thousand kisses, one more passionate than the other, express his ardor, he kisses whatever is presented to his lust: the bomb bursts and the libertine besotted dares taste the sweetest of delights in the sink of incest and infamy. . . .

Rodin sat down to dine; after such exploits he was in need of restoratives. That afternoon there were more lessons and further corrections, I could have observed new scenes had I desired, but I had seen enough to convince myself and to settle upon a reply to make to this villain's offers. The time for giving it approached. Two days after the events I have described, he himself came to my room to ask for it. He surprised me in bed. By employing the excuse of looking to see whether any traces of my wounds remained, he obtained the right, which I was unable to dispute, of performing an examination upon me, naked, and as he had done the same thing twice a day for a month and had never given any offense to my modesty I did not think myself able to resist. But this time Rodin had other plans; when he reaches the object of his worship, he locks his thighs about my waist and squeezes with such force that I find myself, so to speak, quite defenseless.

"Thérèse," says he, the while moving his hands about in such a manner as to erase all doubt of his intents, "you are fully recovered, my dear, and now you can give me evidence of the gratitude with which I have beheld your heart overflowing; nothing simpler than the form your thanks would take; I need nothing beyond this," the traitor continued, binding me with all the strength at his command. ". . . Yes, this will do, merely this, here is my recompense, I never demand anything else from women . . . but," he continued, " 'tis one of the most splendid I have seen in all my life . . . What roundness, fullness! . . . unusual elasticity! . . . what exquisite quality in the skin! . . . Oh my! I absolutely must put this to use. . . ."

Whereupon Rodin, apparently already prepared to put his projects into execution, is obliged, in order to proceed to the next stage, to relax his grip for a moment; I seize my opportunity and extricating myself from his clutches,

"Monsieur," I say, "I beg you to be well persuaded that there is nothing in the entire world which could engage me to consent to the horrors you seem to wish to commit. My gratitude is due to you, indeed it is, but I will not pay my debt in a criminal coin. Needless to say, I am poor and most unfortunate; but no matter; here is the small sum of money I possess," I continue, producing my meager purse, "take what you esteem just and allow me to leave this house, I beg of you, as soon as I am in a fitting state to go."

Rodin, confounded by the opposition he little expected from a girl devoid of means and whom, according to an injustice very ordinary amongst men, he supposed dishonest by the simple fact she was sunk in poverty; Rodin, I say, gazed at me attentively.

"Thérèse," he resumed after a minute's silence, "Thérèse, it is hardly appropriate for you to play the virgin with me; I have, so it would seem to me, some right to your complaisance; but, however, it makes little difference: keep your silver but don't leave me. I am highly pleased to have a well-behaved girl in my house, the conduct of these others I have about me being far from impeccable.

. . . Since you show yourself so virtuous in this instance, you will be equally so, I trust, in every other. My interests would benefit therefrom; my daughter is fond of you, just a short while ago she came and begged me to persuade you not to go; and so rest with us, if you will, I invite you to remain."

"Monsieur," I replied, "I should not be happy here; the two women who serve you aspire to all the affection you are able to give them; they will not behold me without jealousy, and sooner or later I will be forced to leave you."

"Be not apprehensive," Rodin answered, "fear none of the effects of these women's envy, I shall be quite capable of keeping them in their place by maintaining you in yours, and you alone will possess my confidence without any resultant danger to yourself. But in order to continue to deserve it, I believe it would be well for you to know that the first quality, the foremost, I require in you, Thérèse, is an unassailable discretion. Many things take place here, many which do not sort with your virtuous principles; you must be able to witness everything, hear all and never speak a syllable of it. . . . Ah, Thérèse, remain with me, stay here, Thérèse, my child, it will be a joy to have you; in the midst of the many vices to which I am driven by a fiery temper, an unrestrainable imagination and a much rotted heart, at least I will have the comfort of a virtuous being dwelling close by, and upon whose breast I shall be able to cast myself as at the feet of a God when, glutted by my debauches, I . . ." "Oh Heaven!" I did think at this moment, "then Virtue is necessary, it is then indispensable to man, since even the vicious one is obliged to find reassurance in it and make use of it as of a shelter." And then, recollecting Rosalie's requests that I not leave her, and thinking to discern some good principles in Rodin, I resolved to stay with him.

"Thérèse," Rodin said to me several days later, "I am going to install you near my daughter; in this way, you will avoid all frictions with the other two women, and I intend to give you three hundred pounds wages."

Such a post was, in my situation, a kind of godsend; inflamed by the desire to restore Rosalie to righteousness, and perhaps even her father too were I able to attain some influence over him, I repented not of what I had just done . . . Rodin, having had me dress myself, conducted me at once to where his daughter was; Rosalie received me with effusions of joy, and I was promptly established.

Ere a week was gone by I had begun to labor at the conversions after which I thirsted, but Rodin's intransigence defeated all my efforts.

"Do not believe," was the response he made to my wise counsels, "that the kind of deference I showed to the virtue in you proves that I either esteem virtue or have the desire to favor it over vice. Think nothing of the sort, Thérèse, 'twould be to deceive yourself; on the basis of what I have done in your regard, anyone who was to maintain, as consequential to my behavior, the importance or the necessity of virtue would fall into the very largest error, and sorry I would be were you to fancy that such is my fashion of thinking. The rustic hovel to which I repair for shelter when, during the hunt, the excessive heat of the sun's rays falls perpendicularly upon me, that hut is certainly not to be mistaken for a superior building: its worth is merely circumstantial: I am exposed to some sort of danger, I find something which affords protection, I use it, but is this something the grander on that account? can it be the less contemptible? In a totally vicious society, virtue would be totally worthless; our societies not being entirely of this species, one must absolutely either play with virtue or make use of it so as to have less to dread from its faithful followers. If no one adopts the virtuous way, it becomes useless; I am then not mistaken when I affirm that it owes its necessity to naught but opinion or circumstances; virtue is not some kind of mode whose value is incontestable, it is simply a scheme of conduct, a way of getting along, which varies according to accidents of geography and climate and which, consequently, has no reality, the which alone exhibits its futility. Only what is constant is really good; what changes perpetually cannot claim that characterization: that is why they have declared that immutability belongs to the ranks of the Eternal's perfections; but virtue is completely without this quality: there is not, upon the entire globe, two races which are virtuous in the same manner; hence, virtue is not in any sense real, nor in any wise intrinsically good and in no sort deserves our reverence. How is it to be employed? as a prop, as a device: it is politic to adopt the virtue of the country one inhabits, so that those who practice it, either because they have a taste for it or who have to cultivate it because of their station, will leave you in peace, and so that this virtue which happens to be respected in your area will guarantee you, by its conventional preponderance, against the assaults delivered by them who profess vice. But, once again, all that is at the dictation of variable circumstances, and nothing in all that assigns a real merit to virtue. There are, furthermore, such virtues as are impossible to certain men; now, how are you going to persuade me that a virtue in conflict or in contradiction with the passions is to be found in Nature? And if it is not in Nature and natural, how can it be good? In those men we are speaking of there will certainly be vices opposed to these virtues, and these vices will be preferred by these men, since they will be the only modes . . . the only schemes of being which will be thoroughly agreeable to their peculiar physical constitutions or to their uncommon organs; in this hypothesis, there would then be some very useful vices: well, how can virtue be useful if you demonstrate to me that what is contrary to virtue is useful? In reply to that, one hears that virtue is useful to others, and that in this sense it is good; for if it is posited that I must do only what is good to others, in my turn I will receive only good. And this argument is pure sophistry: in return for the small amount of good I receive at the hands of others thanks to the virtue they practice, my obligation to practice virtue in my turn causes me to make a million sacrifices for which I am in no wise compensated. Receiving less than I give, I hence conclude a very disadvantageous bargain, I experience much more ill from the privations I endure in order to be virtuous, than I experience good from those who do it to me; the arrangement being not at all equitable, I therefore must not submit to it, and certain, by being virtuous, not to cause others as much pleasure as I receive pain by compelling myself to be good, would it not be better to give up procuring them a happiness which must cost me so much distress? There now remains the harm I may do others by being vicious and the evil I myself would suffer were everyone to resemble me. Were we to acknowledge an efficient circulation of vices, I am certainly running a grave danger, I concede it; but the grief experienced by what I risk is offset by the pleasure I receive from causing others to be menaced: and there, you see, equality is re-established: and every-one is more or less equally happy: which is not the case and cannot be the case in a society where some are good and others are bad, be-cause, from this mixture, perpetual pitfalls result, and no pitfalls exist in the other instance. In the heterogeneous society, all interests are unalike: there you have the source of an infinite number of miseries; in the contrary association, all interests are identical, each individual composing it is furnished with the same proclivities, the same penchants, each one marches together with all the others and to the same goal; they are all happy. But, idiots complain to you, evil does not make for happiness. No, not when everyone has agreed to idolize good; but merely cease to prize, instead deflate, heap abuse upon what you call good, and you will no longer revere anything but what formerly you had the idiocy to call evil; and every man will have the pleasure of committing it, not at all because it will be permitted (that might be, upon occasion, a reason for the diminishment of its appeal), but because the law will no longer punish it, and it is the law, through the fear it inspires, which lessens the pleasure Nature has seen to it we take in crime. I visualize a society where it will be generally admitted that incest (let us include this offense together with all the others), that incest, I say, is criminal: those who commit incest will be unhappy, because opinion, laws, beliefs, everything will concert to chill their pleasure; those who desist from doing this evil, those who, because of these restraints, will not dare, will be equally unhappy: thus, the law that proscribes incest will have done nothing but cause wretched-ness. Now, I visualize another society neighboring the first; in this one incest is no crime at all: those who do not desist will not be unhappy, and those who desire it will be happy. Hence, the society which permits this act will be better suited to mankind than the one in which the act is represented as a crime; the same pertains to all other deeds clumsily denominated criminal; regard them from this point of view, and you create crowds of unhappy persons; permit them, and not a complaint is to be heard; for he who cherishes this act, whatever it happens to be, goes about performing it in peace and quiet, and he who does not care for it either remains in a kind of neutral indifference toward it, which is certainly not painful, or finds restitution for the hurt he may have sustained by resorting to a host of other injuries wherewith in his turn he belabors whosoever has aggrieved him: thus everyone in a criminal society is either very happy indeed, or else in a paradise of unconcern; consequently, there's nothing good, nothing respectable, nothing that can bring about happiness in what they call virtue. Let those who follow the virtuous track be not boastingly proud of the concessions wrung from us by the structural peculiarities of our society; 'tis purely a matter of circumstance, an accident of convention that the homages demanded of us take a virtuous form; but in fact, this worship is a hallucination, and the virtue which obtains a little pious attention for a moment is not on that account the more noble."

Such was the infernal logic of Rodin's wretched passions; but Rosalie, gentle and less corrupt, Rosalie, detesting the horrors to which she was submitted, was a more docile auditor and more receptive to my opinions. I had the most ardent desire to bring her to discharge her primary religious duties; but we would have been obliged to confide in a priest, and Rodin would not have one in the house; he beheld them, and the beliefs they professed, with horror: nothing in the world would have induced him to suffer one to come near his daughter; to lead the girl to a confessor was equally impossible: Rodin never allowed Rosalie to go abroad unless he accompanied her. We were therefore constrained to bide our time until some occasion might present itself; and while we waited I instructed the young person; by giving her a taste for virtue, I inspired in her another for Religion, I revealed to her its sacred dogmas and its sublime mysteries, and I so intimately attached these two sentiments to her youthful heart that I rendered them indispensable to her life's happiness.

"O Mademoiselle," I said one day, my eyes welling with tears at her compunction, "can man blind himself to the point of believing that he is not destined to some better end? Is not the fact he has been endowed with the capacity of consciousness of his God sufficient evidence that this blessing has not been accorded him save to meet the responsibilities it imposes? Well, what may be the foundation of the veneration we owe the Eternal, if it is not that virtue of which He is the example? Can the Creator of so many wonders have other than good laws? And can our hearts be pleasing unto Him if their element is not good? It seems to me that, for sensitive spirits, the only valid motives for loving that Supreme Being must be those gratitude inspires. Is it not a favor thus to have caused us to enjoy the beauties of this Universe? and do we not owe Him some gratitude in return for such a blessing? But a yet stronger reason establishes, confirms the universal chain of our duties; why should we refuse to fulfill those required by His decrees, since they are the very same which consolidate our happiness amongst mortals? Is it not sweet to feel that one renders oneself worthy of the Supreme Being simply by practicing those virtues which must bring about our contentment on earth, and that the means which render us worthy to live amongst our brethren are the identical ones which give us the assurance of a rebirth, in the life still to come, close by the throne of God! Ah, Rosalie! how blind are they who would strive to ravish away this our hope! Mistaken, benighted, seduced by their wretched passions, they prefer to deny eternal verities rather than abandon what may render them deserving of them. They would rather say, 'These people deceive us,' than admit they deceive themselves; the lingering thought of what they are preparing themselves to lose troubles them in their low riot and sport; it seems to them less dreadful to annihilate hope of Heaven, than to be deprived of what would acquire it for them! But when those tyrannical passions finally weaken and fade in them, when the veil is torn away, when there is no longer any-thing left in their disease-eaten hearts to counter the imperious voice of that God their delirium disregardingly misprized, Oh Rosalie! what must it be, this cruel awakening! and how much its accompanying remorse must inflate the price to be paid for the instant's error that blinded them! Such is the condition wherein man has got to be in order to construe his proper conduct: 'tis neither when in drunkenness, nor when in the transport produced by a burning fever, he ought to be believed or his sayings marked, but when his reason is calmed and enjoys its full lucid energy he must seek after the truth, 'tis then he divines and sees it. 'Tis then with all our being we yearn after that Sacred One of Whom we were once so neglectful; we implore Him, He becomes our whole solace; we pray to Him, He hears our entreaties. Ah, why then should I deny Him, why should I be unheeding of this Object so necessary to happiness? Why should I prefer to say with the misguided man, There is no God, while the heart of the reasoning part of human-kind every instant offers me proofs of this Divine Being's existence? Is it then better to dream amongst the mad than rightly to think with the wise? All derives nevertheless from this initial principle: immediately there exists a God, this God deserves to be worshiped, and the primary basis of this worship indisputably is Virtue."

From these elementary truths I easily deduced the others and the deistic Rosalie was soon made a Christian. But by what means, I repeat, could I join a little practice to the morality? Rosalie, bound to obey her father, could at the very most do no more than display her disgust for him, and with a man like Rodin might that not become dangerous? He was intractable; not one of my doctrines prevailed against him; but although I did not win him over, he for his part at least did not shake me.

However, such an academy, dangers so permanent, so real, caused me to tremble for Rosalie, so much so in fact that I could not find myself in any wise guilty in engaging her to fly from this perverse household. It seemed to me that to snatch her from her incestuous father were a lesser evil than to leave her prey to all the risks she must run by staying with him. I had already delicately hinted at the idea and perhaps I was not so very far from success when all of a sudden Rosalie vanished from the house; all my efforts to find out where she was failed. When I interrogated his women or Rodin himself I was told she had gone to pass the summer months with a relative who lived ten leagues away. When I made inquiries around the neighborhood, they were at first astonished to hear such a question from a member of the household, then, as had Rodin and his domestics, they would answer that she had been seen, everyone had bade her farewell the day before, the day she had left; I received the same replies everywhere. I asked Rodin why this departure had been kept secret from me; why had I not been al-lowed to accompany my mistress? He assured me the unique reason had been to avoid a scene difficult for both Rosalie and me, and that I would certainly see the person I loved very soon. I had to be content with these answers, but it was more difficult to be con-vinced of their truth. Was it presumable that Rosalie—and how great was her affection for me!—could have consented to leave me

without so much as one word? and according to what I knew of
Rodin's character, was there not much to fear for the poor girl's
fate? I resolved to employ every device to learn what had become
of her, and in order to find out, every means seemed justifiable.

The following day, noticing I was alone in the house, I carefully investigated every corner of it; I thought I caught the sound
of moans emanating from a very obscure cellar. . . . I approached;
a pile of firewood seemed to be blocking a narrow door at the end
of a passageway; by removing the obstructions I am able to advance . . . further noises are to be heard . . . I believe I detect a
voice . . . I listen more carefully . . . I am in doubt no longer.

"Thérèse," I hear at last, "O Thérèse, is it you?"

"Yes, my dear, my most tender friend," I cry, recognizing
Rosalie's accents. . . . "Yes, 'tis Thérèse Heaven sends to your
rescue . . ."

And my numerous questions scarcely allow this interesting girl
time to reply. At length I learn that several hours before her dis-
appearance, Rombeau, Rodin's friend and colleague, had examined
her naked and that she had received an order from her father to
ready herself to undergo, at Rombeau's hands, the same horrors
Rodin exposed her to every day; that she had resisted; that Rodin,
furious, had seized her and himself presented her to his companion's frantic attacks; that, next, the two men had spoken together in whispers for a very long time, leaving her naked the
while, and periodically renewing their probings, they had continued to amuse themselves with her in the same criminal fashion
and had maltreated her in a hundred different ways; that, after
this session, which had lasted four or five hours, Rodin had finally
said he was going to send her to the country to visit one of her
family, but that she must leave at once and without speaking to
Thérèse, for reasons he would explain the day afterward, for he
intended to join her immediately. He had given Rosalie to understand he meant to marry her and this accounted for the examination
Rombeau had given her, which was to determine whether she were
capable of becoming a mother. Rosalie had indeed left under an old
woman's guardianship; she had crossed through the town, in passing said farewell to several acquaintances; but immediately night
had fallen, her conductress had led her back to her father's house;

she had entered at midnight. Rodin, who was waiting for her, had seized her, had clapped his hand over her mouth to stifle her voice and, without a word, had plunged her into this cellar where, in truth, she had been decently well fed and looked after.

"I have everything to fear," the poor thing added; "my father's conduct toward me since he put me here, his discourses, what preceded Rombeau's examination, everything, Thérèse, everything suggests that these monsters are going to use me in one of their experiments, and that your poor Rosalie is doomed."

After copious tears had flowed from my eyes, I asked the unhappy girl whether she knew where the key to the cellar was kept; she did not; but she did not believe their custom was to take it with them. I sought for it everywhere; in vain; and by the time the hour arrived for me to return upstairs I had been able to give the dear child no more by way of aid than consoling words, a few hopes, and many tears. She made me swear to come back the next day; I promised, even assuring her that if by that time I had discovered nothing satisfactory regarding her, I would leave the house directly, fetch the police and extricate her, at no matter what price, from the terrible fate threatening her.

I went up; Rombeau was dining with Rodin that evening. Determined to stick at nothing to clarify my mistress' fate, I hid myself near the room where the two friends were at table, and their conversation was more than enough to convince me of the horror of the project wherewith both were occupied.

It was Rodin who was speaking: "Anatomy will never reach its ultimate state of perfection until an examination has been performed upon the vaginal canal of a fourteen- or fifteen-year-old child who has expired from a cruel death; it is only from the contingent contraction we can obtain a complete analysis of a so highly interesting part."

"The same holds true," Rombeau replied, "for the hymeneal membrane; we must, of course, find a young girl for the dissection. What the deuce is there to be seen after the age of puberty? nothing; the menstrual discharges rupture the hymen, and all research is necessarily inexact; your daughter is precisely what we need; although she is fifteen, she is not yet mature; the manner in which we have enjoyed her has done no damage to the membranous tissue, and we will be able to handle her with complete immunity from interference. I am delighted you have made up your mind at last."

"Oh, I certainly have," Rodin rejoined; "I find it odious that futile considerations check the progress of science; did great men ever allow themselves to be enslaved by such contemptible chains? And, when Michelangelo wished to render a Christ after Nature, did he make the crucifixion of a young man the occasion for a fit of remorse? Why no: he copied the boy in his death agonies. But where it is a question of the advance of our art, how absolutely essential such means become! And how the evil in permitting them dwindles to insignificance! Only think of it! you sacrifice one, but you save a million, perhaps; may one hesitate when the price is so modest? Is the murder operated by the law of a species different from the one we are going to perform? and is not the purpose of those laws, which are commonly found so wise, the sacrifice of one in order to save a thousand?"

"But what other way can one approach the problem?" Rombeau demanded; "there is certainly no other by which to obtain any information. In those hospitals where I worked as a young man I saw similar experiments by the thousand; but in view of the ties which attach you to this creature, I must confess I was afraid you would hesitate."

"What! because she is my daughter? A capital reason!" Rodin roared, "and what rank do you then fancy this title must allot her in my heart? I place roughly the same value (weighing the matter very nicely) upon a little semen which has hatched its chick, and upon that I am pleased to waste while enjoying myself. One has the power to take back what one has given; amongst no race that has ever dwelled upon earth has there been any disputing the right to dispose of one's children as one sees fit. The Persians, the Medes, the Armenians, the Greeks enjoyed this right in its fullest latitude. The constitution decreed by Lycurgus, that paragon of lawgivers, not only accorded fathers every right over their offspring, but even condemned to death those children parents did not care to feed, or those which were discovered malformed. A great proportion of savage peoples kill their young immediately they are born. Nearly all the women of Asia, Africa, and America practice abortions, and are not for that reason covered with discredit; Cook discovered the custom widespread in all the South Sea islands. Romulus permitted infanticide; the law of the twelve tables similarly tolerated it and until the era of Constantine the Romans exposed or killed their children with impunity. Aristotle recommended this pretended crime; the Stoic sect regarded it as praiseworthy; it is still very much in use in China. Every day one counts, lying in the streets and floating in the canals of Peking, more than ten thousand individuals immolated or abandoned by their parents, and in that wisely-governed empire whatever be the child's age, a father need but put it into the hands of a judge to be rid of it. According to the laws of the Parthians, one killed one's son, one's daughter, or one's brother, even at the age of nubility; Caesar discovered the custom universal amongst the Gauls; several passages in the Pentateuch prove that amongst the children of God one was allowed to kill one's children; and, finally, God Himself ordered Abraham to do just that. It was long believed, declares a celebrated modern author, that the prosperity of empires depends upon the slavery of children; this opinion is supported by the healthiest logic. Why! a monarch will fancy himself authorized to sacrifice twenty or thirty thousand of his subjects in a single day to achieve his own ends, and a father is not to be allowed, when he esteems it propitious, to become the master of his children's lives! What absurdity! O folly! Oh what is this inconsistency, this feebleness in them upon whom such chains are binding! A father's authority over his children, the only real one, the one that serves as basis to every other, that authority is dictated to us by the voice of Nature herself, and the intelligent study of her operations provides examples of it at every turn and instant. Czar Peter was in no doubt as to this right; he used it habitually and addressed a public declaration to all the orders of his empire, in which he said that, according to laws human and divine, a father had the entire and absolute right to sentence his children to death, without appeal and without consulting the opinion of anyone at all. It is nowhere but in our own barbarous France that a false and ludicrous pity has presumed to suppress this prerogative. No," Rodin pursued with great feeling, "no, my friend, I will never understand how a father, who had the kindness to provide it with life, may not be at liberty to bestow death upon his issue. 'Tis the ridiculous value we attach to this life which eternally makes us speak drivel about the kind of deed to which a man resorts in order to disencumber himself of a fellow creature. Believing that existence is the greatest of all goods, we stupidly fancy we are doing something criminal when we convey someone away from its enjoyment; but the cessation of this existence, or at least what follows it, is no more an evil than life is a good; or rather, if nothing dies, if nothing is destroyed, if nothing is lost to Nature, if all the decomposed parts of any body whatsoever merely await dissolution to reappear immediately under new forms, how indifferent is this act of murder! and how dare one find any evil in it? In this connection I ought to act according to nothing but my own whim; I ought to regard the thing as very simple indeed, especially so when it becomes necessary to an act of such vital importance to mankind . . . when it can furnish such a wealth of knowledge: henceforth it is an evil no longer, my friend, it is no longer a crime, no, not a petty misdemeanor, it is the best, the wisest, the most useful of all actions, and crime would exist only in refusing oneself the pleasure of committing it."

"Ha!" said Rombeau, full of enthusiasm for these appalling maxims, "I applaud you, my dear fellow, your wisdom enchants me, but your indifference is astonishing; I thought you were amorous—"

"I? in love with a girl? . . . Ah, Rombeau! I supposed you knew me better; I employ those creatures when I have nothing better to hand: the extreme penchant I have for pleasures of the variety you have watched me taste makes very precious to me all the temples at which this sort of incense can be offered, and to multiply my devotions, I sometimes assimilate a little girl into a pretty little boy; but should one of these female personages unhappily nourish my illusion for too long, my disgust becomes energetically manifest, and I have never found but one means to satisfy it deliciously . . . you understand me, Rombeau; Chilpéric, the most voluptuous of France's kings, held the same views. His boisterous organ proclaimed aloud that in an emergency one could make use of a woman, but upon the express condition one exterminated her immediately one had done with her.[3] For five years this

---

[3] Cf. a work entitled *The Jesuits in Fine Fettle.*

little wench has been serving my pleasures; the time has come for her to pay for my loss of interest by the loss of her existence."

The meal ended; from those two madmen's behavior, from their words, their actions, their preparations, from their very state, which bordered upon delirium, I was very well able to see that there was not a moment to be lost, and that the hour of the unhappy Rosalie's destruction had been fixed for that evening. I rushed to the cellar, resolved to deliver her or die.

"O dear friend," I cried, "there is not an instant to waste . . . the monsters . . . it is to be tonight . . . they are going to come. . . ."

And upon saying that, I make the most violent efforts to batter down the door. One of my blows dislodges something, I reach out my hand, it is the key, I seize it, I hasten to open the door . . . I embrace Rosalie, I urge her to fly, I promise to follow her, she springs forward . . . Just Heaven! It was again decreed that Virtue was to succumb, and that sentiments of the tenderest commiseration were going to be brutally punished; lit by the governess, Rodin and Rombeau appeared of a sudden, the former grasped his daughter the instant she crossed the threshold of the door beyond which, a few steps away, lay deliverance.

"Ah, wretch, where are you going?" Rodin shouts, bringing her to a halt while Rombeau lays hands upon me. . . . "Why," he continues, glancing at me, "here's the rascal who has encouraged your flight! Thérèse, now we behold the results of your great virtuous principles . . . the kidnaping of a daughter from her father!"

"Certainly," was my steadfast reply, "and I must do so when that father is so barbarous as to plot against his daughter's life."

"Well, well! Espionage and seduction," Rodin pursued; "all a servant's most dangerous vices; upstairs, up with you, I say, the case requires to be judged."

Dragged by the two villains, Rosalie and I are brought back to the apartments; the doors are bolted. The unlucky daughter of Rodin is tied to the posts of a bed, and those two demoniacs turn all their rage upon me, their language is of the most violent, the sentence pronounced upon me appalling: it is nothing less than a question of a vivisection in order to inspect the beating of my heart, and upon this organ to make observations which cannot practicably be made upon a cadaver. Meanwhile, I am undressed, and subjected to the most impudicious fondlings.

"Before all else," says Rombeau, "my opinion is a stout attack ought to be delivered upon the fortress your lenient proceedings have respected. . . . Why, 'tis superb! do you mark that velvet texture, the whiteness of those two half-moons defending the portal! never was there a virgin of such freshness."

"Virgin! but so she is, or nearly," says Rodin, "once raped, and then it was despite her wishes; since then, untouched. Here, let me take the wheel a moment . . ." and the cruel one added to Rombeau's his homage made up of those harsh and savage caresses which degrade rather than honor the idol. Had whips been available I should have been cruelly dealt with; whips were indeed mentioned, but none were found, they limited themselves to what the bare hand could achieve; they set me afire . . . the more I struggled, the more rigidly I was held; when however I saw them about to undertake more serious matters, I flung myself prostrate before my executioners and offered them my life.

"But when you are no longer a virgin," said Rombeau, "what is the difference? What are these qualms? we are only going to violate you as you have been already and not the least peccadillo will sit on your conscience; you will have been vanquished by force . . ." and comforting me in this manner, the infamous one placed me on a couch.

"No," spoke up Rodin, interrupting his colleague's effervescence, of which I was on the brink of becoming the victim, "no, let's not waste our powers with this creature; remember we cannot further postpone the operations scheduled for Rosalie, and our vigor is necessary to carry them out; let's punish this wretch in some other manner."

Upon saying which, Rodin put an iron in the fire. "Yes," he went on, "let's punish her a thousand times more than we would were we to take her life, let's brand her; this disgrace, joined to all the sorry business about her body, will get her hanged if she does not first die of hunger; until then she will suffer, and our more prolonged vengeance will become the more delicious."

Wherewith Rombeau seized me, and the abominable Rodin

applied behind my shoulder the red-hot iron with which thieves are marked.

"Let her dare appear in public, the whore," the monster continued, exhibiting the ignominious letter, "and I'll sufficiently justify my reasons for sending her out of the door with such secrecy and promptitude."

They bandage me, dress me, and fortify me with a few drops of brandy, and under the cover of night the two scientists conduct me to the forest's edge and abandon me cruelly there after once again having sketched what dangers a recrimination would expose me to were I to dare bring complaint in my present state of disgrace.

Anyone else might have been little impressed by the menace; what would I have to fear as soon as I found the means to prove that what I had just suffered had been the work not of a tribunal but of criminals? But my weakness, my natural timidity, the frightful memory of what I had undergone at Paris and recollections of the château de Bressac—it all stunned me, terrified me; I thought only of flight, and was far more stirred by anguish at having to abandon an innocent victim to those two villains, who were without doubt ready to immolate her, than I was touched by my own ills. More irritated, more afflicted morally than in physical pain, I set off at once; but, completely unoriented, never stopping to ask my way, I did but swing in a circle around Paris and on the fourth day of traveling I found I had got no further than Lieursaint. Knowing this road would lead me to the southern provinces, I resolved to follow it and try to reach those distant regions, fancying to myself that the peace and calm so cruelly denied me in those parts of France where I had grown up were, perhaps, awaiting me in others more remote; fatal error! how much there remained of grief and pain yet to experience.

Whatever had been my trials until that time, at least I was in possession of my innocence. Merely the victim of a few monsters' attempts, I was still able to consider myself more or less in the category of an honest girl. The fact was I had never been truly soiled save by a rape operated five years earlier, and its traces had healed . . . a rape consummated at an instant when my numbed state had not even left me the faculty of sensation. Other than that, what was there with which I could reproach myself? Nothing, oh! nothing, doubtless; and my heart was chaste, I was overweeningly proud of it, my presumption was to be punished; the outrages awaiting me were to be such that in a short while it would no longer be possible, however slight had been my participation, for me to form the same comforting ideas in the depths of my heart.

This time I had my entire fortune about me; that is to say, about a hundred crowns, comprising the total of what I had saved from Bressac's clutches and earned from Rodin. In my extreme misery I was able to feel glad that this money, at least, had not been taken from me; I flattered myself with the notion that through the frugality, temperance, and economy to which I was accustomed, this sum would amply suffice until I was so situated as to be able to find a place of some sort. The execration they had just stamped upon my flesh did not show, I imagined I would always be able to disguise it and that this brand would be no bar to making my living. I was twenty-two years old, in good health, and had a face which, to my sorrow, was the object of eulogies all too frequent; I possessed some virtues which, although they had brought me unremitting injury, nevertheless, as I have just told you, were my whole consolation and caused me to hope that Heaven would finally grant me, if not rewards, at least some suspension of the evils they had drawn down upon me. Full of hope and courage, I kept my road until I gained Sens, where I rested several days. A week of this and I was entirely restored; I might perhaps have found work in that city but, penetrated by the necessity of getting further away, I resumed my journeying with the design of seeking my fortune in Dauphiné; I had heard this province much spoken of, I fancied happiness attended me there, and we are going to see with what success I sought it out.

Never, not in a single one of my life's circumstances, had the sentiments of Religion deserted me. Despising the vain casuistries of strong-headed thinkers, believing them all to emanate from libertinage rather than consequent upon firm persuasion, I had dressed my conscience and my heart against them and, by means of the one and the other, I had found what was needed in order to make them stout reply. By my misfortunes often forced to neglect my pious duties, I would make reparation for these faults whenever I could find the opportunity.

I had just, on the 7th of August, left Auxerre; I shall never forget that date. I had walked about two leagues: the noonday heat beginning to incommode me, I climbed a little eminence crowned by a grove of trees; the place was not far removed from the road, I went there with the purpose of refreshing myself and obtaining a few hours of sleep without having to pay the expense of an inn, and up there I was in greater safety than upon the highway. I established myself at the foot of an oak and, after a frugal lunch, I drifted off into sweet sleep. Well did I rest, for a considerable time, and in a state of complete tranquillity; and then, opening my eyes, it was with great pleasure I mused upon the landscape which was visible for a long distance. From out of the middle of a forest that extended upon the right, I thought I could detect, some three or four leagues from where I was, a little bell tower rising modestly into the air. . . . "Beloved solitude," I murmured, "what a desire I have to dwell a time in thee; and thou afar," said I, addressing the abbey, "thou must be the asylum of a few gentle, virtuous recluses who are occupied with none but God . . . with naught but their pious duties; or a retreat unto some holy hermits devoted to Religion alone . . . men who, far removed from that pernicious society where incessant crime, brooding heavily, threatfully over innocence, degrades it, annihilates it . . . ah! there must all virtues dwell, of that I am certain, and when mankind's crimes exile them out of the world, 'tis thither they go in that isolated place to commune with the souls of those fortunate ones who cherish them and cultivate them every day."

I was absorbed in these thoughts when a girl of my age, keeper of a flock of sheep grazing upon the plateau, suddenly appeared before my eyes; I question her about that habitation, she tells me what I see is a Benedictine monastery occupied by four solitary monks of peerless devotion, whose continence and sobriety are without example. Once a year, says the girl, a pilgrimage is made to a miraculous Virgin who is there, and from Her pious folk obtain all their hearts' desire. Singularly eager immediately to go and implore aid at the feet of this holy Mother of God, I ask the girl whether she would like to come and pray with me; 'tis impossible, she replies, for her mother awaits her; but the road there is easy. She indicates it to me, she assures me the superior of the house, the most respectable, the most saintly of men, will receive me with perfect good grace and will offer me all the aid whereof I can possibly stand in need. "Dom Séverino, so he is called," continues the girl, "is an Italian closely related to the Pope, who overwhelms him with kindnesses; he is gentle, honest, correct, obliging, fifty-five years old, and has spent above two-thirds of his life in France . . . you will be satisfied with him, Mademoiselle," the shepherdess concluded, "go and edify yourself in that sacred quiet, and you will only return from it improved."

This recital only inflamed my zeal the more, I became unable to resist the violent desire I felt to pay a visit to this hallowed church and there, by a few acts of piety, to make restitution for the neglect whereof I was guilty. However great was my own need of charities, I gave the girl a crown, and set off down the road leading to Saint Mary-in-the-Wood, as was called the monastery toward which I directed my steps.

When I had descended upon the plain I could see the spire no more; for guide I had nothing but the forest ahead of me, and before long I began to fear that the distance, of which I had forgotten to inform myself, was far greater than I had estimated at first; but was in nowise discouraged. I arrived at the edge of the forest and, some amount of daylight still remaining, I decided to forge on, considering I should be able to reach the monastery before nightfall. However, not a hint of human life presented itself to my gaze, not a house, and all I had for road was a beaten path I followed virtually at random; I had already walked at least five leagues without seeing a thing when, the Star having completely ceased to light the universe, it seemed I heard the tolling of a bell. . . . I harken, I move toward the sound, I hasten, the path widens ever so little, at last I perceive several hedges and soon afterward the monastery; than this isolation nothing could be wilder, more rustic, there is no neighboring habitation, the nearest is six leagues removed, and dense tracts of forest surround the house on all sides; it was situated in a depression, I had a goodly distance to descend in order to get to it, and this was the reason I had lost sight of the tower; a gardener's cabin nestled against the monastery's walls; it was there one applied before entering. I demanded of this gate-keeper whether it were permitted to speak to the superior; he asked to be informed of my errand; I advised him that a religious duty had drawn me to this holy refuge and that I would be well repaid for all the trouble I had experienced to get to it were I able to kneel an instant before the feet of the miraculous Virgin and the saintly ecclesiastics in whose house the divine image was preserved. The gardener rings and I penetrate into the monastery; but as the hour is advanced and the fathers are at supper, he is some time in returning. At last he reappears with one of the monks:

"Mademoiselle," says he, "here is Dom Clément, steward to the house; he has come to see whether what you desire merits inter-rupting the superior."

Clément, whose name could not conceivably have been less descriptive of his physiognomy, was a man of forty-eight years, of an enormous bulk, of a giant's stature; somber was his expression, fierce his eye; the only words he spoke were harsh, and they were expelled by a raucous voice: here was a satyric personage indeed, a tyrant's exterior; he made me tremble. . . . And then despite all I could do to suppress it, the remembrance of my old miseries rose to smite my troubled memory in traits of blood. . . .

"What do you want?" the monk asked me; his air was surly, his mien grim; "is this the hour to come to a church? . . . Indeed, you have the air of an adventuress."

"Saintly man," said I, prostrating myself, "I believed it was always the hour to present oneself at God's door; I have hastened from far off to arrive here; full of fervor and devotion, I ask to confess, if it is possible, and when what my conscience contains is known to you, you will see whether or not I am worthy to humble myself at the feet of the holy image."

"But this is not the time for confession," said the monk, his manner softening; "where are you going to spend the night? We have no hospice . . . it would have been better to have come in the morning." I gave him the reasons which had prevented me from doing so and, without replying, Clément went to report to the superior. Several minutes later the church was opened, Dom

Sévérino himself approached me, and invited me to enter the temple with him.

Dom Sévérino, of whom it would be best to give you an idea at once, was, as I had been told, a man of fifty-five, but endowed with handsome features, a still youthful quality, a vigorous physique, herculean limbs, and all that without harshness; a certain elegance and pliancy reigned over the whole and suggested that in his young years he must have possessed all the traits which constitute a splendid man. There were in all the world no finer eyes than his; nobility shone in his features, and the most genteel, the most courteous tone was there throughout. An agreeable accent which colored every one of his words enabled one to identify his Italian origin and, I admit it, this monk's outward graces did much to dispel the alarm the other had caused me.

"My dear girl," said he very graciously, "although the hour is unseasonable and though it is not our usage to receive so late, I will however hear your confession, and afterward we will confer upon the means whereby you may pass the night in decency; tomorrow you will be able to bow down before the sacred image which brings you here."

We enter the church; the doors are closed; a lamp is lit near the confessional. Sévérino bids me assume my place, he sits down and requests me to tell him everything with complete confidence.

I was perfectly at ease with a man who seemed so mild-mannered, so full of gentle sympathy. I disguised nothing from him: I confessed all my sins; I related all my miseries; I even uncovered the shameful mark wherewith the barbaric Rodin had branded me. Sévérino listened to everything with keenest attention, he even had me repeat several details, wearing always a look of pity and of interest; but a few movements, a few words betrayed him nevertheless—alas! it was only afterward I pondered them thoroughly. Later, when able to reflect calmly upon this interview, it was impossible not to remember that the monk had several times permitted himself certain gestures which dramatized the emotion that had heavy entrance into many of the questions he put to me, and those inquiries not only halted complacently and lingered lovingly over obscene details, but had borne with noticeable insistence upon the following five points:

1. Whether it were really so that I were an orphan and had been born in Paris. 2. Whether it were a certainty I were bereft of kin and had neither friends, nor protection, nor, in a word, anyone to whom I could write. 3. Whether I had confided to anyone, other than to the shepherdess who had pointed out the monastery to me, my purpose in going there, and whether I had not arranged some rendezvous upon my return. 4. Whether it were certain that I had known no one since my rape, and whether I were fully sure the man who had abused me had done so on the side Nature condemns as well as on the side she permits. 5. Whether I thought I had not been followed and whether anyone, according to my belief, might have observed me enter the monastery.

After I had answered these questions in all modesty, with great sincerity, and most naively:

"Very well," said the monk, rising and taking me by the hand, "come, my child, tomorrow I shall procure you the sweet satisfaction of communing at the feet of the image you have come to visit; let us begin by supplying your primary needs," and he led me toward the depths of the church. . . .

"Why!" said I, sensing a vague inquietude arise in me despite myself, "what is this, Father? Why are we going inside?"

"And where else, my charming pilgrim?" answered the monk, introducing me into the sacristy. "Do you really fear to spend the night with four saintly anchorites? Oh, we shall find the means to succor you, my dearest angel, and if we do not procure you very great pleasures, you will at least serve ours in their most extreme amplitude." These words sent a thrill of horror through me; I burst out in a cold sweat, I fell to shivering; it was night, no light guided our footsteps, my terrified imagination raised up the specter of death brandishing its scythe over my head; my knees were buckling . . . and at this point a sudden shift occurred in the monk's speech. He jerked me upright and hissed:

"Whore, pick up your feet and get along; no complaints, don't try resistance, not here, it would be useless."

These cruel words restore my strength, I sense that if I falter I am doomed, I straighten myself. "O Heaven!" I say to the traitor, "must I then be once again my good sentiments' victim, must the desire to approach what is most respectable in Religion be once again punished as a crime! ..."

We continue to walk, we enter obscure byways, I know not where I am, where I am going. I was advancing a pace ahead of Dom Sévérino; his breathing was labored, words flowed incoherently from his lips, one might have thought he was drunk; now and again he stopped me, twined his left arm about my waist while his right hand, sliding beneath my skirts from the rear, wandered impudently over that unseemly part of ourselves which, likening us to men, is the unique object of the homages of those who prefer that sex for their shameful pleasures. Several times the libertine even dared apply his mouth to these areas' most secluded lair; and then we recommenced our march. A stairway appears before us; we climb thirty steps or forty, a door opens, brightness dazzles my eyes, we emerge into a charmingly appointed, magnificently illuminated room; there, I see three monks and four girls grouped around a table served by four other women, completely naked. At the spectacle I recoil, trembling; Sévérino shoves me forward over the threshold and I am in the room with him.

"Gentlemen," says he as we enter, "allow me to present you with one of the veritable wonders of the world, a Lucretia who simultaneously carries upon her shoulder the mark stigmatizing girls who are of evil repute, and, in her conscience, all the candor, all the naïveté of a virgin. ... One lone violation, friends, and that six years ago; hence, practically a vestal ... indeed, I do give her to you as such ... the most beautiful, moreover ... Oh Clément! how that cheerless countenance of yours will light up when you fall to work on those handsome masses ... what elasticity, my good fellow! what rosiness!"

"Ah, fuck!" cried the half-intoxicated Clément, getting to his feet and lurching toward me: "we are pleasantly met, and let us verify the facts."

I will leave you for the briefest possible time in suspense about my situation, Madame, said Thérèse, but the necessity to portray these other persons in whose midst I discovered myself obliges me to interrupt the thread of my story. You have been made acquainted with Dom Sévérino, you suspect what may be his predilections;

alas! in these affairs his depravation was such he had never tasted other pleasures—and what an inconsistency in Nature's operations was here! for with the bizarre fantasy of choosing none but the straiter path, this monster was outfitted with faculties so gigantic that even the broadest thoroughfares would still have appeared too narrow for him.

As for Clément, he has been drawn for you already. To the superficies I have delineated, join ferocity, a disposition to sarcasm, the most dangerous roguishness, intemperance in every point, a mordant, satirical mind, a corrupt heart, the cruel tastes Rodin displayed with his young charges, no feelings, no delicacy, no religion, the temperament of one who for five years had not been in a state to procure himself other joys than those for which savagery gave him an appetite—and you have there the most complete characterization of this horrid man.

Antonin, the third protagonist in these detestable orgies, was forty; small, slight of frame but very vigorous, as formidably organized as Sévérino and almost as wicked as Clément; an enthusiast of that colleague's pleasures, but giving himself over to them with a somewhat less malignant intention; for while Clément, when exercising this curious mania, had no objective but to vex, to tyrannize a woman, and could not enjoy her in any other way, Antonin using it with delight in all its natural purity, had recourse to the flagellative aspect only in order to give additional fire and further energy to her whom he was honoring with his favors. In a word, one was brutal by taste, the other by refinement.

Jérôme, the eldest of the four recluses, was also the most debauched; every taste, every passion, every one of the most bestial irregularities were combined in this monk's soul; to the caprices rampant in the others, he joined that of loving to receive what his comrades distributed amongst the girls, and if he gave (which frequently happened), it was always upon condition of being treated likewise in his turn: all the temples of Venus were, what was more, as one to him, but his powers were beginning to decline and for several years he had preferred that which, requiring no effort of the agent, left to the patient the task of arousing the sensations and of producing the ecstasy. The mouth was his favorite temple, the shrine where he liked best to offer, and while he was in the pursuit of those choice pleasures, he would keep a second woman active: she warmed him with the lash. This man's character was quite as cunning, quite as wicked as that of the others; in whatever shape or aspect vice could exhibit itself, certain it was immediately to find a spectator in this infernal household. You will understand it more easily, Madame, if I explain how the society was organized. Prodigious funds had been poured by the Order into this obscene institution, it had been in existence for above a century, and had always been inhabited by the four richest monks, the most powerful in the Order's hierarchy, they of the highest birth and of a libertinage of sufficient moment to require burial in this obscure retreat, the disclosure of whose secret was well provided against as my further explanations will cause you to see in the sequel; but let us return to the portraits.

The eight girls who were present at the supper were so much separated by age I cannot describe them collectively, but only one by one; that they were so unlike with respect to their years astonished me—I will speak first of the youngest and continue in order.

This youngest one of the girls was scarcely ten: pretty but irregular features, a look of humiliation because of her fate, an air of sorrow and trepidation.

The second was fifteen: the same trouble written over her countenance, a quality of modesty degraded, but a bewitching face, of considerable interest all in all.

The third was twenty: pretty as a picture, the loveliest blond hair; fine, regular, gentle features; she appeared less restive, more broken to the saddle.

The fourth was thirty: she was one of the most beautiful women imaginable; candor, quality, decency in her bearing, and all a gentle spirit's virtues.

The fifth was a girl of thirty-six, six months pregnant; dark-haired, very lively, with beautiful eyes, but having, so it seemed to me, lost all remorse, all decency, all restraint.

The sixth was of the same age: a tall creature of grandiose proportions, a true giantess, fair of face but whose figure was already ruined in excess flesh; when I first saw her she was naked, and I was readily able to notice that not one part of her body was unstamped by signs of the brutality of those villains whose pleasures her unlucky star had fated her to serve.

The seventh and eighth were two very lovely women of about forty.

Let us continue with the story of my arrival in this impure place.

I did tell you that no sooner had I entered than each one approached me: Clément was the most brazen, his foul lips were soon glued to my mouth; I twisted away in horror, but I was advised all resistance was pure affectation, pretense, and useless; I should do best by imitating my companions.

"You may without difficulty imagine," declared Dom Séverino, "that a recalcitrant attitude will be to no purpose in this inaccessible retreat. You have, you say, undergone much suffering; but that greatest of all woes a virtuous girl can know is yet missing from the catalogue of your troubles. Is it not high time that lofty pride be humbled? and may one still expect to be nearly a virgin at twenty-two? You see about you companions who, upon entering here, like yourself thought to resist and who, as prudence will bid you to do, ended by submitting when they noticed that stubbornness could lead them to incur penalties; for I might just as well declare to you, Thérèse," the superior continued, showing me scourges, ferules, withes, cords, and a thousand other instruments of torture, "yes, you might just as well know it: there you see what we use upon unmanageable girls; decide whether you wish to be convinced. What do you expect to find here? Mercy? we know it not; humaneness? our sole pleasure is the violation of its laws. Religion? 'tis as naught to us, our contempt for it grows the better acquainted with it we become; allies . . . kin . . . friends . . . judges? there's none of that in this place, dear girl, you will discover nothing but cruelty, egoism, and the most sustained debauchery and impiety. The completest submissiveness is your lot, and that is all; cast a glance about the impenetrable asylum which shelters you: never has an outsider invaded these premises: the monastery could be taken, searched, sacked, and burned, and this retreat would still be perfectly safe from discovery: we are in an isolated outbuilding, as good as buried within the six walls of incredible thickness surrounding us entirely, and here you are, my child, in the midst of four libertines who surely have no inclination to spare you and whom your entreaties, your tears, your speeches, your genuflections, and your outcries will only further inflame. To whom then will you have recourse? to what? Will it be to that God you have just implored with such earnestness and who, by way of reward for your fervor, only precipitates you into further snares, each more fatal than the last? to that illusory God we ourselves outrage all day long by insulting his vain commandments? ... And so, Thérèse, you conceive that there is no power, of whatever species you may suppose, which could possibly deliver you out of our hands, and there is neither in the category of things real nor in that of miracles, any sort of means which might permit you successfully to retain this virtue you yet glory in; which might, in fine, prevent you from becoming, in every sense and in every manner, the prey of the libidinous excesses to which we, all four of us, are going to abandon ourselves with you. ... Therefore, little slut, off with your clothes, offer your body to our lusts, let it be soiled by them instantly or the severest treatment will prove to you what risks a wretch like yourself runs by disobeying us."

This harangue ... this terrible order, I felt, left me no shifts, but would I not have been guilty had I failed to employ the means my heart prompted in me? my situation left me this last resource: I fall at Dom Séverino's feet, I employ all a despairing soul's eloquence to supplicate him not to take advantage of my state or abuse it; the bitterest tears spring from my eyes and inundate his knees, all I imagine to be of the strongest, all I believe the most pathetic, I try everything with this man. ... Great God! what was the use? could I have not known that tears merely enhance the object of a libertine's coveting? how was I able to doubt that everything I attempted in my efforts to sway those savages had the unique effect of arousing them. ... "Take the bitch," said Séverino in a rage, "seize her, Clément, let her be naked in a minute, and let her learn that it is not in persons like ourselves that compassion stifles Nature." My resistance had animated Clément, he was foaming at the mouth: he took hold of me, his arm shook nervously; interspersing his actions with appalling blasphemies, he had my clothing torn away in a trice.

"A lovely creature," came from the superior, who ran his

fingers over my flanks, "may God blast me if I've ever seen one better made; friends," the monk pursued, "let's put order into our procedures; you know our formula for welcoming newcomers: she might be exposed to the entire ceremony, don't you think? let's omit nothing; and let's have the eight other women stand around us to supply our wants and to excite them."

A circle is formed immediately, I am placed in its center and there, for more than two hours, I am inspected, considered, handled by those four monks, who, one after the other, pronounce either encomiums or criticisms.

You will permit me, Madame, our lovely prisoner said with a blush, to conceal a part of the obscene details of this odious ritual; allow your imagination to figure all that debauch can dictate to villains in such instances; allow it to see them move to and fro between my companions and me, comparing, confronting, contrasting, airing opinions, and indeed it still will not have but a faint idea of what was done in those initial orgies, very mild, to be sure, when matched against all the horrors I was soon to experience.

"Let's to it," says Séverino, whose prodigiously exalted desires will brook no further restraint and who in this dreadful state gives the impression of a tiger about to devour its prey, "let each of us advance to take his favorite pleasure." And placing me upon a couch in the posture expected by his execrable projects and causing me to be held by two of his monks, the infamous man attempts to satisfy himself in that criminal and perverse fashion which makes us to resemble none but the sex we do not possess while degrading the one we have; but either the shameless creature is too strongly proportioned, or Nature revolts in me at the mere suspicion of these pleasures; Séverino cannot overcome the obstacles; he presents himself, and he is repulsed immediately. . . . He spreads, he presses, thrusts, tears, all his efforts are in vain; in his fury the monster lashes out against the altar at which he cannot speak his prayers; he strikes it, he pinches it, he bites it; these brutalities are succeeded by renewed challenges; the chastened flesh yields, the gate cedes, the ram bursts through; terrible screams rise from my throat; the entire mass is swifty engulfed, and darting its venom the next moment, robbed then of its strength, the snake gives ground before the movements I make to expel it, and Sévérino weeps with rage. Never in my life have I suffered so much.

Clément steps forward; he is armed with a cat-o'-nine-tails; his perfidious designs glitter in his eyes.

" 'Tis I," says he to Sévérino, " 'tis I who shall avenge you, Father, I shall correct this silly drab for having resisted your pleasures." He has no need of anyone else to hold me; with one arm he enlaces me and forces me, belly down, across his knees; what is going to serve his caprices is nicely discovered. At first, he tries a few blows, it seems they are merely intended as a prelude; soon inflamed by lust, the beast strikes with all his force; nothing is exempt from his ferocity; everything from the small of my back to the lower part of my thighs, the traitor lays cuts upon it all; daring to mix love with these moments of cruelty, he fastens his mouth to mine and wishes to inhale the sighs agony wrests from me . . . my tears flow, he laps them up, now he kisses, now he threatens, but the rain of blows continues; while he operates, one of the women excites him; kneeling before him, she works with each hand at diverse tasks; the greater her success, the more violent the strokes delivered me; I am nigh to being rent and nothing yet announces the end of my sufferings; he has exhausted every possibility, still he drives on; the end I await is to be the work of his delirium alone; a new cruelty stiffens him: my breasts are at the brute's mercy, he irritates them, uses his teeth upon them, the cannibal snaps, bites, this excess determines the crisis, the incense escapes him. Frightful cries, terrifying blasphemies, shouts characterize its spurtings, and the monk, enervated, turns me over to Jérôme.

"I will be no more of a threat to your virtue than Clément was," said this libertine as he caressed the blood-spattered altar at which Clément had just sacrificed, "but I should indeed like to kiss the furrows where the plow passed; I too am worthy to open them, and should like to pay them my modest respects; but I should like even more," went on the old satyr, inserting a finger where Sévérino had lodged himself, "I should like to have the hen lay, and 'twould be most agreeable to devour its egg . . . does one exist? Why, yes indeed, by God! . . . Oh, my dear, dear little girl! how very soft . . ."

His mouth takes the place of his finger. . . I am told what I have to do, full of disgust I do it. In my situation, alas, am I permitted to refuse? The infamous one is delighted . . . he swallows, then, forcing me to kneel before him, he glues himself to me in this position; his ignominious passion is appeased in a fashion that cannot justify any complaint on my part. While he acts thus, the fat woman flogs him, another puts herself directly above his mouth and acquits herself of the same task I have just been obliged to execute.

" 'Tis not enough," says the monster, "each one of my hands has got to contain . . . for one cannot get one's fill of these goodies." The two prettiest girls approach; they obey: there you have the excesses to which satiety has led Jérôme. At any rate, thanks to impurities he is happy, and at the end of half an hour, my mouth finally receives, with a loathing you must readily appreciate, this evil man's disgusting homage.

Antonin appears. "Well," says he, "let's have a look at this so very spotless virtue; I wonder whether, damaged by a single assault, it is really what the girl maintains." His weapon is raised and trained upon me; he would willingly employ Clément's devices: I have told you that active flagellation pleases him quite as much as it does the other monk but, as he is in a hurry, the state in which his colleague has put me suffices him: he examines this state, relishes it, and leaving me in that attitude of which they are all so fond, he spends an instant pawing the two hemispheres poised at the entrance; in a fury, he rattles the temple's porticos, he is soon at the sanctuary; although quite as violent as Sévérino's, Antonin's assault, launched against a less narrow passage, is not as painful to endure; the energetic athlete seizes my haunches and, supplying the movements I am unable to make, he shakes me, pulls me to him vivaciously; one might judge by this Hercules' redoubling efforts that, not content to be master of the place, he wishes to reduce it to a shambles. Such terrible attacks, so new to me, cause me to succumb; but unconcerned for my pain, the cruel victor thinks of nothing but increasing his pleasure; everything embraces, everything conspires to his voluptuousness; facing him, raised upon my flanks, the fifteen year-old girl, her legs spread open, offers his mouth the altar at which he sacrifices in me: leisurely, he pumps that precious natural juice whose emission Nature has only lately granted the young child; on her knees, one of the older women bends toward my vanquisher's loins, busies herself about them and with her impure tongue animating his desires, she procures them their ecstasy while, to inflame himself yet further, the debauchee excites a woman with either hand; there is not one of his senses which is not tickled, not one which does not concur in the perfection of his delirium; he attains it, but my unwavering horror for all these infamies inhibits me from sharing it. . . . He arrives there alone; his jets, his cries, everything proclaims it and, despite myself, I am flooded with the proofs of a fire I am but one of six to light; and thereupon I fall back upon the throne which has just been the scene of my immolation, no longer conscious of my existence save through my pain and my tears . . . my despair and my remorse.

However, Dom Séverino orders the women to bring me food; but far from being quickened by these attentions, an access of furious grief assails my soul. I, who located all my glory, all my felicity in my virtue, I who thought that, provided I remained well-behaved at all times, I could be consoled for all fortune's ills, I cannot bear the horrible idea of seeing myself so cruelly sullied by those from whom I should have been able to expect the greatest comfort and aid: my tears flowed in abundance, my cries made the vault ring; I rolled upon the floor, I lacerated my breast, tore my hair, invoked my butchers, begged them to bestow death upon me . . . and, Madame, would you believe it? this terrible sight excited them all the more.

"Ah!" said Séverino, "I've never enjoyed a finer spectacle: behold, good friends, see the state it puts me in; it is really unbelievable, what feminine anguish obtains from me."

"Let's go back to work," quoth Clément, "and in order to teach her to bellow at fate, let the bitch be more sharply handled in this second assault."

The project is no sooner conceived than put into execution; up steps Séverino, but his speeches notwithstanding, his desires require a further degree of irritation and it is only after having used Clément's cruel measures that he succeeds in marshaling the forces necessary to accomplish his newest crime. Great God! What excess of ferocity! Could it be that those monsters would carry it to the point of selecting the instant of a crisis of moral agony as violent as that I was undergoing, in order to submit me to so barbarous a physical one! " 'Twould be an injustice to this novice," said Clément, "were we not to employ in its major form what served us so well in its merely episodic dimension," and thereupon he began to act, adding: "My word upon it, I will treat her no better than did you." "One instant," said Antonin to the superior whom he saw about to lay hands upon me again; "while your zeal is exhaled into this pretty maiden's posterior parts, I might, it seems to me, make an offering to the contrary God; we will have her between us two."

The position was so arranged I could still provide Jérôme with a mouth; Clément fitted himself between my hands, I was constrained to arouse him; all the priestesses surrounded this frightful group; each lent an actor what she knew was apt to stir him most profoundly; however, it was I supported them all, the entire weight bore down upon me alone; Séverino gives the signal, the other three follow close after him and there I am a second time infamously defiled by the proofs of those blackguards' disgusting luxury.

"Well," cries the superior, "that should be adequate for the first day; we must now have her remark that her comrades are no better treated than she." I am placed upon an elevated armchair and from there I am compelled to witness those other horrors which are to terminate the orgies.

The monks stand in queue; all the sisters file before them and receive whiplashes from each; next, they are obliged to excite their torturers with their mouths while the latter torment and shower invectives upon them.

The youngest, she of ten, is placed upon a divan and each monk steps forward to expose her to the torture of his choice; near her is the girl of fifteen; it is with her each monk, after having meted out punishment, takes his pleasure; she is the butt; the eldest woman is obliged to stay in close attendance upon the monk presently performing, in order to be of service to him either in this operation or in the act which concludes it. Séverino uses only his hands to molest what is offered him and speeds to engulf himself in the sanctuary of his whole delight and which she whom they have posted nearby presents to him; armed with a handful of nettles, the eldest woman retaliates upon him for what he has a moment ago done to the child; 'tis in the depths of painful titillations the libertine's transports are born. . . . Consult him; will he confess to cruelty? But he has done nothing he does not endure in his turn.

Clément lightly pinches the little girl's flesh; the enjoyment offered within is beyond his capabilities, but he is treated as he has dealt with the girl, and at the feet of the idol he leaves the incense he lacks the strength to fling into its sanctuary.

Antonin entertains himself by kneading the fleshier parts of the victim's body; fired by her convulsive struggling, he precipitates himself into the district offered to his chosen pleasures. In his turn he is mauled, beaten, and ecstasy is the fruit of his torments.

Old Jérôme employs his teeth only, but each bite leaves a wound whence blood leaps instantly forth; after receiving a dozen, the target tenders him her open mouth; therein his fury is appeased while he is himself bitten quite as severely as he did bite.

The saintly fathers drink and recover their strength.

The thirty-six-year-old woman, six months pregnant, as I have told you, is perched upon a pedestal eight feet high; unable to pose but one leg, she is obliged to keep the other in the air; round about her, on the floor, are mattresses garnished three feet deep with thorns, splines, holly; a flexible rod is given to her that she may keep herself erect; it is easy to see, on the one hand, that it is to her interest not to tumble, and on the other, that she cannot possibly retain her balance; the alternatives divert the monks; all four of them cluster around her, during the spectacle each has one or two women to excite him in divers manners; great with child as she is, the luckless creature remains in this attitude for nearly a quarter of an hour; at last, strength deserts her, she falls upon the thorns, and our villains, wild with lust, one last time step forward to lavish upon her body their ferocity's abominable homage . . . the company retires.

The superior put me into the keeping of the thirty-year-old girl of whom I made mention; her name was Omphale; she was charged to instruct me, to settle me in my new domicile. But that night I neither saw nor heard anything. Annihilated, desperate, I thought of nothing but to capture a little rest. In the room where I had been installed I noticed other women who had not been at the supper; I postponed consideration of these new objects until the following day, and occupied myself with naught else but repose. Omphale left me to myself; she went to put herself to bed; scarcely had I stepped into mine when the full horror of my circumstances presented itself to me in yet more lively colors: I could not dispel the thought of the execrations I had suffered, nor of those to which I had been a witness. Alas! if at certain times those pleasures had occurred to my wandering imagination, I had thought them chaste, as is the God Who inspires them, given by Nature in order to comfort human beings; I had fancied them the product of love and delicacy. I had been very far from believing that man, after the example of savage beasts, could only relish them by causing his companion to shudder . . . then, returning to my own black fate . . . "O Just Heaven," I said to myself, "it is then absolutely certain that no virtuous act will emanate from my heart without being answered at once by an agonizing echo! And of what evil was I guilty, Great God! in desiring to come to accomplish some religious duties in this monastery? Do I offend Heaven by wanting to pray? Incomprehensible decrees of Providence, deign," I continued, "deign to open wide my eyes, cause me to see if you do not wish me to rebel against you!" Bitterest tears followed these musings, and I was still inundated with them when daylight appeared; then Omphale approached my bed.

"Dear companion," she said, "I come to exhort you to be courageous; I too wept during my first days, but now the thing has become a habit; as have I, you will become accustomed to it all; the beginnings are terrible: it is not simply the necessity to sate these debauchees' hungers which is our life's torture, it is the loss of our freedom, it is the cruel manner in which we are handled in this terrible house."

The wretched take comfort in seeing other sufferers about them. However trenchant were my anguishes, they were assuaged for an instant; I begged my companion to inform me of the ills I had to expect.

"In a moment," my instructress said, "but first get up and let me show you about our retreat, observe your new companions; then we'll hold our conversation."

Following Omphale's suggestion, I began by examining the

chamber we were in. It was an exceedingly large chamber, containing eight little beds covered with clean calico spreads; by each bed
was a partitioned dressing room; but all the windows which lit both
these closets and the room itself were raised five feet above the
floor and barred inside and out. In the middle of the room was a large
table, secured to the floor, and it was intended for eating or work;
three doors bound and braced with iron closed the room; on our side
no fittings or keyholes were to be seen; on the other, enormous bolts.

"And this is our prison?"

"Alas! yes, my dear," Omphale replied; "such is our unique
dwelling place; not far from here, the eight other girls have a
similar room, and we never communicate with each other save
when the monks are pleased to assemble us all at one time."

I peered into the alcove destined for me; it was eight feet
square, daylight entered it, as in the great room, by a very high
window fitted all over with iron. The only furniture was a bidet, a
lavatory basin and a *chaise percée*. I re-emerged; my companions,
eager to see me, gathered round in a circle: they were seven, I made
the eighth. Omphale, inhabiting the other room, was only in this to
indoctrinate me; were I to wish it, she would remain with me, and
one of the others would take her place in her own chamber; I asked
to have the arrangement made. But before coming to Omphale's
story, it seems to me essential to describe the seven new companions
fate had given me; I will proceed according to age, as I did with
the others.

The youngest was twelve years old: a very animated, very
spirited physiognomy, the loveliest hair, the prettiest mouth.

The second was sixteen: she was one of the most beautiful
blondes imaginable, with truly delicious features and all the grace,
all the sweetness of her age, mingled with a certain interesting quality, the product of her sadness, which rendered her yet a thousand
times more beautiful.

The third was twenty-three; very pretty, but an excessive effrontery, too much impudence degraded, so I thought, the charms
Nature had endowed her with.

The fourth was twenty-six: she had the figure of Venus; but
perhaps her forms were rather too pronounced; a dazzling fair

skin; a sweet, open, laughing countenance, beautiful eyes, a mouth a trifle large but admirably furnished, and superb blond hair.

The fifth was thirty-two; she was four months pregnant; with an oval, somewhat melancholic face, large soulful eyes; she was very pale, her health was delicate, she had a harmonious voice but the rest seemed somehow spoiled. She was naturally libertine: she was, I was told, exhausting herself.

The sixth was thirty-three; a tall strapping woman, the loveliest face in the world, the loveliest flesh.

The seventh was thirty-eight; a true model of figure and beauty: she was the superintendent of my room; Omphale forewarned me of her malicious temper and, principally, of her taste for women.

"To yield is the best way of pleasing her," my companion told me; "resist her, and you will bring down upon your head every misfortune that can befall you in this house. Bear it in mind."

Omphale asked permission of Ursule, which was the superintendent's name, to instruct me; Ursule consented upon condition I kiss her. I approached: her impure tongue sought to attach itself to mine, and meanwhile her fingers labored to determine sensations she was far indeed from obtaining. However, I had to lend myself to everything, my own feelings notwithstanding, and when she believed she had triumphed, she sent me back to my closet where Omphale spoke to me in the following manner:

"All the women you saw yesterday, my dear Thérèse, and those you have just seen, are divided into four classes, each containing four girls; the first is called the children's class: it includes girls ranging from the most tender age to those of sixteen; a white costume distinguishes them.

"The second class, whose color is green, is called the youthful class; it contains girls of from sixteen to twenty-one.

"The third is the class of the age of reason; its vestments are blue; its ages are from twenty-one to thirty, and both you and I belong to it.

"The fourth class, dressed in reddish brown, is intended for those of mature years; it is composed of anyone over thirty.

"These girls are either indiscriminately mingled at the Reverend Fathers' suppers, or they appear there by class: it all depends upon the whims of the monks but, when not at the meals, they are mixed in the two dormitories, as you are able to judge by those who are lodged in ours.

"The instruction I have to give you," said Omphale, "divides under the headings of four primary articles; in the first, we will treat of what pertains to the house; in the second we will place what regards the behavior of the girls, their punishment, their feeding habits, etc., etc., etc.; the third article will inform you of the arrangement of these monks' pleasures, of the manner in which the girls serve them; the fourth will contain observations on personnel changes.

"I will not, Thérèse, describe the environs of this frightful house, for you are as familiar with them as I; I will only discuss the interior; they have shown it all to me so that I can give a picture of it to newcomers, whose education is one of my chores, and in whom, by means of this account, I am expected to dash all hope of escape. Yesterday Séverino explained some of its features and he did not deceive you, my dear. The church and the pavilion form what is properly called the monastery; but you do not know where the building we inhabit is situated and how one gets here; 'tis thus: in the depths of the sacristy, behind the altar, is a door hidden in the wainscoting and opened by a spring; this door is the entrance to a narrow passage, quite as dark as it is long, whose windings your terror, upon entering, prevented you from noticing; the tunnel descends at first, because it must pass beneath a moat thirty feet deep, then it mounts after the moat and, leveling out, continues at a depth of no more than six feet beneath the surface; thus it arrives at the basements of our pavilion having traversed the quarter of a league from the church; six thick enclosures rise to baffle all attempts to see this building from the outside, even were one to climb into the church's tower; the reason for this invisibility is simple: the pavilion hugs the ground, its height does not attain twenty-five feet, and the compounded enclosures, some stone walls, others living palisades formed by trees growing in strait proximity to each other, are, all of them, at least fifty feet high: from whatever direction the place is observed it can only be taken for a dense clump of trees in the forest, never for a habitation; it is, hence, as I have said, by means of a trap door opening into the cellars one emerges from the obscure corridor of which I gave you some idea and of which you cannot possibly have any recollection in view of the state you must have been while walking through it. This pavilion, my dear, has, in all, nothing but basements, a ground floor, an entresol, and a first floor; above it there is a very thick roof covered with a large tray, lined with lead, filled with earth, and in which are planted evergreen shrubberies which, blending with the screens surrounding us, give to everything a yet more realistic look of solidity; the basements form a large hall in the middle, around it are distributed eight smaller rooms of which two serve as dungeons for girls who have merited incarceration, and the other six are reserved for provisions; above are located the dining room, the kitchens, pantries, and two cabinets the monks enter when they wish to isolate their pleasures and taste them with us out of their colleagues' sight; the intervening story is composed of eight chambers, whereof four have each a closet: these are the cells where the monks sleep and introduce us when their lubricity destines us to share their beds; the four other rooms are those of the serving friars, one of whom is our jailer, another the monks' valet, a third the doctor, who has in his cell all he needs for emergencies, and the fourth is the cook; these four friars are deaf and dumb; it would be difficult to expect, as you observe, any comfort or aid from them; furthermore, they never pass time in our company and it is forbidden to accost or attempt to communicate with them. Above the entresol are two seraglios; they are identical; as you see, each is a large chamber edged by eight cubicles; thus, you understand, dear girl, that, supposing one were to break through the bars in the casement and descend by the window, one would still be far from being able to escape, since there would remain five palisades, a stout wall, and a broad moat to get past: and were one even to overcome these obstacles, where would one be? In the monastery's courtyard which, itself securely shut, would not afford, at the first moment, a very safe egress. A perhaps less perilous means of escape would be, I admit, to find, somewhere in our basements, the opening to the tunnel that leads out; but how are we to explore these underground cellars, perpetually locked up as we are? were one even to be able to get down there, this opening would still not be found, for it enters the building in some hidden corner unknown to us and itself barricaded by grills to which

they alone have the key. However, were all these difficulties vanquished, were one in the corridor, the route would still not be any
the more certain for us, for it is strewn with traps with which only
they are familiar and into which anyone who sought to traverse the
passageways would inevitably fall without the guidance of the
monks. And so you must renounce all thought of escape, for it is out
of the question, Thérèse; believe me, were it thinkable, I should
long have fled this detestable place, but that cannot be. They who
come here never leave save upon their death; and thence is born
this impudence, this cruelty, this tyranny these villains use with us;
nothing inflames them, nothing stimulates their imagination like
the impunity guaranteed them by this impregnable retreat; certain
never to have other witnesses to their excesses than the very victims
they feast upon, sure indeed their perversities will never be revealed, they carry them to the most abhorrent extremes; delivered
of the law's restraints, having burst the checks Religion imposes,
unconscious of those of remorse, there is no atrocity in which they
do not indulge themselves, and by this criminal apathy their abominable passions are so much more agreeably pricked that nothing,
they say, incenses them like solitude and silence, like helplessness on
one hand and impunity on the other. The monks regularly sleep
every night in this pavilion, they return here at five in the afternoon
and go to the monastery the following morning at nine, except for
one of the four, chosen daily, who spends the day here: he is known
as the Officer of the Day. We will soon see what his duties are. As
for the four subaltern friars, they never budge from here; in each
chamber we have a bell which communicates with the jailer's cell;
the superintendent alone has the right to ring for him but, when
she does so in time of her need or ours, everyone comes running
instantly; when they return each day, the fathers themselves bring
the necessary victuals and give them to the cook, who prepares our
meals in accordance with their instructions; there is an artesian well
in the basements, abundant wines of every variety in the cellars. We
pass on to the second article which relates to the girls' manners,
bearing, nourishment, punishment, etc.

"Our number is always maintained constant; affairs are so
managed that we are always sixteen, eight in either chamber, and,
as you observe, always in the uniform of our particular class; before

the day is over you will be given the habit appropriate to the one you are entering; during the day we wear a light costume of the color which belongs to us; in the evening, we wear gowns of the same color and dress our hair with all possible elegance. The superintendent of the chamber has complete authority over us, disobedience to her is a crime; her duty is to inspect us before we go to the orgies and if things are not in the desired state she is punished as well as we. The errors we may commit are of several kinds. Each has its particular punishment, and the rules, together with the list of what is to be expected when they are broken, are displayed in each chamber; the Officer of the Day, the person who comes, as I explained a moment ago, to give us orders, to designate the girls for the supper, to visit our living quarters, and to hear the superintendents' complaints, this monk, I say, is the one who, each evening, metes out punishment to whoever has merited it: here are the crimes together with the punishments exacted for them.

"Failure to rise in the morning at the prescribed hour, thirty strokes with the whip (for it is almost always with whipping we are punished; it were perfectly to be expected that an episode in these libertines' pleasures would have become their preferred mode of correction). The presentation during the pleasurable act, either through misunderstanding or for whatsoever may be the reason, of one part of the body instead of some other which was desired, fifty strokes; improper dress or an unsuitable coiffure, twenty strokes; failure to have given prior notice of incapacitation due to menstruation, sixty strokes; upon the day the surgeon confirms the existence of a pregnancy, one hundred strokes are administered; negligence, incompetence, or refusal in connection with luxurious proposals, two hundred strokes. And how often their infernal wickedness finds us wanting on that head, without our having made the least mistake! How frequently it happens that one of them will suddenly demand what he very well knows we have just accorded another and cannot immediately do again! One undergoes the punishment nonetheless; our remonstrances, our pleadings are never heeded; one must either comply or suffer the consequences. Imperfect behavior in the chamber, or disobedience shown the superintendent, sixty strokes; the appearance of tears, chagrin, sorrow, remorse, even the look of the slightest return to Religion, two hundred strokes. If a monk selects you as his partner when he wishes to taste the last crisis of pleasure and if he is unable to achieve it, whether the fault be his, which is most common, or whether it be yours, upon the spot, three hundred strokes; the least hint of revulsion at the monks' propositions, of whatever nature these propositions may be, two hundred strokes; an attempted or concerted escape or revolt, nine days' confinement in a dungeon, entirely naked, and three hundred lashes each day; caballing, the instigation of plots, the sowing of unrest, etc., immediately upon discovery, three hundred strokes; projected suicide, refusal to eat the stipulated food or the proper quantity, two hundred strokes; disrespect shown toward the monks, one hundred eighty strokes. Those only are crimes; beyond what is mentioned there, we can do whatever we please, sleep together, quarrel, fight, carry drunkenness, riot and gourmandizing to their furthest extremes, swear, blaspheme: none of that makes the faintest difference, we may commit those faults and never a word will be said to us; we are rated for none but those I have just mentioned. But if they wish, the superintendents can spare us many of these unpleasantnesses; however, this protection, unfortunately, can be purchased only by complacencies frequently more disagreeable than the sufferings for which they are substitutes; these women, in both chambers, have the same taste, and it is only by according them one's favors that one enters into their good graces. Spurn one of them, and she needs no additional motive to exaggerate her report of your misdeeds, the monks the superintendents serve double their powers, and far from reprimanding them for their injustice, unceasingly encourage it in them; they are themselves bound by all those regulations and are the more severely chastised if they are suspected of leniency: not that the libertines need all that in order to vent their fury upon us, but they welcome excuses; the look of legitimacy that may be given to a piece of viciousness renders it more agreeable in their eyes, adds to its piquancy, its charm. Upon arriving here each of us is provided with a little store of linen; we are given everything by the half-dozen, and our supplies are renewed every year, but we are obliged to surrender what we bring here with us; we are not permitted to keep the least thing. The complaints of the four friars I spoke of are heard just as are the superintendents'; their mere delation is sufficient to procure our punishment; but they at least ask nothing from us and there is less to be feared from that quarter than from the superintendents who, when vengeance informs their maneuvers, are very demanding and very dangerous. Our food is excellent and always copious; were it not that their lust derives benefits thence, this article might not be so satisfactory, but as their filthy debauches profit thereby, they spare themselves no pains to stuff us with food: those who have a bent for flogging seek to fatten us, and those, as Jérôme phrased it yesterday, who like to see the hen lay, are assured by means of abundant feeding, of a greater yield of eggs. Consequently, we eat four times a day; at breakfast, between nine and ten o'clock we are regularly given *volaille au riz*, fresh fruit or compotes, tea, coffee, or chocolate; at one o'clock, dinner is served; each table of eight is served alike; a very good soup, four entrées, a roast of some kind, four second courses, dessert in every season. At five-thirty an afternoon lunch of pastries and fruit arrives. There can be no doubt of the evening meal's excellence if it is taken with the monks; when we do not join them at table, as often happens, since but four of us from each chamber are allowed to go, we are given three roast plates and four entremets; each of us has a daily ration of one bottle of white wine, one of red, and an half-bottle of brandy; they who do not drink that much are at liberty to distribute their quota to the others; among us are some great gourmands who drink astonishing amounts, who get regularly drunk, all of which they do without fear of reprimand; and there are, as well, some for whom these four meals still do not suffice; they have but to ring, and what they ask for will be brought them at once.

"The superintendents require that the food be consumed, and if someone persists in not wishing to eat, for whatever reason, upon the third infraction that person will be severely punished; the monks' supper is composed of three roast dishes, six entrées followed by a cold plate and eight entremets, fruit, three kinds of wine, coffee and liqueurs: sometimes all eight of us are at table with them, sometimes they oblige four of us to wait upon them, and these four dine afterward; it also happens from time to time that they take only four girls for supper; they are, ordinarily, an entire class; when our number is eight, there are always two from each class. I need hardly tell you that no one ever visits us; under no circumstances is any outsider ever admitted into this pavilion. If we fall ill, we are entrusted to the surgeon friar only, and if we die, we leave this world without any religious ministrations; our bodies are flung into one of the spaces between the circumvallations, and that's an end to it; but, and the cruelty is signal, if the sick one's condition becomes too grave or if there is fear of contagion, they do not wait until we are dead to dispose of us; though still alive, we are carried out and dropped in the place I mentioned. During the eighteen years I have been here I have seen more than ten instances of this unexampled ferocity; concerning which they declare it is better to lose one than endanger sixteen; the loss of a girl, they continue, is of very modest import, and it may be so easily repaired there is scant cause to regret it. Let us move on to the arrangements concerning the monks' pleasures and to all of what pertains to the subject.

"We rise at exactly nine every morning, and in every season; we retire at a later or an earlier hour, depending upon the monks' supper. Immediately we are up, the Officer of the Day comes on his rounds; he seats himself in a large armchair and each of us is obliged to advance, stand before him with our skirts raised upon the side he prefers; he touches, he kisses, he examines, and when everyone has carried out this duty, he identifies those who are to participate at the evening's exercises: he prescribes the state in which they must be, he listens to the superintendent's report, and the punishments are imposed. Rarely does the officer leave without a luxurious scene in which all eight usually find roles. The superintendent directs these libidinous activities, and the most entire submission on our part reigns during them. Before breakfast it often occurs that one of the Reverend Fathers has one of us called from bed; the jailer friar brings a card bearing the name of the person desired, the Officer of the Day sees to it she is sent, not even he has the right to withhold her, she leaves and returns when dismissed. This first ceremony concluded, we breakfast; from this moment till evening we have no more to do; but at seven o'clock in summer, at six in winter, they come for those who have been designated; the jailer friar himself escorts them, and after the supper they who have not been retained for the night come back to the seraglio. Often, all return; other girls have been selected for the night, and they are advised several hours in advance in what costume they must make their appearance; sometimes only the Girls of the Watch sleep out of the chamber."

"Girls of the Watch?" I interrupted. "What function this?"

"I will tell you," my historian replied.

"Upon the first day of every month each monk adopts a girl who must serve a term as his servant and as the target of his shameful desires; only the superintendents are exempted, for they have the task of governing their chambers. The monks can neither exchange girls during the month, nor make them serve two months in succession; there is nothing more cruel, more taxing than this drudgery, and I have no idea how you will bear up under it. When five o'clock strikes, the Girl of the Watch promptly descends to the monk she serves and does not leave his side until the next day, at the hour he sets off for the monastery. She rejoins him when he comes back; she employs these few hours to eat and rest, for she must remain awake all night throughout the whole of the term she spends with her master; I repeat to you, the wretch remains constantly on hand to serve as the object of every caprice which may enter the libertine's head; cuffs, slaps, beatings, whippings, hard language, amusements, she has got to endure all of it; she must remain standing all night long in her patron's bedroom, at any instant ready to offer herself to the passions which may stir that tyrant; but the cruelest, the most ignominious aspect of this servitude is the terrible obligation she is under to provide her mouth or her breast for the relief of the one and the other of the monster's needs: he never uses any other vase: she has got to be the willing recipient of everything and the least hesitation or recalcitrance is straightway punished by the most savage reprisals. During all the scenes of lust these are the girls who guarantee pleasure's success, who guide and manage the monks' joys, who tidy up whoever has become covered with filth: for example, a monk dirties himself while enjoying a woman: it is his aide's duty to repair the disorder; he wishes to be excited? the task of rousing him falls to the wretch who accompanies him everywhere, dresses him, undresses him, is ever at his elbow, who is always wrong, always at fault, always beaten; at the suppers her place is behind her master's chair or, like a dog, at his feet under the table, or upon her knees, between his thighs, exciting him with her mouth; sometimes she serves as his cushion, his seat, his torch; at other times all four of them will be grouped around the table in the most lecherous, but, at the same time, the most fatiguing attitudes.

"If they lose their balance, they risk either falling upon the thorns placed near by, or breaking a limb, or being killed, such cases have been known; and meanwhile the villains make merry, enact debauches, peacefully get drunk upon meats, wines, lust, and upon cruelty."

"O Heaven!" said I to my companion, trembling with horror, "is it possible to be transported to such excesses! What infernal place is this!"

"Listen to me, Thérèse, listen, my child, you have not yet heard it all, not by any means," said Omphale. "Pregnancy, reverenced in the world, is the very certitude of reprobation amongst these villains; here, the pregnant woman is given no dispensations: brutalities, punishments, and watches continue; on the contrary, a gravid condition is the certain way to procure oneself troubles, sufferings, humiliations, sorrows; how often do they not by dint of blows cause abortions in them whose fruits they decide not to harvest, and when indeed they do allow the fruit to ripen, it is in order to sport with it: what I am telling you now should be enough to warn you to preserve yourself from this state as best you possibly can."

"But is one able to?"

"Of course, there are certain devices, sponges. . . But if Antonin perceives what you are up to, beware of his wrath; the safest way is to smother whatever might be the natural impression by striving to unhinge the imagination, which with monsters like these is not difficult.

"We have here as well," my instructress continued, "certain dependencies and alliances of which you probably know very little and of which it were well you had some idea; although this has more to do with the fourth article—with, that is to say, the one that treats of our recruitings, our retrenchments, and our exchanges —I am going to anticipate for a moment in order to insert the following details.

"You are not unaware, Thérèse, that the four monks composing this brotherhood stand at the head of their Order; all belong to distinguished families, all four are themselves very rich: independently of the considerable funds allocated by the Benedictines for the maintenance of this bower of bliss into which everyone hopes to enter in his turn, they who do arrive here contribute a large proportion of their property and possessions to the foundation already established. These two sources combined yield more than a hundred thousand crowns annually which is devoted solely to finding recruits and meeting the house's expenses; they have a dozen discreet and reliable women whose sole task is to bring them every month a new subject, no younger than twelve nor older than thirty. The conscriptee must be free of all defects and endowed with the greatest possible number of qualities, but principally with that of eminent birth. These abductions, well paid for and always effected a great distance from here, bring no consequent discomfitures; I have never heard of any that resulted in legal action; their extreme caution protects them against everything. They do not absolutely confine themselves to virgins: a girl who has been seduced already or a married woman may prove equally pleasing, but a forcible abduction has got to take place, rape must be involved, and it must be definitely verified; this circumstance arouses them; they wish to be certain their crimes cost tears; they would send away any girl who was to come here voluntarily; had you not made a prodigious defense, had they not recognized a veritable fund of virtue in you, and, consequently, the possibility of crime, they would not have kept you twenty-four hours. Everyone here, Thérèse, comes of a distinguished line; my dear friend, you see before you the only daughter of the Comte de * * *, carried off from Paris at the age of twelve and destined one day to have a dowry of a hundred thousand crowns: I was ravished from the arms of my governess who was taking me by carriage, unoccupied save for ourselves, from my father's country seat to the Abbey of Panthemont where I was brought up; my guardian disappeared; she was in all likelihood bought; I was fetched hither by post chaise. The same applies to all the others. The girl of twenty belongs to one of the noblest families of Poitou. The one sixteen years old is the daughter of the Baron de * * *, one of the greatest of the Lorraine squires;

Counts, Dukes, and Margraves are the fathers of the girls of twenty-three, twelve, and thirty-two; in a word, there is not one who cannot claim the loftiest titles, not one who is not treated with the greatest ignominy. But these depraved men are not content to stop at these horrors; they have wished to bring dishonor into the very bosom of their own family. The young lady of twenty-six, without doubt one of the most beautiful amongst us, is Clément's daughter; she of thirty-six is the niece of Jérôme.

"As soon as a new girl has arrived in this cloaca, as soon as she has been sealed in here forever to become a stranger to the world, another is immediately retrenched: such is our sufferings' complement; the cruelest of our afflictions is to be in ignorance of what happens to us during these terrible and disquieting dismissals. It is absolutely impossible to say what becomes of one upon leaving this place. From all the evidence we in our isolation are able to assemble, it seems as if the girls the monks retire from service never appear again; they themselves warn us, they do not conceal from us that this retreat is our tomb, but do they assassinate us? Great Heaven! Would murder, the most execrable of crimes, would murder be for them what it was for that celebrated Maréchal de Retz,[4] a species of erotic entertainment whose cruelty, exalting their perfidious imaginations, were able to plunge their senses into a more intense drunkenness! Accustomed to extracting joy from suffering only, to know no delectation save what is derived from inflicting torment and anguish, would it be possible they were distracted to the point of believing that by redoubling, by ameliorating the delirium's primary cause, one would inevitably render it more perfect; and that, without principles as without faith, wanting manners as they are lacking in virtues, the scoundrels, exploiting the miseries into which their earlier crimes plunged us, were able to find satisfaction in the later ones which snatch our lives away from us. . . . I don't know. . . . If one questions them upon the matter, they mumble unintelligibilities, sometimes responding negatively, sometimes in the affirmative; what is certain is that not one of those who has left, despite the promises she made us to denounce these men to the authorities and to strive to procure our liberation,

---

[4] See *L'Historie de Bretagne* by Dom Lobineau. (*Maréchal de Retz:* Gilles de Rais, marshal of Charles VII's army.—*Tr.*)

not one, I say, has ever kept her word. . . . Once again: do they placate us, dissuade us, or do they eliminate the possibility of our preferring charges? What we ask those who arrive for news of them who have gone, they never have any to communicate. What becomes of these wretches? That is what torments me, Thérèse, that is the fatal incertitude which makes for the great unhappiness of our existence. I have been in this house for eighteen years, I have seen more than two hundred girls depart from it. . . . Where are they? All of them having sworn to help us, why has not one kept her vow?

"Nothing, furthermore, justifies our retirement; age, loss of looks, this is not what counts: caprice is their single rule. They will dismiss today the girl they most caressed yesterday, and for ten years they will keep another of whom they are the most weary: such is the story of this chamber's superintendent; she has been twelve years in the house, and to preserve her I have seen them get rid of fifteen-year-old children whose beauty would have rendered the very Graces jealous. She who left a week ago was not yet sixteen; lovely as Venus herself, they had enjoyed her for less than a year, but she became pregnant and, as I told you Thérèse, that is a great sin in this establishment. Last month they retired one of sixteen, a year ago one of twenty, eight months pregnant; and, recently, another when she began to feel the first pangs of childbirth. Do not imagine that conduct has any bearing upon the matter: I have seen some who flew to do their every bidding and who were gone within six months' time; others sullen, peevish, fantastical whom they kept a great number of years; hence, it is useless to prescribe any kind of behavior to our newly arrived; those monsters' whimsy bursts all circumscriptions, and caprice forms the unique law by which their actions are determined.

"When one is going to be dismissed, one is notified the same morning, never earlier: as usual, the Officer of the Day makes his appearance at nine o'clock and says, let us suppose, 'Omphale, the monastery is sending you into retirement; I will come to take you this evening.' Then he continues about his business. But you do not present yourself for his inspection; he examines the others, then he leaves; the person about to be released embraces her comrades, she makes a thousand promises to strive in their behalf, to bring charges, to bruit abroad what transpires in the monastery: the hour strikes, the monk appears, the girl is led away, and not a word is heard of her. Supper takes place in the usual fashion; we have simply been able to remark that upon these days the monks rarely reach pleasure's ultimate episodes, one might say they proceed gingerly and with unwonted care. However, they drink a great deal more, sometimes even to inebriation; they send us to our chamber at a much earlier hour, they take no one to bed with them, even the Girls of the Watch are relegated to the seraglios."

"Very well," I say to my companion, "if no one has helped you it is because you have had to deal with frail, intimidated creatures, or women with children who dared not attempt anything for you. That they will kill us is not my fear; at least, I don't believe they do: that reasoning beings could carry crime to that point . . . it is unthinkable . . . I know that full well. . . . After what I have seen and undergone I perhaps ought not defend mankind as I do, but, my dear, it is simply inconceivable that they can execute horrors the very idea of which defies the imagination. Oh dear companion!" I pursued with great emotion, "would you like to exchange that promise which for my part I swear I will fulfill! . . . Do you wish it?"

"Yes."

"Ah, I swear to you in the name of all I hold most holy, in the name of the God Who makes me to breathe and Whom only I adore . . . I vow to you I will either die in the undertaking or destroy these infamies . . . will you promise me the same?"

"Do not doubt it," Omphale replied, "but be certain of these promises' futility; others more embittered than you, stauncher, no less resolute and not so scrupulous, in a word, friends who would have shed their last drop of blood for us, have not kept identical vows; and so, dear Thérèse, and so allow my cruel experience to consider ours equally vain and to count upon them no more."

"And the monks," I said, "do they also vary, do new ones often come here?"

"No," answered Omphale, "Antonin has been here ten years, Clément eighteen, Jérôme thirty, Séverino twenty-five. The superior was born in Italy, he is closely allied to the Pope with whom he is in intimate contact; only since his arrival have the so-called miracles of the Virgin assured the monastery's reputation and prevented scandalmongers from observing too closely what takes place here; but when he came the house was already furnished as presently you see it to be; it has subsisted in the same style and upon this footing for above a century, and all the superiors who have governed it have perpetuated a system which so amicably smiles upon their pleasures. Séverino, the most libertine man of our times, has only installed himself here in order to lead a life consonant with his tastes. He intends to maintain this abbey's secret privileges as long as he possibly can. We belong to the diocese of Auxerre, but whether or not the bishop is informed, we never see him, never does he set foot in the monastery: generally speaking, very few outsiders come here except toward the time of the festival which is that of Notre Dame d'Août; according to the monks, ten persons do not arrive at this house over the period of a twelvemonth; however, it is very likely that when strangers do present themselves, the superior takes care to receive them with hospitality; by appearances of religion and austerity he imposes upon them, they go away content, the monastery is eulogized, and thus these villains' impunity is established upon the people's good faith and the credulity of the devout."

Omphale had scarcely concluded her instruction when nine o'clock tolled; the superintendent called us to come quickly, and the Officer of the Day did indeed enter. 'Twas Antonin; according to custom, we drew ourselves up in a line. He cast a rapid glance upon the group, counted us, and sat down; then, one by one, we went forward and lifted our skirts, on the one side as high as the navel, on the other up to the middle of the back. Antonin greeted the homage with the blasé unconcern of satiety; then, clapping an eye upon me, he asked how I liked this newest of my adventures. Getting no response but tears, "She'll manage," he said with a laugh; "in all of France there's not a single house where girls are finished as nicely as they are in this." From the superintendent's hands he took the list of girls who had misbehaved, then, addressing himself to me again, he caused me to shudder; each gesture, each movement which seemed to oblige me to submit myself to these libertines was for me as a sentence of death. Antonin commanded me to sit on the edge of a bed and when I was in this posture he bade the superintendent uncover my breast and raise my skirt to above my waist; he himself spread my legs as far apart as possible, he seats himself before this prospect, one of my companions comes and takes up the same pose on top of me in such a way that it is the altar of genera- tion instead of my visage which is offered to Antonin; with these charms raised to the level of his mouth he readies himself for pleasure. A third girl, kneeling before him, begins to excite him with her hands, and a fourth, completely naked, with her fingers indicates where he must strike my body. Gradually, this girl begins to arouse me and what she does to me Antonin does as well, with both his hands, to two other girls on his left and right. One cannot imagine the language, the obscene speeches by which that debauchee stimulates himself; at last he is in the state he desires, he is led to me, but everyone follows him, moves with him, endeavors to in- flame him yet further while he takes his pleasure; his naked hind parts are exposed, Omphale takes possession of them and neglects nothing in order to irritate him: rubbings, kisses, pollutions, she employs them all; completely afire, Antonin leaps toward me. . . . "I wish to stuff her this time," he says, beside himself. . . . These moral deviations determine the physical. Antonin, who has the habit of uttering terrible cries during the final instants of drunkenness, emits dreadful ones; everyone surrounds, everyone serves him, everyone labors to enrich his ecstasy, and the libertine attains it in the midst of the most bizarre episodes of luxury and depravation.

These groupings were frequent; for when a monk indulged in whatever form of pleasure, all the girls regularly surrounded him in order to fire all his parts' sensations, that voluptuousness might, if one may be forgiven the expression, more surely penetrate into him through every pore.

Antonin left, breakfast was brought in; my companions forced me to eat, I did so to please them. We had not quite finished when the superior entered: seeing us still at table, he dispensed us from ceremonies which were to have been identical with those we had just executed for Antonin. "We must give a thought to dressing her," said he, looking at me; and then he opened a wardrobe and threw upon my bed several garments of the color appropriate to my class, and several bundles of linen as well.

"Try that on," he said, "and give me what belongs to you."

I donned the new clothes and surrendered my old; but, in anticipation of having to give them up, I had, during the night, prudently removed my money from my pockets and had concealed it in my hair. With each article of clothing I took off, Sévérino's ardent stare fell upon the feature newly exposed, and his hands wandered to it at once. At length, when I was half-naked, the monk seized me, put me in the position favorable to his pleasure, that is to say, in the one exactly opposite to the attitude Antonin had made me assume; I wish to ask him to spare me, but spying the fury already kindled in his eyes, I decide the obedient is the safer way; I take my place, the others form a ring around me, Sévérino is able to see nothing but a multitude of those obscene altars in which he delights; his hands converge upon mine, his mouth fastens upon it, his eyes devour it . . . he is at the summit of pleasure.

With your approval, Madame, said the beautiful Thérèse, I shall limit myself to a foreshortened account of the first month I spent in that monastery, that is, I will confine myself to the period's principal anecdotes; the rest would be pure repetition; the monotony of that sojourn would make my recital tedious; immediately afterward, I should, it seems to me, move on to the events which finally produced my emergence from this ghastly sewer.

I did not attend supper that first day; I had simply been selected to pass the night with Dom Clément. In accordance with custom, I was outside his cell some few minutes before he was expected to return to it; the jailer opened the door, then locked it when I had gone in.

Clément arrives as warm with wine as lust, he is followed by the twenty-six year-old girl who, at the time was officiating as his watch; previously informed of what I am to do, I fall to my knees as soon as I hear him coming; he nears me, considers me in my humbled posture, then commands me to rise and kiss him upon the mouth; he savors the kiss for several moments and imparts to it all the expression . . . all the amplitude one could possibly conceive. Meanwhile, Armande, as his thrall was named, undresses me by stages; when the lower part of the loins, with which she had begun, is exposed, she bids me turn around and display to her uncle the area his tastes cherish. Clément examines it, feels it, then, reposing himself in an armchair, orders me to bring it close so that he can kiss it; Armande is upon her knees, rousing him with her mouth,

Clément places his at the sanctuary of the temple I present to him and his tongue strays into the path situate at its center; his hands fasten upon the corresponding altar in Armande but, as the clothing the girl is still wearing impedes him, he commands her to be rid of it, this is soon done, and the docile creature returns to her uncle to take up a position in which, while exciting him with only the hand, she finds herself better within reach of Clément's. The impure monk uninterruptedly occupied with me in like fashion, then tells me to give the largest possible vent to whatever winds may be hovering in my bowels, and these I am to direct into his mouth; this eccentricity struck me as revolting, but I was at the time far from perfect acquaintance with all the irregularities of debauch: I obey and straightway feel the effect of this intemperance. More excited, the monk becomes more impassioned: he suddenly applies bites to six different places upon the fleshy globes I have put at his disposal; I emit a cry and start forward involuntarily, whereat he stands, advances toward me, rage blazing in his eyes, and demands whether I know what I am risking by unsettling him. . . . I make a thousand apologies, he grasps the corset still about my torso, rips it away, and my blouse too, in less time than it takes to tell. . . . Ferociously he seizes my breasts, spouting invectives as he squeezes, wrings, crushes them; Armande undresses him, and there we are, all three of us, naked. Upon Armande his attention comes to bear for a moment: he deals her savage blows with his fists; kisses her mouth; nibbles her tongue and lips, she screams; pain now and again sends the girl into uncontrollable gales of weeping; he has her stand upon a chair and extracts from her just what he desired from me. Armande satisfies him, with one hand I excite him, and, during this luxury, I whip him gently with the other, he also bites Armande, but she holds herself somehow in check, not daring to stir a hair. The monster's tooth-marks are soon printed upon the lovely girl's flesh; they are to be seen in a number of places; brusquely wheeling upon me: "Thérèse," he says, "you are going to suffer cruelly"— he had no need to tell me so, for his eyes declared it but too emphatically. "You are going to be lashed everywhere," he continues, "everywhere, without exception," and as he spoke he again laid hands upon my breasts and mauled them brutally, he bruised their extremities with his fingertips and occasioned me very sharp pain; I dared not say a word for fear of irritating him yet more, but sweat bathed my forehead and, willy-nilly, my eyes filled with tears; he turns me about, makes me kneel on the edge of a chair upon whose back I must keep my hands without removing them for a single instant; he promises to inflict the gravest penalties upon me if I lift them; seeing me ready and well within range, he orders Armande to fetch him some birch rods, she presents him with a handful, slender and long; Clément snatches them, and recommending that I not stir, he opens with a score of stripes upon my shoulders and the small of my back; he leaves me for an instant, returns to Armande, brings her back, she too is made to kneel upon a chair six feet from where I am; he declares he is going to flog us simultaneously and the first of the two to release her grip, utter a cry, or shed a tear will be exposed on the spot to whatever torture he is pleased to inflict: he bestows the same number of strokes upon Armande he has just given me, and positively upon the identical places, he returns to me, kisses everything he has just left off molesting, and raising his sticks, says to me, "Steady, little slut, you are going to be used like the last of the damned." Whereupon I receive fifty strokes, all of them directed between the region bordered by the shoulders and the small of the back. He dashes to my comrade and treats her likewise: we pronounce not a word; nothing may be heard but a few stifled groans, we have enough strength to hold back our tears. There was no indication as to what degree the monk's passions were inflamed; he periodically excited himself briskly, but nothing rose. Returning now to me, he spent a moment eyeing those two fatty globes then still intact but about to undergo torture in their turn; he handled them, he could not prevent himself from prying them apart, tickling them, kissing them another thousand times. "Well," said he, "be courageous . . ." and a hail of blows descended upon these masses, lacerating them to the thighs. Extremely animated by the starts, the leaps, the grinding of teeth, the contortions the pain drew from me, examining them, battening upon them rapturously, he comes and expresses, upon my mouth which he kisses with fervor, the sensations agitating him. . . . "This girl entertains me," he cries, "I have never flogged another with as much pleasure," and he goes back to his niece whom he treats with the same barbarity; there remained the space between the upper thigh and the calves and this he struck with identical vehemence: first the one of us, then the other. "Ha!" he said, now approaching me, "let's change hands and visit this place here"; now wielding a cat-o'-nine-tails he gives me twenty cuts from the middle of my belly to the bottom of my thighs; then wrenching them apart, he slashed at the interior of the lair my position bares to his whip. "There it is," says he, "the bird I am going to pluck": several thongs having, through the precautions he had taken, penetrated very deep, I could not suppress my screams. "Well, well!" said the villain, "I must have found the sensitive area at last; steady there, calm yourself, we'll visit it a little more thoroughly"; however, his niece is put in the same posture and treated in the same manner; once again he reaches the most delicate region of a woman's body; but whether through habit, or courage, or dread of incurring treatment yet worse, she has enough strength to master herself, and about her nothing is visible beyond a few shivers and spasmodic twitchings. However, there was by now a slight change in the libertine's physical aspect, and although things were still lacking in substance, thanks to strokings and shakings a gradual improvement was being registered.

"On your knees," the monk said to me, "I am going to whip your titties."

"My titties, oh my Father!"

"Yes, those two lubricious masses which never excite me but I wish to use them thus," and upon saying this, he squeezed them, he compressed them violently.

"Oh Father! They are so delicate! You will kill me!"

"No matter, my dear, provided I am satisfied," and he applied five or six blows which, happily, I parried with my hands. Upon observing that, he binds them behind my back; nothing remains with which to implore his mercy but my countenance and my tears, for he has harshly ordered me to be silent. I strive to melt him . . . but in vain, he strikes out savagely at my now unprotected bosom; terrible bruises are immediately writ out in black and blue; blood appears as his battering continues, my suffering wrings tears from me, they fall upon the vestiges left by the monster's rage, and render them, says he, yet a thousand times more interesting . . . he kisses those marks, he devours them and now and again returns to my mouth, to my eyes whose tears he licks up with lewd delight. Armande takes her place, her hands are tied, she presents breasts of alabaster and the most beautiful roundness; Clément pretends to kiss them, but to bite them is what he wishes. . . . And then he lays on and that lovely flesh, so white, so plump, is soon nothing more in its butcher's eyes but lacerations and bleeding stripes. "Wait one moment," says the berserk monk, "I want to flog simultaneously the most beautiful of behinds and the softest of breasts." He leaves me on my knees and, bringing Armande toward me, makes her stand facing me with her legs spread, in such a way that my mouth touches her womb and my breasts are exposed between her thighs and below her behind; by this means the monk has what he wants before him: Armande's buttocks and my titties in close proximity: furiously he beats them both, but my companion, in order to spare me blows which are becoming far more dangerous for me than for her, has the goodness to lower herself and thus shield me by receiving upon her own person the lashes that would inevitably have wounded me. Clément detects the trick and separates us: "She'll gain nothing by that," he fumes, "and if today I have the graciousness to spare that part of her, 'twill only be so as to molest some other at least as delicate." As I rose I saw that all those infamies had not been in vain: the debauchee was in the most brilliant state; and it made him only the more furious; he changes weapons—opens a cabinet where several martinets are to be found and draws out one armed with iron tips. I fall to trembling. "There, Thérèse," says he showing me the martinet, "you'll see how delicious it is to be whipped with this . . . you'll feel it, you'll feel it, my rascal, but for the instant I prefer to use this other one . . ." It was composed of small knotted cords, twelve in all; at the end of each was a knot somewhat larger than the others, about the size of a plum pit. "Come there! Up! The cavalcade! . . . the cavalcade!" says he to his niece; she, knowing what is meant, quickly gets down on all fours, her rump raised as high as possible, and tells me to imitate her; I do. Clément leaps upon my back, riding facing my rear; Armande, her own presented to him, finds herself directly ahead of Clément: the villain then discovering us both well within reach, furiously cuts at the charms we offer him; but, as this position obliges us to open as wide as possible that delicate part of ourselves which distinguishes our sex from men's, the barbarian aims stinging blows in this direction: the whip's long and supple strands, penetrating into the interior with much more facility than could withes or ferules, leave deep traces of his rage; now he strikes one, now his blows fly at the other; as skilled a horseman as he is an intrepid flagellator, he several times changes his mount; we are exhausted, and the pangs of pain are of such violence that it is almost impossible to bear them any longer. "Stand up," he tells us, catching up the martinet again, "yes, get up and stand in fear of me"—his eyes glitter, foam flecks his lips—like persons distracted, we run about the room, here, there, he follows after us, indiscriminately striking Armande, myself; the villain brings us to blood; at last he traps us both between the bed and the wall: the blows are redoubled: the unhappy Armande receives one upon the breast which staggers her, this last horror determines his ecstasy, and while my back is flailed by its cruel effects, my loins are flooded by the proofs of a delirium whose results are so dangerous.

"We are going to bed," Clément finally says to me; "that has perhaps been rather too much for you, Thérèse, and certainly not enough for me; one never tires of this mania notwithstanding the fact it is a very pale image of what one should really like to do; ah, dear girl! you have no idea to what lengths this depravity leads us, you cannot imagine the drunkenness into which it plunges us, the violent commotion in the electrical fluid which results from the irritation produced by the suffering of the object that serves our passions; how one is needled by its agonies! The desire to increase them . . . 'tis, I know, the reef upon which the fantasy is doomed to wreck, but is this peril to be dreaded by him who cares not a damn for anything?"

Although Clément's mind was still in the grip of enthusiasm, I observed that his senses were much more calm, and by way of reply to what he had just said, I dared reproach him his tastes' depravation, and the manner in which this libertine justified them merits inclusion, it seems to me, amidst the confessions you wish to have from me.

"Without question the silliest thing in the world, my dear Thérèse," Clément said to me, "is to wish to dispute a man's tastes, to wish to contradict, thwart, discredit, condemn, or punish them if they do not conform either with the laws of the country he inhabits on with the prejudices of social convention. Why indeed! Will it never be understood that there is no variety of taste, however bizarre, however outlandish, however criminal it may be supposed, which does not derive directly from and depend upon the kind of organization we have individually received from Nature? That posed, I ask with what right one man will dare require another either to curb or get rid of his tastes or model them upon those of the social order? With what right will the law itself, which is created for man's happiness only, dare pursue him who cannot mend his ways, or who would succeed in altering his behavior only at the price of forgoing that happiness whose protection the law is obliged to guarantee him? Even were one to desire to change those tastes could one do so? Have we the power to remake ourselves? Can we become other than what we are? Would you demand the same thing from someone born a cripple? and is this inconformity of our tastes anything in the moral sphere but what the ill-made man's imperfection is in the physical?

"Shall we enter into details? Why, very well. The keen mind I recognize in you, Thérèse, will enable you to appreciate them. I believe you have been arrested by two irregularities you have remarked in us: you are astonished at the piquant sensation experienced by some of our friends where it is a question of matters commonly beheld as fetid or impure, and you are similarly surprised that our voluptuous faculties are susceptible of powerful excitation by actions which, in your view, bear none but the emblem of ferocity; let us analyze both these tastes and attempt, if 'tis possible, to convince you that there is nothing simpler or more normal in this world than the pleasures which are their result.

"Extraordinary, you declare, that things decayed, noisome, and filthy are able to produce upon our senses the irritation essential to precipitate their complete delirium; but before allowing oneself to be startled by this, it would be better to realize, Thérèse, that objects have no value for us save that which our imagination imparts to them; it is therefore very possible, bearing this constant truth well in mind, that not only the most curious but even the vilest and most appalling things may affect us very appreciably. The human imagination is a faculty of man's mind whereupon, through the senses' agency, objects are painted, whereby they are modified, and wherein, next, ideas become formed, all in reason of the initial glimpsing of those external objects. But this imagination, itself the result of the peculiar organization a particular individual is endowed with, only adopts the received objects in such-and-such a manner and afterward only creates ideas according to the effects produced by perceived objects' impact: let me give you a comparison to help you grasp what I am exposing. Thérèse, have you not seen those differently formed mirrors, some of which diminish objects, others of which enlarge them; some give back frightful images of things, some beautify things; do you now imagine that were each of these types of mirrors to possess both a creative and an objective faculty, they would not each give a completely different portrait of the same man who stands before them, and would not that portrait be different thanks to the manner in which each mirror had perceived the object? If to the two faculties we have just ascribed to the mirror, there were added a third of sensation, would not this man, seen by it in such-and-such a manner, be the source of that one kind of feeling the mirror would be able, indeed would be obliged, to conceive for the sort of being the mirror had perceived? The mirror sees the man as beautiful, the mirror loves the man; another mirror sees the man as frightful and hates him, and it is always the same being who produces various impressions.

"Such is the human imagination, Thérèse; the same object is represented to it under as many forms as that imagination has various facets and moods, and according to the effect upon the imagination received from whatsoever be the object, the imagination is made to love or to hate it; if the perceived object's impact strikes it in an agreeable manner, the object is loved, preferred, even if this object has nothing really attractive about it; and if the object, though of a certain high value in the eyes of someone else, has only struck in a disagreeable manner the imagination we are discussing, hostility will be the result, because not one of our sentiments is formed save in reason of what various objects produce upon the imagination; these fundamentals once grasped, should not by any means be cause for astonishment that what distinctly pleases some is able to displease others, and, conversely, that the most extraordinary thing is able to find admirers. . . . The cripple also discovers certain mirrors which make him handsome.

"Now, if we admit that the senses' joy is always dependent upon the imagination, always regulated by the imagination, one must not be amazed by the numerous variations the imagination is apt to suggest during the pleasurable episode, by the infinite multitude of different tastes and passions the imagination's various extravagances will bring to light. Luxurious though these tastes may be, they are never intrinsically strange; there is no reason to find a mealtime eccentricity more or less extraordinary than a bedroom whim; and in the one and the other, it is not more astonishing to idolize what the common run of mankind holds detestable than it is to love something generally recognized as pleasant. To like what others like proves organic conformity, but demonstrates nothing in favor of the beloved object. Three-quarters of the universe may find the rose's scent delicious without that serving either as evidence upon which to condemn the remaining quarter which might find the smell offensive, or as proof that this odor is truly agreeable.

"If then in this world there exist persons whose tastes conflict with accepted prejudices, not only must one not be surprised by the fact, not only must one not scold these dissenters or punish them, but one must aid them, procure them contentment, remove obstacles which impede them, and afford them, if you wish to be just, all the means to satisfy themselves without risk; because they are no more responsible for having this curious taste than you are responsible for being live-spirited or dull-witted, prettily made or knock-kneed. It is in the mother's womb that there are fashioned the organs which must render us susceptible of such-and-such a fantasy; the first objects which we encounter, the first conversations we overhear determine the pattern; once tastes are formed nothing in the world can destroy them. Do what it will, education is incapable of altering the pattern, and he who has got to be a villain just as surely becomes a villain, the good education you give him notwithstanding; quite as he, however much he has lacked good example, flies unerringly toward virtue if his organs dispose him to the doing of good. Both have acted in accordance with their organic structure, in accordance with the impressions they have received from Nature, and the one is no more deserving of punishment than the other is of reward.

"Curiously enough, so long as it is merely a question of trifles, we are never in the least astonished by the differences existing among tastes; but let the subject take on an erotic tincture, and listen to the word spread about! rumors fly, women, always thoughtful of guarding their rights—women whose feebleness and inconsequence make them especially prone to seeing enemies everywhere about—, women, I say, are all constantly trembling and quivering lest something be snatched away from them and if, when taking one's pleasure, one unfortunately puts practices to use which conflict with woman-worship, lo! there you have crimes which merit the noose. And what an injustice! Must sensual pleasure render a man better than life's other pleasures? In one word, must our penchants be any more concentrated upon the temple of generation, must it necessarily more certainly awaken our desires, than some other part of the body either the most contrary to or at the furthest remove from it? than some emanation of the body either the most fetid or the most disgusting? It should not, in my opinion, appear any more astonishing to see a man introduce singularity into his libertine pleasures than it should appear strange to see him employ the uncommon in any other of life's activities. Once again, in either case, his singularity is the result of his organs: is it his fault if what affects you is naught to him, or if he is only moved by what repels you? What living man would not instantly revise his tastes, his affections, his penchants and bring them into harmony with the general scheme, what man, rather than continue a freak, would not prefer to be like everyone else, were it in his power to do so? It is the most barbarous and most stupid intolerance to wish to fly at such a man's throat; he is no more guilty toward society, regardless of what may be his extravagances, than is, as I have just said, the person who came blind and lame into the world. And it would be quite as unjust to punish or deride the latter as to afflict or berate the other. The man endowed with uncommon tastes is sick; if you prefer, he is like a woman subject to hysterical vapors. Has the idea to punish such a person ever occurred to us? let us be equally fair when dealing with the man whose caprices startle us; perfectly like unto the ill man or the woman suffering from vapors, he is deserving of sympathy and not of blame; that is the moral apology for the persons whom we are discussing; a physical explanation will without doubt be found as easily, and when the study of anatomy reaches perfection they will without any trouble be able to demonstrate the relationship of the human constitution to the tastes which it affects. Ah, you pedants, hangmen, turnkeys, lawmakers, you shavepate rabble, what will you do when we have arrived there? what is to become of your laws, your ethics, your religion, your gallows, your Gods and your Heavens and your Hell when it shall be proven that such a flow of liquids, this variety of fibers, that degree of pungency in the blood or in the animal spirits are sufficient to make a man the object of your givings and your takings away? We continue. Cruel tastes astonish you.

"What is the aim of the man who seeks his joy? is it not to give his senses all the irritation of which they are susceptible in order, by this means, better and more warmly to reach the ultimate crisis . . . the precious crisis which characterizes the enjoyment as good or bad, depending upon the greater or lesser activity which occurs during the crisis? Well, is one not guilty of an untenable sophistry when one dares affirm it is necessary, in order to ameliorate it, that it be shared with the woman? Is it not plain enough that the woman can share nothing with us without taking something from us? and that all she makes away with must necessarily be had by her at our expense? And what then is this necessity, I ask, that a woman enjoy herself when we are enjoying ourselves? in this arrangement is there any sentiment but pride which may be flattered? and does one not savor this proud feeling in a far more piquant manner when, on the contrary, one harshly constrains this woman to abandon her quest for pleasure and to devote herself to making you alone feel it? Does not tyranny flatter the pride in a far more lively way than does beneficence? In one word, is not he who imposes much more surely the master than he who shares? But how could it ever have entered a reasonable man's head that delicacy is of any value during enjoyment? 'Tis absurd, to maintain it is necessary at such a time; it never adds anything to the pleasure of the senses, why, I contend that it detracts therefrom. To love and to enjoy are two very different things: the proof whereof is that one loves every day without enjoying, and that even more often one enjoys without loving. Anything by way of consideration for the woman one stirs into the broth has got to dilute its strength and impair its flavor for the man; so long as the latter spends his time giving enjoyment, he assuredly does not himself do any enjoying, or his enjoyment is merely intellectual, that is to say, chimerical and far inferior to sensual enjoyment. No, Thérèse, no, I will not cease repeating it, there is absolutely no necessity that, in order to be keen, an enjoyment must be shared; and in order that this kind of pleasure may be rendered piquant to the utmost, it is, on the contrary, very essential that the man never take his pleasure save at the expense of the woman, that he take from her (without regard for the sensation she may experience thereby) everything which may in any way improve or increase the voluptuous exercise he wants to relish, and this without the slightest concern for whatever may be the effects of all this upon the woman, for preoccupation of that sort will prove bothersome to him; he either wants the woman to partake of pleasure, and thereupon his joys are at an end; or he fears lest she will suffer, and he is hurled into confusion, all's brought to a stop. If egoism is Nature's fundamental commandment, it is very surely most of all during our lubricious delights that this celestial Mother desires us to be most absolutely under its rule; why, it's a very small evil, is it not, that, in the interests of the augmentation of the man's lecherous delights he has got either to neglect or upset the woman's; for if this upsetting of her pleasure causes him to gain any, what is lost to the object which serves him affects him in no wise, save profitably: it must be a matter of indifference to him whether that object is happy or unhappy, provided it be delectable to him; in truth, there is no relation at all between that object and himself. He would hence be a fool to trouble himself about the object's sensations and forget his own; he would be entirely mad if, in order to modify those sensations foreign to him, he were to renounce improvement of his. That much established, if the individual in question is, unhappily, organized in such a fashion he cannot be stirred save by producing painful sensations in the object employed, you will admit he is forced to go ruthlessly to work, since the point of it all is to have the best possible time, the consequences for the object being entirely excluded from consideration. . . . We will return to the problem; let us continue in an orderly fashion.

"Isolated enjoyment therefore has its charms, it may therefore have more of them than all other kinds; why! if it were not so, how should the aged and so many deformed or defective persons be able to enjoy themselves? for they know full well they are not loved nor lovable; perfectly certain it is impossible to share what they experience, is their joy any the less powerful on that account? Do they desire even the illusion? Behaving with utter selfishness in their riots, you will observe them seeking pleasure, you will see them sacrifice everything to obtain it, and in the object they put to use never other than passive properties. Therefore, it is in no wise necessary to give pleasures in order to receive them; the happy or unhappy situation of the victim of our debauch is, therefore, absolutely as one from the point of view of our senses, there is never any question of the state in which his heart or mind may be; it matters not one whit, the object may be pleased by what you do to it, the object may suffer, it may love or detest you: all these considerations are nullified immediately it is only a question of your sensation. Women, I concede, may establish contrary theories, but women, who are nothing but machines designed for voluptuousness, who ought to be nothing but the targets of lust, are untrustworthy authorities whenever one has got to construct an authentic doctrine upon this kind of pleasure. Is there a single reasonable man who is eager to have a whore partake of his joy? And, however, are there not millions of men who amuse themselves hugely with these creatures? Well, there you have that many individuals convinced of what I am urging, who unhesitatingly put it into practice, and who scorn those who use good principles to legitimate their deeds, those ridiculous fools, the world is stuffed to overflowing with them, who go and come, who do this and that, who eat, who digest, without ever sensing a thing.

"Having proven that solitary pleasures are as delicious as any others and much more likely to delight, it becomes perfectly clear that this enjoyment, taken in independence of the object we employ, is not merely of a nature very remote from what could be pleasurable to that object, but is even found to be inimical to that object's pleasure: what is more, it may become an imposed suffering, a vexation, or a torture, and the only thing that results from this abuse is a very certain increase of pleasure for the despot who does the tormenting or vexing; let us attempt to demonstrate this.

"Voluptuous emotion is nothing but a kind of vibration produced in our soul by shocks which the imagination, inflamed by the remembrance of a lubricious object, registers upon our senses, either through this object's presence, or better still by this object's being exposed to that particular kind of irritation which most profoundly stirs us; thus, our voluptuous transport—this indescribable convulsive needling which drives us wild, which lifts us to the highest pitch of happiness at which man is able to arrive—is never ignited save by two causes: either by the perception in the object we use of a real or imaginary beauty, the beauty in which we delight the most, or by the sight of that object undergoing the strongest possible sensation; now, there is no more lively sensation than that of pain; its impressions are certain and dependable, they never deceive as may those of the pleasure women perpetually feign and almost never experience; and, furthermore, how much self-confidence, youth, vigor, health are not needed in order to be sure of producing this dubious and hardly very satisfying impression of pleasure in a woman. To produce the painful impression, on the contrary, requires no virtues at all: the more defects a man may have, the older he is, the less lovable, the more resounding his success. With what regards the objective, it will be far more certainly attained since we are establishing the fact that one never better touches, I wish to say, that one never better irritates one's senses than when the greatest possible impression has been produced in the employed object, by no matter what devices; therefore, he who will cause the most tumultuous impression to be born in a woman, he who will most thoroughly convulse this woman's entire frame, very decidedly will have managed to procure himself the heaviest possible dose of voluptuousness, because the shock resultant upon us by the impressions others experience, which shock in turn is necessitated by the impression we have of those others, will necessarily be more vigorous if the impression these others receive be painful, than if the impression they receive be sweet and mild; and it follows that the voluptuous egoist, who is persuaded his pleasures will be keen only insofar as they are entire, will therefore impose, when he has it in his power to do so, the strongest possible dose of pain upon the employed object, fully certain that what by way of voluptuous pleasure he extracts will be his only by dint of the very lively impression he has produced."

"Oh, Father," I said to Clément, "these doctrines are dreadful, they lead to the cultivation of cruel tastes, horrible tastes."

"Why, what does it matter?" demanded the barbarian; "and, once again, have we any control over our tastes? Must we not yield to the dominion of those Nature has inserted in us as when before the tempest's force the proud oak bends its head? Were Nature offended by these proclivities, she would not have inspired them in us; that we can receive from her hands a sentiment such as would outrage her is impossible, and, extremely certain of this, we can give ourselves up to our passions, whatever their sort and of whatever their violence, wholly sure that all the discomfitures their shock may occasion are naught but the designs of Nature, of whom we are the involuntary instruments. And what to us are these passions' consequences? When one wishes to delight in any action whatsoever, there is never any question of consequences."

"I am not speaking to you of consequences," I put in abruptly, "but of the thing itself; if indeed you are the stronger and if through atrocious principles of cruelty you love to take your pleasure only by means of causing suffering with the intention of augmenting your sensations, you will gradually come to the point of producing them with such a degree of violence that you will certainly risk killing the employed object."

"So be it; that is to say that, by means of tastes given me by Nature, I shall have carried out the intentions of Nature who, never affecting her creations save through destructions, never inspires the thought of the latter in me save when she is in need of the former; that is to say that from an oblong portion of matter I shall have formed three or four thousand round or square ones. Oh Thérèse, is there any crime here? Is this the name with which to designate what serves Nature? Is it in man's power to commit crimes? And when, preferring his own happiness to that of others, he overthrows or destroys whatever he finds in his path, has he done anything but serve Nature whose primary and most imperious inspirations enjoin him to pursue his happiness at no matter whose expense? The doctrine of brotherly love is a fiction we owe to Christianity and not to Nature; the exponent of the Nazarene's cult, tormented, wretched and consequently in an enfeebled state which prompted him to cry out for tolerance and compassion, had no choice but to allege this fabulous relationship between one person and another; by gaining acceptance for the notion he was able to save his life. But the philosopher does not acknowledge these gigantic rapports; to his consideration, he is alone in the universe, he judges everything subjectively, he only is of importance. If he is thoughtful of or caresses another for one instant, it is never but in strait connection with what profit he thinks to draw from the business; when he is no longer in need of others, when he can forcefully assert his empire, he then abjures forever those pretty humanitarian doctrines of doing good deeds to which he only submitted himself for reasons of policy; he no longer fears to be selfish, to reduce everyone about him, and he sates his appetites without inquiring to know what his enjoyments may cost others, and without remorse."

"But the man you describe is a monster."

"The man I describe is in tune with Nature."

"He is a savage beast."

"Why, is not the tiger or the leopard, of whom this man is, if you wish, a replica, like man created by Nature and created to prosecute Nature's intentions? The wolf who devours the lamb accomplishes what this common mother designs, just as does the malefactor who destroys the object of his revenge or his lubricity."

"Oh, Father, say what you will, I shall never accept this destructive lubricity."

"Because you are afraid of becoming its object—there you have it: egoism. Let's exchange our roles and you will fancy it very nicely. Ask the lamb, and you will find he does not understand why the wolf is allowed to devour him; ask the wolf what the lamb is for: to feed me, he will reply. Wolves which batten upon lambs, lambs consumed by wolves, the strong who immolate the weak, the weak victims of the strong: there you have Nature, there you have her intentions, there you have her scheme: a perpetual action and reaction, a host of vices, a host of virtues, in one word, a perfect equilibrium resulting from the equality of good and evil on earth; the equilibrium essential to the maintenance of the stars, of vegetation and, lacking which, everything would be instantly in ruins. O

Thérèse, mightily astonished she would be, this Nature, were she to be able to converse with us for a moment and were we to tell her that these crimes which serve her, these atrocities she demands and inspires in us are punished by laws they assure us are made in imitation of hers. 'Idiots' she would reply to us, 'sleep, eat, and fearlessly commit whatever crimes you like whenever you like: every one of those alleged infamies pleases me, and I would have them all, since it is I who inspire them in you. It is within your province to regulate what annoys me and what delights, indeed! be advised that there is nothing in you which is not my own, nothing I did not place in you for reasons it is not fitting you be acquainted with; know that the most abominable of your deeds is, like the most virtuous of some other, but one of the manners of serving me. So do not restrain yourself, flout your laws, a fig for your social conventions and your Gods; listen to me and to none other, and believe that if there exists a crime to be committed against me it is the resistance you oppose, in the forms of stubbornness or casuistries, to what I inspire in you.' "

"Oh, Just Heaven!" I cried, "you make me shudder! Were there no crimes against Nature, whence would come that insurmountable loathing we experience for certain misdeeds?"

"That loathing is not dictated by Nature," the villain replied with feeling, "its one source is in the total lack of habit; does not the same hold true for certain foods? Although they are excellent, is not our repugnance merely caused by our being unaccustomed to them? would you dare say, upon the basis of your prejudices or ignorance, that they are good or bad? If we make the effort, we will soon become convinced and will find they suit our palate; we have a hostility toward medicaments, do we not, although they are salutary; in the same fashion, let us accustom ourselves to evil and it will not be long before we find it charming; this momentary revulsion is certainly a shrewdness, a kind of coquetry on the part of Nature, rather than a warning that the thing outrages her: thus she prepares the pleasures of our triumph; she even manages thus to augment those of the deed itself: better still, Thérèse, better still: the more the deed seems appalling to us, the more it is in contradiction with our manners and customs, the more it runs headlong against restraints and shatters them, the more it conflicts with social conventions and affronts them, the more it clashes with what we mistake for Nature's laws, then the more, on the contrary, it is useful to this same Nature. It is never but by way of crimes that she regains possession of the rights Virtue incessantly steals away from her. If the crime is slight, if it is at no great variance with Virtue, its weight will be less in re-establishing the balance indispensable to Nature; but the more capital the crime, the more deadly, the more it dresses the scales and the better it offsets the influence of Virtue which, without this, would destroy everything. Let him then cease to be in a fright, he who meditates a crime or he who has just committed one: the vaster his crime, the better it will serve Nature."

These frightful theories soon led me to think of Omphale's doubts upon the manner in which we left the terrible house we were in. And it was then I conceived the plans you will see me execute in the sequel. However, to complete my enlightenment I could not prevent myself from putting yet a few more questions to Father Clément.

"But surely," I said, "you do not keep your passions' unhappy victims forever; you surely send them away when you are wearied of them?"

"Certainly, Thérèse," the monk replied; "you only entered this establishment in order to leave it when the four of us agree to grant your retirement. Which will most certainly be granted."

"But do you not fear," I continued, "lest the younger and less discreet girls sometimes go and reveal what is done here?"

" 'Tis impossible."

"Impossible?"

"Absolutely."

"Could you explain . . ."

"No, that's our secret, but I can assure you of this much: that whether you are discreet or indiscreet, you will find it perfectly impossible ever to say a word about what is done here when you are here no longer. And thus you see, Thérèse, I recommend no discretion to you, just as my own desires are governed by no restraining policy. . . ."

And, having uttterd these words, the monk fell asleep. From that moment onward, I could no longer avoid realizing that the most violent measures were used with those unhappy ones of us who were retrenched and that this terrible security they boasted of was only the fruit of our death. I was only the more confirmed in my resolve; we will soon see its effect.

As soon as Clément was asleep, Armande came near to me.

"He will awake shortly," she said; "he will behave like a madman: Nature only puts his senses to sleep in order to give them, after a little rest, a much greater energy; one more scene and we will have peace until tomorrow."

"But you," I said to my companion, "aren't you going to sleep a little while?"

"How can I?" Armande replied, "when, were I not to remain awake and standing by his side, and were my negligence to be perceived, he would be the man to stab me to death."

"O Heaven!" I sighed, "why! even as he sleeps the villain would that those around him remain in a state of suffering!"

"Yes," my companion responded, "it is the very barbarity of the idea which procures the furious awakening you are going to witness; upon this he is like unto those perverse writers whose corruption is so dangerous, so active, that their single aim is, by causing their appalling doctrines to be printed, to immortalize the sum of their crimes after their own lives are at an end; they themselves can do no more, but their accursed writings will instigate the commission of crimes, and they carry this sweet idea with them to their graves: it comforts them for the obligation, enjoined by death, to relinquish the doing of evil."

"The monsters!" I cried. . . .

Armande, who was a very gentle creature, kissed me as she shed a few tears, then went back to pacing about the roué's bed.

Two hours passed and then the monk did indeed awake in a prodigious agitation and seized me with such force I thought he was going to strangle me; his respiration was quick and labored, his eyes glittered, he uttered incoherent words which were exclusively blasphemous or libertine expressions; he summoned Armande, called for whips, and started in again with his flogging of us both, but in a yet more vigorous manner than before having gone to sleep. It seemed as if he wished to end matters with me; shrill cries burst from his mouth; to abridge my sufferings, Armande excited him violently, he lost his head entirely, and finally made rigid by the most violent sensations, the monster lost both his ardor and his desires together with smoking floods of semen.

Nothing transpired during the rest of the night; upon getting up, the monk was content to touch and examine each of us; and as he was going to say Mass, we returned to the seraglio. The superintendent could not be prevented from desiring me in the inflamed state she swore I must be in; exhausted I indeed was and, thus weakened, how could I defend myself? She did all she wished, enough to convince me that even a woman, in such a school, soon losing all the delicacy and restraint native to her sex, could only, after those tyrants' example, become obscene and cruel.

Two nights later, I slept with Jérôme; I will not describe his horrors to you; they were still more terrifying. What an academy, great God! by week's end I had finally made the circuit, and then Omphale asked me whether it were not true that of them all, Clément was the one about whom I had the most to complain.

"Alas!" was my response, "in the midst of a crowd of horrors and messes of filth which now disgust and now revolt, it is very difficult to pronounce upon these villains' individual odiousness; I am mortally weary of them all and would that I were gone from here, whatever be the fate that awaits me."

"It might be possible that you will soon be satisfied," my companion answered; "we are nearing the period of the festival: this circumstance rarely takes place without bringing them victims; they either seduce girls by means of the confessional, or, if they can, they cause them to disappear: which means so many new recruits, each of whom always supposes a retrenchment."

The famous holiday arrived . . . will you be able to believe, Madame, what monstrous impieties the monks were guilty of during this event! They fancied a visible miracle would double the brilliance of their reputation; and so they dressed Florette, the youngest of the girls, in all the Virgin's attire and adornments; by means of concealed strings they tied her against the wall of the niche and ordered her to elevate her arms very suddenly and with compunction toward heaven simultaneously the host was raised. As the little creature was threatened with the cruelest chastising if she were to speak a single word or mismanage in her role, she carried it off marvelously well, and the fraud enjoyed all the success that could possibly have been expected. The people cried aloud the miracle, left rich offerings to the Virgin, and went home more convinced than ever of the efficacity of the celestial Mother's mercies. In order to increase their impiety, our libertines wanted to have Florette appear at the orgies that evening, dressed in the same costume that had attracted so many homages, and each one inflamed his odious desires to submit her, in this guise, to the irregularity of his caprices. Aroused by this initial crime, the sacrilegious ones go considerably further: they have the child stripped naked, they have her lie on her stomach upon a large table; they light candles, they place the image of our Saviour squarely upon the little girl's back and upon her buttocks they dare consummate the most redoubtable of our mysteries. I swooned away at this horrible spectacle, 'twas impossible to bear the sight. Séverino, seeing me unconscious, says that, to bring me to heel, I must serve as the altar in my turn. I am seized; I am placed where Florette was lying; the sacrifice is consummated, and the host . . . that sacred symbol of our august Religion . . . Séverino catches it up and thrusts it deep into the obscene locale of his sodomistic pleasures . . . crushes it with oaths and insults . . . ignominiously drives it further with the intensified blows of his monstrous dart and as he blasphemes, spurts, upon our Saviour's very Body, the impure floods of his lubricity's torrents. . . .

I was insensible when they drew me from his hands; I had to be carried to my room, where for a week I shed uninterrupted tears over the hideous crime for which, against my will, I had been employed. The memory still gnaws at my soul, I never think back upon that scene without shuddering. . . . In me, Religion is the effect of sentiment; all that offends or outrages it makes my very heart bleed.

The end of the month was close at hand when one morning toward nine Séverino entered our chamber; he appeared greatly aroused; a certain crazed look hovered in his eyes; he examines us, one after the other, places us in his cherished attitude, and especially lingers over Omphale; for several minutes he stands, contemplating her in the posture she has assumed, he excites himself, mutters dully, secretly, kisses what is offered him, allows everyone to see he is in a state to consummate, and consummates nothing;

next, he has her straighten up, casts upon her glances filled with
rage and wickedness; then, swinging his foot, with all his strength
he kicks her in the belly, she reels backward and falls six yards
away.

"The company is retrenching you, whore," he says, "we are
tired of you, be ready by this afternoon. I will come to fetch you
myself." And he leaves.

When he is gone Omphale gets up and, weeping, casts herself
into my arms.

"Ah!" she says, "by the infamy, by the cruelty of the preliminaries . . . can you still blind yourself as to what follows? Great
God! what is to become of me?"

"Be easy," I say to the miserable girl, "I have made up my
mind about everything; I only await the opportunity; it may perhaps present itself sooner than you think; I will divulge these
horrors; if it is true the measures they take are as cruel as we have
reason to believe, strive to obtain some delays, postpone it, and I
will wrest you from their clutches."

In the event Omphale were to be released, she swore in the
same way to aid me, and both of us fell to weeping. The day passed,
nothing happened during it; at five o'clock Séverino returned.

"Well," he asked Omphale, "are you ready?"

"Yes, Father," she answered between sobs, "permit me to
embrace my friends."

" 'Tis useless," replied the monk; "we have no time for lachry-
mose scenes; they are waiting for us; come." Then she asked
whether she were obliged to take her belongings with her.

"No," said the superior; "does not everything belong to the
house? You have no further need of any of it"; then, checking
himself, as might one who has said too much:

"Those old clothes have become useless; you will have some
cut to fit your size, they will be more becoming to you; be content
to take along only what you are wearing."

I asked the monk whether I might be allowed to accompany
Omphale to the door of the house; his reply was a glance that made
me recoil in terror. . . . Omphale goes out, she turns toward us
eyes filled with uneasiness and tears, and the minute she is gone I
fling myself down upon the bed, desperate.

Accustomed to these occurrences or blind to their significance, my companions were less affected by Omphale's departure than I; the superior returned an hour later to lead away the supper's girls of whom I was one—we were only four: the girl of twelve, she of sixteen, she of twenty-three, and me. Everything went more or less as upon other days; I only noticed that the Girls of the Watch were not on hand, that the monks often whispered in each other's ears, that they drank much, that they limited themselves violently to exciting desires they did not once consummate, and that they sent us away at an early hour without retaining any of us for their own beds. . . . I deduced what I could from what I observed, because, under such circumstances, one keeps a sharp eye upon everything, but what did this evidence augur? Ah, such was my perplexity that no clear idea presented itself to my mind but it was not immediately offset by another; recollecting Clément's words, I felt there was everything to fear . . . of course; but then, hope . . . that treacherous hope which comforts us, which blinds us, and which thus does us almost as much ill as good . . . hope finally surged up to reassure me. . . . Such a quantity of horrors were so alien to me that I was simply unable to conceive of them. In this terrible state of confusion, I lay down in bed; now I was persuaded Omphale would not fail to keep her word; and the next instant I was convinced the cruel devices they would use against her would deprive her of all power to help us, and that was my final opinion when I saw an end come to the third day of having heard nothing at all.

Upon the fourth I found myself again called to supper; the company was numerous and select: the eight most beautiful women were there that evening, I had been paid the honor of being included amongst them; the Girls of the Watch attended too. Immediately we entered we caught sight of our new companion.

"Here is the young lady the corporation has destined to replace Omphale, Mesdemoiselles," said Sévérino.

And as the words escaped his lips he tore away the mantlets and lawn which covered the girl's bust, and we beheld a maiden of fifteen, with the most agreeable and delicate face: she raised her lovely eyes and graciously regarded each of us; those eyes were still moist with tears, but they contained the liveliest expression; her figure was supple and light, her skin of a dazzling whiteness, she had the world's most beautiful hair, and there was something so seductive about the whole that it was impossible not to feel oneself automatically drawn to her. Her name was Octavie; we were soon informed she was a girl of the highest quality, born in Paris, and had just emerged from a convent in order to wed the Comte de * * *: she had been kidnaped while en route in the company of two governesses and three lackeys; she did not know what had become of her retinue; it had been toward nightfall and she alone had been taken; after having been blindfolded, she had been brought to where we were and it had not been possible to know more of the matter.

As yet no one had spoken a word to her. Our libertine quartet, confronted by so much charm, knew an instant of ecstasy; they had only the strength to admire her. Beauty's dominion commands respect; despite his heartlessness, the most corrupt villain must bow before it or else suffer the stings of an obscure remorse; but monsters of the breed with which we had to cope do not long languish under such restraints.

"Come, pretty child," quoth the superior, impudently drawing her toward the chair in which he was settled, "come hither and let's have a look to see whether the rest of your charms match those Nature has so profusely distributed in your countenance."

And as the lovely girl was sore troubled, as she flushed crimson and strove to fend him off, Séverino grasped her rudely round the waist.

"Understand, my artless one," he said, "understand that what I want to tell you is simply this: get undressed. Strip. Instantly."

And thereupon the libertine slid one hand beneath her skirts while he grasped her with the other. Clément approached, he raised Octavie's clothes to above her waist and by this maneuver exposed the softest, the most appetizing features it is possible anywhere to find; Séverino touches, perceives nothing, bends to scrutinize more narrowly, and all four agree they have never seen anything as beautiful. However, the modest Octavie, little accustomed to usage of this sort, gushes tears, and struggles.

"Undress, undress," cries Antonin, "we can't see a thing this way."

He assists Séverino and in a trice we have displayed to us all the maiden's unadorned charms. Never, without any doubt, was there a fairer skin, never were there more happily modeled forms. . . . God! the crime of it! . . . So many beauties, such chaste freshness, so much innocence and daintiness—all to become prey to these barbarians! Covered with shame, Octavie knows not where to fly to hide her charms, she finds naught but hungering eyes everywhere about, nothing but brutal hands which sully those treasures; the circle closes around her, and, as did I, she rushes hither and thither; the savage Antonin lacks the strength to resist; a cruel attack determines the homage, and the incense smokes at the goddess' feet. Jérôme compares her to our young colleague of sixteen, doubtless the seraglio's prettiest; he places the two altars of his devotion one next to the other.

"Ha! what whiteness! what grace!" says he as he fingers Octavie, "but what gentility and freshness may be discerned in this other one: indeed," continues the monk all afire, "I am uncertain"; then imprinting his mouth upon the charms his eyes behold, "Octavie," he cries, "to you the apple, it belongs to none but you, give me the precious fruit of this tree my heart adores. . . . Ah, yes! yes, one of you, give it me, and I will forever assure beauty's prize to who serves me sooner."

Sévérino observes the time has come to meditate on more serious matters; absolutely in no condition to be kept waiting, he lays hands upon the unlucky child, places her as he desires her to be; not yet being able to have full confidence in Octavie's aid, he calls for Clément to lend him a hand. Octavie weeps and weeps unheeded; fire gleams in the impudicious monk's glance; master of the terrain, one might say he casts about a roving eye only to consider the avenues whereby he may launch the fiercest assault; no ruses, no preparations are employed; will he be able to gather these so charming roses? will he be able to battle past the thorns? Whatever the enormous disproportion between the conquest and the assailant, the latter is not the less in a sweat to give fight; a piercing cry announces victory, but nothing mollifies the enemy's chilly heart; the more the captive implores mercy, the less quarter is granted her, the more vigorously she is pressed; the ill-starred one fences in vain: she is soon transpierced.

"Never was laurel with greater difficulty won," says Sévérino, retreating, "I thought indeed that for the first time in my life I would fall before the gate . . . ah! 'twas never so narrow, that way, nor so hot; 'tis the God's own Ganymede."

"I had better bring her round to the sex you have just soiled," cries Antonin, seizing Octavie where she is, and not wishing to let her stand up; "there's more than one breach to a rampart," says he, and proudly, boldly marching up, he carries the day and is within the sanctuary in no time at all. Further screams are heard.

"Praise be to God," quoth the indecent man, "I thought I was alone; and would have doubted of my success without a groan or two from the victim; but my triumph is sealed. Do you observe? Blood and tears."

"In truth," says Clément, who steps up with whip in hand, "I'll not disturb her sweet posture either, it is too favorable to my desires." Jérôme's Girl of the Watch and the twenty-year-old girl hold Octavie: Clément considers, fingers; terrified, the little girl beseeches him, and is not listened to.

"Ah, my friends!" says the exalted monk, "how are we to avoid flogging a schoolgirl who exhibits an ass of such splendor!"

The air immediately resounds to the whistle of lashes and the thud of stripes sinking into lovely flesh; Octavie's screams mingle with the sounds of leather, the monk's curses reply: what a scene for these libertines surrendering themselves to a thousand obscenities in the midst of us all! They applaud him, they cheer him on; however, Octavie's skin changes color, the brightest tints incarnadine join the lily sparkle; but what might perhaps divert Love for an instant, were moderation to have direction of the sacrifice, becomes, thanks to severity, a frightful crime against Love's laws; nothing stops or slows the perfidious monk, the more the young student complains, the more the professor's harshness explodes; from the back to the knee, everything is treated in the same way, and it is at last upon his barbaric pleasures' blood-drenched vestiges the savage quenches his flames.

"I shall be less impolite, I think," says Jérôme, laying hands upon the lovely thing and adjusting himself between her coral lips; "where is the temple where I would sacrifice? Why, in this enchanting mouth. . . ."

I fall silent. . . . 'Tis the impure reptile withering the rose—my figure of speech relates it all.

The rest of the *soirée* would have resembled all the others had it not been for the beauty and the touching age of this young maiden who more than usually inflamed those villains and caused them to multiply their infamies; it was satiety rather than commiseration that sent the unhappy child back to her room and gave her, for a few hours at least, the rest and quiet she needed.

I should indeed have liked to have been able to comfort her that first night, but, obliged to spend it with Séverino, it may well have been I on the contrary who stood in the greater need of help, for I had the misfortune, no, not to please, the word would not be suitable, no, but in a most lively manner to excite that sodomite's infamous passions; at this period he desired me almost every night; being exhausted on this particular one, he conducted some researches; doubtless afraid the appalling sword with which he was endowed would not cause me an adequate amount of pain, he fancied, this time, he might perforate me with one of those articles of furniture usually found in nunneries, which decency forbids me from naming and which was of an exorbitant thickness; here, one was obliged to be ready for anything. He himself made the weapon penetrate into his beloved shrine; thanks to powerful blows, it was driven very deep; I screamed; the monk was amused, after a few backward and forward passes, he suddenly snapped the instrument free and plunged his own into the gulf he had just dug open . . . what whimsy! Is that not positively the contrary of everything men are able to desire! But who can define the spirit of libertinage? For a long time we have realized this to be an enigma of Nature; she has not yet pronounced the magic word.

In the morning, feeling somewhat renewed, he wanted to try out another torture: he produced a far more massy machine: this one was hollow and fitted with a high-pressure pump that squirted an incredibly powerful stream of water through an orifice which gave the jet a circumference of over three inches; the enormous instrument itself was nine inches around by twelve long. Séverino loaded it with steaming hot water and prepared to bury it in my front end; terrified by such a project, I throw myself at his knees to ask for mercy, but he is in one of those accursed situations where pity cannot be heard, where far more eloquent passions stifle it and substitute an often exceedingly dangerous cruelty. The monk threatens me with all his rage if I do not acquiesce; I have to obey. The perfidious machine penetrates to the two-thirds mark and the tearing it causes combined with its extreme heat are about to deprive me of the use of my senses; meanwhile, the superior, showering an uninterrupted stream of invectives upon the parts he is molesting, has himself excited by his follower; after fifteen minutes of rubbing which lacerates me, he releases the spring, a quart of nearly boiling water is fired into the last depths of my womb . . . I fall into a faint. Séverino was in an ecstasy . . . he was in a delirium at least the equal of my agony.

"Why," said the traitor, "that's nothing at all. When I recover my wits, we'll treat those charms much more harshly . . . a salad of thorns, by Jesus! well peppered, a copious admixture of vinegar, all that tamped in with the point of a knife, that's what they need to buck them up; the next mistake you make, I condemn you to the treatment," said the villain while he continued to handle the object of his worship; but two or three homages after the preceeding night's debauches had near worked him to death, and I was sent packing.

Upon returning to my chamber I found my new companion in tears; I did what I could to soothe her, but it is not easy to adjust to so frightful a change of situation; this girl had, furthermore, a great fund of religious feeling, of virtue, and of sensitivity; owing to it, her state only appeared to her the more terrible. Omphale had been right when she told me seniority in no way influenced retirement; that, simply by the monks' caprice, or by their fear of ulterior inquiries, one could undergo dismissal at the end of a week as easily as at the end of twenty years. Octavie had not been with us four months when Jérôme came to announce her departure; although 'twas he who had most enjoyed her during her sojourn at the monastery, he who had seemed to cherish her and seek her more than any other, the poor child left, making us the same promises Omphale had given; she kept them just as poorly.

From that moment on, my every thought was bent upon the plan I had been devising since Omphale's departure; determined to do everything possible to escape from this den of savages, nothing that might help me succeed held any terrors for me. What was there to dread by putting my scheme into execution? Death. And were I to remain, of what could I be certain? Of death. And successful flight would save me; there could be no hesitation for there was no alternative; but it were necessary that, before I launched my enterprise, fatal examples of vice rewarded be yet again reproduced before my eyes; it was inscribed in the great book of fate, in that obscure tome whereof no mortal has intelligence, 'twas set down there, I say, that upon all those who had tormented me, humiliated me, bound me in iron chains, there were to be heaped unceasing bounties and rewards for what they had done with regard to me, as if Providence had assumed the task of demonstrating to me the inutility of virtue. . . . Baleful lessons which however did not correct me, no, I wavered not; lessons which, should I once again escape from the blade poised above my head, will not prevent me from forever remaining the slave of my heart's Divinity.

One morning, quite unexpectedly, Antonin appeared in our chamber and announced that the Reverend Father Sévérino, allied to the Pope and his protégé, had just been named General of the Benedictine Order by His Holiness. The next day that monk did in effect depart, without taking his leave of us; 'twas said another was expected to replace him, and he would be far superior in debauch to all who remained; additional reasons to hasten ahead with my plans.

The day following Sévérino's departure, the monks decided to retrench one more of my companions; I chose for my escape the very day when sentence was pronounced against the wretched girl, so that the monks, preoccupied with her, would pay less attention to me.

It was the beginning of spring; the length of the nights still somewhat favored my designs: for two months I had been preparing them, they were completely unsuspected; little by little I sawed through the bars over my window, using a dull pair of scissors I had found; my head could already pass through the hole; with sheets and linen I had made a cord of more than sufficient length to carry me down the twenty or twenty-five feet Omphale had told me was the building's height. When they had taken my old belongings, I had been careful, as I told you, to remove my little fortune which came to about six *louis,* and these I had always kept hidden with extreme caution; as I left, I put them into my hair, and nearly all of our chamber having left for that night's supper, finding no one about but one of my companions who had gone to bed as soon as the others had descended, I entered my cabinet; there, clearing the hole I had scrupulously kept covered at all times, I knotted my cord to one of the undamaged bars, then, sliding down outside, I soon touched the ground—'twas not this part which troubled me: the six enclosures of stone and trees my companion had mentioned were what intrigued me far more.

Once there, I discovered that each concentric space between one barrier and the next was no more than eight feet wide, and it was this proximity which assured a casual glance that there was nothing in the area but a dense cluster of trees. The night was very dark; as I turned round the first alley to discover where I might not find a gap in the palisade, I passed beneath the dining hall, which seemed deserted; my inquietude increased; however, I continued my search and thus at last came abreast the window to the main underground room, located directly below that in which the orgies were staged. Much light flooded from the basement, I was bold enough to approach the window and had a perfect view of the interior. My poor companion was stretched out upon a trestle table, her hair in disarray; she was doubtless destined for some terrible torture by which she was going to find freedom, the eternal end of her miseries. . . . I shuddered, but what my glances fell upon soon astonished me more: Omphale had either not known everything, or had not told all she knew; I spied four naked girls in the basement, and they certainly did not belong to our group; and so there were other victims of these monsters' lechery in this horrible asylum . . . other wretches unknown to us. . . . I fled away and continued my circuit until I was on the side opposite the basement window; not yet having found a breach, I resolved to make one; all unobserved, I had furnished myself with a long knife; I set to work; despite my gloves, my hands were soon scratched and torn; but nothing daunted me; the hedge was two feet thick, I opened a passage, went through, and entered the second ring; there, I was surprised to find nothing but soft earth underfoot; with each step I sank in ankle-deep: the further I advanced into these copses, the more profound the darkness became. Curious to know whence came the change of terrain, I felt about with my hands ... O Just Heaven! my fingers seized the head of a cadaver! Great God! I thought, whelmed with horror, this must then be the cemetery, as indeed I was told, into which those murderers fling their victims; they have scarcely gone to the bother of covering them with earth! ... this skull perhaps belongs to my dear Omphale, perhaps it is that of the unhappy Octavie, so lovely, so sweet, so good, and who while she lived was like unto the rose of which her charms were the image. And I, alas! might that this have been my resting place! Wouldst that I had submitted to my fate! What had I to gain by going on in pursuit of new pitfalls? Had I not committed evil enough? Had I not been the occasion of a number of crimes sufficiently vast? Ah! fulfill my destiny! O Earth, gape wide and swallow me up! Ah, 'tis madness, when one is so forsaken, so poor, so utterly abandoned, madness to go to such pains in order to vegetate yet a few more instants amongst monsters! ... But no! I must avenge Virtue in irons. ... She expects it of my courage. ... Let her not be struck down ... let us advance: it is essential that the universe be ridded of villains as dangerous as these. Ought I fear causing the doom of three or four men in order to save the millions of individuals their policy or their ferocity sacrifice?

And therewith I pierce the next hedge; this one was thicker than the first: the further I progressed, the stouter they became. The hole was made, however, but there was firm ground beyond ... nothing more betrayed the same horrors I had just encountered; and thus I arrived at the brink of the moat without having met with the wall Omphale had spoken of; indeed, there turned out to be none at all, and it is likely that the monks mentioned it merely to add to our fear. Less shut in when beyond the sextuple enclosure, I was better able to distinguish objects: my eyes at once beheld the church and the bulk of the adjacent building; the moat bordered each of them; I was careful not to attempt to cross it at this point; I moved along the edge and finally discovering myself opposite one of the forest roads, I resolved to make my crossing there and to dash down that road as soon as I had climbed up the other side of the ditch; it was very deep but, to my good fortune, dry and lined with brick, which eliminated all possibilities of slipping; then I leapt: a little dazed by my fall, it was a few moments before I got to my feet . . . I went ahead, got to the further side without meeting any obstacle, but how was I to climb it! I spent some time seeking a means and at last found one where several broken bricks at once gave me the opportunity to use the others as steps and to dig footholds in order to mount; I had almost reached the top when something gave way beneath my weight and I fell back into the moat under the debris I dragged with me; I thought myself dead; this involuntary fall had been more severe than the other; I was, as well, entirely covered with the material which had followed me; some had struck my head . . . it was cut and bleeding. O God! I cried out in despair, go no further; stay there; 'tis a warning sent from Heaven; God does not want me to go on: perhaps I am deceived in my ideas, perhaps evil is useful on earth, and when God's hand desires it, perhaps it is a sin to resist it! But, soon revolted by that doctrine, the too wretched fruit of the corruption which had surrounded me, I extricated myself from the pile of rubble on top of me and finding it easier to climb by the breach I had just made, for now there were new holes, I try once again, I take courage, a moment later I find myself at the crest. Because of all this I had strayed away from the path I had seen, but having taken careful note of its position, I found it again, and began to run. Before daybreak I reached the forest's edge and was soon upon that little hill from which, six long months before, I had, to my sorrow, espied that frightful monastery; I rest a few minutes, I am bathed in perspiration; my first thought is to fall upon my knees and beg God to forgive the sins I unwillingly committed in that odious asylum of crime and impurity; tears of regret soon flowed from my eyes. Alas! I said, I was far less a criminal when last year I left this same road, guided by a devout principle so fatally deceived! O God! In what state may I now behold myself! These lugubrious reflections were in some wise mitigated by the pleasure of discovering I was free; I continued along the road toward Dijon, supposing it would only be in that capital my complaints could be legitimately lodged. . . .

At this point Madame de Lorsange persuaded Thérèse to catch her breath for a few minutes at least; she needed the rest; the emotion she put into her narrative, the wounds these dreadful recitals reopened in her soul, everything, in short, obliged her to resort to a brief respite. Monsieur de Corville had refreshments brought in, and after collecting her forces, our heroine set out again to pursue her deplorable adventures in great detail, as you shall see.

$\mathcal{B}$y the second day all my initial fears of pursuit had dissipated; the weather was extremely warm and, following my thrifty habit, I left the road to find a sheltered place where I could eat a light meal that would fortify me till evening. Off the road to the right stood a little grove of trees through which wound a limpid stream; this seemed a good spot for my lunch. My thirst quenched by this pure cool water, nourished by a little bread, my back leaning against a tree trunk, I breathed deep draughts of clear, serene air which relaxed me and was soothing. Resting there, my thoughts dwelled upon the almost unexampled fatality which, despite the thorns strewn thick along the career of Virtue, repeatedly brought me back, whatever might happen, to the worship of that Divinity and to acts of love and resignation toward the Supreme Being from Whom Virtue emanates and of Whom it is the image. A kind of enthusiasm came and took possession of me; alas! I said to myself, He abandons me not, this God I adore, for even at this instant I find the means to recover my strength. Is it not to Him I owe this merciful favor? And are there not persons in the world to whom it is refused? I am then not completely unfortunate because there are some who have more to complain of than I. . . . Ah! am I not much less so than the unlucky ones I left in that den of iniquity and vice from which God's kindness caused me to emerge as if by some sort of miracle? . . . And full of gratitude I threw myself upon my knees, raised my eyes, and fixing the sun, for it seemed to me the Divinity's most splendid achievement, the one which best manifests His greatness, I was drawing from that Star's sublimity new motives for prayer and good works when all of a sudden I felt myself seized by two men who, having cast something over my head to

179

prevent me from seeing and crying out, bound me like a criminal and dragged me away without uttering a word.

And thus had we walked for nearly two hours during which I knew not whither my escorts were taking me when one of them, hearing me gasp for air, proposed to his comrade that I be freed of the sack covering my head; he agreed, I drank in fresh air and observed that we were in the midst of a forest through which we were traveling along a fairly broad although little frequented road. A thousand dark ideas rushed straightway into my mind. I feared I was being led back to their odious monastery.

"Ah," I say to one of my guides, "ah Monsieur, will you tell me where I am being conducted? May I not ask what you intend to do with me?"

"Be at ease, my child," the man replied, "and do not let the precautions we are obliged to take cause you any fright; we are leading you to a good master; weighty considerations engage him to procure a maid for his wife by means of this mysterious process, but never fear, you will find yourself well off."

"Alas! Messieurs," I answered, "if 'tis my welfare for which you labor it is to no purpose I am constrained; I am a poor orphan, no doubt much to be commiserated; I ask for nothing but a place and since you are giving me one, I have no cause to run away, do I?"

"She's right," said one of my escorts, "let's make her more comfortable; untie everything but her hands."

They do so and we resume our march. Seeing me calmed, they even respond to my questions, and I finally learn that I am destined to have for master one Comte de Gernande, a native of Paris, but owning considerable property in this country and rich to the tune of five hundred thousand pounds a year, all of which he consumes alone—so said one of my guides.

"Alone?"

"Yes, he is a solitary man, a philosopher: he never sees a soul; but on the other hand he is one of Europe's greatest epicures; there is not an eater in all the world who can hold a candle to him. But I'll say no more about it; you'll see."

"But what do these cautious measures signify, Monsieur?"

"Well, simply this. Our master has the misfortune to have a wife who has become insane; a strict watch must be kept over her, she never leaves her room, no one wishes to be her servant; it would have done no good to propose the work to you, for had you been forewarned you'd never have accepted it. We are obliged to carry girls off by force in order to have someone to exercise this unpleasant function."

"What? I will be made this lady's captive?"

"Why, forsooth, yes, you will, and that's why we have you tied this way; but you'll get on . . . don't fret, you'll get on perfectly; apart from this annoyance, you'll lack nothing."

"Ah! Merciful Heaven! what thralldom!"

"Come, come, my child, courage, you'll get out of it someday and you'll have made your fortune."

My guide had no sooner finished speaking than we caught sight of the château. It was a superb and vast building isolated in the middle of the forest, but this great edifice which could have accommodated hundreds of persons, seemed to be inhabited hardly at all. I only noticed a few signs of life coming from kitchens situated in the vaults below the central part of the structure; all the rest was as deserted as the château's site was lonely. No one was there to greet us when we entered; one of my guides went off in the direction of the kitchens, the other presented me to the Count. He was at the far end of a spacious and superb apartment, his body enveloped in an oriental satin dressing gown, reclining upon an ottoman, and having hard by him two young men so indecently, or rather so ridiculously, costumed, their hair dressed with such elegance and skill, that at first I took them for girls; a closer inspection allowed me to recognize them for two youths, one of about fifteen, the other perhaps sixteen. Their faces struck me as charming, but in such a state of dissipated softness and weariness, that at the outset I thought they were ill.

"My Lord, here is a girl," said my guide, "she seems to us to be what might suit you: she is properly bred and gentle and asks only to find a situation; we hope you will be content with her."

" 'Tis well," the Count said with scarcely a glance in my direction; "you, Saint-Louis, will close the doors when you go out and you will say that no one is to enter unless I ring."

Then the Count rose to his feet and came up to examine me. While he makes a detailed investigation I can describe him to you:

the portrait's singularity merits an instant's attention. Monsieur de Gernande was at that time a man of fifty, almost six feet tall and monstrously fat. Nothing could be more terrifying than his face, the length of his nose, his wicked black eyes, his large ill-furnished mouth, his formidable high forehead, the sound of his fearful raucous voice, his enormous hands; all combined to make a gigantic individual whose presence inspired much more fear than reassurance. We will soon be able to decide whether the morals and actions of this species of centaur were in keeping with his awesome looks. After the most abrupt and cavalier scrutiny, the Count demanded to know my age.

"I am twenty-three, Monsieur," I replied.

And to this first question he added some others of a personal nature. I made him privy to everything that concerned me; I did not even omit the brand I had received from Rodin, and when I had represented my misery to him, when I had proven to him that unhappiness had constantly dogged my footsteps:

"So much the better," the dreadful man replied, "so much the better, it will have made you more pliable—adaptability counts heavily toward success in this household—; I see nothing to regret in the wretchedness that hounds an abject race of plebeians Nature has doomed to grovel at our feet throughout the period allotted them to live on the same earth as we. Your sort is more energetic and less insolent, the pressures of adversity help you fulfill your duties toward us."

"But, Monsieur, I told you that I am not of mean birth."

"Yes, yes, I have heard that before, they always pass themselves off for all kinds of things when in fact they are nothing or miserable. Oh indeed, pride's illusions are of the highest usefulness to console fortune's ills, and then, you see, it is up to us to believe what we please about these lofty estates beaten down by the blows of destiny. Pish, d'ye know, it's all the same to me if you fancy yourself a princess. To my consideration you have the look and more or less the costume of a servant, and as such you may enter my hire, if it suits you. However," the hard-hearted man continued, "your welfare, your happiness—they are your concern, they depend on your performance: a little patience, some discretion, and in a few years you will be sent forth in a way to avoid further service."

Then he took one after the other of my arms, rolled my sleeves to the elbows, and examined them attentively while asking me how many times I had been bled.

"Twice, Monsieur," I told him, rather surprised at the question, and I mentioned when and under what circumstances it had happened. He pressed his fingers against the veins as one does when one wishes to inflate them, and when they were swollen to the desired point, he fastened his lips to them and sucked. From that instant I ceased to doubt libertinage was involved in this dreadful person's habits, and tormenting anxieties were awakened in my heart.

"I have got to know how you are made," continued the Count, staring at me in a way that set me to trembling; "the post you are to occupy precludes any corporeal defects; show me what you have about you."

I recoiled; but the Count, all his facial muscles beginning to twitch with anger, brutally informed me that I should be ill-advised to play the prude with him, for, said he, there are infallible methods of bringing women to their senses.

"What you have related to me does not betoken a virtue of the highest order; and so your resistance would be quite as misplaced as ludicrous."

Whereupon he made a sign to his young boys who, approaching immediately, fell to undressing me. Against persons as enfeebled, as enervated as those who surrounded me, it is certainly not difficult to defend oneself; but what good would it have done? The cannibal who had cast me into their hands could have pulverized me, had he wished to, with one blow of his fist. I therefore understood I had to yield: an instant later I was unclothed; 'twas scarcely done when I perceived I was exciting those two Ganymedes to gales of laughter.

"Look ye, friend," said the younger, "a girl's a pretty thing, eh? But what a shame there's that cavity there."

"Oh!" cried the other, "nothing nastier than that hole, I'd not touch a woman even were my fortune at stake."

And while my fore end was the subject of their sarcasms, the Count, an intimate partisan of the behind (unhappily, alas! like every libertine), examined mine with the keenest interest: he handled it brutally, he browsed about with avidity; taking handfuls of flesh between his fingers, he rubbed and kneaded them to the point of drawing blood. Then he made me walk away from him, halt, walk backward in his direction, keeping my behind turned toward him while he dwelled upon the sight of it. When I had returned to him, he made me bend, stoop, squat, stand erect, squeeze and spread. Now and again he slipped to his knees before that part which was his sole concern. He applied kisses to several different areas of it, even a few upon that most secret orifice; but all his kisses were distinguished by suction, his lips felt like leeches. While he was applying them here and there and everywhere he solicited numerous details concerning what had been done to me at the monastery of Saint Mary-in-the-Wood, and without noticing that my recitations doubled his warmth, I was candid enough to give them all with naïveté. He summoned up one of his youths and placing him beside me, he untied the bow securing a great red ribbon which gathered in white gauze pantaloons, and brought to light all the charms this garment concealed. After some deft caresses bestowed upon the same altar at which, in me, the Count had signaled his devotion, he suddenly exchanged the object and fell to sucking that part which characterized the child's sex. He continued to finger me: whether because of habit in the youth, whether because of the satyr's dexterity, in a very brief space Nature, vanquished, caused there to flow into the mouth of the one what was ejected from the member of the other. That was how the libertine exhausted the unfortunate children he kept in his house, whose number we will shortly see; 'twas thus he sapped their strength, and that was what caused the languor in which I beheld them to be. And now let us see how he managed to keep women in the same state of prostration and what was the true cause of his own vigor's preservation.

The homage the Count rendered me had been protracted, but during it not a trace of infidelity to his chosen temple had he revealed; neither his glances, nor his kisses, nor his hands, nor his desires strayed away from it for an instant; after having sucked the other lad and having in likewise gathered and devoured his sperm:

"Come," he said to me, drawing me into an adjacent room

before I could gather up my clothes, "come, I am going to show you how we manage."

I was unable to dissimulate my anxiety, it was terrible; but there was no other way to put a different aspect upon my fate, I had to quaff to the lees the potion in the chalice tendered to me.

Two other boys of sixteen, quite as handsome, quite as peaked as the first two we had left in the salon, were working upon a tapestry when we entered the room. Upon our entrance they rose.

"Narcisse," said the Count to one of them, "here is the Countess' new chambermaid; I must test her; hand me the lancets."

Narcisse opens a cupboard and immediately produces all a surgeon's gear. I allow your imagination to fancy my state; my executioner spied my embarrassment, and it merely excited his mirth.

"Put her in place, Zéphire," Monsieur de Gernande said to another of the youths, and this boy approached me with a smile.

"Don't be afraid, Mademoiselle," said he, "it can only do you the greatest good. Take your place here."

It was a question of kneeling lightly upon the edge of a tabouret located in the middle of the room; one's arms were elevated and attached to two black straps which descended from the ceiling.

No sooner have I assumed the posture than the Count steps up scalpel in hand: he can scarcely breathe, his eyes are alive with sparks, his face smites me with terror; he ties bands about both my arms, and in a flash he has lanced each of them. A cry bursts from between his teeth, it is accompanied by two or three blasphemies when he catches sight of my blood; he retires to a distance of six feet and sits down. The light garment covering him is soon deployed; Zéphire kneels between his thighs and sucks him; Narcisse, his feet planted on his master's armchair, presents the same object to him to suckle he is himself having drained by Zéphire. Gernande gets his hands upon the boy's loins, squeezes them, presses them to him, but quits them long enough to cast his inflamed eyes toward me. My blood is escaping in floods and is falling into two white basins situated underneath my arms. I soon feel myself growing faint.

"Monsieur, Monsieur," I cry, "have pity on me, I am about to collapse."

I sway, totter, am held up by the straps, am unable to fall; but my arms having shifted, and my head slumping upon my shoulder, my face is now washed with blood. The Count is drunk with joy . . . however, I see nothing like the end of his operation approaching, I swoon before he reaches his goal; he was perhaps only able to attain it upon seeing me in this state, perhaps his supreme ecstasy depended upon this morbid picture. . . . At any rate, when I returned to my senses I found myself in an excellent bed, with two old women standing near me; as soon as they saw me open my eyes, they brought me a cup of bouillon and, at three-hour intervals, rich broths; this continued for two days, at the end of which Monsieur de Gernande sent to have me get up and come for a conversation in the same salon where I had been received upon my arrival. I was led to him; I was still a little weak and giddy, but otherwise well; I arrived.

"Thérèse," said the Count, bidding me be seated, "I shall not very often repeat such exercises with you, your person is useful for other purposes; but it was of the highest importance I acquaint you with my tastes and the manner in which you will expire in this house should you betray me one of these days, should you be unlucky enough to let yourself be suborned by the woman in whose society you are going to be placed.

"That woman belongs to me, Thérèse, she is my wife and that title is doubtless the most baleful she could have, since it obliges her to lend herself to the bizarre passion whereof you have been a recent victim; do not suppose it is vengeance that prompts me to treat her thus, scorn, or any sentiment of hostility or hatred; it is merely a question of passion. Nothing equals the pleasure I experience upon shedding her blood . . . I go mad when it flows; I have never enjoyed this woman in any other fashion. Three years have gone by since I married her, and for three years she has been regularly exposed every four days to the treatment you have undergone. Her youth (she is not yet twenty), the special care given her, all this keeps her aright; and as the reservoir is replenished at the same rate it is tapped, she has been in fairly good health since the regime began. Our relations being what they are, you perfectly well appreciate why I can neither allow her to go out nor to receive visitors. And so I represent her as insane and her mother, the only living member of her family, who resides in a château six leagues from here, is so firmly convinced of her derangement that she dares not even come to see her. Not infrequently the Countess implores my mercy, there is nothing she omits to do in order to soften me; but I doubt whether she shall ever succeed. My lust decreed her fate, it is immutable, she will go on in this fashion so long as she is able; while she lives she will want nothing and as I am incredibly fond of what can be drained from her living body, I will keep her alive as long as possible; when finally she can stand it no more, well, tush, Nature will take its course. She's my fourth; I'll soon have a fifth. Nothing disturbs me less than to lose a wife. There are so many women about, and it is so pleasant to change.

"In any event, Thérèse, your task is to look after her. Her blood is let once every ninety-six hours; she loses two bowls of it each time and nowadays no longer faints, having got accustomed to it. Her prostration lasts twenty-four hours; she is bedridden one day out of every four, but during the remaining three she gets on tolerably well. But you may easily understand this life displeases her; at the outset there was nothing she would not try to deliver herself from it, nothing she did not undertake to acquaint her mother with her real situation: she seduced two of her maid-servants whose maneuvers were detected early enough to defeat their success: she was the cause of these two unhappy creatures' ruin, today she repents what she did and, recognizing the irremediable character of her destiny, she is co-operating cheerfully and has promised not to make confederates of the help I hire to care for her. But this secret and what becomes of those who conspire to betray me, these matters, Thérèse, oblige me to put no one in her neighborhood but persons who, like yourself, have been impressed; and thus inquiries are avoided. Not having carried you off from anyone's house, not having to render an account of you to anyone at all, nothing stands in the way of my punishing you, if you deserve to be, in a manner which, although you will be deprived of mortal breath, cannot nevertheless expose me to interrogations or embroil me in any unpleasantnesses. As of the present moment you inhabit the world no longer, since the least impulse of my will can cause you to disappear from it. What can you expect at my hands? Happiness if you behave properly, death if you seek to play me false.

Were these alternatives not so clear, were they not so few, I would ask for your response; but in your present situation we can dispense with questions and answers. I have you, Thérèse, and hence you must obey me. . . . Let us go to my wife's apartment."

Having nothing to object to a discourse as precise as this, I followed my master: we traversed a long gallery, as dark, as solitary as the rest of the château; a door opens, we enter an antechamber where I recognize the two elderly women who waited upon me during my coma and recovery. They got up and introduced us into a superb apartment where we found the unlucky Countess doing tambour brocade as she reclined upon a chaise longue; she rose when she saw her husband.

"Be seated," the Count said to her, "I permit you to listen to me thus. Here at last we have a maid for you, Madame," he continued, "and I trust you will remember what has befallen the others —and that you will not try to plunge this one into an identical misfortune."

"It would be useless," I said, full eager to be of help to this poor woman and wishing to disguise my designs, "yes, Madame, I dare certify in your presence that it would be to no purpose, you will not speak one word to me I shall not report immediately to his Lordship, and I shall certainly not jeopardize my life in order to serve you."

"I will undertake nothing, Mademoiselle, which might force you into that position," said this poor woman who did not yet grasp my motives for speaking in this wise; "rest assured: I solicit nothing but your care."

"It will be entirely yours, Madame," I answered, "but beyond that, nothing."

And the Count, enchanted with me, squeezed my hand as he whispered: "Nicely done, Thérèse, your prosperity is guaranteed if you conduct yourself as you say you will." The Count then showed me to my room which adjoined the Countess' and he showed me as well that the entirety of this apartment, closed by stout doors and double grilled at every window, left no hope of escape.

"And here you have a terrace," Monsieur de Gernande went on, leading me out into a little garden on a level with the apartment, "but its elevation above the ground ought not, I believe, give you the idea of measuring the walls; the Countess is permitted to take fresh air out here whenever she wishes, you will keep her company . . . adieu."

I returned to my mistress and, as at first we spent a few moments examining one another without speaking, I obtained a good picture of her—but let me paint it for you.

Madame de Gernande, aged nineteen and a half, had the most lovely, the most noble, the most majestic figure one could hope to see, not one of her gestures, not a single movement was without gracefulness, not one of her glances lacked depth of senti- ment: nothing could equal the expression of her eyes, which were a beautiful dark brown although her hair was blond; but a certain languor, a lassitude entailed by her misfortunes, dimmed their *éclat,* and thereby rendered them a thousand times more interesting; her skin was very fair, her hair very rich; her mouth was very small, perhaps too small, and I was little surprised to find this defect in her: 'twas a pretty rose not yet in full bloom; but teeth so white . . . lips of a vermillion . . . one might have said Love had colored them with tints borrowed from the goddess of flowers; her nose was aquiline, straight, delicately modeled; upon her brow curved two ebony eyebrows; a perfectly lovely chin; a visage, in one word, of the finest oval shape, over whose entirety reigned a kind of attractiveness, a naïveté, an openness which might well have made one take this adorable face for an angelic rather than mortal physiognomy. Her arms, her breasts, her flanks were of a splendor . . . of a round fullness fit to serve as models to an artist; a black silken fleece covered her *mons veneris,* which was sustained by two superbly cast thighs; and what astonished me was that, despite the slenderness of the Countess' figure, despite her sufferings, nothing had impaired the firm quality of her flesh: her round, plump but- tocks were as smooth, as ripe, as firm as if her figure were heavier and as if she had always dwelled in the depths of happiness. How- ever, frightful traces of her husband's libertinage were scattered thickly about; but, I repeat, nothing spoiled, nothing damaged . . . the very image of a beautiful lily upon which the honeybee has inflicted some scratches. To so many gifts Madame de Gernande added a gentle nature, a romantic and tender mind, a heart of such sensibility! . . . well-educated, with talents . . . a native art for seduction which no one but her infamous husband could resist, a charming timbre in her voice and much piety: such was the unhappy wife of the Comte de Gernande, such was the heavenly creature against whom he had plotted; it seemed that the more she inspired ideas, the more she inflamed his ferocity, and that the abundant gifts she had received from Nature only became further motives for that villain's cruelties.

"When were you last bled, Madame?" I asked in order to have her understand I was acquainted with everything.

"Three days ago," she said, "and it is to be tomorrow. . . ." Then, with a sigh: ". . . yes, tomorrow . . . Mademoiselle, tomorrow you will witness the pretty scene."

"And Madame is not growing weak?"

"Oh, Great Heaven! I am not twenty and am sure I shall be no weaker at seventy. But it will come to an end, I flatter myself in the belief, for it is perfectly impossible for me to live much longer this way: I will go to my Father, in the arms of the Supreme Being I will seek a place of rest men have so cruelly denied me on earth."

These words clove my heart; wishing to maintain my role, I disguised my trouble, but upon the instant I made an inward promise to lay down my life a thousand times, if necessary, rather than leave this ill-starred victim in the clutches of this monstrous debauchee.

The Countess was on the point of taking her dinner. The two old women came to tell me to conduct her into her cabinet; I transmitted the message; she was accustomed to it all, she went out at once, and the two women, aided by the two valets who had carried me off, served a sumptuous meal upon a table at which my place was set opposite my mistress. The valets retired and the women informed me that they would not stir from the antechamber so as to be near at hand to receive whatever might be Madame's orders. I relayed this to the Countess, she took her place and, with an air of friendliness and affability which entirely won my heart, invited me to join her. There were at least twenty dishes upon the table.

"With what regards this aspect of things, Mademoiselle, you see that they treat me well."

"Yes, Madame," I replied, "and I know it is the wish of Monsieur le Comte that you lack nothing."

"Oh yes! But as these attentions are motivated only by cruelty, my feelings are scarcely of gratitude."

Her constant state of debilitation and perpetual need of what would revive her strength obliged Madame de Gernande to eat copiously. She desired partridge and Rouen duckling; they were brought to her in a trice. After the meal, she went for some air on the terrace, but upon rising she took my arm, for she was quite unable to take ten steps without someone to lean upon. It was at this moment she showed me all those parts of her body I have just described to you; she exhibited her arms: they were covered with small scars.

"Ah, he does not confine himself to that," she said, "there is not a single spot on my wretched person whence he does not love to see blood flow."

And she allowed me to see her feet, her neck, the lower part of her breasts and several other fleshy areas equally speckled with healed punctures. That first day I limited myself to murmuring a few sympathetic words and we retired for the night.

The morrow was the Countess' fatal day. Monsieur de Gernande, who only performed the operation after his dinner—which he always took before his wife ate hers—had me join him at table; it was then, Madame, I beheld that ogre fall to in a manner so terrifying that I could hardly believe my eyes. Four domestics, amongst them the pair who had led me to the château, served this amazing feast. It deserves a thorough description: I shall give it you without exaggeration. The meal was certainly not intended simply to overawe me. What I witnessed then was an everyday affair.

Two soups were brought on, one a consommé flavored with saffron, the other a ham bisque; then a sirloin of English roast beef, eight hors d'oeuvres, five substantial entrées, five others only apparently lighter, a boar's head in the midst of eight braised dishes which were relieved by two services of entremets, then sixteen plates of fruit; ices, six brands of wine, four varieties of liqueur and coffee. Monsieur de Gernande attacked every dish, and several were polished off to the last scrap; he drank a round dozen bottles of wine, four, to begin with, of Burgundy, four of Champagne with the roasts; Tokay, Mulseau, Hermitage and Madeira were downed with the fruit. He finished with two bottles of West Indies rum and ten cups of coffee.

As fresh after this performance as he might have been had he just waked from sleep, Monsieur de Gernande said:

"Off we go to bleed your mistress; I trust you will let me know if I manage as nicely with her as I did with you."

Two young boys I had not hitherto seen, and who were of the same age as the others, were awaiting at the door of the Countess' apartment; it was then the Count informed me he had twelve minions and renewed them every year. These seemed yet prettier than the ones I had seen hitherto; they were livelier . . . we went in. . . . All the ceremonies I am going to describe now, Madame, were part of a ritual from which the Count never deviated, they were scrupulously observed upon each occasion, and nothing ever changed except the place where the incisions were made.

The Countess, dressed only in a loose-floating muslin robe, fell to her knees instantly the Count entered.

"Are you ready?" her husband inquired.

"For everything, Monsieur," was the humble reply; "you know full well I am your victim and you have but to command me."

Monsieur de Gernande thereupon told me to undress his wife and lead her to him. Whatever the loathing I sensed for all these horrors, you understand, Madame, I had no choice but to submit with the most entire resignation. In all I have still to tell you, do not, I beseech you, do not at any time regard me as anything but a slave; I complied simply because I could not do otherwise, but never did I act willingly in anything whatsoever.

I removed my mistress' simar, and when she was naked conducted her to her husband who had already taken his place in a large armchair: as part of the ritual she perched upon this armchair and herself presented to his kisses that favorite part over which he had made such a to-do with me and which, regardless of person or sex, seemed to affect him in the same way.

"And now spread them, Madame," the Count said brutally.

And for a long time he rollicked about with what he enjoyed the sight of; he had it assume various positions, he opened it, he snapped it shut; with tongue and fingertip he tickled the narrow aperture; and soon carried away by his passions' ferocity, he plucked up a pinch of flesh, squeezed it, scratched it. Immediately he produced a small wound he fastened his mouth to the spot. I held his unhappy victim during these preliminaries, the two boys, completely naked, toiled upon him in relays; now one, now the other knelt between Gernande's thighs and employed his mouth to excite him. It was then I noticed, not without astonishment, that this giant, this species of monster whose aspect alone was enough to strike terror, was howbeit barely a man; the most meager, the most minuscule excrescence of flesh or, to make a juster comparison, what one might find in a child of three was all one discovered upon this so very enormous and otherwise so corpulent individual; but its sensations were not for that the less keen and each pleasurable vibration was as a spasmodic attack. After this prologue he stretched out upon a couch and wanted his wife, seated astride his chest, to keep her behind poised over his visage while with her mouth she rendered him, by means of suckings, the same service he had just received from the youthful Ganymedes who were simultaneously, one to the left, one to the right, being excited by him; my hands meanwhile worked upon his behind: I titillated it, I polluted it in every sense; this phase of activities lasted more than a quarter of an hour but, producing no results, had to be given up for another; upon her husband's instructions I stretched the Countess upon a chaise longue: she lay on her back, her legs spread as wide as possible. The sight of what she exposed put her husband in a kind of rage, he dwelt upon the perspective . . . his eyes blaze, he curses; like one crazed he leaps upon his wife, with his scalpel pricks her in several places, but these were all superficial gashes, a drop or two of blood, no more, seeped from each. These minor cruelties came to an end at last; others began. The Count sits down again, he allows his wife a moment's respite, and, turning his attention to his two little followers, he now obliges them to suck each other, and now he arranges them in such a way that while he sucks one, the other sucks him, and now again the one he sucked first brings round his mouth to render the same service to him by whom he was sucked: the Count received much but gave little. Such was his satiety, such his impotence that the extremest efforts availed not at all, and he remained in his torpor: he did indeed seem to experience some very violent reverberations, but nothing manifested itself; he several

times ordered me to suck his little friends and immediately to convey to his mouth whatever incense I drained from them; finally he
flung them one after the other at the miserable Countess. These
young men accosted her, insulted her, carried insolence to the point
of beating her, slapping her, and the more they molested her, the
more loudly the Count praised and egged them on.

Then Gernande turned to me; I was in front of him, my
buttocks at the level of his face, and he paid his respects to his
God; but he did not abuse me; nor do I know why he did not torment his Ganymedes; he chose to reserve all his unkindness for the
Countess. Perhaps the honor of being allied to him established one's
right to suffer mistreatment at his hands; perhaps he was moved to
cruelty only by attachments which contributed energy to his outrages. One can imagine anything about such minds, and almost
always safely wager that what seems most apt to be criminal is
what will inflame them most. At last he places his young friends
and me beside his wife and enlaces our bodies; here a man, there a
woman, etc., all four dressing their behinds; he takes his stand some
distance away and muses upon the panorama, then he comes near,
touches, feels, compares, caresses; the youths and I were not persecuted, but each time he came to his wife, he fussed and bothered
and vexed her in some way or other. Again the scene changes: he
has the Countess lie belly down upon a divan and taking each boy in
turn, he introduces each of them into the narrow avenue Madame's
posture exposes: he allows them to become aroused, but it is nowhere but in his mouth the sacrifice is to be consummated; as one
after another they emerge he sucks each. While one acts, he has
himself sucked by the other, and his tongue wanders to the throne
of voluptuousness the agent presents to him. This activity continues
a long time, it irritates the Count, he gets to his feet and wishes
me to take the Countess' place; I instantly beg him not to require
it of me, but he insists. He lays his wife upon her back, has me
superimpose myself upon her with my flanks raised in his direction
and thereupon he orders his aides to plumb me by the forbidden
passage: he brings them up, his hands guide their introduction;
meanwhile, I have got to stimulate the Countess with my fingers
and kiss her mouth; as for the Count, his offertory is still the same;
as each of the boys cannot act without exhibiting to him one of the

sweetest objects of his veneration, he turns it all to his profit and, as with the Countess, he who has just perforated me is obliged to go, after a few lunges and retreats, and spill into his mouth the incense I have warmed. When the boys are finished, seemingly inclined to replace them, the Count glues himself to my buttocks.

"Superfluous efforts," he cries, "this is not what I must have . . . to the business . . . the business . . . however pitiable my state . . . I can hold back no longer . . . come, Countess, your arms!"

He seizes her ferociously, places her as I was placed, arms suspended by two black straps; mine is the task of securing the bands; he inspects the knots: finding them too loose, he tightens them, "So that," he says, "the blood will spurt out under greater pressure"; he feels the veins, and lances them, on each arm, at almost the same moment. Blood leaps far: he is in an ecstasy; and adjusting himself so that he has a clear view of these two fountains, he has me kneel between his legs so I can suck him; he does as much for first one and then the other of his little friends, incessantly eyeing the jets of blood which inflame him. For my part, certain the instant at which the hoped for crisis occurs will bring a conclusion to the Countess' torments, I bring all my efforts to bear upon precipitating this denouement, and I become, as, Madame, you observe, I become a whore from kindness, a libertine through virtue. The much awaited moment arrives at last; I am not familiar with its dangers or violence, for the last time it had taken place I had been unconscious. . . . Oh, Madame! what extravagance! Gernande remained delirious for ten minutes, flailing his arms, staggering, reeling like one falling in a fit of epilepsy, and uttering screams which must have been audible for a league around; his oaths were excessive; lashing out at everyone at hand, his strugglings were dreadful. The two little ones are sent tumbling head over heels; he wishes to fly at his wife, I restrain him: I pump the last drop from him, his need of me makes him respect me; at last I bring him to his senses by ridding him of that fiery liquid, whose heat, whose viscosity, and above all whose abundance puts him in such a frenzy I believe he is going to expire; seven or eight tablespoons would scarcely have contained the discharge, and the thickest gruel would hardly give a notion of its consistency; and with all that, no appearance of an erection at all, rather, the limp look and feel of exhaustion: there you have the contrarieties which, better than might I, explain artists of the Count's breed. The Count ate excessively and only dissipated each time he bled his wife, every four days, that is to say. Would this be the cause of the phenomenon? I have no idea, and not daring to ascribe a reason to what I do not understand, I will be content to relate what I saw.

However, I rush to the Countess, I stanch her blood, untie her, and deposit her upon a couch in a state of extreme weakness; but the Count, totally indifferent to her, without condescending to cast even a glance at this victim stricken by his rage, abruptly goes out with his aides, leaving me to put things in whatever order I please. Such is the fatal apathy which better than all else characterizes the true libertine soul: if he is merely carried away by passion's heat, limned with remorse will be his face when, calmed again, he beholds the baleful effects of delirium; but if his soul is utterly corrupt? then such consequences will affright him not: he will observe them with as little trouble as regret, perhaps even with some of the emotion of those infamous lusts which produced them.

I put Madame de Gernande to bed. She had, so she said, lost much more this time than she ordinarily did; but such good care and so many restoratives were lavished upon her, that she appeared well two days later. That same evening, when I had completed all my chores in the Countess' apartment, word arrived that the Count desired to speak to me; Gernande was taking supper; I was obliged to wait upon him while he fed with a much greater intemperance than at dinner; four of his pretty little friends were seated round the table with him and there, every evening, he regularly drank himself into drunkenness; but to that end, twenty bottles of the most excellent wine were scarcely sufficient and I often saw him empty thirty. And every evening, propped up by his minions, the debauchee went to bed, and took one or two of the boys with him; these were nothing but vehicles which disposed him for the great scene.

But I had discovered the secret of winning this man's very highest esteem: he frankly avowed to me that few women had pleased him so much; and thereby I acquired the right to his confidence, which I only exploited in order to serve my mistress.

One morning Gernande called me to his room to inform me of

some new libertine schemes; after having listened closely and approved enthusiastically, and seeing him in a relatively calm state, I undertook to persuade him to mitigate his poor wife's fate. "Is it possible, Monsieur," I said to him, "that one may treat a woman in this manner, even setting aside all the ties which bind you to her? Condescend to reflect upon her sex's touching graces."

"Oh Thérèse!" the Count answered with alacrity, "why in order to pacify me do you bring me arguments which could not more positively arouse me? Listen to me, my dear girl," he continued, having me take a place beside him, "and whatever the invectives you may hear me utter against your sex, don't lose your temper; no, a reasoned discussion; I'll yield to your arguments if they're logically sound.

"How are you justified, pray tell me, Thérèse, in asserting that a husband lies under the obligation to make his wife happy? and what titles dares this woman cite in order to extort this happiness from her husband? The necessity mutually to render one another happy cannot legitimately exist save between two persons equally furnished with the capacity to do one another hurt and, consequently, between two persons of commensurate strength: such an association can never come into being unless a contract is immediately formed between these two persons, which obligates each to employ against the other no kind of force but what will not be injurious to either; but this ridiculous convention assuredly can never obtain between two persons one of whom is strong and the other weak. What entitles the latter to require the former to treat kindly with him? and what sort of a fool would the stronger have to be in order to subscribe to such an agreement? I can agree not to employ force against him whose own strength makes him to be feared; but what could motivate me to moderate the effects of my strength upon the being Nature subordinates to me? Pity, do you say? That sentiment is fitting for no one but the person who resembles me and as he is an egoist too, pity's effects only occur under the tacit circumstances in which the individual who inspires my commiseration has sympathy for me in his turn; but if my superiority assures me a constant ascendancy over him, his sympathy becoming valueless to me, I need never, in order to excite it, consent to any sacrifice. Would I not be a fool to feel pity for the chicken they slaughtered for my dinner? That object, too inferior to me, lacking any relation to me, can never excite any feelings in me; well, the relationships of a wife to her husband and that of the chicken to myself are of identical consequence, the one and the other are household chattels which one must use, which one must employ for the purpose indicated by Nature, without any differentiation whatsoever. But, I ask, had it been Nature's intention to create your sex for the happiness of ours and vice versa, would this blind Nature have caused the existence of so many ineptitudes in the construction of the one and the other of those sexes? Would she have implanted faults so grave in each that mutual estrangement and antipathy were bound infallibly to be their result? Without going any further in search of examples, be so good as to tell me, Thérèse, knowing my organization to be what it is, what woman could I render happy? and, reversibly, to what man can the enjoyment of a woman be sweet when he is not endowed with the gigantic proportions necessary to satisfy her? In your opinion, will they be moral qualities which will compensate his physical shortcomings? And what thinking being, upon knowing a woman to her depths, will not cry with Euripides: 'That one amongst the Gods who brought women into the world may boast of having produced the worst of all creatures and the most afflicting to man.' If then it is demonstrated that the two sexes do not at all sort agreeably with each other and that there is not one well-founded grievance of the one which could not equally and immediately be voiced by the other, it is therefore false, from this moment, to say that Nature created them for their reciprocal happiness. She may have permitted them the desire to attain each other's vicinity in order to conjugate in the interests of propagation, but in no wise in order to form attachments with the design of discovering a mutual felicity. The weaker therefore having no right to mouth complaints with the object of wresting pity from the stronger and no longer being able to raise the objection that the stronger depends for his happiness upon her, the weaker, I say, has no alternative but to submit; and as, despite the difficulty of achieving that bilateral happiness, it is natural that individuals of both sexes labor at nothing but to procure it for themselves, the weaker must reconcile herself to distilling from her submissiveness the only dose of happiness she can possibly hope to cull, and the stronger must strive after his by whatever oppressive methods he is pleased to employ, since it is proven that the mighty's sole happiness is yielded him by the exercise of his strong faculties, by, that is to say, the most thorough-going tyranny; thus, that happiness the two sexes cannot find with each other they will find, one in blind obedience, the other in the most energetic expression of his domination. Why! were it not Nature's intention that one of the sexes tyrannize the other, would she not have created them equally strong? By rendering one in every particular inferior to the other, has she not adequately indicated that she wills the mightier to exploit the rights she has given him? the more the latter broadens his authority, the more, by means of his preponderance, he worsens the misery of the woman enthralled by her destiny, the better he answers Nature's intentions; the frail being's complaints do not provide a correct basis for analyzing the process; judgments thus come by would be nothing if not vicious, since, to reach them, you would have to appropriate none but the feeble's ideas: the suit must be judged upon the stronger party's power, upon the scope he has given to his power, and when this power's effects are brought to bear upon a woman, one must examine the question, What is a woman? and how has this contemptible sex been viewed in ancient times and in our own by seventy-five per cent of the peoples of this earth?

"Now, what do I observe upon coolly proceeding to this investigation? A puny creature, always inferior to man, infinitely less attractive than he, less ingenious, less wise, constructed in a disgusting manner entirely opposite to what is capable of pleasing a man, to what is able to delight him . . . a being three-quarters of her life untouchable, unwholesome, unable to satisfy her mate throughout the entire period Nature constrains her to childbearing, of a sharp turn of humor, shrill, shrewish, bitter, and thwart; a tyrant if you allow her privileges, mean, vile, and a sneak in bondage; always false, forever mischievous, constantly dangerous; in short, a being so perverse that during several convocations the question was very soberly agitated at the Council of Mâcon whether or not this peculiar creature, as distinct from man as is man from the ape, had any reasonably legitimate pretensions to classification as a human; but this quandary might be merely an error of the times; were women more favorably viewed in earlier ages? Did the Persians, the Medes, the Babylonians, the Greeks, the Romans honor this odious sex we are able to dare make our idol today? Alas! I see it oppressed everywhere, everywhere rigorously banished from affairs, contemned everywhere, vilified, sequestered, locked up; women treated, in a word, like beasts one stables in the barn and puts to use when the need arises. Do I pause a moment at Rome? then I hear the wise Cato exclaim from the heart of the ancient world's capital: 'Were women lacking to men, they would yet hold conversation with the Gods.' I hear a Roman censor begin his harangue with these words: 'Gentlemen, were we ever to find a means to live without women, thereupon unto us should true happiness be known.' I hear the Greek theater resound to these lines intoned: 'O Zeus! what reason was it obliged thee to create women? couldst not have given being to humankind by better devices and wiser, by schemes which in a word would have spared us this female pestilence?' I see this same Greek race hold that sex in such high contempt legislation was needed to oblige a Spartan to reproduce, and one of the penalties decreed in those enlightened republics was to compel a malefactor to garb himself in a woman's attire, that is to say, to wear the raiments of the vilest and most scorned creature of which man had acquaintance.

"But without inquiring for examples in ages at such a great remove from ours, with what sort of an eye is this wretched sex still viewed upon the earth's surface? How is it dealt with? I behold it imprisoned throughout Asia and serving there as slave to the barbarous whims of a despot who molests it, torments it, and turns its sufferings into a game. In America I find a naturally humane race, the Eskimos, practicing all possible acts of beneficence amongst men and treating women with all imaginable severity: I see them humiliated, prostituted to strangers in one part of the world, used as currency in another. In Africa, where without doubt their station is yet further degraded, I notice them toiling in the manner of beasts of burden, tilling the soil, fertilizing it and sowing seed, and serving their husbands on their knees only. Will I follow Captain Cook in his newest discoveries? Is the charming isle of Tahiti, where pregnancy is a crime sometimes meriting death for the mother and almost always for the child, to offer me women enjoying a happier lot? In the other islands this same mariner charted, I find them beaten, harassed by their own offspring, and bullied by the husband himself who collaborates with his family to torment them with additional rigor.

"Oh, Thérèse! let not all this astonish you, nor be more surprised by the general pre-eminence accorded men over their wives in all epochs: the more a people is in harmony with Nature, the better will be its use of her laws; the wife can have no relation to her husband but that of a slave to his master; very decidedly she has no right to pretend to more cherished titles. One must not mistake for a prerogative the ridiculous abuses which, by degrading our sex, momentarily elevates yours: the cause for these travesties must be sought out, enunciated, and afterward one must only the more constantly return to reason's sagacious counsels. Well, Thérèse, here is the cause of the temporary respect your sex once upon a time enjoyed and which it still misuses today while they who perpetuate it are unaware of what they are doing.

"In the Gaul of long ago, that is to say, in that one part of the world where women were not totally treated as slaves, women had the habit of prophesying, of predicting the happy event: the people fancied they plied their trade successfully only because of the intimate commerce they doubtless had with the Gods; whence they were, so to speak, associated with the sacerdotal and enjoyed a measure of the consideration lavished upon priests. French chivalry was founded upon these inanities and finding them favorable to its spirit, adopted them: but what happened next was what happens always: the causes became extinct, the effects were preserved; chivalry vanished, the prejudices it nourished persevered. This ancient veneration accorded for no sound reason could not itself be annihilated when what founded the illusion had dissipated: we no longer stand in awe of witches, but we reverence whores and, what is worse, we continue to kill each other for them. May such platitudes cease to influence these our philosophers' minds, and restoring women to their true position, may the intelligent spirit conceive them, as Nature indicates, as the wisest peoples acknowledge, to be nothing but individuals created for their pleasures, submitted to their caprices, objects whose frailty and wickedness make them deserving of naught but contempt.

"But not only, Thérèse, did all the peoples of the earth enjoy the most extensive rights over their women, there were even to be found certain races which condemned women to death immediately they were born into the world, and of their numbers retained only those few necessary to the race's reproduction. The Arabs known as Koreish interred their daughters at the age of seven upon a mountain near Mecca, because, said they, so vile a sex appeared to them unworthy of seeing the light; in the seraglio of the King of Achem, the most appalling tortures are applied as punishment for the mere suspicion of infidelity, for the slightest disobedience in the service of the prince's lusts, or as soon as his women inspire his distaste; upon the banks of the River Ganges they are obliged to immolate themselves over their husbands' ashes, for they are esteemed of no further purpose in the world once their lords are able to enjoy them no more; in other regions they are hunted like wild beasts, 'tis an honor to kill a quantity of them; in Egypt they are sacrificed to the Gods; they are trampled under foot in Formosa if they become pregnant; German law condemned the man who killed a foreign woman to pay a fine of about ten crowns, nothing at all if the woman was his own or a courtesan; everywhere, to be brief, everywhere, I repeat, I see women humiliated, molested, everywhere sacrificed to the superstition of priests, to the savagery of husbands, to the playfulness of libertines. And because I have the misfortune to live amidst a people still so uncouth as not to dare abolish the most ludicrous of prejudices, I should deprive myself of the rights Nature has granted me! I should forgo all the pleasures to which these privileges give birth! ... Come, come, Thérèse, that's not just, no, 'tis unfair: I will conceal my behavior because I must, but I will be compensated, in the retreat where I have exiled myself, and silently, for the absurd chains to which I am condemned by legislation, and here I will treat my wife as I like, for I find my right to do so lettered in all the universe's codes, graved in my heart, and sealed in Nature."

"Oh Monsieur," said I, "your conversion is impossible."

"And I advise you not to attempt it, Thérèse," Gernande answered; "the tree is too long out of the nursery; at my age one can advance a few steps in the career of evil, but not one toward good. My principles and my tastes have brought me joy since childhood, they have always been the unique bases of my conduct and actions: I will, who knows? go further, I have the feeling it could be done, but return? never; I have too great a horror for mankind's prejudices, I too sincerely hate their civilization, their virtue and their Gods ever to sacrifice my penchants to them."

From this moment I saw very clearly that nothing remained for me, in order either to extricate myself from this house or to save the Countess, but the employment of stratagems and joint action with her.

During the year I had spent in the house, what I had allowed her to read in my heart was more than sufficient to dispel any doubts she might have of my desire to serve her, and now she could not fail to divine what had at first prompted me to act differently. I became less guarded, then spoke; she assented; we settled upon a plan: it was to inform her mother, to expose the Count's infamies to her eyes. Madame de Gernande was certain that unfortunate lady would hasten with all expedition to sever her daughter's bonds; but how were we to approach her? for we were so securely imprisoned, so closely watched! Accustomed to coping with ramparts, I gauged those upon which the terrace was raised: their height was scarcely thirty feet; there was no other enclosure in sight; once at the foot of the wall I thought one would find oneself already on the road through the forest; but the Countess, having been brought to this apartment at night and never having left it since, was unable to confirm my ideas. I agreed to attempt the descent; the letter Madame de Gernande wrote to her mother could not have been better phrased to melt and persuade her to come to the rescue of her most unhappy daughter; I slipped the letter into my bosom, I embraced that dear and attractive woman, then, as soon as night had fallen, aided by our bed linen, I slid to the ground outside the fortress. What had become of me, O Heaven! I discovered that instead of being outside the enclosure I was simply in a park, and in a park girt by walls which the quantity and dense foliage of trees had camouflaged from sight: these battlements were more than forty feet high, all of them garnished at the top with broken glass, and of a prodigious thickness . . . what was to become of me? Dawn was not far off: what would they think when I was found in a place into which I could not have come without a certain plan of escape?

Would I be able to keep the Count's fury at bay? Was it not very likely that ogre would drink my blood to punish such an offense? To return was out of the question, the Countess had drawn back the sheets; to knock at the door would be still more certainly to betray myself; a little more and I would have lost my head altogether and ceded to the violent effects of my despair. Had I been able to recognize some pity in the Count's soul, I might perhaps have been lulled into hopefulness, but a tyrant, a barbarian, a man who detested women and who, he said, had long been seeking the occasion to immolate one by draining away her blood drop by drop in order to find out how many hours she would be able to last . . . No doubt about it, he was going to put me to the test. Knowing not what would happen or what to do, discovering dangers everywhere, I threw myself down beside a tree, determined to await my fate and silently resigning myself to the Eternal's will. . . . The sun rose at last; merciful Heaven! the first object to present itself to me . . . is the Count himself: it had been frightfully warm during the night, he had stepped out to take a breath of air. He believes he is in error, he supposes this a specter, he recoils, rarely is courage a traitor's virtue: I get trembling to my feet, I fling myself at his knees.

"Thérèse! What are you doing here?" he demands.

"Oh, Monsieur, punish me," I reply, "I am guilty and have nothing to answer you."

Unhappily, in my fright I had forgotten to destroy the Countess' letter: he suspects its existence, asks for it, I wish to deny I have it; but Gernande sees the fatal letter protruding above my kerchief, snatches, it, reads it, and orders me to follow him.

We enter the château, descend a hidden stairway leading down to the vaults: the most profound stillness reigns there below ground; after several detours, the Count opens a dungeon and casts me into it.

"Impudent girl," says he, "I gave you warning that the crime you have just committed is punished here by death: therefore prepare yourself to undergo the penalty you have been pleased to incur. When tomorrow I rise from dinner I am going to dispatch you."

Once again I fall prostrate before him but, seizing me by the hair, he drags me along the ground, pulls me several times around my prison, and ends by hurling me against the wall in such a manner I am nigh to having my brains dashed out.

"You deserve to have me open your four veins this instant," says he as he closes the door, "and if I postpone your death, be very sure it is only in order to render it the more horrible."

He has left; I am in a state of the most violent agitation; I shall not describe the night I passed: my tormented imagination together with the physical hurt done me by the monster's initial cruelties made it one of the most dreadful I had ever gone through. One has no conception of what anguish is suffered by the wretch who from hour to hour awaits his ordeal, from whom hope has fled, and who knows not whether this breath he draws may not be his last. Uncertain of the torture, he pictures it in a thousand forms, one more frightful than the other; the least noise he hears may be that of his approaching assassins; the blood freezes in his veins, his heart grows faint, and the blade which is to put a period to his days is less cruel than those terrible instants swollen with the menace of death.

In all likelihood the Count began by revenging himself upon his wife: you will be as convinced of it as I by the event which saved me. For thirty-six hours I lingered in the critical condition I have just described; during that time I was brought no relief; and then my door was opened and the Count appeared: he was alone, fury glittered in his eyes.

"You must be fully cognizant of the death you are going to undergo: this perverse blood has got to be made to seep out of you: you will be bled three times a day, I want to see how long you can survive the treatment. 'Tis an experiment I have been all afire to make, you know; my thanks to you for furnishing me the means."

And, for the time being occupying himself with no passion but his vengeance, the monster made me stretch forth an arm, pricked it and stopped the wound after he had drawn two bowls of blood. He had scarcely finished when cries were heard.

"Oh, my Lord, my Lord!" exclaimed one of the servants who came running up to him, "come as quick as ever you can, Madame is dying, she wishes to speak to you before she gives up her soul."

And the old woman turned and flew back to her mistress.

However habituated one may be to crime, it is rarely that news of its accomplishment does not strike terror into him who has committed it; this fear avenges Virtue: Virtue resumes possession of its rights: Gernande goes out in alarm, he forgets to secure the dungeon's doors; although enfeebled by a forty hours' fast and the blood I have lost, I exploit my opportunity, leap from my cell, find my way unimpeded, traverse the court, the park, and reach the forest without having been perceived. Walk, I say to myself, walk, walk, be courageous; if the mighty scorn the weak, there is an omnipotent God Who shields the latter and Who never abandons them. My head crowded with these ideas, I advance with a stout heart and before night closes I find myself in a cottage four leagues from the château. Some money remained to me, my needs were attended to, in a few hours I was rested. I left at daybreak and, renouncing all plans to register old or new complaints with the authorities, I asked to be directed toward Lyon; the road was pointed out to me and on the eighth day I reached that city, very weak, suffering much, but happy and unpursued; once arrived, I turned all my thoughts to recovery before striking out for Grenoble where, according to one of my persistent notions, happiness awaited me.

One day my eye fell upon a gazette printed in some distant place; what was my surprise to behold crime crowned once again and to see one of the principal authors of my miseries arrived at the pinnacle of success. Rodin, the surgeon of Saint-Michel, that infamous wretch who had punished me with such cruelty for having wished to spare him the murder of his daughter, had just, the newspaper declared, been named First Surgeon to the Empress of Russia with the considerable emoluments accompanying that post. May he prosper, the villain, I muttered to myself, may he be so whilst Providence so wills it; and thou, unhappy creature, suffer, suffer uncomplainingly, since it is decreed that tribulations and pain must be Virtue's frightful share; no matter, I shall never lose my taste for it.

But I was far from done with these striking examples of the triumph of vice, examples so disheartening for Virtue, and the flourishing condition of the personage whose acquaintance I was about to renew was surely to exasperate and amaze me more than any other, since it was that of one of the men at whose hands I had endured the bloodiest outrages. I was exclusively busied with preparing my departure when one evening a lackey clad in gray and completely unknown to me brought me a note; upon presenting it, he said his master had charged him to obtain my response without fail. The missive was worded this way: "A man who has somewhat wronged you, who believes he recognized you in the Place de Bellecour, is most desirous to see you and to make amends for his conduct: hasten to come to meet him; he has things to tell you which may help liquidate his entire indebtedness to you."

The message carried no signature and the lackey offered no explanations. Having declared I was resolved to make no answer at all lest I was informed of who his master was:

"He is Monsieur de Saint-Florent, Mademoiselle," the lackey said; "he has had the honor to know you formerly in the neighborhood of Paris; you rendered him, he maintains, services for which he burns to attest his gratitude. Presently risen to a position of undisputed eminence in this city's commercial circles, he at once enjoys the consideration and the means which put him in a position to prove his regard for you. He awaits you."

My deliberations were soon completed. If this man had other than good intentions, I said to myself, would he be apt to write to me, to have me spoken to in this fashion? He repented his past infamies, was covered with remorse, it was with horror he remembered having torn from me what I cherished most and, by inaugurating a sequence of nightmares, having reduced me to the cruelest circumstances a woman may know . . . yes, yes, no doubt of it, this is repentance, I should be culpable before the Supreme Being were I not to consent to assuage his sufferings. Am I in a position, furthermore, to spurn the support that is proposed here? Rather, ought I not eagerly snatch at all that is offered to relieve me? This man wishes to see me in his town house: his prosperity must surround him with servants before whom he will have to act with enough dignity to prevent him from daring to fail me again, and in my state, Great God! can I inspire anything but sympathy in him? Therefore I assured Saint-Florent's lackey that upon the morrow at eleven o'clock I would take the privilege of going to salute his master; that I congratulated him upon his good fortune, and added that luck had treated me in nothing approaching the same manner.

I returned to my room, but I was so preoccupied with what this man might wish to say to me that I slept not a wink all night; the next day I arrived at the indicated address: a superb mansion, a throng of domestics, that insolent *canaille*'s contemptuous glances at the poverty it scorned, everything afflicts me and I am about ready to retreat when up comes the same liveryman who had spoken to me the previous evening, and, reassuring me, he conducts me into a sumptuous drawing room where, although it is nine years since I have set eyes on him, I perfectly recognize my butcher who has now reached the age of forty-five. He does not rise upon my entrance, but gives the order we be left alone, and gestures me to come and seat myself near the vast armchair where he is enthroned.

"I wanted to see you again, my child," says he with a humiliating tone of superiority, "not that I thought I had much wronged you, not that a troublesome recollection bids me make restitutions from which I believe my position exempts me; but I remember that, however brief was our acquaintance, you exhibited some parts during it: wit and character are needed for what I have to propose to you and if you accept, the need I will then have of you will insure your discovery of the resources which are necessary to you, and upon which it should be in vain you were to count without signifying your agreement."

I wished to reply with some reproaches for the levity of this beginning, but Saint-Florent imposed silence upon me.

"'Tis water under the bridge," says he, "a purely emotional episode, and my principles support the belief I have, that no brake should be applied to passion; when the appetites speak, they must be heard: that's my law. When I was captured by the thieves with whom you were, did you see me burst into tears? Swallow the bitter pill and act with diligence if one is weak, enjoy all one's rights if powerful: that's my doctrine. You were young and pretty, Thérèse, we found ourselves in the middle of a forest, nothing so arouses me sensually as the rape of a young virgin girl; such you were, I raped you; I might perhaps have done worse had what I attempted not met with success and had you put up any resistance. But I raped you, then left you naked and robbed in the middle of the night, upon a perilous road: two motives gave rise to that further villainy: I needed money and had none; as for the other reason which drove me to do this, 'twould be in vain were I to explain it, Thérèse, it would surpass your understanding. Only those spirits who are deep-learned in the heart of man, who have studied its innermost recesses, gained access to the most impenetrable nooks of this dim-lit labyrinth, they alone might be able to account for this consequence of an aberration."

"What, Monsieur! the money I gave you . . . the service I had just rendered you . . . to be paid for what I did in your behalf by the blackest treachery . . . that may, you think, be understood, justified?"

"Why yes, Thérèse! yes indeed! the proof an explanation exists for all I did is that, having just pillaged you, molested you . . . (for, Thérèse, I did beat you, you know), why! having taken twenty steps, I stopped and, meditating upon the state in which I had left you, I at once found strength in these ideas, enough to perpetrate additional outrages I might not have committed had it not been for that: you had lost but one maidenhead. . . . I turned, retraced my steps, and made short work of the other. . . . And so it is true that in certain souls lust may be born from the womb of crime! What do I say? it is thus true that only crime awakes and stiffens lust and that there is not a single voluptuous pleasure it does not inflame and improve. . . ."

"Oh Monsieur! what horror is this?"

"Could I not have acquitted myself of a still greater? I was close enough to it, I confess, but I was amply sure you were going to be reduced to the last extremities: the thought satisfied me, I left you. Well, Thérèse, let's leave the subject and continue to my reason for desiring to see you.

"My incredible appetite for both of a little girl's maidenheads has not deserted me, Thérèse," Saint-Florent pursued; "with this it is as with all libertinage's other extravagances: the older you grow, the more deeply they take root; from former misdeeds fresh desires are born, and new crimes from these desires. There would be nothing to the matter, my dear, were not the means one employs to succeed exceedingly culpable. But as the desire of evil is the *primum mobile* of our caprices, the more criminal the thing we are led to do, the better our irritation. When one arrives at this stage, one merely complains of the mediocrity of the means: the more encompassing their atrociousness, the more piquant our joy becomes, and thus one sinks in the quagmire without the slightest desire to emerge.

"That, Thérèse, is my own history: two young children are necessary for my daily sacrifices; having once enjoyed them, not only do I never again set eyes upon these objects, but it even becomes essential to my fantasies' entire satisfaction that they instantly leave the city: I should not at all savor the following day's pleasures were I to imagine that yesterday's victims still breathed the same air I inhale; the method for being rid of them is not complicated. Would you believe it, Thérèse? They are my debauches which populate Languedoc and Provence with the multitude of objects of libertinage with which those regions are teeming:[5] one hour after these little girls have served me, reliable emissaries pack them off and sell them to the matchmakers of Montpellier, Toulouse, Nîmes, Aix, and Marseilles: this trade, two-thirds of whose net profits go to me, amply recompenses the outlay required to procure my subjects, and thus I satisfy two of my most cherished passions, lust and greed; but reconnoitering and seduction are bothersome. Furthermore, the kind of subject is of infinite importance to my lubricity: I must have them all procured from those asylums of misery where the need to live and the impossibility of managing to do so eat away courage, pride, delicacy, finally rot the soul, and, in the hope of an indispensable subsistence, steel a person to undertake whatever appears likely to provide it. I have all these nests ransacked, all these dungheaps combed pitilessly: you've no idea what they yield; I would even go further, Thérèse: I say that civil activity, industry, a little social ease would defeat my subornations and divest me of a great pro-

---

[5] Let this not be mistaken for a fable: this wretched figure existed in this same Lyon. What is herein related of his maneuvers is exact and authentic: he cost the honor of between fifteen and twenty thousand unhappy little creatures: upon the completion of each operation, the victim was embarked on the Rhône, and for thirty years the above-mentioned cities were peopled with the objects of this villain's debauchery, with girls undone by him. There is nothing fictitious about this episode but the gentleman's name.

portion of my subjects: I combat these perils with the influence I
enjoy in this city, I promote commercial and economic fluctuations
or instigate the rise of prices which, enlarging the poverty-stricken
class, depriving it, on the one hand, of possibilities of work and on
the other rendering difficult those of survival, increases according
to a predictable ratio the total number of the subjects misery puts
into my clutches. The strategy is a familiar one, Thérèse: these
scarcities of firewood, dearths of wheat and of other edibles wherefrom Paris has been trembling for so many years, have been created
for the identical purposes which animate me: avarice, libertinage:
such are the passions which, from the gilded halls of the rich, extend
a multitude of nets to ensnare the poor in their humble dwellings.
But whatever skill I employ to press hard in this sector, if dexterous
hands do not pluck nimbly in another, I get nothing for my troubles,
and the machine goes quite as badly as if I were to cease to exhaust
my imagination in devising and my credit in operating. And so I
need a clever woman, young and intelligent, who, having herself
found her way through misery's thorny pathways, is more familiar
than anyone else with the methods for debauching those who are
in the toils; a woman whose keen eyes will descry adversity in its
darkest caves and attics, whose suborning intelligence will determine destitution's victims to extricate themselves from oppression
by the means I make available; a spirited woman, in a word, un-
scrupulous and ruthless, who will stop at nothing in order to succeed, who will even go to the point of cutting away the scanty
reserves which, still bolstering up those wretches' hopes, inhibit
them from taking the final step. I had an excellent woman and
trustworthy, she has just died: it cannot be imagined to what
lengths that brilliant creature carried effrontery; not only did she
use to isolate these wretches until they would be forced to come
begging on their knees, but if these devices did not succeed in ac-
celerating their fall, the impatient villain would hasten matters by
kidnaping them. She was a treasure; I need but two subjects a day,
she would have got me ten had I wanted them. The result was I
used to be able to make better selections, and the superabundance of
raw material consumed by my operations reimbursed me for inflated
labor costs. That's the woman I have got to replace, my dear, you'll
have four people under your command and ten thousand crowns

wages for your trouble; I have had my say, Thérèse; give me your answer, and above all do not let your illusions prevent you from accepting happiness when chance and my hand offer it to you."

"Oh Monsieur," I say to this dishonest man, shuddering at his speech, "is it possible you have been able to conceive such joys and that you dare propose that I serve them? What horrors you have just uttered in my hearing! Cruel man, were you to be miserable for but two days, you would see these doctrines upon humanity swiftly obliterated from your heart: it is prosperity blinds and hardens you: mightily blasé you are before the spectacle of the evils whence you suppose yourself sheltered, and because you hope never to suffer them, you consider you have the right to inflict them; may happiness never come nigh unto me if it can produce this degree of corruption! O Just Heaven! not merely to be content to abuse the misfortunate! To drive audacity and ferocity to the point of increasing it, of prolonging it for the unique gratification of one's desires! What cruelty, Monsieur! the wildest animals do not give us the example of a comparable barbarity."

"You are mistaken, Thérèse, there is no roguery the wolf will not invent to draw the lamb into his clutches: these are natural ruses, while benevolence has nothing to do with Nature: charity is but an appurtenance of the weakness recommended by the slave who would propitiate his master and dispose him to leniency; it never proclaimed itself in man save in two cases: in the event he is weak, or in the event he fears he will become weak; that this alleged virtue is not natural is proven by the fact it is unknown to the man who lives in a state of Nature. The savage expresses his contempt for charity when pitilessly he massacres his brethren from motives of either revenge or cupidity . . . would he not respect that virtue were it etched in his heart? but never does it appear there, never will it be found wherever men are equal. Civilization, by weeding certain individuals out of society, by establishing rank and class, by giving the rich man a glimpse of the poor, by making the former dread any change of circumstances which might precipitate him into the latter's misery, civilization immediately puts the desire into his head to relieve the poor in order that he may be helped in his turn should he chance to lose his wealth; and thus was benevolence born, the fruit of civilization and fear: hence it is merely a circumstantial virtue, but nowise a sentiment originating in Nature, who never inserted any other desire in us but that of satisfying ourselves at no matter what the price. It is thus by confounding every sentiment, it is by continually refusing to analyze a single one of them that these people are able to linger in total darkness about them all and deprive themselves of every pleasurable enjoyment."

"Ah, Monsieur," I interrupted with great emotion, "may there be one any sweeter than the succoring of misfortune? Leaving aside the dread lest someday one have to endure suffering oneself, is there any more substantial satisfaction than that to be had from obliging others? . . . from relishing gratitude's tearful thanks, from partaking of the well-being you have just distributed like manna to the downtrodden who, your own fellow creatures, nevertheless want those things which you take airily for granted; oh! to hear them sing your praise and call you their father, to restore serenity to brows clouded by failure, destitution, and despair; no, Monsieur, not one of this world's lewd pleasures can equal this: it is that of the Divinity Himself, and the happiness He promises to those who on earth will serve Him, is naught other than the possibility to behold or make happy creatures in Heaven. All virtues stem directly from that one, Monsieur; one is a better father, a better son, a better husband when one knows the charm of alleviating misfortune's lot. One might say that like unto the sun's rays, the charitable man's presence sheds fertility, sweetness, and joy everywhere about and upon all, and the miracle of Nature, after this source of celestial light, is the honest, delicate, and sensitive soul whose supreme felicity consists in laboring in behalf of that of others."

"Feeble Phoebus stuff, Thérèse," Saint-Florent smiled; "the character of man's enjoyment is determined by the kind of organs he has received from Nature; a weak individual's, and hence every woman's, incline in the direction of procuring moral ecstasies which are more keenly felt than any other by these persons whose physical constitution happens to be entirely devoid of energy; quite the opposite is the case for vigorous spirits who are far more delighted by powerful shocks imparted to what surround them than they would be by the delicate impressions the feeble creatures by whom they are surrounded inevitably prefer, as befits their constitution; similarly the vigorous spirits delight more in what affects others painfully than in what affects them agreeably: such is the only difference between the cruel and the meek; both groups are endowed with sensibility, but each is endowed with it in a special manner. I do not deny that each class knows its pleasures, but I, together with a host of philosophers, maintain of course that those of the individual constructed in the more vigorous fashion are incontestably more lively than all his adversary's; and, these axioms established, there may and there must be men of one sort who take as much joy in everything cruelty suggests, as the other category of persons tastes delight in benevolence; but the pleasures of the latter will be mild, those of the former keen and strong: these will be the most sure, the most reliable, and doubtless the most authentic, since they characterize the penchants of every man who is still a creature of Nature, and indeed of all children before they have fallen under the sway of civilization; the others will merely be the effect of this civilization and, consequently, of deceiving and vapid delights. Well, my child, since we are met not so much in order to philosophize as to conclude a bargain, be so kind as to give me your final decision . . . do you or do you not accept the post I propose to you?"

"I very decidedly reject it, Monsieur," I replied, getting to my feet, ". . . indeed I am poor . . . oh yes! very poor, Monsieur; but richer in my heart's sentiments than I could be in all fortune's blessings; never will I sacrifice the one in order to possess the other; I may die in indigence, but I will not betray Virtue."

"Get out," the detestable man said to me, "and, above all, should I have anything to fear from your indiscretion, you will be promptly conveyed to a place where I need dread it no longer."

Nothing heartens Virtue like the fear of vice; a good deal less timorous than I should have thought, I dared, upon promising he would have nothing to dread at my hands, remind him of what he had stolen from me in the forest of Bondy and apprise him of my present circumstances which, I said, made this money indispensable to me. The monster gave me harsh answer, declaring it was up to me to earn it and that I had refused.

"No Monsieur, no," I replied firmly, "no, I repeat, I would rather perish a thousand times over than preserve my life at that price."

"And as for myself," Saint-Florent rejoined, "there is in the same way nothing I would not prefer to the chagrin of disbursing unearned money: despite the refusal you have the insolence to give me, I should relish passing another fifteen minutes in your company; and so if you please, we will move into my boudoir and a few moments of obedience will go far to straighten out your pecuniary difficulties."

"I am no more eager to serve your debauches in one sense than in another, Monsieur," I proudly retorted; "it is not charity I ask, cruel man; no, I should not procure you the pleasure of it; what I demand is simply what is my due: that is what you stole from me in the most infamous manner. . . . Keep it, cruel wretch, keep it if you see fit: unpityingly observe my tears; hear, if you are able, hear without emotion need's sorrowing accents, but bear in mind that if you commit this newest outrage, I will have bought, for the price it costs me, the right to scorn you forever."

Furious, Saint-Florent ordered me to leave and I was able to read in his dreadful countenance that, had it not been for what he had confided in me and were he not afraid lest it get abroad, my bold plain speaking might perhaps have been repaid by some brutality. . . . I left. At the same instant they were bringing the debauchee one of the luckless victims of his sordid profligacy. One of those women whose horrible state he had suggested I share was leading into the house a poor little girl of about nine who displayed every attribute of wretchedness and dereliction: she scarcely seemed to have enough strength to keep erect. . . . O Heaven! I thought upon beholding this, is it conceivable that such objects can inspire any feelings but those of pity? Woe unto the depraved one who will be able to suspect pleasures in the womb want consumes, who will seek to gather kisses from lips withered by hunger and which open only to curse him!

Tears spilled from my eyes; I should have liked to snatch that victim from the tiger awaiting her; I dared not. Could I have done it? I returned directly to my hotel, quite as humiliated by the misfortune which attracted such proposals as revolted by the opulence which ventured to make them.

The following day I left Lyon by way of the road to Dauphiné, still filled with the mad faith which allowed me to believe happiness awaited me in that province. Traveling afoot as usual, with a pair of blouses and some handkerchiefs in my pockets, I had not proceeded two leagues when I met an old woman; she approached me with a look of suffering and implored alms. Far from having the miserliness of which I had just received such cruel examples, and knowing no greater worldly happiness than what comes of obliging a poor person, I instantly drew forth my purse with the intention of selecting a crown and giving it to this woman; but the unworthy creature, much quicker than I, although I had at first judged her aged and crippled, leaps nimbly at my purse, seizes it, aims a powerful blow of her fist at my stomach, topples me, and the next I see of her, she has put a hundred yards betwixt us; there she is, surrounded by four rascals who gesture threateningly and warn me not to come near.

"Great God!" I cried with much bitterness, "then it is impossible for my soul to give vent to any virtuous impulse without my being instantly and very severely punished for it!" At this fatal moment all my courage deserted me; today I beg Heaven's forgiveness in all sincerity, for I faltered; but I was blinded by despair. I felt myself ready to give up a career beset with so many obstacles. I envisioned two alternatives: that of going to join the scoundrels who had just robbed me, or that of returning to Lyon to accept Saint-Florent's offer. God had mercy upon me; I did not succumb, and though the fresh hope He quickened in me was misleading, since so many adversities yet lay in store for me, I nevertheless thank Him for having held me upright: the unlucky star which guides me, although innocent, to the gallows, will never lead me to worse than death; other supervision might have brought me to infamy, and the one is far less cruel than the other.

I continue to direct my steps toward Vienne, having decided to sell what remains to me in order to get on to Grenoble: I was walking along sadly when, at a quarter league's distance from this city, I spied a plain to the right of the highway, and in the fields were two riders busily trampling a man beneath their horses' hooves; after having left him for dead, the pair rode off at a gallop. This appalling spectacle melted me to the point of tears. "Alas!" I said to myself, "there is an unluckier person than I; health and strength at least remain to me, I can earn my living, and if that poor fellow is not rich, what is to become of him?"

However much I ought to have forbidden myself the self-indulgence of sympathy, however perilous it was for me to surrender to the impulse, I could not vanquish my extreme desire to approach the man and to lavish upon him what care I could offer. I rush to his side, I aid him to inhale some spirits I had kept about me: at last he opens his eyes and his first accents are those of gratitude. Still more eager to be of use to him, I tear up one of my blouses in order to bandage his wounds, to stanch his blood: I sacrificed for this wretched man one of the few belongings I still owned. These first attentions completed, I give him a little wine to drink: the unlucky one has completely come back to his senses, I cast an eye upon him and observe him more closely. Although traveling on foot and without baggage, he had some valuable effects—rings, a watch, a snuff box—but the latter two have been badly damaged during his encounter. As soon as he is able to speak he asks me what angel of charity has come to his rescue and what he can do to express his gratitude. Still having the simplicity to believe that a soul enchained by indebtedness ought to be eternally beholden to me, I judge it safe to enjoy the sweet pleasure of sharing my tears with him who has just shed some in my arms: I instruct him of my numerous reverses, he listens with interest, and when I have concluded with the latest catastrophe that has befallen me, the recital provides him with a glimpse of my poverty.

"How happy I am," he exclaims, "to be able at least to acknowledge all you have just done for me; my name is Roland," the adventurer continues, "I am the owner of an exceedingly fine château in the mountains fifteen leagues hence, I invite you to follow me there; and that this proposal cause your delicacy no alarm, I am going to explain immediately in what way you will be of service to me. I am unwedded, but I have a sister I love passionately: she has dedicated herself to sharing my solitude; I need someone to wait upon her; we have recently lost the person who held that office until now, I offer her post to you."

I thanked my protector and took the liberty to ask him how it chanced that a man such as he exposed himself to the dangers of journeying alone, and, as had just occurred, to being molested by bandits.

"A stout, youthful, and vigorous fellow, for several years," said Roland, "I have been in the habit of traveling this way between the place where I reside and Vienne. My health and pocketbook benefit from walking. It is not that I need avoid the expense of a coach, for I am wealthy, and you will soon see proof of it if you are good enough to return home with me; but thriftiness never hurts. As for those two men who insulted me a short while ago, they are two would-be gentlemen of this canton from whom I won a hundred *louis* last week in a gaming house at Vienne; I was content to accept their word of honor, then I met them today, asked for what they owe me, and you witnessed in what coin they paid me."

Together with this man I was deploring the double misfortune of which he was the victim when he proposed we continue our way.

"Thanks to your attentions I feel a little better," said Roland; "night is approaching, let's get on to a house which should be two leagues away; by means of the horses we will secure tomorrow, we might be able to arrive at my château the same afternoon."

Absolutely resolved to profit from the aid Heaven seemed to have sent me, I help Roland to get up, I give him my arm while we walk, and indeed, after progressing two leagues we find the inn he had mentioned. We take supper together, 'tis very proper and nice; after our meal Roland entrusts me to the mistress of the place, and the following day we set off on two mules we have rented and which are led by a boy from the inn; we reach the frontier of Dauphiné, ever heading into the highlands. We were not yet at our destination when the day ended, so we stopped at Virieu, where my patron showed me the same consideration and provided me with the same care; the next morning we resumed our way toward the mountains. We arrived at their foot toward four in the afternoon; there, the road becoming almost impassable, Roland requested my muleteer not to leave me for fear of an accident, and we penetrated into the gorges. We did but turn, wind, climb for the space of more than four leagues, and by then we had left all habitations and all traveled roads so far behind us I thought myself come to the end of the world; despite myself, I was seized by a twinge of uneasiness; Roland could not avoid seeing it, but he said nothing, and I was made yet more uncomfortable by his silence. We finally came to a castle perched upon the crest of a mountain; it beetled over a dreadful precipice into which it seemed ready to plunge: no road seemed to lead up to it; the one we had followed, frequently by goats only, strewn with pebbles and stones, however did at last take us to this awful eyrie which much more resembled the hideaway of thieves than the dwelling place of virtuous folk.

"That is where I live," said Roland, noticing I was gazing up at his castle.

I confessed my astonishment to see that he lived in such isolation.

"It suits me," was his abrupt reply.

This response redoubled my forebodings. Not a syllable is lost upon the miserable; a word, a shift of inflection and, when 'tis a question of the speech of the person upon whom one depends, 'tis enough to stifle hope or revive it; but, being completely unable to do anything, I held my tongue and waited. We mounted by zigzags; the strange pile suddenly loomed up before us: roughly a quarter of a league still separated it from us: Roland dismounted and having told me to do likewise, he returned both mules to the boy, paid him and ordered him to return. This latest maneuver was even more displeasing to me; Roland observed my anxiety.

"What is the trouble, Thérèse?" he demanded, urging me on toward his fortress; "you are not out of France; we are on the Dauphiné border and within the bishopric of Grenoble."

"Very well, Monsieur," I answered; "but why did it ever occur to you to take up your abode in a place befitting brigands and robbers?"

"Because they who inhabit it are not very honest people," said Roland; "it might be altogether possible you will not be edified by their conduct."

"Ah, Monsieur!" said I with a shudder, "you make me tremble; where then are you leading me?"

"I am leading you into the service of the counterfeiters of whom I am the chief," said Roland, grasping my arm and driving me over a little drawbridge that was lowered at our approach and raised immediately we had traversed it; "do you see that well?" he continued when we had entered; he was pointing to a large and deep grotto situated toward the back of the courtyard, where four women, nude and manacled, were turning a wheel; "there are your companions and there your task, which involves the rotation of

that wheel for ten hours each day, and which also involves the
satisfaction of all the caprices I am pleased to submit you and the
other ladies to; for which you will be granted six ounces of black
bread and a plate of kidney beans without fail each day; as for your
freedom, forget it; you will never recover it. When you are dead
from overwork, you will be flung into that hole you notice beside
the well, where the remains of between sixty and eighty other rascals of your breed await yours, and your place will be taken by
somebody else."

"Oh, Great God!" I exclaimed, casting myself at Roland's
feet, "deign to remember, Monsieur, that I saved your life, that,
moved by gratitude for an instant, you seemed to offer me happiness and that it is by precipitating me into an eternal abyss of evils
you reward my services. Is what you are doing just? and has not
remorse already begun to avenge me in the depths of your heart?"

"What, pray tell, do you mean by this feeling of gratitude with
which you fancy you have captivated me?" Roland inquired. "Be
more reasonable, wretched creature; what were you doing when you
came to my rescue? Between the two possibilities, of continuing on
your way and of coming up to me, did you not choose the latter
as an impulse dictated by your heart? You therefore gave yourself
up to a pleasure? How in the devil's name can you maintain I am
obliged to recompense you for the joys in which you indulge yourself? And how did you ever get it into your head that a man like myself, who is swimming in gold and opulence, should condescend to
lower himself to owing something to a wretch of your species? Even
had you resurrected me, I should owe you nothing immediately it
were plain you had acted out of selfishness only: to work, slave, to
work; learn that though civilization may overthrow the principles
of Nature, it cannot however divest her of her rights; in the beginning she wrought strong beings and weak and intended that the
lowly should be forever subordinated to the great; human skill and
intelligence made various the positions of individuals, it was no
longer physical force alone that determined rank, 'twas gold; the
richest became the mightiest man, the most penurious the weakest;
if the causes which establish power are not to be found in Nature's
ordinations, the priority of the mighty has always been inscribed
therein, and to Nature it made no difference whether the weak

danced at the end of a leash held by the richest or the most energetic, and little she cared whether the yoke crushed the poorest or the most enfeebled; but these grateful impulses out of which you would forge chains for me, why, Thérèse, Nature recognizes them not; it has never been one of her laws that the pleasure whereunto someone surrenders when he acts obligingly must become a cause for the recipient of his gratuitous kindness to renounce his rights over the donor; do you detect these sentiments you demand in the animals which serve us as examples? When I dominate you by my wealth or might is it natural for me to abandon my rights to you, either because you have enjoyed yourself while obliging me or because, being unhappy, you fancied you had something to gain from your action? Even were service to be rendered by one equal to another, never would a lofty spirit's pride allow him to stoop to acknowledge it; is not he who receives always humiliated? And is this humiliation not sufficient payment for the benefactor who, by this alone, finds himself superior to the other? Is it not pride's delight to be raised above one's fellow? Is any other necessary to the person who obliges? And if the obligation, by causing humiliation to him who receives, becomes a burden to him, by what right is he to be forced to continue to shoulder it? Why must I consent to let myself be humiliated every time my eyes fall upon him who has obliged me? Instead of being a vice, ingratitude is as certainly a virtue in proud spirits as gratitude is one in humble; let them do what they will for me if doing it gives them pleasure, but let them expect nothing from me simply because they have enjoyed themselves."

Having uttered these words, to which Roland gave me no opportunity to reply, he summoned two valets who upon his instructions seized me, despoiled me, and shackled me next to my companions, so was I set to work at once, without a moment's rest after the fatiguing journey I had just made. Then Roland approaches me, he brutally handles all those parts of me designation of which modesty forbids, heaps sarcasms upon me, makes impertinent reference to the damning and little merited brand Rodin printed upon me, then, catching up a bull's pizzle always kept in readiness nearby, he applies twenty cuts to my behind.

"That is how you will be treated, bitch," says he, "when you lag at the job; I'm not giving you this for anything you've already done, but only to show you how I cope with those who make mistakes."

I screamed, struggled against my manacles; my contortions, my cries, my tears, the cruel expressions of my pain merely entertained my executioner. . . .

"Oh, little whore, you'll see other things," says Roland, "you're not by a long shot at the end of your troubles and I want you to make the acquaintance of even the most barbaric refinements of misery."

He leaves me.

Located in a cave on the edge of that vast well were six dark kennels; they were barred like dungeons, and they served us as shelters for the night, which arrived not long after I was enlisted in this dreadful chain gang. They came to remove my fetters and my companions', and after we had been given the ration of water, beans, and dry bread Roland had mentioned, we were locked up.

I was no sooner alone than, undistracted, I abandoned myself to contemplating my situation in all its horror. Is it possible, I wondered, can it be that there are men so hardened as to have stifled in themselves their capacity for gratitude? This virtue to which I surrender myself with such charm whenever an upright spirit gives me the chance to feel it . . . can this virtue be unknown to certain beings, can they be utter strangers to it? and may they who have suppressed it so inhumanly in themselves be anything but monsters?

I was absorbed in these musings when suddenly I heard the door to my cell open; 'tis Roland: the villain has come to complete his outraging of me by making me serve his odious eccentricities: you may well imagine, Madame, that they were to be as ferocious as his other proceedings and that such a man's love-makings are necessarily tainted by his abhorrent character. But how can I abuse your patience by relating these new horrors? Have I not already more than soiled your imagination with infamous recitations? Dare I hazard additional ones?

"Yes, Thérèse," Monsieur de Corville put in, "yes, we insist upon these details, you veil them with a decency that removes all their edge of horror; there remains only what is useful to whoever seeks to perfect his understanding of enigmatic man. You may not fully apprehend how these tableaux help toward the development of the human spirit; our backwardness in this branch of learning may very well be due to the stupid restraint of those who venture to write upon such matters. Inhibited by absurd fears, they only discuss the puerilities with which every fool is familiar, and dare not, by addressing themselves boldly to the investigation of the human heart, offer its gigantic idiosyncrasies to our view."

"Very well, Monsieur, I shall proceed," Thérèse resumed, deeply affected, "and proceeding as I have done until this point, I will strive to offer my sketches in the least revolting colors."

Roland, with whose portrait I ought to begin, was a short, heavy-set man, thirty-five years old, incredibly vigorous and as hirsute as a bear, with a glowering mien and fierce eye; very dark, with masculine features, a long nose, bearded to the eyes, black, shaggy brows; and in him that part which differentiates men from our sex was of such length and exorbitant circumference, that not only had I never laid eyes upon anything comparable, but was even absolutely convinced Nature had never fashioned another as prodigious; I could scarcely surround it with both hands, and its length matched that of my forearm. To this physique Roland joined all the vices which may be the issue of a fiery temperament, of considerable imagination, and of a luxurious life undisturbed by anything likely to distract from one's leisure pursuits. From his father Roland had inherited a fortune; very early on in life he had become surfeited by ordinary pleasures, and begun to resort to nothing but horrors; these alone were able to revive desires in a person jaded by excessive pleasure; the women who served him were all employed in his secret debauches and to satisfy appetites only slightly less dishonest within which, nevertheless, this libertine was able to find the criminal spice wherein above all his taste delighted; Roland kept his own sister as a mistress, and it was with her he brought to a climax the passions he ignited in our company.

He was virtually naked when he entered; his inflamed visage was evidence simultaneously of the epicurean intemperance to which he had just given himself over, and the abominable lust which consumed him; for an instant he considers me with eyes that unstring my limbs.

"Get out of those clothes," says he, himself tearing off what I was wearing to cover me during the night . . . "yes, get rid of all that and follow me; a little while ago I made you sense what you risk by laziness; but should you desire to betray us, as that crime would be of greater magnitude, its punishment would have to be proportionally heavier; come along and see of what sort it would be."

I was in a state difficult to describe, but Roland, affording my spirit no time in which to burst forth, immediately grasped my arm and dragged me out; he pulls me along with his right hand, in his left he holds a little lantern that emits a feeble light; after winding this way and that, we reach a cellar door; he opens it, thrusts me ahead of him, tells me to descend while he closes this first barrier; I obey; a hundred paces further, a second door; he opens and shuts it in the same way; but after this one there is no stairway, only a narrow passage hewn in the rock, filled with sinuosities, whose downward slope is extremely abrupt. Not a word from Roland; the silence affrights me still more; he lights us along with his lantern; thus we travel for about fifteen minutes; my frame of mind makes me yet more sensitive to these subterranean passages' terrible humidity. At last, we had descended to such a depth that it is without fear of exaggeration I assure you the place at which we were to arrive must have been more than a furlong below the surface of the earth; on either side of the path we followed were occasional niches where I saw coffers containing those criminals' wealth: one last bronze door appeared, Roland unlocked it, and I nearly fell backward upon perceiving the dreadful place to which this evil man had brought me. Seeing me falter, he pushed me rudely ahead, and thus, without wishing to be there, I found myself in the middle of that appalling sepulcher. Imagine, Madame, a circular cavern, twenty-five feet in diameter, whose walls, hung in black, were decorated by none but the most lugubrious objects, skeletons of all sizes, crossed bones, several heads, bundles of whips and collections of martinets, sabers, cutlasses, poignards, firearms: such were the horrors one spied on the walls illuminated by a three-wicked oil lamp suspended in one corner of the vault; from a transverse beam dangled a rope which fell to within eight or ten feet of the ground in the center of this dungeon and which, as very soon you will see, was there for no other purpose than to facilitate dreadful expeditions: to the right was an open coffin wherein glinted an effigy of death brandishing a threatful scythe; a prayer stool was beside it; above it was visible a crucifix bracketed by candles of jet; to the left, the waxen dummy of a naked woman, so lifelike I was for a long time deceived by it; she was attached to a cross, posed with her chest facing it so that one had a full view of her posterior and cruelly molested parts; blood seemed to ooze from several wounds and to flow down her thighs; she had the most beautiful hair in all the world, her lovely head was turned toward us and seemed to implore our mercy; all of suffering's contortions were plainly wrought upon her lovely face, and there were even tears flowing down her cheeks: the sight of this terrible image was again enough to make me think I would collapse; the further part of the cavern was filled by a vast black divan which eloquently bespoke all the atrocities which occurred in this infernal place.

"And here is where you will perish, Thérèse," quoth Roland, "if ever you conceive the fatal notion of leaving my establishment; yes, it is here I will myself put you to death, here I will make you reverberate to the anguishes inflicted by everything of the most appalling I can possibly devise."

As he gave vent to this threat Roland became aroused; his agitation, his disorder made him resemble a tiger about to spring upon its prey: 'twas then he brought to light the formidable member wherewith he was outfitted; he had me touch it, asked me whether I had ever beheld its peer.

"Such as you see it, whore," said he in a rage, "in that shape it has, however, got to be introduced into the narrowest part of your body even if I must split you in half; my sister, considerably your junior, manages it in the same sector; never do I enjoy women in any other fashion," and so as to leave me in no doubt of the locale he had in mind, he inserted into it three fingers armed with exceedingly long nails, the while saying:

"Yes, 'tis there, Thérèse, it will be shortly into this hole I will drive this member which affrights you; it will be run every inch of the way in, it will tear you, you'll bleed and I will be beside myself."

Foam flecked his lips as he spoke these words interspersed with revolting oaths and blasphemies. The hand, which had been prying open the shrine he seemed to want to attack, now strayed over all the adjacent parts; he scratched them, he did as much to my breast, he clawed me so badly I was not to get over the pain for a fortnight. Next, he placed me on the edge of the couch, rubbed alcohol upon that mossy tonsure with which Nature ornaments the altar wherein our species finds regeneration; he set it afire and burned it. His fingers closed upon the fleshy protuberance which surmounts this same altar, he snatched at it and scraped roughly, then he inserted his fingers within and his nails ripped the membrane which lines it. Losing all control over himself, he told me that, since he had me in his lair, I might just as well not leave it, for that would spare him the nuisance of bringing me back down again; I fell to my knees and dared remind him again of what I had done in his behalf. . . . I observed I but further excited him by harping again upon the rights to his pity I fancied were mine; he told me to be silent, bringing up his knee and giving me a tremendous blow in the pit of the stomach which sent me sprawling on the flagstones. He seized a handful of my hair and jerked me erect.

"Very well!" he said, "come now! prepare yourself; it is a certainty, I am going to kill you. . . ."

"Oh, Monsieur!"

"No, no, you've got to die; I do not want to hear you reproach me with your good little deeds; I don't like owing anything to anybody, others have got to rely upon me for everything. . . . You're going to perish, I tell you, get into that coffin, let's see if it fits."

He lifts me, thrusts me into it and shuts it, then quits the cavern and gives me the impression I have been left there. Never had I thought myself so near to death; alas! it was nonetheless to be presented to me under a yet more real aspect. Roland returns, he fetches me out of the coffin.

"You'll be well off in there," says he, "one would say 'twas made for you; but to let you finish peacefully in that box would be a death too sweet; I'm going to expose you to one of a different variety which, all the same, will have its agreeable qualities; so implore your God, whore, pray to him to come posthaste and avenge you if he really has it in him. . . ."

I cast myself down upon the *prie-dieu,* and while aloud I open my heart to the Eternal, Roland in a still crueler manner intensifies, upon the hindquarters I expose to him, his vexations and his torments; with all his strength he flogs those parts with a steel-tipped martinet, each blow draws a gush of blood which springs to the walls.

"Why," he continued with a curse, "he doesn't much aid you, your God, does he? and thus he allows unhappy virtue to suffer, he abandons it to villainy's hands; ah! what a bloody fine God you've got there, Thérèse, what a superb God he is! Come," he says, "come here, whore, your prayer should be done," and at the same time he places me upon the divan at the back of that cell; "I told you Thérèse, you have got to die!"

He seizes my arms, binds them to my side, then he slips a black silken noose about my neck; he holds both ends of the cord and, by tightening, he can strangle and dispatch me to the other world either quickly or slowly, depending upon his pleasure.

"This torture is sweeter than you may imagine, Thérèse," says Roland; "you will only approach death by way of unspeakably pleasurable sensations; the pressure this noose will bring to bear upon your nervous system will set fire to the organs of voluptuousness; the effect is certain; were all the people who are condemned to this torture to know in what an intoxication of joy it makes one die, less terrified by this retribution for their crimes, they would commit them more often and with much greater self-assurance; this delicious operation, Thérèse, by causing, as well, the contraction of the locale in which I am going to fit myself," he added as he presented himself to a criminal avenue so worthy of such a villain, "is also going to double my pleasure."

He thrusts, he sweats, 'tis in vain; he prepares the road, 'tis futile; he is too monstrously proportioned, his enterprises are repeatedly frustrated; and then his wrath exceeds all limits; his nails, his hands, his feet fly to revenge him upon the opposition Nature puts up against him; he returns to the assault, the glowing blade slides to the edge of the neighboring canal and smiting vigorously, penetrates to nigh the midway mark; I utter a cry; Roland, enraged by his mistake, withdraws petulantly, and this time hammers at the other gate with such force the moistened dart plunges in, rending me. Roland exploits this first sally's success; his efforts become more violent; he gains ground; as he advances, he gradually

tightens the fatal cord he has passed round my neck, hideous
screams burst from my lips; amused by them, the ferocious Roland
urges me to redouble my howlings, for he is but too confident of
their insufficiency, he is perfectly able to put a stop to them when
he wishes; their shrill sharp notes inflame him, the noose's pressure
is modulated by his degrees of delight; little by little my voice waxes
faint; the tightenings now become so intense that my senses weaken
although I do not lose the power to feel; brutally shaken by the
enormous instrument with which Roland is rending my entrails,
despite my frightful circumstances, I feel myself flooded by his
lust's jetted outpourings; I still hear the cries he mouths as he
discharges; an instant of stupor followed, I knew not what had
happened to me, but soon my eyes open again to the light, I find
myself free, untied, and my sensory organs seem to come back to
life.

"Well, Thérèse," says my butcher, "I dare swear that if you'll
tell the truth you'll say you felt pleasure only?"

"Only horror, Monsieur, only disgust, only anguish and
despair."

"You are lying, I am fully acquainted with the effects you have
just experienced, but what does it matter what they were? I fancy
you already know me well enough to be damned certain that when
I undertake something with you, the joy you reap from it concerns
me infinitely less than my own, and this voluptuousness I seek has
been so keen that in an instant I am going to procure some more of
it. It is now upon yourself, Thérèse," declares this signal libertine,
"it is upon you alone your life is going to depend."

Whereupon he hitches about my neck the rope that hangs
from the ceiling; he has me stand upon a stool, pulls the rope
taut, secures it, and to the stool he attaches a string whose end he
keeps in his hand as he sits down in an armchair facing me; I am
given a sickle which I am to use to sever the rope at the moment
when, by means of the string, he jerks the stool from beneath my
feet.

"Notice, Thérèse," he says when all is ready, "that though
you may miss your blow, I'll not miss mine; and so I am not mistaken when I say your life depends upon you."

He excites himself; it is at his intoxication's critical moment he is to snatch away the stool which, removed, will leave me dangling from the beam; he does everything possible to pretend the instant has come; he would be beside himself were I to miss my cue; but do what he will, I divine the crisis, the violence of his ecstasy betrays him, I see him make the telltale movement, the stool flies away, I cut the rope and fall to the ground; there I am, completely detached, and although five yards divide us, would you believe it, Madame? I feel my entire body drenched with the evidence of his delirium and his frenzy.

Anyone but I, taking advantage of the weapon she clutched in her hand, would doubtless have leapt upon that monster; but what might I have gained by this brave feat? for I did not have the keys to those subterranean passages, I was ignorant of their scheme, I should have perished before being able to emerge from them; Roland, furthermore, was armed; and so I got up, leaving the sickle on the ground so that he might not conceive the slightest suspicion of my intentions, and indeed he had none, for he had savored the full extent of pleasure and, far more content with my tractability, with my resignation, than with my agility, he signaled to me and we left.

The next day I cast an appraising eye upon my companions: those four girls ranged from twenty-five to thirty years of age; although bestialized and besotted by misery and warped by excessive drudgery, they still had the remnants of beauty; their figures were handsome, and the youngest, called Suzanne, still had, together with charming eyes, very fine hair; Roland had seized her in Lyon, he had deflowered her, and after having sworn to her family he would marry her, he had brought her to this frightful château, where she had been three years his slave, and during that period she had been especially singled out to be the object of the monster's ferocities: by dint of blows from the bull's pizzle, her buttocks had become as calloused and toughened as would be cow's hide dried in the sun; she had a cancer upon her left breast and an abscess in her matrix which caused her unspeakable suffering; all that was the perfidious Roland's achievement; each of those horrors was the fruit of his lecheries.

It was she who informed me Roland was on the eve of departing for Venice if the considerable sums he had very recently shipped to Spain could be converted into letters of credit he needed for Italy, for he did not want to transport his gold east across the Alps; never did he send any in that direction: it was in a different country from the one he had decided to inhabit that he circulated his false coins; by this device, rich to be sure but only in the bank-notes of another kingdom, his rascalities could never be detected in the land where he planned to take up his next abode. But everything could be overthrown within the space of an instant and the retirement he envisioned wholly depended upon this latest transaction in which the bulk of his treasure was compromised. Were Cadiz to accept his false *piasters, sequins,* and *louis,* and against them send him letters negotiable in Venice, Roland would be established for the rest of his days; were the fraud to be detected, one single day would suffice to demolish the fragile edifice of his fortune.

"Alas!" I remarked upon learning these details, "Providence will be just for once. It will not countenance the success of such a monster, and all of us will be revenged. . . ."

Great God! in view of the experience I had acquired, how was I able thus to reason!

Toward noon we were given a two-hour respite, which we always used to good advantage to go for a little individual rest and food in our cells; at two o'clock we were reattached to the wheel and were made to work till nightfall; never were we allowed to enter the château; if we were naked, 'twas not only because of the heat, but so as better to be able to receive the bull's pizzle beatings our savage master periodically came to inflict upon us; in winter we were given pantaloons and a light sweater which so closely hugged the skin that our bodies were not the less exposed to the blows of a villain whose unique pleasure was to beat us half-senseless.

A week passed during which I saw no sign of Roland; on the ninth day he visited us at work and maintained Suzanne and I were improperly applying ourselves to our task; he distributed thirty cuts with the pizzle upon each of us, slashing us from back to calf.

At midnight on that same day, the evil man came to get me in my kennel and, warmed by the sight of what his cruelties had produced, he once again introduced his terrible bludgeon into the shadowy lair I exposed by the posture he made me assume in order to inspect the vestiges of his rage. When his hungers were appeased I thought to profit from his momentary calm to supplicate him to mitigate my lot. Alas! I was unaware that in such a genius, whereas the delirious interlude stimulates the penchant for cruelty into greater activity, the subsequent reflux does not by any means restore the honest man's pacific virtues to it; 'tis a fire more or less quickened by the fuel wherewith it is fed, but one whose embers, though covered with cinder, burn nonetheless.

"And what right have you," Roland replied to me, "to expect me to sweeten your circumstances? Because of the fantasies I am pleased to put into execution with you? But am I to throw myself at your feet and implore you to accord favors for the granting of which you can implore some recompense? I ask nothing from you, I take, and I simply do not see that, because I exercise one right over you, it must result that I have to abstain from demanding a second; there is no love in what I do: love is a chivalric sentiment I hold in sovereign contempt and to whose assaults my heart is always impervious; I employ a woman out of necessity, as one employs a round and hollow vessel for a different purpose but an analogous need; but never according this individual, which my money and authority make subject to me, either esteem or tenderness, owing to myself what I get from her and never exacting from her anything but submission, I cannot be constrained, in the light of all this, to acknowledge any gratitude toward her. I ask them who would like to compel me to be thankful whether a thief who snatches a man's purse in the woods because he, the thief, is the stronger of the two, owes this man any gratitude for the wrong he has just done him; the same holds true for an outrage committed against a woman: it may justify a repetition of the abuse, but never is it a sufficient reason to grant her compensation."

"Oh, Monsieur," I said to him, "to what limits you do carry your villainy!"

"To the ultimate periods," Roland answered; "there is not a single extravagance in the world in which I have not indulged, not a crime I have not committed, and not one that my doctrines do not excuse or legitimate; unceasingly, I have found in evil a kind of attractiveness which always redounds to my lust's advantage; crime ignites my appetites; the more frightful it is, the more it stimulates; in committing it, I enjoy the same sort of pleasure ordinary folk taste in naught but libricity, and a hundred times I have discovered myself, while thinking of crime, while surrendering to it, or just after having executed it, in precisely the same state in which one is when confronted by a beautiful naked woman; it irritates my senses in the same way, and I have committed it in order to arouse myself as, when one is filled with impudicious designs, one approaches a beautiful object."

"Oh, Monsieur! 'tis frightful, what you say, but I have beheld examples of it."

"There are a thousand, Thérèse. It must not be supposed that it is a woman's beauty which best stirs a libertine mind, it is rather the species of crime that the law has associated with possession of her: the proof of which is that the more criminal this possession the more one is inflamed by it; the man who enjoys a woman he steals from her husband, a daughter he snatches from her parents, knows a far greater delectation, no doubt of it, than does the husband who enjoys no one but his wife, and the more the ties one breaks appear to be respected, the more the voluptuousness is compounded. If 'tis one's mother, or one's daughter, so many additional charms to the pleasures experienced; when you've savored all this, then you truly would have interdictions further increase in order to give the violation of them added difficulty and greater charm; now, if pleasure-taking is seasoned by a criminal flavoring, crime, dissociated from this pleasure, may become a joy in itself; there will then be a certain delight in naked crime. Well, it is impossible that what contributes the saline tang not itself be very salty. Thus, let me imagine, the abduction of a girl on one's own account will give a very lively pleasure, but abduction in the interests of someone else will give all that pleasure with which the enjoyment of this girl is improved by rape; the theft of a watch, the rape of a purse will also give the same pleasure, and if I have accustomed my senses to being moved by the rape of some girl *qua* rape, that same pleasure, that same delight will be found again in the seizing of the watch or of the purse, etc.; and that explains the eccentricity in so many honest folk who steal without needing to steal. Nothing more common; from this moment on, one both tastes the greatest pleasure in everything criminal, and, by every imaginable device, one renders simple enjoyments as criminal as they can possibly be rendered; by conducting oneself in this style, one but adds to enjoyment the dash of salt which was wanting and which became indispensable to happiness' perfection. These doctrines lead far, I know; perhaps, Thérèse, I shall even show you how far before too long, but what matter? enjoyment's the thing. Was there, for example, dear girl, anything more ordinary or more natural than for me to enjoy you? But you oppose it, you ask that it stop; it would seem that, in the light of my obligations toward you, I ought to grant what you request; however, I surrender to nothing, I listen to nothing, I slash through all the knots that bind fools, I submit you to my desires, and out of the most elementary, the most monotonous enjoyment I evolve one that is really delicious; therefore submit, Thérèse, submit, and if ever you are reincarnated and return to the world in the guise of the mighty, exploit your privileges in the same way and you will know every one of the most lively and most piquant pleasures."

These words gone out of his mouth, Roland went away and left me to ponder thoughts which, as you may well believe, presented him in no favorable aspect.

I had been six months in this household, from time to time serving the villain's disgraceful debauches, when one night I beheld him enter my prison with Suzanne.

"Come, Thérèse," said he, " 'tis already a long time, I find, since I took you down to that cavern which impressed you so deeply; both of you are going to accompany me there, but don't expect to climb back together, for I absolutely must leave one of you behind; well, we'll see which one fate designates."

I get to my feet, cast alarmed glances at my companion, I see tears rolling from her eyes . . . and we set off.

When we were locked into the underground vault, Roland examined each of us with ferocious eyes; he amused himself by reiterating our sentence and persuading us both that one of the two would certainly remain there below.

"Well," said he, seating himself and having us stand directly before him, "each of you take your turn and set to work exorcising this disabled object; there's a devil in it keeps it limp, and woe unto the one of you who restores its energy."

" 'Tis an injustice," quoth Suzanne; "she who arouses you most should be the one to obtain your mercy."

"Not at all," Roland retorted, "once it is manifest which of you arouses me most, it is established which one's death will give me the greater pleasure . . . and I'm aiming at pleasure, nothing else. Moreover, by sparing her who inflames me the more rapidly, you would both proceed with such industry that you might perhaps plunge my senses into their ecstasy before the sacrifice were consummated, and that must not happen."

" 'Tis to want evil for evil's sake, Monsieur," I said to Roland, "the completion of your ecstasy ought to be the only thing you desire, and if you attain it without crime, why do you want to commit one?"

"Because I only deliciously reach the critical stage in this way, and because I only came down here in order to commit one. I know perfectly well I might succeed without it, but I want it in order to succeed."

And, during this dialogue, having chosen me to begin, I start exciting his behind with one hand, his front with the other, while he touches at his leisure every part of my body offered him by my nakedness.

"You've still a long way to go, Thérèse," said he, fingering my buttocks, "before this fine flesh is in the state of petrified callosity and mortification apparent in Suzanne's; one might light a fire under that dear girl's cheeks without her feeling a thing; but you, Thérèse, you . . . these are yet roses bound in lilies: we'll get to them in good time, in good time."

You simply have no idea, Madame, how much that threat set me at ease; Roland doubtless did not suspect, as he uttered it, the peace it sent flooding through me, for was it not clear that, since he planned to expose me to further cruelties, he was not yet eager to immolate me? I have told you, Madame, that everything the wretched hear drives home, and thenceforth I was reassured. Another increase of happiness! I was performing in vain, and that enormous mass telescoped into itself resisted all my shakings;

Suzanne was in the same posture, she was palpated in the same areas, but as her flesh was toughened in a very different way, Roland treated it with much less consideration; however, Suzanne was younger.

"I am convinced," our persecutor was saying, "that the most awesome whips would now fail to draw a drop of blood from that ass."

He made each of us bend over and, our angle of inclination providing him with the four avenues of pleasure, his tongue danced wriggling into the two narrowest; the villain spat into the others; he turned us about, had us kneel between his thighs in such a manner our breasts found themselves at a level with what of him we were stimulating.

"Oh! as regards breasts," said Roland, "you've got to yield to Suzanne; never had you such fine teats; now then, let's take a look at this noble endowment."

And with those words he pressed the poor girl's breasts till, beneath his fingers, they were covered with bruises. At this point it was no longer I who was exciting him, Suzanne had replaced me; scarcely had she fallen into his clutches when his dart, springing from its quiver, began to menace everything surrounding it.

"Suzanne," said Roland, "behold an appalling triumph. . . . 'tis your death decreed, Suzanne; I feared as much," added that ferocious man as he nipped and clawed her breasts.

As for mine, he only sucked and chewed them. At length, he placed Suzanne on her knees at the edge of the sofa, he made her bend her head and in this attitude he enjoyed her according to the frightful manner natural to him; awakened by new pains, Suzanne struggles and Roland, who simply wishes to skirmish, is content with a brisk passage of arms, and comes to take refuge in me at the same shrine at which he has sacrificed in my companion whom he does not cease to vex and molest the while.

"There's a whore who excites me cruelly," he says to me, "I don't know what to do with her."

"Oh, Monsieur," say I, "have pity upon her; her sufferings could not be more intense."

"Oh, but you're wrong!" the villain replies, "one might . . . ah! if only I had with me that celebrated Emperor Kié, one of the

greatest scoundrels ever to have sat on the Chinese throne,[6] with
Kié we'd really be able to perform wonders. Both he and his wife,
they say, immolated victims daily and would have them live twenty-
four hours in death's cruelest agonies, and in such a state of suffering that they were constantly on the verge of expiring but never
quite able to die, for those monsters administered that kind of aid
which made them flutter between relief and torture and only
brought them back to life for one minute in order to kill them the
next. . . . I, Thérèse, I am too gentle, I know nothing of those arts,
I'm a mere apprentice."

Roland retires without completing the sacrifice and hurts me
almost as much by this precipitous withdrawal as he had upon
inserting himself. He throws himself into Suzanne's arms, and
joining sarcasm to outrage:

"Amiable creature," he apostrophizes, "with such delight I
remember the first instants of our union; never had woman given
me such thrilling pleasures, never had I loved one as I did you . . .
let us embrace, Suzanne, for we're going to part, perhaps the
season of our separation will be long."

"Monster!" my companion retorts, thrusting him away with
horror, "begone; to the torments you inflict upon me, join not the
despair of hearing your terrible remarks; sate your rage, tigerish
one, but at least respect my sufferings."

Roland laid hands on her, stretched her upon the couch, her
legs widespread, and the workshop of generation ideally within
range.

"Temple of my ancient pleasures," the infamous creature intoned, "you who procured me delights so sweet when I plucked
your first roses, I must indeed address to you my farewells. . . ."

The villain! he drove his fingernails into it and, rummaging

---

[6] Kié, the Emperor of China, had a wife as cruel and debauched as he; bloodshed
was as naught to them, and for their exclusive pleasure they spilled rivers of it every
day; within their palace they had a secret chamber where victims were put to death
before their eyes and while they enjoyed themselves. Théo, one of this Prince's suc-
cessors, had, like him, a very bloodthirsty wife; they invented a brass column and
this great cylinder they would heat red hot; unlucky persons were bound to it while
the royal couple looked on: "The Princess," writes the historian from whom we have
borrowed these touches, "was infinitely entertained by these melancholy victims'
contortions and screams; she was not content unless her husband gave her this
spectacle frequently." *Hist. des Conj.* vol. 7, page 43.

about inside for a few minutes while screams burst from Suzanne's mouth, he did not withdraw them until they were covered with blood. Glutted and wearied by these horrors, and feeling, indeed, he could restrain himself no longer:

"Come, Thérèse, come," he said, "let's conclude all this with a little scene of funambulism: it'll be cut-the-cord,[7] dear girl."

That was the name he gave that deadly legerdemain of which I gave you a description when I mentioned Roland's cavern for the first time. I mount the three-legged stool, the evil fellow fits the halter about my neck, he takes his place opposite me; although in a frightful state, Suzanne excites him manually; an instant passes, then he snaps the stool from beneath me, but equipped with the sickle, I sever the cord immediately and fall uninjured to the ground.

"Nicely done, very neat," says Roland, "your turn, Suzanne, there it is, and I'll spare you, if you manage as cleverly."

Suzanne takes my place. Oh, Madame, allow me to pass over that dreadful scene's details. . . . The poor thing did not recover from it.

"And now off we go, Thérèse," says Roland, "you'll not return to this place until your time has come."

"Whenever you like, Monsieur, whenever you like," I reply; "I prefer death to the frightful life you have me lead. Are there wretches such as we for whom life can be valuable? . . ."

And Roland locked me into my cell. The next day my companions asked what had become of Suzanne and I told them; they were hardly surprised; all were awaiting the same fate and each,

---

[7] This game, described above, was in great use amongst the Celts from whom we are descended (see Monsieur Peloutier's *Histoire des Celtes*); virtually all these extravagances of debauchery, these extraordinary libertine passions, some part of which are described in this book and which, how ridiculously! today awaken the law's attention, were, in days bygone, either our ancestors' sports, games far superior to our contemporary amusements, or legalized customs, or again, religious ceremonies; currently, they are transformed into crimes. In how many pious rituals did not the pagans employ flagellation! Several people used these identical tortures, or passions, to initiate their warriors; this was known as *huscanaver* (*viz.*, the religious ceremonies of every race on earth). These pleasantries, whose maximum inconvenience may be at the very most the death of a slut, are capital crimes at the moment. Three cheers for the progress of civilization! How it conspires to the happiness of man, and how much more fortunate than our forebears we are!

238 THE MARQUIS DE SADE

like me, seeing therein a term to their suffering, passionately longed for it.

And thus two years went by, Roland indulging in his customary debauchery, I lingering on with the prospect of a cruel death, when one day the news went about the château that not only were our master's expectations satisfied, not only had he received the immense quantity of Venetian funds he had wished, but that he had even obtained a further order for another six millions in counterfeit coin for which he would be reimbursed in Italy when he arrived to claim payment; the scoundrel could not possibly have enjoyed better luck; he was going to leave with an income of two millions, not to mention his hopes of getting more: this was the new piece of evidence Providence had prepared for me. This was the latest manner in which it wished to convince me that prosperity belongs to Crime only and indigence to Virtue.

Matters were at this stage when Roland came to take me to his cavern a third time. I recollect what he threatened me with on my previous visit, I shudder. . . .

"Rest assured," he says, "you've nothing to fear, 'tis a question of something which concerns me alone . . . an uncommon joy I'd like to taste and from which you will incur no risks."

I follow him. When the doors are shut:

"Thérèse," says Roland, "there's no one in the house but you to whom I dare confide the problem; I've got to have a woman of impeccable honesty. . . . I've no one about but you, I confess that I prefer you to my sister. . . .

Taken aback, I entreat him to clarify himself.

"Then listen," says he; "my fortune is made, but whatever be the favors I have received from fate, it can desert me at any instant; I may be trapped, I could be caught while transporting my bullion, and if that misfortune occurs, Thérèse, it's the rope that's waiting for me: 'tis the same delight I am pleased to have women savor: that's the one will serve as my undoing; I am as firmly persuaded as I can possibly be that this death is infinitely sweeter than cruel; but as the women upon whom I have tested its initial anguishes have never really wished to tell me the truth, it is in person I wish to be made acquainted with the sensation. By way of the experience itself I want to find out whether it is not very certain this asphyxiation impels, in the individual who undergoes it, the erectory nerve to produce an ejaculation; once convinced this death is but a game, I'll brave it with far greater courage, for it is not my existence's cessation terrifies me: my principles are determined upon that head and well persuaded matter can never become anything but matter again, I have no greater dread of Hell than I have expectation of Paradise; but a cruel death's torments make me apprehensive; I don't wish to suffer when I perish; so let's have a try. You will do to me everything I did to you; I'll strip; I'll mount the stool, you'll adjust the rope, I'll excite myself for a moment, then, as soon as you see things assume a certain consistency, you'll jerk the stool free and I'll remain hanging; you'll leave me there until you either discern my semen's emission or symptoms of death's throes; in the latter case, you'll cut me down at once; in the other, you'll allow Nature to take her course and you'll not detach me until afterward. You observe, Thérèse, I'm putting my life in your hands; your freedom, your fortune will be your good conduct's reward."

"Ah, Monsieur, there's folly in the proposition."

"No, Thérèse, I insist the thing be done," he answered, undressing himself, "but behave yourself well; behold what proof I give you of my confidence and high regard!"

What possibility of hesitation had I? Was he not my master? Furthermore, it seemed to me the evil I was going to do him would be immediately offset by the extreme care I would take to save his life: I was going to be mistress of that life, but whatever might be his intentions with respect to me, it would certainly only be in order to restore it to him.

We take our stations; Roland is stimulated by a few of his usual caresses; he climbs upon the stool, I put the halter round his neck; he tells me he wants me to curse him during the process, I am to reproach him with all his life's horrors, I do so; his dart soon rises to menace Heaven, he himself gives me the sign to remove the stool, I obey; would you believe it, Madame? nothing more true than what Roland had conjectured: nothing but symptoms of pleasure ornament his countenance and at practically the same instant rapid jets of semen spring nigh to the vault. When 'tis all shot out without any assistance whatsoever from me, I rush to cut him down, he falls, unconscious, but thanks to my ministrations he quickly recovers his senses.

"Oh Thérèse!" he exclaims upon opening his eyes, "oh, those sensations are not to be described; they transcend all one can possibly say: let them now do what they wish with me, I stand unflinching before Themis' sword!

"You're going to find me guilty yet another time, Thérèse," Roland went on, tying my hands behind my back, "no thanks for you, but, dear girl, what can one expect? a man doesn't correct himself at my age. . . . Beloved creature, you have just saved my life and never have I so powerfully conspired against yours; you lamented Suzanne's fate; ah well, I'll arrange for you to meet again; I'm going to plunge you alive into the dungeon where she expired."

I will not describe my state of mind, Madame, you fancy what it was; in vain did I weep, groan, I was not heeded. Roland opened the fatal dungeon, he hangs out a lamp so that I can still better discern the multitude of corpses wherewith it is filled; next, he passes a cord under my arms which, as you know, are bound behind my back, and by means of this cord he lowers me thirty feet: I am twenty more from the bottom of the pit: in this position I suffer hideously, it is as if my arms are being torn from their sockets. With what terror was I not seized! what a prospect confronted my eyes! Heaps of bodies in the midst of which I was going to finish my life and whose stench was already infecting me. Roland cinches the rope about a stick fitted above the hole then, brandishing a knife, I hear him exciting himself.

"Well, Thérèse," he cries, "recommend your soul to God, the instant my delirium supervenes will be that when I plunge you into the eternal abyss awaiting you; ah . . . ah . . . Thérèse, ah . . ." and I feel my head covered with proof of his ecstasy; but, happily, he has not parted the rope: he lifts me out.

"Ha," says he, "were you afraid?"

"Oh, Monsieur—"

" 'Tis thus you'll die, be sure of it, Thérèse, be sure of it, and 'twas pleasant to familiarize you with your egress."

We climb back to the light. . . . Was I to complain? or be thankful? What a reward for what I had just done for him! But had the monster not been in a position to do more? Could he not have killed me? Oh, what a man!

Roland prepared his departure; on the eve of setting out he pays me a visit; I fall before his feet, most urgently I beg him to free me and to give me whatever little sum of money he would like, that I might be able to reach Grenoble.

"Grenoble! Certainly not, Thérèse, you'd denounce us when you got there."

"Very well, Monsieur," I say, sprinkling his knees with my tears, "I swear to you I'll never go there and, to be sure of me, condescend to take me to Venice with you; I will perhaps find gentler hearts there than in my native land, and once you are so kind as to set me free, I swear to you by all that is holy I will never importune you."

"I'll not aid you, not a pennyworth of aid will you get from me," that peerless rogue answered; "everything connected with pity, commiseration, gratitude is so alien to my heart that were I three times as rich as I am, they'd not see me give one crown to the poor; the spectacle of misery irritates me, amuses me, and when I am unable to do evil myself, I have a delicious time enjoying that accomplished by the hand of destiny. Upon all this I have principles to which, Thérèse, I adhere faithfully; poverty is part of the natural order; by creating men of dissimilar strength, Nature has convinced us of her desire that inequality be preserved even in those modifications our culture might bring to Nature's laws. To relieve indigence is to violate the established order, to imperil it, it is to enter into revolt against that which Nature has decreed, it is to undermine the equilibrium that is fundamental to her sublimest arrangements; it is to strive to erect an equality very perilous to society, it is to encourage indolence and flatter drones, it is to teach the poor to rob the rich man when the latter is pleased to refuse the former alms, for it's a dangerous habit, and gratuities encourage it."

"Oh, Monsieur, how harsh these principles are! Would you speak thus had you not always been wealthy?"

"Who knows, Thérèse? everyone has a right to his opinion, that's mine, and I'll not change it. They complain about beggars in France: if they wished to be rid of them, the thing could soon be done; hang seven or eight thousand of 'em and the infamous breed will vanish overnight. The Body Politic should be governed by the same rules that apply to the Body Physical. Would a man devoured by vermin allow them to feed upon him out of sympathy? In our gardens do we not uproot the parasitic plant which harms useful vegetation? Why then should one choose to act otherwise in this case?"

"But Religion," I expostulated, "benevolence, Monsieur, humanity..."

"... are the chopping blocks of all who pretend to happiness," said Roland; "if I have consolidated my own, it is only upon the debris of all those infamous prejudices of mankind; 'tis by mocking laws human and divine; 'tis by constantly sacrificing the weak when I find them in my path, 'tis by abusing the public's good faith; 'tis by ruining the poor and stealing from the rich I have arrived at the summit of that precipice whereupon sits the temple sacred to the divinity I adore; why not imitate me? The narrow road leading to that shrine is as plainly offered to your eyes as mine; the hallucinatory virtues you have preferred to it, have they consoled you for your sacrifices? 'Tis too late, luckless one, 'tis too late, weep for your sins, suffer, and strive to find in the depths of the phantoms you worship, if any finding there is to be done, what the reverence you have shown them has caused you to lose."

With these words, the cruel Roland leaps upon me and I am again forced to serve the unworthy pleasures of a monster I had such good reason to abhor; this time I thought he would strangle me; when his passions were satisfied, he caught up the bull's pizzle and with it smote me above a hundred blows all over my body, the while assuring me I was fortunate he lacked the time to do more.

On the morrow, before setting out, the wretch presented us with a new scene of cruelty and of barbarity whereof no example is furnished by the annals of Andronicus, Nero, Tiberius, or Wenceslaus. Everyone at the château supposed Roland's sister would leave with him, and he had indeed told her to dress and ready herself for the journey; at the moment of mounting his horse, he leads her toward us. "There's your post, vile creature," says he, ordering her to take off her clothes, "I want my comrades to remember me by leaving them as a token the woman for whom they thought I had a fancy; but as we need only a certain number and as I am going to follow a dangerous road upon which my weapons will perhaps be useful, I must try my pistols upon one of these rascals." Whereupon he loads one of his guns, aims it at each of our breasts, and comes at last to his sister. "Off you go, whore," says he, blasting out her brains, "go advise the devil that Roland, the richest villain on earth, is he who most insolently taunts the hand of Heaven and challenges Satan's own!" The poor girl did not expire at once: she writhed in her death throes for a considerable period: 'twas a hideous spectacle: that infamous scoundrel calmly considered it and did not tear his eyes away until he had left us forever.

Everything changed the day after Roland went away. His successor, a gentle and very reasonable man, had us released at once.

"That is hardly fit work for a frail and delicate sex," he said to us with kindness; "animals should be employed at this machine; our trade is criminal enough without further offending the Supreme Being with gratuitous atrocities."

He installed us in the château and, without requiring me to do so, suggested I assume possession of the duties Roland's sister had performed; the other women were busied cutting out counterfeit coins, a much less fatiguing task, no doubt, and one for which they were rewarded, as was I, with good lodgings and excellent food.

At the end of two months, Dalville, Roland's successor, informed us of his colleague's happy arrival at Venice; there he had established himself and there realized his fortune and there he enjoyed it in peace and quiet, wholly content, full of the felicity he had anticipated. The fate of the man who replaced him was of a distinctly different character. The unfortunate Dalville was honest in his profession, indeed, even more honest than was necessary in order to be destroyed.

One day, while all was calm at the château, while, under the direction of that good master, the work, although criminal, was however being carried on with gaiety, one day the gates were stormed, the moats bridged and the house, before our men had a moment's opportunity to look to their defense, found itself invaded by soldiers of the constabulary, sixty strong. Surrender was our sole alternative; we were shackled like beasts; we were attached to the horses and marches down to Grenoble. "O Heaven!" I said to myself as we entered, " 'tis then the scaffold destiny holds for me in this city wherein I wildly fancied my happiness was to be born. . . . Oh! how deceived is man by his intuitions!"

The court was not long tarrying over the counterfeiters' case; they were all sentenced to the gallows; when the mark that branded me was detected, they scarcely gave themselves the trouble of interrogating me and I was about to be hanged along with the others when I made a last effort to obtain some pity from that famous magistrate who proved to be an honor to his tribunal, a judge of integrity, a beloved citizen, an enlightened philosopher whose wisdom and benevolence will grave his name for all time in letters of gold upon Themis' temple. He listened to me; convinced of my good faith and the authenticity of my wretched plight, he deigned to give my case a little more attention than his cohorts saw fit to lavish upon it. . . . O great man, 'tis to thee I owe an homage: a miserable creature's gratitude would not sit onerously with thee and the tribute she offers thee, by publishing abroad thy goodness of heart, will always be her sweetest joy.

Monsieur S*** himself became my advocate; my testimony was heard, and his male eloquence illumined the mind of the court. The general depositions of the false coiners they were going to execute fortified the zeal of the man who had the kindness to take an interest in me: I was declared an unwilling party to crime, innocent, and fully acquitted of all charges, was set at complete liberty to become what I wished; to those services my protector added a collection he had taken for my relief, and it totaled more than fifty *louis;* I began to see a dawning of happiness at last; my presentiments seemed finally about to be realized and I thought I had reached an end of my tribulations when it pleased Providence to convince me they were still far from their definitive cessation.

Upon emerging from jail I took up lodgings at an inn facing the Isère bridge on the side of the *faubourgs* where, I had been assured, I might find proper quarters. My plan, suggested by the advice of Monsieur S***, was to stay there awhile in order to try to find a situation in the town; in the event the letters of recommendation Monsieur S*** had so kindly given me produced no results, I was to return to Lyon. On the second day I was dining at my inn—'twas what is called table d'hôte—when I noticed I was being closely scrutinized by a tall, very handsomely attired woman who went under a baroness' title; upon examining her in my turn, I believed I recognized her; we both rose and approached each other, we embraced like two people who once knew each other but cannot remember under what circumstances.

Then the baroness drew me aside.

"Thérèse," says she, "am I in error? are you not the person I saved from the Conciergerie ten years ago? have you entirely forgotten your Dubois?"

Little flattered by this discovery, I however replied to it with politeness, but I was dealing with the most subtle, the most adroit woman in contemporary France; there was no way of eluding her. Dubois overwhelmed me with attentions, she said that she, like the entire town, had taken an interest in my fate but that had she known who I really was, she would have resorted to all sorts of measures and made many a representation to the magistrates, amongst whom, she declared, she had several friends. As usual, I was weak, I permitted myself to be led to this woman's room and there I related my sufferings to her.

"My dear friend," said she, renewing her embraces, "if I have desired to see you more intimately, it is to tell you I have made my fortune and that all I possess is at your disposal; look here," she said, opening some caskets brimming with gold and diamonds, "these are the fruits of my industry; had I worshiped Virtue like you, I should be in prison today, or hanged."

"O Madame," I cried, "if you owe all that to naught but crime, Providence, which eventually is always just, will not suffer you to enjoy it for long."

"An error," said Dubois; "do not imagine that Providence invariably favors Virtue; do not let a brief interlude of prosperity blind you to this point. It is as one to the maintenance of Providence's scheme whether 'tis Peter or Paul who follows the evil career while the other surrenders himself to good; Nature must have an equal quantity of each, and the exercise of crime rather than the commission of good is a matter of you've no idea what indifference to her; listen Thérèse, pay a little attention to me," continued that corruptor, seating herself and bidding me take a nearby chair; "you have some wit, my child, and your intelligence will be speedily convinced.

" 'Tis not man's election of Virtue which brings him happiness, dear girl, for Virtue, like vice, is nothing beyond a scheme of getting along in the world; 'tis not, hence, a question of adopting one course rather than another; 'tis merely a matter of following the road generally taken; he who wanders away from it is always wrong; in an entirely virtuous world, I would recommend virtue to you, because worldly rewards being associated therewith, happiness would infallibly be connected with it too; in a totally corrupt world, I would never advise anything but vice. He who does not walk along with others has inevitably to perish; everyone he encounters he collides with, and, as he is weak, he has necessarily to be crushed. It is in vain the law wishes to re-establish order and restore men to righteousness; too unjust to undertake the task, too insufficient to succeed in it, those laws will lure you away from the beaten path, but only temporarily; never will they make man abandon it. While the general interest of mankind drives it to corruption, he who does not wish to be corrupted with the rest will therefore be fighting against the general interest; well, what happiness can he expect who is in perpetual conflict with the interest of everyone else? Are you going to tell me it is vice which is at odds with mankind's welfare? I would grant this true in a world composed of equal proportions of good and bad people, because in this instance, the interest of the one category would be in clear contradiction with that of the other; however, that does not hold true in a completely corrupt society; in it, my vices outrage the vicious only and provoke in them other vices which they use to square matters: and thus all of us are happy: the vibration becomes general: we have a multitude of conflicts and mutual injuries whereby everyone, immediately recovering what he has just lost, incessantly discovers himself in a happy position. Vice is dangerous to naught but Virtue which, frail and timorous, dares undertake nothing; but when it shall no longer exist on earth, when its wearisome reign shall reach its end, vice thereafter outraging no one but the vicious, will cause other vices to burgeon but will cause no further damage to the virtuous. How could you help but have foundered a thousand times over in the course of your life, Thérèse? for have you not continually driven up the one-way street all the world has crowded down? Had you turned and abandoned yourself to the tide you would have made a safe port as well as I. Will he who wishes to climb upstream cover as much distance in a day as he who moves with the current? You constantly talk about Providence; ha! what proves to you this Providence is a friend of order and consequently enamored of Virtue? Does It not give you uninterrupted examples of Its injustices and Its irregularities? Is it by sending mankind war, plagues, and famine, is it by having formed a universe vicious in every one of its particulars It manifests to your view Its extreme fondness of good? Why would you have it that vicious individuals displease It since Providence Itself acts only through the intermediary of vices? since all is vice and corruption in Its works? since all is crime and disorder in what It wills? Moreover, whence do we derive those impulses which lead us to do evil? is it not Providence's hand which gives them to us? is there a single one of our sensations which does not come from It? one of our desires which is not Its artifact? is it then reasonable to say that It would allow us or give us penchants for something which might be harmful to It or useless? if then vices serve Providence, why should we wish to disown them, disclaim them, resist them? what would justify our labors to destroy them? and whence comes the right to stifle their voice? A little more philosophy in the world would soon restore all to order and would cause magistrates and legislators to see that the crimes they condemn and punish with such rigor sometimes have a far greater degree of utility than those virtues they preach without practicing and without ever rewarding."

"But when I become sufficiently enfeebled, Madame," I replied, "to be able to embrace your appalling doctrines, how will you manage to suppress the feelings of guilt in my heart whose birth they will cause at every instant?"

"Guilt is an illusion," Dubois answered; "my dear Thérèse, it it naught but the idiotic murmuring of a soul too debilitated to dare annihilate it."

"Annihilate it! May one?"

"Nothing simpler; one repents only of what one is not in the habit of doing; frequently repeat what makes you remorseful and you'll quickly have done with the business; against your qualms oppose the torch of your passions and self-interest's potent laws: they'll be put to rout in a trice. Remorse is no index of criminality; it merely denotes an easily subjugated spirit; let some absurd command be given you, which forbids you to leave this room, and you'll not depart without guilty feelings however certain it is your departure will cause no one any harm. And so it is not true that it is exclusively crime which excites remorse. By convincing yourself of crime's nullity, of its necessity with what regards Nature's universal scheme, it would therefore be as possible to vanquish the guilt one would sense after having committed it as it would be to throttle that which would be born from your leaving this room after having received the illegal order to stay here. One must begin with a precise analysis of everything mankind denominates as criminal; by convincing oneself that it is merely the infraction of its laws and national manners they characterize thus, that what is called crime in France ceases to be crime two hundred leagues away, that there is no act really considered criminal everywhere upon earth, none which, vicious or criminal here, is not praiseworthy and virtuous a few miles hence, that it is all a matter of opinion and of geography and that it is therefore absurd to tie oneself down to practicing virtues which are only vices somewhere else, and to flying from crimes which are excellent deeds in another climate—I ask you now if, after these reflections, I can still retain any feelings of guilt for having committed, either for the sake of pleasure or of self-interest, a crime in France which is nothing but a virtue in China? or if I ought to make myself very miserable or be prodigiously troubled about practicing actions in France which would have me burned in Siam? Now, if remorse exists only in reason of prohibition, if it is never but born of the wreckage of the inhibitory check and in no wise of the committed act, is it so very wise to allow the impulse in itself to subsist? is it not stupid not to extirpate it at once? Let one become accustomed to considering as inconsequential the act which has just excited remorse; let the scrupulously meditated study of the manners and customs of all the world's nations culminate in one's judging the act indifferent; as a result of this research, let one repeat this act, whatever it is, as often as possible; or, better still, let one commit more powerful versions of the act one is concerting so as better to habituate oneself to it, do this, and familiarity together with reason will soon destroy remorse for it; they will rapidly annihilate this shadowy, furtive impulse, issue of naught but ignorance and education. One will straightway feel that there being nothing really criminal in anything whatsoever, there is stupidity in repentance and pusillanimity in not daring to do everything that may be useful or agreeable to us, whatever be the dikes one must breach, the fences one must topple in order to do it. I am forty-five, Thérèse; I committed my first crime at four-teen. That one emancipated me from all the bonds that hampered me; since then I have not ceased to chase fortune throughout a career sown with crimes, there's not a single one I've not done or had done . . . and never have I known any remorse. However that may be, I am reaching my term, yet another two or three neat strokes and I pass from the mediocre condition wherein I was to have spent my life, to an income of above fifty thousand a year. I repeat, my dear, never upon this happily traveled road has remorse made me feel its stings; a catastrophic miscarriage might this instant plunge me from the pinnacle into the abyss, I'd not feel remorse, no: I would lament my want of skill or accuse men, but I should always be at peace with my conscience."

"Very well," I replied, "very well, Madame, but let's spend a moment reasoning in terms of your own principles: what right have you to require that my conscience be as impregnable as yours when since childhood it has not been accustomed to vanquishing the same prejudices? By what title do you require that my mind, which is not constituted like your own, be able to adopt the same systems? You acknowledge sums of good and evil in Nature, you admit that, in consequence, there must be a certain quantity of beings who practice good and another group which devotes itself to evil; the course I elect is hence natural; therefore, how would you be able to demand that I take leave of the rules Nature prescribes to me? You say you find happiness in the career you pursue; very well, Madame, why should it be that I do not also find it in the career I pursue? Do not suppose, furthermore, that the law's vigilance long leaves in peace him who violates its codes, you have just had a striking example of the contrary; of the fifteen scoundrels with whom I was living, fourteen perish ignominiously. . . ."

"And is that what you call a misfortune?" Dubois asked. "But what does this ignominy mean to him who has principles no longer? When one has trespassed every frontier, when in our eyes honor is no more than a hallucination, reputation of perfect indifference, religion an illusion, death a total annihilation; is it then not the same thing, to die on the scaffold or in bed? There are two varieties of rascals in the world, Thérèse: the one a powerful fortune or prodigious influence shelters from this tragic end; the other one who is unable to avoid it when taken. The latter, born unprovided with possessions, must have but one desire if he has any *esprit*: to become rich at no matter what price; if he succeeds, he obtains what he wanted and should be content; if he is put on the rack, what's he to regret since he has nothing to lose? Those laws decreed against banditry are null if they are not extended to apply to the powerful bandit; that the law inspire any dread in the miserable is impossible, for the sword is the miserable man's only resource."

"And do you believe," I broke in, "that in another world Celestial Justice does not await him whom crime has not affrighted in this one?"

"I believe," this dangerous woman answered, "that if there were a God there would be less evil on earth; I believe that since evil exists, these disorders are either expressly ordained by this God, and there you have a barbarous fellow, or he is incapable of preventing them and right away you have a feeble God; in either case, an abominable being, a being whose lightning I should defy and whose laws contemn. Ah, Thérèse! is not atheism preferable to the one and the other of these extremes? that's my doctrine, dear lass, it's been mine since childhood and I'll surely not renounce it while I live."

"You make me shudder, Madame," I said, getting to my feet; "will you pardon me? for I am unable to listen any longer to your sophistries and blasphemies."

"One moment, Thérèse," said Dubois, holding me back, "if I cannot conquer your reason, I may at least captivate your heart. I have need of you, do not refuse me your aid; here are a thousand *louis*: they will be yours as soon as the blow is struck."

Heedless of all but my penchant for doing good, I immediately asked Dubois what was involved so as to forestall, if 'twere possible, the crime she was getting ready to commit.

"Here it is," she said: "have you noticed that young tradesman from Lyon who has been taking his meals here for the past four or five days?"

"Who? Dubreuil?"

"Precisely."

"Well?"

"He is in love with you, he told me so in confidence, your modest and gentle air pleases him infinitely, he adores your candor, your virtue enchants him; this romantic fellow has eight hundred thousand francs in gold or paper, it's all in a little coffer he keeps near his bed; let me give the man to understand you consent to hear him, whether that be true or not; for, does it matter? I'll get him to propose you a drive, you'll take a carriage out of the town, I'll persuade him he will advance matters with you during your promenade; you'll amuse him, you'll keep him away as long as possible, meanwhile I'll rob him, but I'll not flee; his belongings will reach Turin before I quit Grenoble, we will employ all imaginable art to dissuade him from settling his eyes upon us, we'll pretend to assist his searches; however, my departure will be announced, he'll not be surprised thereby, you'll follow me, and the thousand *louis* will be counted out to you immediately we get to the Piedmont."

"Agreed, Madame," I said to Dubois, fully determined to warn Dubreuil of the concerted theft, "but consider," I added in order more thoroughly to deceive this villain, "that if Dubreuil is fond of me, by revealing the business or by giving myself to him, I might get much more from him than you offer me to betray him."

"Bravo," replied Dubois, "that's what I call an adept scholar, I'm beginning to believe Heaven gave you a greater talent for crime than you pretend: ah well," she continued, picking up a quill, "here's my note for twenty thousand crowns, now dare say no to me."

"Not for the world, Madame," quoth I, taking her note, "but, at least, my weakness and my wrong in surrendering to your seductions are to be attributed only to my impecunious circumstances."

"I'd prefer to interpret it as a meritorious act of your

intelligence," said Dubois, "but if you prefer me to blame your poverty, why then, as you like; serve me and you will always be content."

Everything was arranged; the same evening I began in earnest to play my game with Dubreuil, and indeed I discovered he had some taste for me.

Nothing could have been more embarrassing than my situation: I was without any doubt far from lending myself to the proposed crime even had it been worth ten thousand times as much gold; but the idea of denouncing this woman was also painful for me; I was exceedingly loath to expose to death a creature to whom I had owed my freedom ten years before. I should have liked to have been able to find a way of preventing the crime without having it punished, and with anyone else but a consummate villain like Dubois I should have succeeded; here then is what I resolved to do, all the while unaware that this horrible woman's base maneuvers would not only topple the entire edifice of my honorable schemes but even punish me for having dreamt of them.

Upon the day fixed for the projected outing, Dubois invites us both to dine in her room, we accept, and the meal over, Dubreuil and I descend to summon the carriage that has been prepared for us; Dubois does not accompany us, I find myself alone with Dubreuil the moment before we set out.

"Monsieur," I say, speaking very rapidly, "listen closely to me, don't be alarmed, no noise, and above all pay strict attention to what I am going to recommend; have you a reliable friend at this hotel?"

"Yes, I have a young associate upon whom I can count with absolute confidence."

"Then, Monsieur, go promptly and order him not to leave your room for a second while we are on our drive."

"But I have the key to the room; what does this excess of precaution signify?"

"It is more essential than you believe, Monsieur, I beg you to employ it, or else I shall not go out with you; the woman with whom we dined is a bandit, she only arranged our outing in order more easily to rob you while we are gone; make haste, Monsieur, she is watching us, she is dangerous; quickly, turn your key over to your friend, have him go and install himself in your room and let him not budge until we're back. I'll explain the rest as soon as we are in the carriage."

Dubreuil heeds me, presses my hand in token of thanks, flies to give orders relative to the warning he has received, and returns; we leave; when en route, I disclose the entire adventure to him, I recite mine and inform him of the unhappy circumstances in my life which have caused me to make the acquaintance of such a woman. This correct and sensible young man expresses the deepest gratitude for the service I have just so kindly rendered him, he takes an interest in my misfortunes, and proposes to alleviate them with the bestowal of his hand.

"I am only too happy to be able to make you restitution for the wrongs fortune has done you, Mademoiselle," says he; "I am my own master, dependent upon no one, I am going on to Geneva to make a considerable investment with the funds your timely warning has saved me from losing; accompany me to Switzerland; when we arrive there I shall become your husband and you will not appear in Lyon under any other title, or, if you prefer, Mademoiselle, if you have any misgivings, it will only be in my own country I will give you my name."

Such an offer, so very flattering, was one I dared not refuse; but it did not on the other hand become me to accept it without making Dubreuil aware of all that might cause him to repent it; he was grateful for my delicacy and only insisted the more urgently ... unhappy creature that I was! 'twas necessary that happiness be offered me only in order that I be more deeply penetrated with grief at never being able to seize it! it was then ordained that no virtue could be born in my heart without preparing torments for me!

Our conversation had already taken us two leagues from the city, and we were about to dismount in order to enjoy the fresh air along the bank of the Isère, when all of a sudden Dubreuil told me he felt very ill. . . . He got down, he was seized by dreadful vomitings; I had him climb into the carriage at once and we flew back posthaste to Grenoble. Dubreuil is so sick he has to be borne to his room; his condition startles his associate whom we find there and who, in accordance with instructions, has not stirred from the chamber; a doctor comes, Just Heaven! Dubreuil has been poisoned! I no sooner learn the fatal news than I dash to Dubois' apartment; the infamous creature! she's gone; I rush to my room, my armoire has been forced open, the little money and odds and ends I possess have been removed; Dubois, they tell me, left three hours ago in the direction of Turin. There was no doubt she was the author of this multitude of crimes; she had gone to Dubreuil's door; annoyed to find his room occupied, she revenged herself upon me and had envenomed Dubreuil at dinner so that upon our return, if she had succeeded with her theft, that unhappy young man would be more busied with his own failing life than concerned to pursue her who had made off with his fortune and would let her fly in safety; the accident of his death, occurring, so to speak, while he was in my arms, would make me appear more suspect than herself; nothing directly informed us of the scheme she had contrived, but could it have been different?

And then I rush back to Dubreuil's room; I am not allowed to approach his bedside. "But why?" I demand and am given the reason: the poor man is expiring and is no longer occupied with anyone save his God. However, he exonerates me, he gives assurance of my innocence; he expressly forbids that I be pursued; he dies. Hardly has he closed his eyes when his associate hastens to bring me the news and begs me to be easy. Alas! how could I be? how was I not to weep bitterly for the loss of a man who had so generously offered to extricate me from misery! how was I not to deplore a theft which forced me back into the wretchedness whence I had only a moment before emerged! Frightful creature! I cried; if 'tis to this your principles lead you, is it any wonder they are abhorred and that honest folk punish them! But I was arguing from the injured party's viewpoint and Dubois, who had only reaped happiness therefrom and saw nothing but her interest in what she had undertaken, Dubois, I say, had doubtless reached a very different conclusion.

To Dubreuil's associate, whose name was Valbois, I divulged everything, both what had been concerted against the man we had lost and what had happened to me. He sympathized with me, most sincerely regretted Dubreuil and blamed the overly nice scruples which had prevented me from lodging a complaint instantly I had been advised of Dubois' schemes; we agreed that this monster who needed but four hours to get to another country and security would arrive there before we would be able to organize her pursuit, that to follow her would involve considerable expense, that the innkeeper, heavily compromised by the proceedings we would launch, by defending himself with vehemence might perhaps end by having me crushed, I . . . who seemed to be living in Grenoble as one who had missed the gallows by a hairsbreadth. These reasons convinced me and even terrified me to the point I resolved to leave the town without even saying farewell to my protector, Monsieur S * * *. Dubreuil's friend approved the idea; he did not conceal from me that if the entire adventure were to be revealed he would be obliged to make depositions which, his precautions notwithstanding, would involve me as much by my intimacy with Dubreuil as in reason of my last outing with his friend; in the light of which he urged me to leave at once without a word to anyone, and I could be perfectly sure that, on his side, he would never take steps against me, whom he believed innocent, and, in all that had just occurred, whom he could only accuse of weakness.

Upon pondering Valbois' opinions, I recognized they were that much better the more certain it appeared I would be beheld with suspicion; the less my guilt, the wiser his suggestions; the one thing that spoke in my behalf, the recommendation I had made to Dubreuil at the outset of our promenade, which had, so they told me, been unsatisfactorily explained by the article of his death, would not appear so conclusive as I might hope; whereupon I promptly made my decision; I imparted it to Valbois.

"Would," said he, "that my friend had charged me with some dispositions favorable to you, I should carry out such requests with the greatest pleasure; I am sorry indeed he did not tell me 'twas to you he owed the advice to guard his room; but he said nothing of the sort, not a word did I have from him, and consequently I am obliged to limit myself to merely complying with his orders. What you have suffered by his loss would persuade me to do something in my own name were I able to, Mademoiselle, but I am just setting up in business, I am young, my fortune is not boundless, I am compelled to render an account of Dubreuil to his family and without delay; allow me then to confine myself to the one little service I beg you to accept: here are five *louis* and I have here as well an honest merchant from Chalon-sur-Saône, my native city; she is going to return there after a day and a night's stop at Lyon where she is called by business matters; I put you into her keeping."

"Madame Bertrand," Valbois continued, "here is the young lady I spoke of; I recommend her to you, she wishes to procure herself a situation. With the same earnestness which would apply were she my own sister, I beg you to take all possible steps to find something in our city which will be suitable to her person, her birth, and her upbringing; that until she is properly installed she incur no expense; do see to her requirements and I shall reimburse you immediately I am home."

Valbois besought me leave to embrace me. "Adieu, Mademoiselle," he continued, "Madame Bertrand sets off tomorrow at daybreak; accompany her and may a little more happiness attend you in a city where I shall perhaps soon have the satisfaction of seeing you again."

The courtesy of this young man, who was in no sort indebted to me, brought tears to my eyes. Kind treatment is sweet indeed when for so long one has experienced naught but the most odious. I accepted his gifts, at the same time swearing I was going to work at nothing but to put myself in a way to be able someday to reciprocate. Alas! I thought as I retired, though the exercise of yet another virtue has just flung me into destitution, at least, for the first time in my life, the hope of consolation looms out of this appalling pit of evil into which Virtue has cast me again.

The hour was not advanced; I needed a breath of air and so went down to the Isère embankment, desiring to stroll there for several instants; and, as almost always happens under similar circumstances, my thoughts, absorbing me entirely, led me far. Finding myself, at length, in an isolated place, I sat down, more leisurely to ponder. However, night descended before I thought to return; of a sudden I felt myself seized by three men: one clapped a hand over my mouth, the other two precipitated me into a carriage, climbed in, and for three full hours we sped along, during which time not one of these brigands deigned either to say a word to me or respond to any of my questions. The blinds were drawn down, I saw nothing; the carriage came to a halt before a house, gates swung wide, we entered, the gates clanged to immediately. My abductors pick me up, lead me through several unlit apartments, and finally leave me in one near which is a room wherein I perceive a light.

"Stay here," says one of my ravishers as he withdraws with his companions, "you're soon going to see an old acquaintance."

And they disappear, carefully shutting all the doors. At almost the same time, that leading into the room where I had spied illumination is opened, and carrying a candle in her hand, I see emerge ... oh, Madame, fancy who it was ... Dubois ... Dubois herself, that frightful monster, devoured, no question of it, by the most ardent desire to be revenged.

"Hither, charming girl," said she in an arrogant tone, "come here and receive the reward for the virtues in which you indulged yourself at my expense. ..." And angrily clutching my hand: "... ah, you wretch! I'll teach you to betray me!"

"No, Madame, no," I say in great haste, " I betrayed you not at all: inform yourself: I uttered not one word which could cause you any inquietude, no, I spoke not the least word which might compromise you."

"But did you not offer resistance to the crime I meditated? have you not thwarted its execution, worthless creature! You've got to be chastened. ..."

And, as we were entering, she had no time to say more. The apartment into which I was made to pass was lit with equal sumptuousness and magnificence; at the further end, reclining upon an ottoman, was a man of about forty, wearing a billowing taffeta dressing robe.

"Monseigneur," said Dubois, presenting me to him, "here is the young lady you wanted, she in whom all Grenoble has become interested ... the celebrated Thérèse, to be brief, condemned to hang with the counterfeiters, then delivered thanks to her innocence and her virtue. Acknowledge that I serve you with skill, Monseigneur; not four days ago you evinced your extreme desire to immolate her to your passions; and today I put her into your hands; you will perhaps prefer her to that pretty little pensionnaire from the Benedictine convent at Lyon you also desired and who should be arriving any minute: the latter has her physical and moral integrity this one here has nothing but a sentimental chastity; but it is deep-grained in her being and nowhere will you find a creature more heavily ballasted with candor and honesty. They are both at your disposition, Monseigneur: you'll either dispatch each this evening, or one today and the other tomorrow. As for myself, I am leaving you: your kindnesses in my regard engaged me to make you privy to my Grenoble adventure. One man dead, Monseigneur, one dead man; I must fly—"

"Ah no, no, charming woman!" cried the master of the place; "no, stay, and fear nothing while you have my protection! You are as a soul unto my pleasures; you alone possess the art of exciting and satisfying them, and the more you multiply your crimes, the more the thought of you inflames my mind. . . . But this Thérèse is a pretty thing. . . ." and addressing himself to me: "what is your age, my child?"

"Twenty-six, Monseigneur," I replied, "and much grief."

"Ha, yes, grief indeed, lots of distress, excellent, I'm familiar with all that, hugely amusing, just what I like; we're going to straighten everything out, we'll put a stop to these tumbles; I guarantee you that in twenty-four hours you'll be unhappy no longer, ha! . . ." and, with that, dreadful flights of laughter . . . " 'tis true, eh, Dubois? I've a sure method for ending a young girl's misfortunes, haven't I?"

"Indeed you do," the odious creature replied; "and if Thérèse weren't a friend of mine, I'd never have brought her to you; but it is only fair I reward her for what she did for me. You'd never imagine how useful this dear thing was to me during my latest enterprise at Grenoble; you, Monseigneur, have had the kindness to accept my expression of gratitude, and, I pray you, repay what I owe her with interest."

The opaque ambiguity of these phrases, what Dubois had said to me upon entering, the species of gentleman with whom I had to do, this other girl whose forthcoming appearance had been announced, all this instantly troubled my imagination to a degree it would be difficult to describe. A cold sweat seeped from my pores and I was about to fall in a swoon—'twas at that instant this man's projects finally became clear to me. He calls me to him, begins with two or three kisses whereby our mouths are obliged to unite; he seeks my tongue, finds and sucks it and his, running deep into my throat, seems to be pumping the very breath from my lungs. He has me bend my head upon his chest, he lifts my hair and closely observes the nape of my neck.

"Oh, 'tis delicious!" he cries, squeezing it vigorously; "I've never seen one so nicely attached; 'twill be divine to make it jump free."

This last remark confirmed all my intimations; I saw very clearly I was once again in the clutches of one of those libertines moved by cruel passions, whose most cherished delights consist in enjoying the agonies or the death of the luckless victims procured them by money; I observed I was in danger of losing my life.

And then a knock at the door; Dubois leaves and an instant later ushers in the young Lyonnaise she had mentioned shortly before. I'll now try to sketch the two personages in whose company you are going to see me for a while. The Monseigneur, whose name and estate I never discovered, was, as I told you, a man of forty years, slender, indeed slight of frame, but vigorously constituted, sinewy, with his muscles almost constantly tensed, powerful biceps showing upon arms that were covered with a growth of thick black hair; everything about him proclaimed strength and good health; his face was animated, his gaze ardent, his eyes small, black, and wicked, there were splendid white teeth in his mouth, and liveliness in his every feature; his height was above average, and this man's amatory goad, which I was to have but too frequent occasion to see and feel, was roughly a foot long and above eight inches around. This incisive, nervous, constantly alerted and oozing instrument, ribboned with great purple veins that rendered its aspect still more formidable, was levitated throughout the séance, which lasted five or six hours; never once did it sink or falter. I had never before or since found a more hirsute man: he resembled those fauns described in fables. His powerful hands ended in fingers whose strength was that of a vice; as for his character, it seemed to me harsh, abrupt, cruel, his mind was inclined to that sarcasm and teasing of a sort calculated to redouble the sufferings one was perfectly well able to see one had to expect such a man would strive to inflict.

The little Lyonnaise was called Eulalie. A glimpse of her was enough to convince one of her distinguished birth and virtue: she was the daughter of one of the city's foremost families from whose house Dubois' criminal hirelings had abducted her under the pretext of conveying her to a rendezvous with the lover she idolized; together with an enchanting forthrightness and naïveté, she possessed one of the most delightful countenances imaginable. Barely sixteen years old, Eulalie had the face of a genuine Madonna; her features were embellished by an enviable innocence and modesty; she had little color but was only the more fetching for that; and the sparkle in her superb eyes endowed her pretty face with all the fire and warmth whereof, at first glance, this pallor seemed to deprive her; her rather generous mouth was filled with the prettiest teeth, her already fully matured breasts seemed yet whiter than her complexion; but she was no sense lacking in plumpness: her form was round and well furnished, all her flesh was firm, sweet, and succulent. Dubois asserted it were impossible to behold a more beautiful ass: little expert in these matters, you will permit me to abstain from judging here. A fine mossy growth shadowed her fore end; majestic blond hair floated about all those charms, rendering them still more piquant; and to complete the masterpiece, Nature, who seemed to have created it for pleasure, had endowed her with the sweetest and most lovable temperament. Tender and delicate flower, thus were you to grace the world for but an instant in order more swiftly to be withered!

"Oh, Madame!" she said upon recognizing Dubois, "is it in this way you have deceived me! . . . Just Heaven! where have you brought me?"

"You shall see, my child," put in the master of the house, abruptly seizing Eulalie, drawing her to him and forthwith beginning his kisses while, upon his orders, I excited him with one hand.

Eulalie sought to protect herself, but, thrusting the girl toward the libertine, Dubois eliminated all possibility of her escape. The sitting was long; for very fresh, new-blown was that flower, and the hornet's desire to drain its pollen was commensurately great. His iterated suckings were succeeded by an inspection of Eulalie's neck; betimes, I palpated his member and felt it throb with growing insistence.

"Well," said Monseigneur, "here are two victims who shall fill my cup of joy to overflowing: Dubois, you shall be well paid, for I am well served. Let's move into my boudoir; follow us, dear woman, come," he continued as he led us away; "you'll leave to-night, but I need you for the party."

Dubois resigns herself, and we pass into the debauchee's pleasure chamber, where we are stripped naked.

Oh, Madame, I shall not attempt to represent the infamies of which I was at once victim and witness. This monster's pleasures were those of the executioner; his unique joy consisted in decapitating. My luckless companion . . . oh, no! Madame . . . no! do not require me to finish . . . I was about to share her fate; spurred on by Dubois, the villain had decided to render my torture yet more horrible when both experienced a need to revive their strength; whereupon they sat down to eat. . . . What a debauch! But ought I complain? for did it not save my life? Besotted with wine, exhausted by overeating, both fell dead drunk and slumbered amidst the litter that remained from their feast. No sooner do I see them collapse than I leap to the skirt and mantle Dubois had just removed in order to appear more immodest in her patron's view; I snatch up a candle and spring toward the stairway: this house, divested, or nearly so, of servants, contains nothing to frustrate my escape, I do encounter someone, I put on a terrified air and cry to him to make all haste to relieve his master who is dying, and I reach the door without meeting further obstacles. I have no acquaintance with the roads, I'd not been allowed to see the one whereby we had come, I take the first I see . . . 'tis the one leading to Grenoble; there is nothing denied us when fortune deigns momentarily to smile upon us; at the inn everyone was still abed, I enter secretly and fly to Valbois' room, knock, Valbois wakes and scarcely recognizes me in my disordered state; he demands to know what has befallen me, I relate the horrors whereof I was simultaneously an observer and object.

"You can have Dubois arrested," I tell him, "she's not far from here, I might even be able to point out the way. . . . Quite apart from all her other crimes, the wretch has taken both my clothing and the five *louis* you gave me."

"O Thérèse," says Valbois, "there's no denying it, you are without doubt the unluckiest girl on earth, but, nevertheless, my honest creature, do you not perceive, amidst all these afflictions which beset you, a celestial arm that saves you? may that be unto you as one additional motive for perpetual virtuousness, for never do good deeds go unrewarded. We will not chase after Dubois, my reasons for letting her go in peace are the same you expounded yesterday, let us simply repair the harm she has done you: here, first of all, is the money she stole from you. In an hour's time I'll have a seamstress bring two complete outfits for you, and some linen.

"But you have got to leave, Thérèse, you must leave this very day, Bertrand expects you, I've persuaded her to delay her departure a few hours more, join her. . . ."

"O virtuous young man," I cried, falling into my benefactor's arms, "may Heaven someday repay you for the kindness you have done me."

"Ah, Thérèse," said Valbois, embracing me, "the happiness you wish me . . . I've enjoyed it already, 'tis presently mine, since your own is my doing . . . fare thee well."

And thus it was I left Grenoble, Madame, and though I had not found in that city all the felicity I had imagined was awaiting me there, at least I had never met in another so many kindly and goodhearted people assembled to sympathize with or assuage my woes.

My conductress and I were in a small covered carriage drawn by one horse we drove from within; we had with us, beside Madame Bertrand's baggage, her baby girl of fifteen months whom she was still suckling and for whom I straightway, to my vast misfortune, formed an attachment quite as deep as was that of the mother who had brought the infant into the world.

She was, this Bertrand, an unattractive person, suspicious, gossipy, noisy, monotonous, and dull-witted. Every night we regularly emptied the carriage and transported everything into our inn and then went to sleep in the same room. Until Lyon, everything went along very smoothly, but during the three days this woman needed for her business dealings, I fell upon someone I was far from expecting to encounter in that city.

Together with girls from the hotel whom I had got to accompany me, I would take walks on the Rhône quay; one day I all of a sudden espied the Reverend Father Antonin formerly of Saint

Mary-in-the-Wood, now superior in charge of his order's establishment located in that city. That monk accosted me and after rebuking me in a very low and still sharper tone for my flight, and having given me to understand I would be running great risks of recapture were he to relay information to the Burgundian monastery, he added, softening his manner, that he would not breathe a word if I should be willing that very instant to come to visit him in his new quarters and to bring with me the girl I was with, who struck him as worth having; then repeating his proposal aloud, and to this other creature: "We shall reward you handsomely, both of you," quoth the monster; "there are ten of us in our house, and I promise you a minimum of one *louis* from each if your complacency is unlimited." I flush crimson upon hearing these words; I spend a moment trying to convince the monk he has made a mistake; failing at that, I attempt to use signs to induce him to be silent, but nothing prevails with this insolent fellow, and his solicitations become only the more heated; at last having received repeated refusals, he demands to know our address; in order to get rid of him, I immediately give a fictitious one, he writes it down, and leaves us with the assurance we will soon meet again.

Upon returning to our inn I explained as best I could the history of this unfortunate acquaintance; but whether my companion was not at all satisfied by what I told her, or whether she may perhaps have been exceedingly annoyed by my virtuous performance which deprived her of an adventure wherefrom she might have earned much, she waggled her tongue, the effects of which were only too plainly revealed by Bertrand's remarks upon the occasion of the deplorable catastrophe I am going to relate to you in a moment; however, the monk never did reappear, and we left Lyon.

Having quit the city late, we could get no further than Villefranche that day, and there we stopped for the night; 'twas in that town, Madame, there took place the horrible event which today causes me to appear before you in a criminal guise, although I was no more a malefactor in that one of my life's fateful circumstances than in any other of those where you have observed me so unjustly assaulted by the blows of fate; and as in many another instance, so this time I was flung into the abyss by nothing other than the goodness of my heart and the wickedness of men.

Having made Villefranche toward six o'clock in the evening, we supped in haste and retired directly, that we might be able to undertake a longer stage on the morrow; we had not been two hours in bed when a dreadful smell of smoke roused us from sleep; convinced the flames are near at hand, we get instantly from bed. Just Heaven! the havoc wrought by the fire was already but too frightful; half-naked, we open our door and all around us hear nothing but the fracas of collapsing walls, the noise of burning timbers and woodwork and the shrieks of those who had fallen into the blaze; surrounded by devouring flames we have no idea in which direction to run; to escape their violence, we rush past them and soon find ourselves lost in a milling crush of wretches who, like ourselves, are seeking salvation in flight; at this point I remember that my conductress, more concerned for her own than for her child's safety, has not thought of preserving it from death; without a word to the woman, I fly to our chamber, having to pass through the conflagration and to sustain burns in several places: I snatch up the poor little creature, spring forward to restore her to her mother: I advance along a half-consumed beam, miss my footing, instinctively thrust out my hands, this natural reflex forces me to release the precious burden in my arms . . . it slips from my grasp and the unlucky child falls into the inferno before its own mother's eyes; at this instant I am myself seized . . . carried away; too upset to be able to distinguish anything, I am unaware whether 'tis aid or peril which surrounds me but, to my grief, I am but too fully enlightened when, flung into a post chaise, I discover myself beside Dubois who, clapping a pistol to my head, threatens to blow out my brains if I utter a syllable . . .

"Ah, little villain," says she, "I've got you now and this time for good."

"Oh, Madame! you?" I exclaim. "Here?"

"Everything that has just transpired is my doing," the monster replies, " 'twas by arson I saved your life; and by a fire you're going to lose it: in order to catch you I'd have followed you to Hell had it been necessary. Monseigneur was furious, believe me, when he found out you had escaped; I get two hundred *louis* for every girl

I procure him, and not only did he not want to pay me for Eulalie, but he menaced me with all his anger could produce were I to fail to bring you back. I discovered I'd missed you by two hours at Lyon; yesterday I reached Villefranche an hour after your arrival, I had the hotel burned by the henchmen I always have in my employ, I wanted to incinerate you or get you back; I've got you, I'm returning you to a house your flight has plunged into trouble and unquiet, and I'm taking you there, Thérèse, to be treated in a cruel manner. Monseigneur swore he'd not have tortures terrible enough for you, and we'll not step from this carriage until we are at his seat. Well, Thérèse, what is your present opinion of Virtue?"

"Oh, Madame! that it is very frequently crime's prey; that it is happy when triumphant; but that it ought to be the unique object of the Heavenly God's rewards even though human atrocities bring about its downfall upon earth."

"You've not long to wait before you know, Thérèse, whether there is really a God who punishes or recompenses the deeds of mortals. . . . Ah! if, in the eternal inexistence you are shortly going to enter, if 'twere possible to cogitate in that state of annihilation, how much you would regret the fruitless sacrifices your inflexible stubbornness has forced you to make to phantoms who have never doled out any but the wages of sorrow. . . . Thérèse, there is yet time left to you: if you wish to be my accomplice I'll save you, for, I avow, 'tis more than I can bear to see you break down ever and ever again upon Virtue's routes all beset by perils. What! are you not yet sufficiently punished for your good behavior and false principles? What kind of misery do you have to know in order to be persuaded to mend your ways? What then are the examples you require in order to be convinced the attitude you have adopted is the worst of all and that, as I have told you a hundred times over, one must expect nothing but calamity when, breasting the crowd's headlong stampede, one wishes to be virtuous and alone in a completely corrupt society. You count upon an avenging God; cease to be a gull, Thérèse, disabuse yourself, the God you fabricate for yourself is but a fiction whose stupid existence is never found elsewhere but in the heads of the crazed; 'tis a phantom invented by human wickedness; the solitary purpose of this illusion is to deceive mankind or to create armed divisions among men. The greatest

service it were possible to render humankind would have been instantly to cut the throat of the first impostor who took it into his
head to speak of God to men. How much blood that one murder
would have spared the universe! Get on, get on with you, Thérèse,
perpetually active Nature, Nature acting always, has no need of a
master for her government. And if indeed this master did exist,
after all the faults and sins with which he has stuffed creation, would
he, think you, would he merit anything from us but scorn and outrage? Ah, if he exists, your God, how I do hate him! Thérèse, how
I abhor him! Yes, were this existence authentic, I affirm that the
mere pleasure of perpetually irritating whatever I found that bore
his impress or bespoke his touch would become for me the most
precious compensation for the necessity in which I would find myself
to acknowledge some belief in him. . . . Once again, Thérèse, do you
wish to become my confederate? A superb possibility presents itself,
with courage we can execute the thing; I'll save your life if you'll
undertake it. This Monseigneur to whose house we are going, and
whom you know, lives alone in the country house where he gives his
parties; their species, with which you are familiar, requires isolation; a single valet lives with him when he takes up residence there
for the sake of his pleasures: the man riding ahead of the coach,
you and I, dear girl, that's three of us against two; when that
libertine is inflamed by his lecheries, I'll snatch away the saber with
which he decapitates his victims, you'll hold him, we'll kill him, and
meanwhile my man will have done in the valet. There's money
hidden in that house; more than eight hundred thousand francs,
Thérèse, I'm sure of it, the thing's well worth the trouble. . . .
Choose, clever creature, decide: death or an alliance; if you betray
me, if you expose my plan to him, I'll accuse you of having contrived
it alone, and don't doubt for a moment that the confidence he has
always had in me will tip the balance my way . . . think carefully
before you give me your answer: this man is a villain; hence, by
assassinating him we merely aid the law whose rigorous treatment
he deserves. A day does not go by, Thérèse, without this rascal
murdering a girl; is it then to outrage Virtue by punishing Crime?
And does the reasonable proposition I make you still alarm your
wild principles?"

"Be certain of it, Madame," I answered; "it is not with the

object of chastening crime you propose this deed, it is rather with the sole intention of committing one yourself; consequently there cannot be but great evil in doing what you suggest, and no semblance of legitimacy can appear thereupon; better still, even were you to intend to avenge humanity for this man's horrors, you would still be committing evil by doing so, for this is not a problem which concerns you: there are laws decreed to punish the guilty; let those laws take their course, it is not unto our feeble hands the Supreme Being has entrusted their sword, never might we wield that blade without affronting justice."

"Well, then you'll have to die, worthless creature," retorted the furious Dubois, "you'll die; don't tease yourself with hopes of escaping your fate."

"What matters it to me?" I calmly answered, "I shall be delivered of all the ills that assail me; death holds no terrors for me, 'tis life's last sleep, 'tis the downtrodden's haven of repose...."

And, upon these words, that savage beast sprang at me, I thought she was going to strangle me; she struck several blows upon my breast, but released me, however, immediately I cried out, for she feared lest the postilion hear me.

We were moving along at a brisk pace; the man who was riding ahead arranged for new horses and we stopped only long enough to change teams. As the new pair was being harnessed, Dubois suddenly raised her weapon and clapped it to my heart ... what was she about to do? ... Indeed, my exhaustion and my situation had beaten me down to the point of preferring death to the ordeal of keeping it at bay.

We were then preparing to enter Dauphiné, of a sudden six horsemen, galloping at top speed behind our coach, overtook it and, with drawn cutlasses, forced our driver to halt. Thirty feet off the highway was a cottage to which these cavaliers, whom we soon identified as constables, ordered the driver to lead the carriage; when we were alongside it, we were told to get out, and all three of us entered the peasant's dwelling. With an effrontery unthinkable in a woman soiled with unnumbered crimes, Dubois, who found herself arrested, archly demanded of these officers whether she were known to them, and with what right they comported themselves thus with a woman of her rank.

"We have not the honor of your acquaintance, Madame," replied the officer in charge of the squadron; "but we are certain you have in your carriage the wretch who yesterday set fire to the principal hotel in Villefranche"; then, eyeing me closely: "she answers the description, Madame, we are not in error; have the kindness to surrender her to us and to inform us how a person as respectable as you appear to be could have such a woman in your keeping."

"Why, 'tis very readily accounted for," replied Dubois with yet greater insolence, "and, I declare, I'll neither hide her from you nor take her side in the matter if 'tis certain she is guilty of the horrible crime you speak of. I too was staying at that hotel in Villefranche, I left in the midst of all the commotion and as I am getting into my coach, this girl runs up, begs my compassion, says she has just lost everything in the fire, and implores me to take her with me to Lyon where she hopes to be able to find a place. Far less attentive to my reason than to my heart's promptings, I acquiesced, consented to fetch her along; once in the carriage she offered herself as my servant; once again imprudence led me to agree to everything and I have been taking her to Dauphiné where I have my properties and family: 'tis a lesson, assuredly, I presently recognize with utmost clarity all of pity's shortcomings; I shall not again be guilty of them. There she is, gentlemen, there she is; God forbid that I should be interested in such a monster, I abandon her to the law's severest penalties, and, I beseech you, take every step to prevent it from being known that I committed the unfortunate mistake of lending an instant's credence to a single word she uttered."

I wished to defend myself, I wanted to denounce the true villain; my speeches were interpreted as calumniatory recriminations to which Dubois opposed nothing but a contemptuous smile. O fatal effects of misery and biased prepossession, of wealth and of insolence! Were it thinkable that a woman who had herself called Madame la Baronne de Fulconis, who proclaimed a high degree and displayed opulence, who asserted she owned extensive holdings and arrogated a family to herself; were it to be conceived that such a personage could be guilty of a crime wherefrom she did not appear to have the slightest thing to gain? And, on the other hand, did not everything condemn me? I was unprotected, I was poor, 'twas a very sure thing I'd done a fell deed.

The squadron officer read me the catalogue of Bertrand's deposed charges. 'Twas she had accused me; I'd set the inn afire to pillage her with greater ease, and she'd been robbed indeed to her last penny; I'd flung her infant into the flames in order that, blinded by the despair with which this event would overwhelm her, she'd forget all else and give not a thought to my maneuvers; and, further- more, Bertrand had added, I was a girl of suspect virtue and bad habits who had escaped the gallows at Grenoble and whom she had only taken in charge, very foolishly, thanks to the excessive kindness she had shown a young man from her own district, my lover, no doubt. I had publicly and in broad daylight solicited monks in Lyon: in one word, there was nothing the unworthy creature had not ex- ploited in order to seal my doom, nothing that calumny whetted by despair had not invented in order to besmirch me. Upon the woman's insistence, a juridical examination had been conducted on the premises. The fire had begun in a hayloft into which several persons had taken oath I had entered the evening of that fatal day, and that was true. Searching for a water closet to which I had not been very clearly directed by a maid I had consulted, I had entered this loft having failed to locate the sought after place, and there I had remained long enough to make what I was accused of plausible, or at least to furnish probabilities of its truth; and 'tis well known: in this day and age those are proofs. And so, do what I could to defend myself, the officer's single response was to ready his mana- cles.

"But, Monsieur," I expostulated before allowing him to put me in irons, "if I robbed my traveling companion at Villefranche, the money ought to be found upon my person; search me."

This ingenuous defense merely excited laughter; I was assured I'd not been alone, that they were certain I had accomplices to whom, as I fled, I had transferred the stolen funds. Then the malicious Dubois, who knew of the brand which to my misfortune Rodin had burned upon my flesh long ago, in one instant Dubois put all sympathy to rout.

"Monsieur," said she to the officer, "so many mistakes are committed every day in affairs of this sort that you will forgive me for the idea that occurs to me: if this girl is guilty of the atrocity she is accused of it is surely not her first; the character required to execute crimes of this variety is not attained in a night: and so I beg you to examine this girl, Monsieur . . . were you to find, by chance, something upon her wretched body . . . but if nothing denounces her, allow me to defend and protect her."

The officer agreed to the verification . . . it was about to be carried out . . .

"One moment, Monsieur," said I, "stay; this search is to no purpose; Madame knows full well I bear the frightful mark; she also knows very well what misfortune caused it to be put on me: this subterfuge of hers is the crowning horror which will, together with all the rest, be revealed at Themis' own temple. Lead me away, Messieurs: here are my hands, load them with chains; only Crime blushes to carry them, stricken Virtue is made to groan thereby, but is not terrified."

"Truth to tell," quoth Dubois, "I'd never have dreamt my idea would have such success; but as this creature repays my kindness by insidious inculpations, I am willing to return with her if you deem it necessary."

"There's no need whatsoever to do so, Madame la Baronne," rejoined the officer, "this girl is our quarry: her avowals, the mark branded on her body, it all condemns her; we need no one else, and we beg your pardon a thousand times over for having caused you this protracted inconvenience."

I was handcuffed immediately, flung upon the crupper of one of the constables' mounts, and Dubois went off, not before she had completed her insults by giving a few crowns to my guards, which generously bestowed silver was to aid me during my melancholy sojourn while awaiting trial.

O Virtue! I cried when I perceived myself brought to this dreadful humiliation; couldst thou suffer a more penetrating outrage! Were it possible that Crime might dare affront thee and vanquish thee with so much insolence and impunity!

We were soon come to Lyon; upon arrival I was cast into the keep reserved for criminals and there I was inscribed as an arsonist, harlot, child-murderer, and thief.

Seven persons had been burned to death in the hotel; I had

myself thought I might be; I had been on the verge of perishing; but she who had been the cause of this horror was eluding the law's vigilance and Heaven's justice: she was triumphant, she was flying on to new crimes whereas, innocent and unlucky, I had naught for prospect but dishonor, castigation, and death.

For such a long time habituated to calumny, injustice, and wretchedness; destined, since childhood, to acquit myself of not a single virtuous deed or feel a single righteous sentiment without suffering instant retribution therefor, my anguish was rather mute and blunted than rending, and I shed fewer tears than I might have supposed . . . however, as 'tis instinctive in the distressed creature to seek after every possible device to extricate himself from the chasm into which his ill-fortune has plunged him, Father Antonin came to my mind; whatever the mediocre relief I could hope from him, I did not deny to myself I was anxious to see him: I asked for him, he appeared. He had not been informed of by whom he was desired; he affected not to recognize me; whereupon I told the turn-key that it was indeed possible he had forgotten me, having been my confessor only when I was very young, but, I continued, it was as my soul's director I solicited a private interview with him. 'Twas agreed by both parties. As soon as I was alone with this holy man I cast myself at his knees, rained tears upon them and besought him to save me from my cruel situation; I proved my innocence to him; I did not conceal that the culpable proposals he had made me some days before had provoked my young companion's enmity, and presently, said I, she accused me out of spite. The monk listened attentively.

"Thérèse," said he when I was done, "don't lose control of yourself as you customarily do when someone contradicts your damnable prejudices; you notice to what a pass they've brought you, and you can at present readily convince yourself that it's a hundred times better to be a rascal and happy than well-behaved and unprosperous; your case is as bad as it possibly could be, dear girl, there's nothing to be gained by hiding the fact from you: this Dubois you speak of, having the largest benefits to reap from your doom, will unquestionably labor behind the scene to ruin you: Bertrand will accuse you, all appearances stand against you, and, these days, appearances are sufficient grounds for decreeing the death sentence: you are, hence, lost, 'tis plain: one single means might save you: I get on well with the bailiff, he has considerable influence with this city's magistrature; I'm going to tell him you are my niece, and that by this title I am claiming you: he'll dismiss the entire business: I'll ask to send you back to my family; I'll have you taken away, but 'twill be to our monastery and incarceration there, whence you'll never emerge . . . and there, why conceal it? you, Thérèse, will be the bounden slave of my caprices, you'll sate them all without a murmur; as well, you will submit yourself to my colleagues: in a word, you will be as utterly mine as the most subordinated of victims . . . you heed me: the task is hard; you know what are the passions of libertines of our variety; so make up your mind, and make me prompt answer."

"Begone, Father," I replied, horror-struck, "begone, you are a monster to dare so cruelly take advantage of my circumstances in order to force upon me the alternatives of death or infamy; I shall know how to die, if die I must, but 'twill be to die sinless."

"As you like," quoth the cruel man as he prepared to withdraw; "I have never been one to impose happiness upon reluctant people. . . . Virtue has so handsomely served you until the present, Thérèse, you are quite right to worship at its altar . . . good-bye: above all, let it not occur to you to ask for me again."

He was leaving; an unconquerable impulse drew me to his knees yet another time.

"Tiger!" I exclaimed through my tears, "open your granite heart, let my appalling misadventures melt it, and do not, in order to conclude them, do not impose conditions more dreadful to me than death itself. . . ."

The violence of my movements had disturbed what veiled my breast, it was naked, my disheveled hair fell in cascades upon it, it was wetted thoroughly by my tears; I quicken desires in the dishonest man . . . desires he wants to satisfy on the spot; he dares discover to me to what point my state arouses them; he dares dream of pleasures lying in the middle of the chains binding me and beneath the sword which is poised to smite me . . . I was upon my knees . . . he flings me backward, leaps upon me, there we lie upon the wretched straw I use for a bed; I wish to cry out, he stuffs his handkerchief into my mouth; he ties my arms; master of me, the infamous creature examines me everywhere . . . everything becomes prey to his gaze, his fingerings, his perfidious caresses; at last, he appeases his desires.

"Listen to me," says he, untying me and readjusting his costume, "you do not want me to be helpful, all very well; I am leaving you; I'll neither aid nor harm you, but if it enters your head to breathe a word of what has just happened, I will, by charging you with yet more enormous crimes, instantly deprive you of all means of defending yourself; reflect carefully before jabbering . . . I am taken for your confessor . . . now hark: we are permitted to reveal anything and all when 'tis a question of a criminal; fully approve what I am going to say to your warden, or else I'll crush you like a fly."

He knocks, the jailer appears.

"Monsieur," says the traitor, "the nice young lady is in error; she wished to speak to a Father Antonin who is now in Bordeaux; I have no acquaintance of her, never have I even set eyes upon her: she besought me to hear her confession, I did so, I salute you and her and shall always be ready to present myself when my ministry is esteemed important."

Upon uttering these words, Antonin departs and leaves me as much bewildered by his fraudulence as revolted by his libertinage and insolence.

My situation was so dreadful that, whatever it might be, I could ill afford not to employ every means at my disposal; I recollected Monsieur de Saint-Florent: in the light of my behavior toward him, I was incapable of believing this man could underestimate my character; once long ago I had rendered him a most important service, he had dealt most cruelly with me, and therefore I imagined he could not, in my presently critical plight, very well refuse to make reparation for the wrongs he had done me; no, I was sure he would at least have to acknowledge, as best he were able, what I had so generously done in his behalf; passions' heat might have blinded him upon the two occasions I had held commerce with him; there had been some sort of excuse for his former horrors, but in this instance, it seemed to me, no feeling should prevent him from coming to my aid. . . . Would he renew his last proposals? to the assistance I was going to request from him would he attach the condition I must agree to the frightful employments he had outlined to me before? ah, very well! I'd accept and, once free, I should easily discover the means to extricate myself from the abominable kind of existence into which he might have the baseness to lure me. Full of these ideas, I write a letter to him, I describe my miseries, I beg him to visit me; but I had not devoted adequate thought to analyzing this man's soul when I supposed it susceptible of infiltration by beneficence; I either did not sufficiently remember his appalling theories, or my wretched weakness constantly forcing me to use my own heart as the standard by which to judge others, fancied this man was bound to comport himself toward me as I should certainly have done toward him.

He arrives; and, as I have asked to see him alone, he is freely introduced into my cell. From the marks of respect showered profusely upon him it was easy to determine the eminent position he held in Lyon.

"Why, it's you!" said he, casting scornful eyes upon me, "I was deceived by the letter; I thought it written by a woman more honest than you and whom I would have helped with all my heart; but what would you have me do for an imbecile of your breed? What! you're guilty of a hundred crimes one more shocking than the other, and when someone suggests a way for you to earn your livelihood you stubbornly reject the proposal? Never has stupidity been carried to these lengths."

"Oh, Monsieur!" I cried, "I am not in the least guilty."

"Then what the devil must one do in order to be?" the harsh creature sharply rejoined. "The first time in my life I clapped eyes on you, there you were, in the thick of a pack of bandits who wanted to assassinate me; and now it is in the municipal prison I discover you, accused of three or four new crimes and wearing, so they tell me, a mark on your shoulder which proclaims your former misdeeds. If that is what you designate by the word honest, do inform me of what it would require not to be."

"Just Heaven, Monsieur!" I replied, "can you excoriate that period in my life when I knew you, and should it not rather be for me to make you blush at the memory of what passed then? You know very well, Monsieur, the bandits who captured you, and amongst whom you found me, kept me with them by force; they wanted to kill you, I saved your life by facilitating your escape while making mine; and what, cruel man, did you do to thank me for my aid? is it possible you can recall your actions without horror? You yourself wanted to murder me; you dazed me by terrible blows and, profiting from my half-unconscious state, you snatched from me what I prized most highly; through an unexampled refinement of cruelty, you plundered me of the little money I possessed quite as if you had desired to summon humiliation and misery to complete your victim's obliteration! And great was your success, barbaric one! indeed, it has been entire; 'tis you who precipitated me into desolation; 'tis you who made the abyss to yawn, and 'tis thanks to you I fell into it and have not ceased to fall since that accursed moment.

"Nevertheless, Monsieur, I would forget it all, yes, everything is effaced from my memory, I even ask your pardon for daring to upbraid you for what is past, but can you hide from yourself the fact that some recompense, some gratitude is owing to me? Ah, deign not to seal up your heart when the wing of death brushes its shadow over my unhappy days; 'tis not death I fear, but disgrace; save me from the dread horror of a criminal's end: all I demand from you comes to that single mercy, refuse me it not, and both Heaven and my heart will reward you someday."

I was weeping, I was upon my knees before this ferocious man and, far from reading upon his face the effect I thought I should be able to expect from the disturbances I flattered myself I was producing in his soul, I distinguished nothing but a muscular altera-tion caused by that sort of lust whose germinal origins are in cruelty. Saint-Florent was seated opposite me; his wicked dark eyes considered me in a dreadful manner, and I noticed his hand glide to a certain sector and his fingers begin to perform those cer-tain motions which indicated I was putting him in a state which was by no means that of pity; he concealed himself withal, and, getting to his feet:

"Look here," he said, "your case rests entirely in the hands of Monsieur de Cardoville; I need not tell you what official post he occupies; it suffices that you know your fate depends absolutely upon him; he and I have been intimate friends since childhood; I shall speak to him; if he agrees to a few arrangements, you will be called for at sunset and in order that he may see you, you'll be brought to either his home or mine; such an interrogation, wrapped in secrecy, will make it much simpler to turn matters in your favor, which could not possibly be done here. If he consents to bestow the favor, justify yourself when you have your interview with him, prove your innocence to him in a persuasive manner; that is all I can do for you. Adieu, Thérèse, keep yourself ready for any eventuality and above all do not have me waste my time taking futile measures." Saint-Florent left.

Nothing could have equaled my perplexity; there had been so little harmony between that man's remarks, the character I knew him to have, and his actual conduct, that I dreaded yet further pitfalls; but, Madame, pause a moment and decide whether I was right or wrong; was I in a position to hesitate? for my position was desperate; and was I not obliged to leap at everything which had the semblance of assistance? Hence I decided to accompany the persons who would come to fetch me; should I be compelled to prostitute myself, I would put up what defense I could; was it to death I was to be led? too bad; it would not, at least, be ignominious, and I would be rid of all my sufferings. Nine o'clock strikes, the jailer appears, I tremble.

"Follow me," that Cerberus says; "you are wanted by Messieurs Saint-Florent and de Cardoville; consider well and take advantage, as it befits you, of the favor Heaven offers you; there are many here who might desire such a blessing and who will never obtain it."

Arrayed as best I am able, I follow the warden who puts me into the keeping of two strange tall fellows whose savage aspect doubles my fright; not a word do they utter; the carriage rolls off and we halt before an immense mansion I soon recognize as Saint-Florent's. Silence enshrouds everything; it augments my dread, however, my guides grasp my arms, hustle me along, and we climb to the fourth floor; there we discover a number of small decorated apartments; they seem to me very mysterious indeed. As we progress through them every door closes shut behind us, and thus we advance till we reach a remote room in which, I notice, there are no windows; Saint-Florent awaits me, and also the man I am told is Monsieur de Cardoville, in whose hands my case rests; this heavy-

set, fleshy personage, provided with a somber and feral countenance, could have been about fifty years of age; although he was in
lounging costume, 'twas readily to be seen he was a gentleman of the
bar. An air of severity seemed to distinguish his entire aspect; it
made a deep impression upon me. O cruel injustice of Providence!
'tis then possible Virtue may be overawed by Crime. The two men
who had led me hither, and whom I was better able to make out by
the gleam of the twenty candles which lit this room, were not above
twenty-five and thirty years old. The first, referred to as La Rose,
was a dark handsome chap with Hercules' own figure; he seemed
to me the elder; the other had more effeminate features, the loveliest chestnut locks and large brown eyes; he was at least five feet
ten inches tall, a very Adonis, had the finest skin to be seen, and was
called Julien. As for Saint-Florent, you are acquainted with him; as
much of coarseness in his traits as in his character, yet, nevertheless,
certain splendid features.

"Everything is secured fast?" Saint-Florent asked Julien.

"We're well shut in, yes, Monsieur," the young man replied;
"your servants are off for the night in accordance with your orders
and the gatekeeper, who alone is on watch, will follow his instructions to admit no one under any circumstances." These few
words enlightened me, I shivered, but what could I have done, confronted as I was by four men?

"Sit down over there, my friends," said Cardoville, kissing the
two men, "we'll call for your co-operation when the need arises."

Whereupon Saint-Florent spoke up: "Thérèse," said he, presenting me to Cardoville, "here is your judge, this is the man upon
whom your fate depends; we have discussed your problem; but it
appears to me that your crimes are of such a nature we will have
much to do to come to terms about them."

"She has exactly forty-two witnesses against her," remarks
Cardoville, who takes a seat upon Julien's knees, who kisses him
upon the lips, and who permits his fingers to stray over the young
man's body in the most immodest fashion; "it's a perfect age since
we condemned anyone to die for crimes more conclusively established."

"I? Conclusively established crimes?"

"Conclusively established or inconclusively established," quoth

Cardoville, getting to his feet and coming up to shout, with much effrontery, at my very nose, "you're going to burn pissing if you do not, with an entire resignation and the blindest obedience, instantly lend yourself to everything we are going to require of you."

"Yet further horrors!" I cried; "ah indeed! 'tis then only by yielding to infamies innocence can escape the snares set for it by the wicked!"

"That's it; 'tis ordained," Saint-Florent broke in; "you know, my dear: the weak yield to the strong's desires, or fall victims to their wickedness: that's all: that's your whole story, Thérèse, therefore obey."

And while he spoke the libertine nimbly pulled up my skirts. I recoiled, fended him off, horrified, but, having reeled backward into Cardoville's arms, the latter grasped my hands and thereupon exposed me, defenseless, to his colleague's assaults. The ribbons holding up my skirts were cut, my bodice torn away, my kerchief, my blouse, all were removed, and in no time I found myself before those monsters' eyes as naked as the day I came into the world.

"Resistance . . ." said one. "Resistance," chimed in the other, both proceeding to despoil me, "the whore fancies she can resist us. . . ." and not a garment was ripped from my body without my receiving a few blows.

When I was in the state they wished, they drew up their chairs, which were provided with protruding armrests; thus a narrow space between the chairs was left and into it I was deposited; and thus they were able to study me at their leisure: while one regarded my fore end, the other mused upon my behind; then they turned me round, and turned me again. In this way I was stared at, handled, kissed for thirty minutes and more; during this examination not one lubricious episode was neglected, and I thought it safe to conjecture, upon the basis of those preliminaries, that each had roughly the same idiosyncrasies.

"Well, now," Saint-Florent said to his friend, "did I not tell you she had a splendid ass!"

"Yes, by God! her behind is sublime," said the jurist who thereupon kissed it; "I've seen damned few buttocks molded like these: why! look ye! solid and fresh at the same time! . . . how d'ye suppose that fits with such a tempestuous career?"

"Why, it's simply that she's never given herself of her own accord; I told you there's nothing as whimsical as this girl's exploits! She's never been had but by rape"—and then he drives his five fingers simultaneously into the peristyle of Love's temple—"but she's been had . . . unfortunately, for it's much too capacious for me: accustomed to virgins, I could never put up with this."

Then, swinging me around, he repeated the same ceremony with my behind wherein he found the same flaws.

"Ah well, you know our secret," said Cardoville.

"And I'll employ it too," replied Saint-Florent; "and you who have no need of the same resource, you, who are content with a factitious activity which, although painful for the woman, nevertheless brings enjoyment of her to perfection, you, I hope, will not have her till I'm done."

"Fair enough," Cardoville answered, "while watching you, I'll busy myself with those preludes so cherished by my lechery; I'll play the girl with Julien and La Rose while you masculinize Thérèse, and, so I think, the one's as good as the other."

"Doubtless a thousand times better; for you've no idea how fed up I am with women! . . . do you suppose I would be capable of enjoying those whores without the help of the auxiliary episodes we both use to add a tart flavor to the business?"

With these words, having afforded me clear evidence their state called for more substantial pleasures, the impudicious creatures rose and made me mount upon a large chair, my forearms leaning upon its back, my knees propped upon its arms, and my behind arched so that it was prominently thrust toward them. I was no sooner placed in this attitude than they stepped out of their breeches, tucked up their shirts, and save for their shoes, they thus discovered themselves completely naked from the waist down; they exhibited themselves to me, passed several times to and fro before my eyes, making boastful display of their behinds of which they were overweeningly proud, for, they declared, they had parts far superior to anything I could offer; indeed, each was womanishly made in this region: 'twas especially Cardoville who was possessed of elegant lines and majestic form, snowy white color and enviable plumpness; they whiled away a minute or two polluting themselves in full view of me, but did not ejaculate: about Cardoville, nothing

that was not of the most ordinary; as for Saint-Florent, 'twas monstrous: I shuddered to think that such was the dart which had
immolated me. Oh Just Heaven! what need of maidenheads had
a man of those dimensions? Could it be anything other than ferocity
which governed such caprices? But what, alas! were the other
weapons I was going to be confronted by! Julien and La Rose,
plainly aroused by these exhibitions, also ridded themselves of their
clothes and advanced pike in hand. . . . Oh, Madame! never had
anything similar soiled my gaze, and whatever may have been my
previous representations, what now I beheld surpassed everything I
have been able to describe until the present: 'tis like unto the ascendancy the imperious eagle enjoys over the dove. Our two debauchees soon laid hands upon those menacing spears: they caressed
them, polluted them, drew them to their mouths, and the combat
straightway became more in earnest. Saint-Florent crouches upon
the armchair supporting me; he is so adjusted my widespread buttocks are on an exact level with his mouth; he kisses them, his
tongue penetrates into first one then the other temple. Saint-Florent
provided Cardoville with amusement, the latter offers himself to
the pleasures of La Rose whose terrific member instantly vanishes
into the redoubt dressed before him, and Julien, situated beneath
Saint-Florent, excites him with his mouth the while grasping his
haunches and modulating them before the resolute blows of Cardoville who, treating his friend with intransigent rudeness, does not
quit him before having wetted the sanctuary with his incense. Nothing could equal Cardoville's transports when the crisis deprives
him of his senses; softly abandoning himself to the man who is
serving as husband to him, but pressing hard after him of whom
he is making a wife, this dastardly libertine, with hoarse gasps like
unto those of a dying man, thereupon pronounces indescribable
blasphemies; as for Saint-Florent, measure governs his evolutions,
he restrains himself, and the tableau is dissolved without his having
performed his *beau geste.*

"Truly," Cardoville says to his comrade, "you still give me as
much pleasure as you did when you were fifteen. . . . Indeed," he
continues, turning and kissing La Rose, " 'tis true this fine lad knows
how to arouse me too. . . . Have you not found me rather gulfy
this evening, angelic boy? . . . would you believe it, Saint-Florent?

'tis the thirty-sixth time I've had it today . . . only natural that the thing be somewhat dilated; I'm all yours, dear friend," the abominable man pursues, fitting himself into Julien's mouth, his nose glued to my behind, and his own offered to Saint-Florent, "I'm yours for the thirty-seventh." Saint-Florent takes his pleasure with Cardoville, La Rose his with Saint-Florent, and after a quick skirmish the latter burns in his friend the same offering his friend had burned in him. If Saint-Florent's ecstasy was of briefer duration, it was no less intense, less noisy, less criminal than Cardoville's; the one shouted, roared out everything that came to his mouth, the other restricted his transports' scope without their being the less energetic for that; Saint-Florent chose his words with care, but they were simply yet filthier and more impure: distraction and rage, to select precise terms, seemed to characterize the delirium of the one, wickedness and ferocity were the eminent qualities announced in the other's.

"To work, Thérèse, revive us," says Cardoville; "you see the lamps are extinguished, they've got to be lit again."

While Julien enjoyed Cardoville and La Rose Saint-Florent, the two libertines inclined over me and one after the other inserted their languishing instruments into my mouth; while I pumped one, I was obliged to go to the rescue of the other and pollute it with my hands, then I had to anoint the member itself and the adjacent parts with an alcoholic liquid I had been given; but I was not to limit myself to sucking, I had to revolve my tongue about the heads and I was required to nibble them with my teeth while my lips squeezed tightly about them. However, our two patients were being vigorously thumped and jolted; Julien and La Rose shifted in order to increase the sensations produced by entrances and exits. When at length two or three homages had flowed into those impure temples I began to perceive a degree of firmness; although the elder of the two, Cardoville's was the first to manifest solidity; he swung his hand and with all the strength at his command slapped one of my titties: that was my reward. Saint-Florent was not far behind him; he repaid my efforts by nearly tearing one of my ears from my head. They backed away, reviewed the situation, and then warned me to prepare to receive the treatment I richly deserved. An analysis of these libertines' appalling language allowed to me to conclude that vexations were about to descend like a hailstorm upon me. To have besought mercy in the state to which they had just reduced me would have been to have further aroused them: and so they placed me, completely naked as I was, in the center of the circle they formed by all four drawing up chairs. I was obliged to parade from one to the next and to receive the penance each in his turn chose to order me to do; I had no more compassion from the youths than from the older men, but 'twas above all Cardoville who distinguished himself by refined teasings which Saint-Florent, cruel as he was, was unable to duplicate without an effort.

A brief respite succeeded these vicious orgies, I was given a few instants to catch my breath; I had been beaten black and blue, but what surprised me was that they doctored and healed the damage done me in less time than it had taken to inflict it, whereof not the slightest trace remained. The lubricities were resumed.

There were moments when all those bodies seemed to form but one and when Saint-Florent, lover and mistress, received copious quantities of what the impotent Cardoville doled out with sparing economy: the next instant, no longer active but lending himself in every manner, both his mouth and hindquarters served as altars to frightful homages. Cardoville cannot resist such a profusion of libertine scenes. Seeing his friend brilliantly elevated, he comes up to offer himself to Saint-Florent's lust, and the tradesman enjoys him; I sharpen the spears, I steer them in the direction they are to thrust, and my exposed buttocks provide a perspective to the lubricity of some, a target for the bestiality of others. As all this wears on our two libertines become more circumspect, for considerable efforts are the price of reanimation; they emerge unscathed from their joustings and their new state is such to terrify me even more.

"Very well, La Rose," says Saint-Florent, "take the bitch; we'll tighten her up: it's time for the stricturing."

I am not familiar with the expression: a cruel experiment soon reveals its meaning. La Rose seizes me, he places my flanks upon a small circular repentance stool not a foot in diameter: once there, lacking any other support, my legs fall on one side, my head and arms on the other; my four limbs, stretched as far apart as possible, are tied to the floor; the executioner who is going to perform the stricturing catches up a long needle through whose eye he passes a stout waxed thread, and with complete unconcern for either the blood he is to shed or the sufferings he is going to cause me, the monster, directly before the two colleagues whom the spectacle amuses, sews shut the entrance to the temple of Love; when finished, he turns me over, now my belly rests upon the repentance stool; my limbs hang free, they are attached as before, and the indecent shrine of Sodom is barricaded in the same manner: I do not speak of my agonies, Madame, you must yourself fancy what they were, I was on the verge of losing consciousness.

"Splendid, that's how I must have them," quoth Saint-Florent when I had been turned over again and was lying on my buttocks, and when, in this posture, he spied well within striking range the fortress he wanted to invade. "Accustomed to reaping nothing but the first fruits, how, without this ceremony, should I be able to harvest any pleasures from this creature?"

Saint-Florent had the most violent erection, they were currying and drubbing his device to keep it rampant; grasping that pike, he advances: in order to excite him further, Julien enjoys Cardoville before his eyes; Saint-Florent opens the attack, maddened by the resistance he encounters, he presses ahead with incredible vigor, the threads are strained, some snap. Hell's tortures are as naught to mine; the keener my agonies, the more piquant seem to be my tormenter's delights. At length, everything capitulates before his efforts, I am ripped asunder, the glittering dart sinks to the ultimate depths, but Saint-Florent, anxious to husband his strength, merely touches bottom and withdraws; I am turned over; the same obstacles: the savage one scouts them as he stands heating his engine and with his ferocious hands he molests the environs in order to put the place in fit condition for assault. He presents himself, the natural smallness of the locale renders his campaign more arduous to wage, my redoubtable vanquisher soon storms the gates, clears the entry; I am bleeding; but what does it matter to the conquering hero? Two vigorous heaves carry him into the sanctuary and there the villain consummates a dreadful sacrifice whose racking pains I should not have been able to endure another second.

"My turn," cries up Cardoville, causing me to be untied, "I'll have no tailoring done, but I'm going to place the dear girl upon a camping bed which should restore her circulation, and bring out

all the warmth and mobility her temperament or her virtue refuse us."

Upon the spot La Rose opens a closet and draws out a cross
made of gnarled, thorny, spiny wood. 'Tis thereon the infamous
debauchee wishes to place me, but by means of what episode will he
improve his cruel enjoyment? Before attaching me, Cardoville inserts into my behind a silver-colored ball the size of an egg; he
lubricates it and drives it home: it disappears. Immediately it is in
my body I feel it enlarge and begin to burn; without heeding my
complaints, I am lashed securely to this thorn-studded frame;
Cardoville penetrates as he fastens himself to me: he presses my
back, my flanks, my buttocks on the protuberances upon which they
are suspended. Julien fits himself into Cardoville; obliged to bear
the weight of these two bodies, and having nothing to support myself upon but these accursed knots and knurs which gouge into my
flesh, you may easily conceive what I suffered; the more I thrust
up against those who press down upon me, the more I am driven
upon the irregularities which stab and lacerate me. Meanwhile the
terrible globe has worked its way deep into my bowels and is cramp-
ing them, burning them, tearing them; I scream again and again:
no words exist which can describe what I am undergoing; all the
same and all the while, my murderer frolics joyfully, his mouth
glued to mine, he seems to inhale my pain in order that it may
magnify his pleasures: his intoxication is not to be rendered; but,
as in his friend's instance, he feels his forces about to desert him,
and like Saint-Florent wants to taste everything before they are
gone entirely. I am turned over again, am made to eject the ardent
sphere, and it is set to producing in the vagina itself, the same conflagration it ignited in the place whence it has just been flushed;
the ball enters, sears, scorches the matrix to its depths; I am not
spared, they fasten me belly-down upon the perfidious cross, and far
more delicate parts of me are exposed to molestation by the thorny
excrescences awaiting them. Cardoville penetrates into the forbidden passage; he perforates it while another enjoys him in similar wise: and at last delirium holds my persecutor in its grasp, his
appalling shrieks announce the crime's completion; I am inundated,
then untied.

"Off you go, dear friends," Cardoville says to the pair of

young men, "get your hands on this whore and amuse yourselves in whatever way your whims advise: she's yours, we're done with her." The two youthful libertines seize me. While one entertains himself with the front, the other buries himself in the rear; they change places and change again; I am more gravely torn by their prodigious thickness than I have been by Saint-Florent's artificial barricadings; both he and Cardoville toy with the young men while they occupy themselves with me. Saint-Florent sodomizes La Rose who deals in like manner with me, and Cardoville does as much to Julien who employs a more decent place to excite himself in me. I am the focal point of these execrable orgies, their absolute center and mainspring; La Rose and Julien have each four times done reverence at my altars, whilst Cardoville and Saint-Florent, less vigorous or more enervated, are content with one sacrifice offered to each of my lovers. And then the last measure of seed is sown by La Rose—'twas high time, for I was ready to swoon.

"My comrade has certainly hurt you, Thérèse," says Julien, "and I am going to repair all the damage." He picks up a flask of spirits and several times rubs all my wounds. The traces of my executioners' atrocities vanish, but nothing assuages my pain, and never had I experienced any as sharp.

"What with our skill at making the evidence of our cruelties disappear, the ladies who would like to lodge complaints against us must have the devil's own time getting themselves believed, eh, Thérèse?" says Cardoville. "What proofs do you fancy could be presented to support an accusation?"

"Oh," Saint-Florent interrupts, "the charming Thérèse is in no condition to level charges; on the eve of being immolated herself, we ought to expect nothing but prayers from her."

"Well, she'd be ill-advised to undertake the one or the other," Cardoville replies; "she might inculpate us; but would she be heard? I doubt it; our consequence and eminent stations in this city would scarcely allow anyone to notice suits which, anyhow, always come before us and whereof we are at all times the masters. Her final torture would simply be made crueler and more prolonged. Thérèse must surely sense we have amused ourselves with her person for the natural, common, and uncomplex reason which engages might to abuse feebleness; she must surely sense she cannot escape her sentence, that it must be undergone, that she will undergo it, that it would be in vain she might divulge this evening's absence from jail; she'd not be believed; the jailer—for he's ours —would deny it at once. And so may this lovely and gentle girl, so penetrated with the grandeur of Providence, peacefully offer up to Heaven all she has just suffered and all that yet awaits her; these will be as so many expiations for the frightful crimes which deliver her into the hands of the law; put on your clothes, Thérèse, day is not yet come, the two men who brought you hither are going to conduct you back to your prison."

I wanted to say a word, I wanted to cast myself a suppliant at these ogres' feet, either to unbend their hearts, or ask that their hands smite away my life. But I am dragged off, pitched into a cab, and my two guides climb in after me; we had hardly started off when infamous desires inflamed them again.

"Hold her for me," quoth Julien to La Rose, "I simply must sodomize her; I have never laid eyes on a behind which could squeeze me so voluptuously; I'll render you the same service."

There is nothing I can do to defend myself, the project is executed, Julien triumphs, and it is not without atrocious agonies I sustain this newest attack: the assailant's exorbitant bulk, the lacerated condition of those parts, the fire with which that accursed ball had devoured my intestines, everything combined to make me suffer tortures which La Rose renewed immediately his companion was finished. Before arriving I was thus yet another time victim of those wretched valets' criminal libertinage; we reached our destination at last. The jailer greeted us, he was alone, it was still night, no one saw me enter.

"Go to sleep, Thérèse," said he, restoring me to my cell, "and if ever you wish to tell, it makes no difference whom, that on this night you left prison, remember that I will contradict you, and that this useless accusation will get you nowhere. . . ."

And, said I to myself when I was left alone, I should regret departing this world! I should dread to leave a universe freighted with such monsters! Ah! were the hand of God to snatch me from their clutches at whatever instant and in whatever manner He sees fit! why! I'd complain no more; the unique consolation which may remain to the luckless one bred up in this den of savage beasts, his one comfort is the hope of leaving it soon.

The next day I heard nothing and resolved to abandon myself to Providence, I languished and would touch no food. The day after that, Cardoville came to question me; I could not repress a shudder upon beholding the nonchalance wherewith that scoundrel walked in to execute his judiciary duties—he, Cardoville, the most villainous of mortals, he who, contrary to every article of the justice in which he was cloaked, had just so cruelly abused my innocence and exploited my misery; it was in vain I pled my cause, the dishonest man's artfulness devised more crimes than I could invent defenses; when all the charges had been well established in the view of this iniquitous judge, and when the case was made, he had the impudence to ask me whether I knew in Lyon one Monsieur de Saint-Florent, a wealthy and estimable citizen; I answered that I knew him, yes.

"Excellent," said Cardoville, "no more is needed. This Monsieur de Saint-Florent, whom you declare you know, also has a perfect knowledge of you; he has deposed that he saw you in a band of thieves, that you were the first to steal his money and his pocketbook. He further deposes that your comrades wished to spare his life, that you recommended they take it from him; nevertheless, he managed to escape. Saint-Florent adds that, several years later, having recognized you in Lyon, he yielded to your importunings and permitted you to come to pay him a call at his home upon condition you would give him your word to behave well in future and that, while he was delivering a lecture on manners to you, while he was seeking to persuade you to persist along the paths of righteousness, you carried insolence and crime to the point of choosing these moments of kindness to steal a watch and one hundred *louis* he had left lying upon the mantel. . . ."

And, profiting from the resentment and anger such atrocious calumnies provoked in me, Cardoville ordered the court clerk to write that my silence and my facial expressions were ample acknowledgment of my guilt and were tantamount to a confession.

I threw myself upon the ground, I made the walls resound with my cries, I struck my head against the stone floor, hoping to obtain a speedier death, unable to find vehicles to give expression to my rage: "Villain!" I screamed, "I put my faith in the God of Justice who will revenge me for your crimes; He shall cry out innocence, He shall make you repent your disgraceful abuse of the authority vested in you!" Cardoville rings and tells the jailer to take me away, I appear, says he, to be unsettled by despair and remorse and, at any rate, in no state to follow the interrogation; "But, on the other hand, what remains to be asked or said? The dossier is complete; she has confessed to all her crimes." And the villain leaves peacefully! And divine lightning strikes him not!

The case was tried in short order; motivated and directed by hatred, vengeance, and lust, the court promptly condemned me and I was dispatched to Paris for the confirmation of my sentence. While on this fatal journey, which, though guiltless, I made in the character of the last of criminals, the most bitter and the most dolorous thoughts gathered in my head and completed the desolation of my heart. Under what doom-spelling star must I have been born, I wondered, in order that I be utterly incapable of conceiving a single generous sentiment without immediately being drowned in a sea of misfortunes! And why is it that this enlightened Providence whose justice I am pleased to worship, the while punishing me for my virtues, simultaneously shows me those who crush me with their crimes carried to the pinnacle of happiness!

During my childhood I meet a usurer; he seeks to induce me to commit a theft, I refuse, he becomes rich. I fall amongst a band of thieves, I escape from them with a man whose life I save; by way of thanks, he rapes me. I reach the property of an aristocratic debauchee who has me set upon and devoured by his dogs for not having wanted to poison his aunt. From there I go to the home of a murderous and incestuous surgeon whom I strive to spare from doing a horrible deed: the butcher brands me for a criminal; he doubtless consummates his atrocities, makes his fortune, whilst I am obliged to beg for my bread. I wish to have the sacraments made available to me, I wish fervently to implore the Supreme Being whence howbeit I receive so many ills, and the august tribunal, at which I hope to find purification in our most holy mysteries, becomes the bloody theater of my ignominy: the monster who abuses and plunders me is elevated to his order's highest honors and I fall back into the appalling abyss of misery. I attempt to preserve a woman from her husband's fury, the cruel one wishes to put me to death by draining away my blood drop by drop. I wish to relieve a poor woman, she robs me. I give aid to a man whom adversaries have struck down and left unconscious, the thankless creature makes me turn a wheel like an animal; he hangs me for his pleasure's sake; all fortune's blessings accrue to him, and I come within an ace of dying on the gallows for having been compelled to work for him. An unworthy woman seeks to seduce me for a new crime, a second time I lose the little I own in order to rescue her victim's treasure. A gentleman, a kind spirit wishes to compensate me for all my sufferings by the offer of his hand, he dies in my arms before being able to do anything for me. I risk my life in a fire in order to snatch a child, who does not belong to me, from the flames; the infant's mother accuses and launches legal proceedings against me. I fall into my most mortal enemy's hands; she wishes to carry me off by force and take me to a man whose passion is to cut off heads: if I avoid that villain's sword it is so that I can trip and fall under Themis'. I implore the protection of a man whose life and fortune I once saved; I dare expect gratitude from him, he lures me to his house, he submits me to horrors, and there I find the iniquitous judge upon whom my case depends; both abuse me, both outrage me, both accelerate my doom; fortune overwhelms them with favors, I hasten on to death.

That is what I have received from mankind, that is what I have learned of the danger of trafficking with men; is it any wonder that my soul, stung, whipsawed by unhappiness, revolted by outrage and injustice, aspires to nothing more than bursting from its mortal confines?

A thousand pardons, Madame, said this unlucky girl, terminating her adventures at this point; a thousand times over I ask to be forgiven for having sullied your spirit with such a host of obscenities, for having, in a word, so long abused your patience. I have, perhaps, offended Heaven with impure recitals, I have laid open my old wounds, I have disturbed your ease and rest; farewell, Madame, Godspeed; the Star rises above the horizon, I hear my guards summon me to come, let me run on to meet my destiny, I fear it no more, 'twill abridge my torment: this last mortal instant is dreaded only by the favored being whose days have passed unclouded; but the wretched creature who has breathed naught but the venomous effluvia of reptiles, whose tottering feet have trod only upon nettles, who has never beheld the torch of dawn save with feelings like unto those of the lost traveler who, trembling, perceives the thunderbolt's forked track; she from whom cruel accident has snatched away parents, all kin, friends, fortune, protection, aid; she who in all this world has nothing more than tears to quench her thirst and for sustenance her tribulations; she, I say, undismayed sees death advance, she even yearns for it as for a safe haven, a port wherein tranquillity will be born again unto her when she is clasped to the breast of a God too just to permit that innocence, defiled and ground under the heel on earth, may not find recompense for so many evils in another world.

The honest Monsieur de Corville had not heard this tale without profound emotion; as for Madame de Lorsange in whom, as we have said, the monstrous errors of her youth had not by any means extinguished sensibility, as for Madame de Lorsange, she was ready to swoon.

"Mademoiselle," said she to Justine, "it is difficult to listen to you without taking the keenest interest in you; but, and I must avow it! an inexplicable sentiment, one far more tender than this I describe, draws me invincibly toward you and does make of your ills my very own. You have disguised your name, you have concealed your birth, I beg you to disclose your secret to me; think not that it is a vain curiosity which bids me speak thus to you . . . Great God! may what I suspect be true? . . . O Thérèse! were you Justine? . . . were it that you would be my sister!"

"Justine! Madame! 'tis a strange name."

"She would have been your age—"

"Juliette! is it you I hear?" cried the unhappy prisoner, casting herself into Madame de Lorsange's arms; ". . . you . . . my sister! . . . ah, I shall die far less miserable, for I have been able to embrace you again! . . ."

And the two sisters, clasped in each other's arms, were prevented by their sobs from hearing one another, and found expression in naught but tears.

Monsieur de Corville was unable to hold back his own; aware

of the overpowering significance of this affair and sensing his in-
volvement in it, he moves into an adjoining room, sits down and
writes a letter to the Lord Chancellor, with fiery strokes, in ardent
ciphers he paints in all its horror the fate of poor Justine, whom
we shall continue to call Thérèse; he takes upon himself responsibility for her innocence, he will guarantee it under oath; he asks
that, until the time her case has been finally clarified, the allegedly
guilty party be confined to no other prison but his château, and
Corville gives his word he will produce her in court the instant the
Chief Justice signals his desire to have her appear there; he makes
himself known unto Thérèse's two guards, entrusts his corres-
pondence to them, makes himself answerable for their prisoner; he
is obeyed, Thérèse is confided to him; a carriage is called for.

"Come, my too unfortunate creature," Monsieur de Corville
says to Madame de Lorsange's interesting sister, "come hither; all
is going to be changed; it shall not be said your virtues ever remained unrewarded and that the beautiful soul you had from Nature ever encountered but steel; follow us, 'tis upon me you depend
henceforth. . . ."

And Monsieur de Corville gave a brief account of what he
had just done.

"Dearly beloved and respectable man," said Madame de Lorsange, casting herself down before her lover, "this is the most
splendid gesture you have performed in your life, it is such as comes
from one who has true acquaintance with the human heart and the
spirit of the law which is the avenger of oppressed innocence. There
she stands, Monsieur, behold, there is your captive; go, Thérèse,
go, run, fly at once and kneel down before this equitable protector
who will not, as have all others, abandon you. O, Monsieur, if those
attachments of love which have bound me to you have been cherished, how much more so are they to become now that they are
strengthened by the most tender esteem. . . ."

And one after the other the two women embraced the knees
of a so generous friend, and upon him they did shed their tears.

A few hours later they arrived at the château; once there,
Monsieur de Corville and Madame de Lorsange both strove with
might and main to raise Thérèse from the ultimate deeps of un-

happiness to the pure sunshine of contentment and well-being. They took greatest joy in giving her to eat of the most succulent foods, they laid her to sleep in the finest of beds, they did urge her to command and they made her will to be done, and into their hospitable proceedings they introduced all the gentility and understanding it were possible to expect from two sensitive souls. She was given medicines for several days, she was bathed, dressed, arrayed in elegant attire, embellished, the two lovers worshiped her, each labored at nothing but to make her forget her sorrows as quickly as might be. An excellent surgeon was fetched; he undertook to make the ignominious mark disappear, and soon the cruel result of Rodin's villainy was effectively gone; and everything responded to the cares her benefactors lavished upon Thérèse: the shadowed memories of misery were already effaced from that amiable girl's brow; already the Graces had re-established their empire thereupon. For the livid tints on her cheeks of alabaster were substituted the rosy hue appropriate to her years; what had been withered by such a multitude of griefs was called back to fresh new life. Laughter, for so many years banished from her lips, reappeared again under the wings of Pleasure. The very best news came from the Court; Monsieur de Corville had put all of France in action, he had reanimated the zeal of Monsieur S* * *, who collaborated with him to publicize Thérèse's ill-treatment and to restore her to a tranquillity to which she was so heavily entitled. At length letters came from the King, they nullified all the legal proceedings unjustly initiated against her, they gave her back the name of an honest citizen, imposed silence upon all the realm's tribunals before which efforts had been made to defame her, and accorded her a thousand crowns a year, interest realized upon the gold seized in the counterfeiters' Dauphiné workshop. They wished to make Cardoville and Saint-Florent answer for their misdeeds but, in accordance with the fatality of the star intending upon all of Thérèse's persecutors, one of them, Cardoville, had just, before his crimes were made known, been named to the administration of the Province of * * *, and the other to general supervision of Colonial Trade; each had already reached his destination, the edicts affected no one but the powerful families who soon found means to quiet the storm and, pacifically installed in Fortune's sanctuary, those monsters' depredations were quickly forgotten.[8]

With what regards Thérèse, as soon as she learned of so many agreeable developments she came well-nigh to expiring from joy; for several days on end the sweetest tears flowed from her eyes and she rejoiced upon her guardians' breasts, and then, all of a sudden, her humor altered, and 'twas impossible to ferret out the cause. She became somber, uneasy, troubled, was given to dreaming, sometimes she burst into weeping before her friends, and was not herself able to explain what was the subject of her woe. "I was not born for such felicity," said she to Madame de Lorsange, ". . . oh, dear sister, 'tis impossible it last much longer." She was assured all her troubles were over, none remained, said they, no more inquietude for her; 'twas all in vain, nothing would quiet her; one might have said that this melancholy creature, uniquely destined for sorrow, and feeling the hand of misery forever raised above her head, already foresaw the final blow whereby she was going to be smitten down.

Monsieur de Corville was still residing on his country estate; 'twas toward summer's end, they had planned an outing when the approach of a dreadful storm obliged them to postpone their promenade; the excessive heat had constrained them to leave all the windows open. Lightning glitters, shakes, hail slashes down, winds blow wrathfully, heaven's fire convulses the clouds, in the most hideous manner makes them to seethe; it seems as if Nature were wearied out of patience with what she has wrought, as if she were ready to confound all the elements that she might wrench new forms from them. Terrified, Madame de Lorsange begs her sister to make all haste and close the shutters; anxious to calm her, Thérèse dashes to the windows which are already being broken; she would do battle with the wind, she gives a minute's fight, is driven back and at that instant a blazing thunderbolt reaches her where she stands in the middle of the room . . . transfixes her.

Madame de Lorsange emits a terrible cry and falls in a faint; Monsieur de Corville calls for help, attentions are given each woman, Madame de Lorsange is revived, but the unhappy Thérèse

---

[8] As for the monks of Saint Mary-in-the-Wood, suppression of the religious orders will expose the atrocious crimes of that horrible crew.

has been struck in such wise hope itself can no longer subsist for her; the lightning entered her right breast, found the heart, and after having consumed her chest and face, burst out through her belly. The miserable thing was hideous to look upon; Monsieur de Corville orders that she be borne away....

"No," says Madame de Lorsange, getting to her feet with the utmost calm; "no, leave her here before my eyes, Monsieur, I have got to contemplate her in order to be confirmed in the resolves I have just taken. Listen to me, Corville, and above all do not oppose the decision I am adopting; for the present, nothing in the world could swerve my designs.

"The unheard of sufferings this luckless creature has experienced although she has always respected her duties, have something about them which is too extraordinary for me not to open my eyes upon my own self; think not I am blinded by that false-gleaming felicity which, in the course of Thérèse's adventures, we have seen enjoyed by the villains who battened upon her. These caprices of Heaven's hand are enigmas it is not for us to sound, but which ought never seduce us. O thou my friend! The prosperity of Crime is but an ordeal to which Providence would expose Virtue, it is like unto the lightning, whose traitorous brilliancies but for an instant embellish the atmosphere, in order to hurl into death's very deeps the luckless one they have dazzled. And there, before our eyes, is the example of it; that charming girl's incredible calamities, her terrifying reversals and uninterrupted disasters are a warning issued me by the Eternal, Who would that I heed the voice of mine guilt and cast myself into His arms. Ah, what must be the punishment I have got to fear from Him, I, whose libertinage, irreligion, and abandon of every principle have stamped every instant of my life! What must I not expect if 'tis thus He has treated her who in all her days had not a single sin whereof to repent! Let us separate, Corville, the time has come, no chain binds us one to the other, forget me, and approve that I go and by an eternal penance abjure, at the Supreme Being's feet, the infamies wherewith I am soiled absolutely. That appalling stroke was necessary to my conversion in this life, it was needed for the happiness I dare hope for in another. Farewell, Monsieur; the last mark of your friendship I ask is that you institute no perquisitions to discover what shall have become of me. Oh, Corville! I await you in a better world, your virtues should lead you unto it; may the atonements I make, to expiate my crimes, in this place where I go to spend the unhappy years that remain to me, permit me to encounter you again someday."

Madame de Lorsange leaves the house immediately; she takes some money with her, leaps into a carriage, to Monsieur de Corville abandons the rest of her ownings after having recommended that they be turned into a pious legacy, and flies to Paris, where she takes a Carmelite's veil; not many years go by before she becomes the example of her order and the edification, as much by her great piety as by the wisdom of her mind and the regularity of her manners.

Monsieur de Corville, worthy of his country's highest posts, attained to them, and, whatever were his honors, he employed them for no end but to bring happiness to the people, glory to his master, whom, "although a minister," he served well, and fortune to his friends.

O you who have wept tears upon hearing of Virtue's miseries; you who have been moved to sympathy for the woe-ridden Justine; the while forgiving the perhaps too heavy brushstrokes we have found ourselves compelled to employ, may you at least extract from this story the same moral which determined Madame de Lorsange! May you be convinced, with her, that true happiness is to be found nowhere but in Virtue's womb, and that if, in keeping with designs it is not for us to fathom, God permits that it be persecuted on Earth, it is so that Virtue may be compensated by Heaven's most dazzling rewards.